SECOND STRIKE

Chris Ryan was born in Newcastle. In 1984 he joined 22 SAS. After completing the year-long Alpine Guides Course, he was the troop guide for B Squadron Mountain Troop. He completed three tours with the anti-terrorist team, serving as an assaulter, sniper and finally Sniper Team Commander.

Chris was part of the SAS eight-man team chosen for the famous Bravo Two Zero mission during the 1991 Gulf War. He was the only member of the unit to escape from Iraq, where three of his colleagues were killed and four captured, for which he was awarded the Military Medal. Chris wrote about his experiences in his book *The One That Got Away*, which became an immediate bestseller. Since then he has written over fifty books and presented a number of very successful TV programmes.

To hear more about Chris Ryan's books, sign up to his Readers' Club at bit.ly/ChrisRyanClub

You can also follow him on social media:
X: @exSASChrisRyan
Instagram: @exsaschrisryan
Facebook: ChrisRyanBooks

Also by Chris Ryan

Manhunter
Outcast
Cold Red
Traitor

CHRIS RYAN

SECOND STRIKE

ZAFFRE

First published in the UK in 2025 by
ZAFFRE
An imprint of Bonnier Books UK
5th Floor, HYLO, 105 Bunhill Row, London, EC1Y 8LZ

Copyright © Chris Ryan, 2025

All rights reserved.
No part of this publication may be reproduced,
stored or transmitted in any form by any means, electronic,
mechanical, photocopying or otherwise, without the
prior written permission of the publisher.

The right of Chris Ryan to be identified as Author of this
work has been asserted by him in accordance with the
Copyright, Designs and Patents Act, 1988.

This is a work of fiction. Names, places, events and
incidents are either the products of the author's
imagination or used fictitiously. Any resemblance to
actual persons, living or dead, or actual
events is purely coincidental.

A CIP catalogue record for this book is
available from the British Library.

Hardback ISBN: 978-1-83877-979-5
Trade paperback ISBN: 978-1-83877-980-1

Also available as an ebook and an audiobook

1 3 5 7 9 10 8 6 4 2

Typeset by IDSUK (Data Connection) Ltd
Printed and bound in Great Britain by Clays Ltd, Elcograf S.p.A.

The authorised representative in the EEA is Bonnier Books
UK (Ireland) Limited.
Registered office address: Floor 3, Block 3, Miesian Plaza,
Dublin 2, D02 Y754, Ireland
compliance@bonnierbooks.ie
www.bonnierbooks.co.uk

One

Plymouth, England. September 2024

Matt King stared at the message on his phone and felt a hot thrill of anticipation.

Finally. After the longest dry spell of his life, his luck was about to change.

Big time.

An hour ago, he had been facing another depressing weekend at home, trawling through crappy streaming shows and uploading his latest runs. Now he had the prospect of a date.

Not just any date, King corrected himself. A date with the most jaw-thuddingly gorgeous woman he'd ever set eyes on. Helina was movie-star hot. Her profile pictures looked like something out of a modelling portfolio. She had curves in all the right places and none in the wrong ones. The kind of figure that could make a Buddhist punch a hole in a wall. And now she wanted to meet up with him.

Excitement swept through King's veins as he read the brief message again.

Hey, my sexy genius. Can we meet? Please??? I really really want you!! ☺

King figured it was about time life threw him a bone. Especially when it came to women. He'd had his fair share of disappointments down the years. Wasn't his fault. Most women just didn't understand him. They weren't on his wavelength. Either that, or they felt intimidated in the presence of his special genius. He guessed all great minds suffered the same problem. When you thought in maths and physics, how could you hope to communicate with normies?

King knew that among his colleagues he had a reputation as something of a paranoid loner. In truth, he saw no point in making friends with any of them. He disliked banter and idle chit-chat. But there were times when he wished he could have been less socially awkward. Maybe then, King reflected, he wouldn't be so lonely.

From a young age King had known that his brain was wired differently to everyone else. A question of genetic engineering. He interpreted the world through equations and formulas. Numbers. Massively complex systems he could understand. They were neat, efficient, logical. They behaved according to certain principles.

Unlike people.

People, in King's experience, could be messy, irrational, contradictory. Or all of the above. So he tried to avoid them wherever possible. He swerved office parties and after-work drinks. He kept to himself, spent his weekends going for runs and reading Substack feeds.

But avoiding social situations made it difficult to meet anyone. His latest drought had lasted for more than two years. At the office, several of his co-workers had started calling him 'The Welsh Incel' behind his back. They joked about buying him a sex doll for his next birthday.

King knew he shouldn't let that stuff bother him, but it did. Sometimes, when he felt the anger boiling in his veins, threatening to explode, he would imagine punching his piss-taking colleagues in the face. Breaking noses, mashing teeth. Teaching them a lesson.

He knew he would never actually do that, of course. King was slightly built, tall and gangly. Skin and bone. He wouldn't stand a chance in a fight. So he didn't react. Instead, he smiled and went about his business. Pretended not to care about the taunts.

In desperation he had turned to online dating. The thought of meeting some random stranger filled him with terror, but he figured he might stand a better chance of finding someone with the help of an algorithm. Someone on his level. After all, King had reminded himself, he had plenty going for him. He was incredibly smart, made good wedge as an engineer at DeepSpear Defence Industries, a major supplier to the Ministry of Defence. He rented an apartment in Plymouth's fashionable Stonehouse district, drove a Tesla and kept himself in good shape. He'd even completed his first half-marathon recently.

Okay, so he wouldn't give Paul Mescal a run for his money in the looks department. But so what? Plenty of his workmates had met people online. Some had even found their soul mates, or so they said. Why not him?

So King had shoved aside his built-in caution. He'd filled out the dating profile, taken the personality quiz, selected photos that made him look (he hoped) fun and interesting. Stumped up the £99 fee for premium membership, so women wouldn't think he was a cheapskate. Then he'd waited for the messages to roll in.

Except they hadn't.

There had been a handful of approaches over the past several months. Fake profiles, mostly. King could spot them from a mile off. Some acne-faced kid in a basement flat in Krasnodar, looking to fleece a horny Brit out of a few quid. The few genuine flickers of interest had come to nothing. First dates had gone nowhere. Messages had gone unanswered.

After a while King had simply given up. He stopped checking the app each day. Let his subscription lapse. Threw himself back into his running. Considered taking up road cycling to fill his spare time. Maybe dabble in flipping properties.

Then Helina had reached out to him.

At first, King had hesitated to reply. Mainly because she looked way out of his league.

Her profile shot showed Helina at some sort of black-tie event, wearing a black velvet mini dress, clutching a flute of champagne.

Hair the colour of autumn leaf-fall, heart-shaped face. Pouting lips formed a teasing smile. Soft green eyes burned fiercely at the camera. Other snaps showed Helina at weddings, or on holiday. In every single one she looked drop-dead stunning. She looked like someone who knew that she was beautiful and understood how to use it to get what she wanted from life.

Naturally, King had assumed she'd messaged him by mistake. Either that, or this was another Romanian scammer. He decided to ignore her.

Then he'd considered his life in the round. The many evenings he'd spent alone in front of the TV. The meals-for-one. He didn't even have a pet, for Chrissakes.

Fuck it, he thought. *What have I got to lose?*

To his amazement, Helina had replied at once. Their first conversations had gone surprisingly well. Helina Tullus, he learned, had grown up in Estonia; she had completed a degree in Geography at the University of Tartu before moving to England to study an MA at Plymouth in environmental consultancy. She was passionate about the climate, loved to ski, had been a promising basketball player at school before a knee injury curtailed her career. Her father owned a pharmacy in Tallinn; her mother was a retired maths teacher. She was smart, funny, sports-mad, but also into video games and Wordle. They shared many of the same interests.

King was not stupid. Long experience had taught him to be wary of beautiful women taking a liking to him. So he'd done his homework. Took a deep dive into Helina's digital life. Background research on Google, Instagram, LinkedIn and Facebook confirmed everything Helina had told him. Her story checked out. She was clean.

One hundred per cent.

Most importantly, she understood King. Recognised his genius-level intellect. She loved listening to him talk about the philosophies of John Gray and Richard Dawkins; admired his thoughts on artificial general intelligence, quantum entanglement and the merits of establishing a colony on Mars. 'You're so smart you should be Elon Musk's boss,' she had told him.

Late one night, during one of their conversations, Helina had hinted at a toxic relationship in her past. There had been some trouble with an aggressive ex-boyfriend back in Estonia. She had complained that she always seemed to pick the wrong guy. Now she wanted someone different, she said.

I'm done dating jocks.

I just want to be with someone smart. Someone who thinks with their big brain instead of their small one.

That sounded just fine to King. His chance to shine. In their chats she had referred to him as her 'hot geek'.

He liked that.

Now she wanted to meet.

I'm in here, thought King.

He could scarcely control his heartbeat as he typed out his response.

I want you too . . . When do you want to meet?

He tapped send. Waited. Speech dots bobbed up and down at the bottom of the screen. King's palms became sweaty. His pulse quickened with nervous anticipation.

Helina's next message popped up.

Tomorrow? The White Horse Tavern on Cremyll? I'm meeting with friends in the morning but can meet you at say 2pm??

King knew the place. A short hop on the ferry from Admiral's Hard.

He replied. Fingers danced excitedly over the scratched glass. King knew he should be following the advice he'd gleaned from dating podcasts and Reddit forums. Pretend that he'd have to check his diary, maybe hint at needing to shift around a few things before he could confirm the date. *Don't look too eager. Don't look like you've got absolutely nothing going on in your life.* But King had gone too long without any action. He wasn't interested in playing mind games.

Great, he wrote. Sounds good!

He sent the message. One beat passed. Then another. Then a third. Then Helina replied.

Ok!!! Can't wait.
PS I'm so wet for you right now.

A photo quickly followed. A selfie. Taken in what King guessed was Helina's bathroom. She was dressed in a white plunge bra and a crotchless laced thong. Blood-red lips parted a little as she smiled sweetly at the camera.
Something stirred in King's pants.
Another message quickly followed.

See you tomorrow.

King sent a grinning emoticon, got a pair of winking kisses back. He ignored his raging-hard on and visualised the jealous looks on the faces of his co-workers when he told them about Helina. And, most importantly, when he showed them photos of her.
He would have to go shopping later on. Smarten up for his date. Maybe pop a couple of Viagra. It had been a while. He wanted to make sure he could perform.
The long drought was almost over.
Tomorrow, Matt King was going to have the shag of a lifetime.

* * *

At one thirty the following afternoon, King stepped outside the entrance to his apartment building, a converted victualling yard with tall arched windows and exposed granite walls. A faint breeze muttered in from the harbour, rustling through King's thinning hair as he made his way north-east towards Admiralty Road. He continued north on Cremyll Street at a quick trot, his heart beating quickly now at the thought of meeting Helina.

Soon, he hoped, he would have another reason to celebrate.

In recent weeks King had uncovered a crisis at his office. People he worked with had been caught sneaking around the building. Poking around in areas that were strictly off-limits to unauthorised personnel. King suspected they were up to no good, so he'd decided to keep a close eye on them. Find out what they were doing, and why. A dangerous move. But also necessary. He had a duty to his employers.

Then he had gotten careless. King had been spotted following one of them around. He'd seen the look in the other man's eyes. That guy knew King was onto them. Fact.

Also a fact: they were not the kind of people you wanted to cross.

At first King had gone to his managers. A waste of time. They had shown no interest in listening to him or taking his concerns higher up the ladder. A combination of corporate inertia and a disinclination to believe someone with a reputation around the office as a paranoid loner.

So King had decided to bypass the chain of command. Go right to the top of the food chain. Drastic action. The nuclear option. But he had no alternative. Someone needed to be alerted.

King had to assume that they had eyes on him the whole time. But he knew how to protect himself. How to disguise his movements. How to make sure he didn't leave a trace of his footprints online.

Nothing had happened yet, but he felt sure it was only a matter of time before his actions bore fruit. They wouldn't be able to ignore him. Not this time. Not with the stakes so high.

Soon, he would be vindicated.

Once everyone realised what had been going on King was going to be the hero of the hour. The guy who had helped to avert a major security disaster. They'd give him a big bump in salary, maybe a promotion. He could treat Helina to a five-star break in the Maldives.

He carried on up Cremyll Street until he reached the junction with Admiral's Hard. Whereupon he hooked a left and headed west, resisting the temptation to pop into the Bunch of Grapes for a quick pint to calm his nerves before his date.

A loose throng of passengers waited to board the ferry. Tourists, mostly. Ramblers and families heading across the water for a Sunday afternoon stroll around the park. King clambered aboard and made his way round to the aft deck. Found an empty space on one of the bench seats and bought a return ticket from a weathered deck-hand with a bristly moustache.

The tourists crowded around the bows, jostling for the best view as the boat chuntered lazily across the Hamoaze towards Cremyll. King had taken this route hundreds of times – he liked to go running along Rame Head when the weather permitted – but he never grew tired of the view. Oldest ferry service in the country, someone had told him.

East of the Sound was Drake's Island. A mile to the north stood the sprawling Royal Navy base at Devonport. The biggest of its kind in Europe. DeepSpear's offices were just about visible from the deck, towering above the tiled roofs of the terraced houses. The DeepSpear corporate logo, a bold red 'D' set against a plain white background, gleamed down the side of the building.

The boat scudded across the water, creamy trail in its wake. There was just enough time for the deck-hand to collect the rest of the fares before the engine dialled down as the skipper steered towards Cremyll Quay. The deck-hand lassoed a painter round the mooring post; the skipper gave the all-clear. King disembarked and followed the other passengers up the slipway. He passed the old stone-walled ticket office and made straight for the boozer across the road.

The White House looked like it had been taken from a Wikipedia entry about traditional English pubs. A handful of drinkers sat around the outdoor picnic tables, guzzling pints of cider. Weeds poked through the block paving. Bright sprays of petunias adorned the window boxes beneath old sash windows. The flag of St Piran's flickered like a black tongue in the gentle breeze.

King made for the main entrance. A chalk pavement board outside the main entrance promised good ales and a warm welcome, but King was excited about something else waiting inside for him.

He tugged open the door and ducked his head under the low lintel, swept into a gloomy interior that looked like it pre-dated the invention of the combustion engine. Worn leather armchairs and rickety tables had been arranged either side of the central space. Landscape paintings hung from oakwood panelled walls. Beer mats covered the wall behind the main bar. Couples and families were tucking into Sunday roasts, roaring with laughter. At the far end of the room, a separate door led outside to the rear car park.

A group of walkers sat around a table in one corner of the bar. Hikers who'd flocked to the pub after a long walk around Rame Head, he presumed. Decked out in their unofficial uniform of Craghopper trousers, Gore-Tex boots and telescopic hiking poles.

King looked round. There was no sign of Helina, but that didn't worry him.

You're early.

Plenty of time yet.

He beelined for the bar, ordered a pint of Hicks Special Draught from a glum-looking barmaid with a lazy eye. Tapped his watch against the card machine, took a hit of strong Cornish ale and planted himself down at an empty table near the entrance. Through the grimy window he could see the waterfront. A family of four loitered close to the water's edge, the parents pointing out landmarks across the drink, teenage kids staring at their phones.

King took another swig of his pint. Waited.

Six minutes later, Helina Tullus walked through the door.

She looked better in real life than she did in her profile pics. Which King had assumed would be scientifically impossible. But the evidence was right there in front of him. Undeniable.

Helina stood in the doorway, strands of flame-coloured hair playfully caressing her pale skin. Bright red lips reminded King of holly berries in midwinter snow. Jade eyes glowed in high-boned cheeks. Helina wore a sleeveless daisy print sundress, finishing just above the knee and cut low to reveal a triangle of naked flesh between small rounded breasts.

She looked round the bar, caught sight of King and sauntered over to his table, carrying herself in a way that seemed at once both highly sexual and completely natural, oblivious to the leery looks from the blokes in the hiking group. There was nothing rehearsed or forced about her appearance. Nothing that implied she was trying to mask insecurities or project false confidence.

King wished his workmates could see him now.

He rose to greet Helina. They hugged, kissed each other lightly on the cheeks. King ordered Helina a rhubarb-flavoured gin and tonic at the bar, carried her glass over to the table, eased back into his chair. Realised he was as nervous as fuck despite sinking half his beer before Helina had showed up.

Helina must have detected his nerves, because she smiled sweetly at him. The smile spread from her cherry lips to her eyes. Her whole face radiated. When she looked at him, King felt like he was the most important person in the universe.

'Your profile didn't say anything about being so tall,' Helina said. She spoke perfect English, but with a slight melodic accent that King found deeply alluring.

'Sorry,' he mumbled. 'Er, is that a problem?'

As soon as the words left his mouth King cursed himself for his stupidity. Not for the first time in his life, he feared his social awkwardness might wreck his chances of getting laid.

Helina's smile broadened.

'Don't be silly,' she said. 'I like tall men. It's sexy.'

King grinned. He felt himself begin to relax.

They finished their drinks, and then Helina suggested they order a bottle of prosecco. King hated frivolous spending, but he didn't want to look tight-fisted, so he splashed out on a bottle of Bottega Gold. They migrated to one of the sofas and passed the next few hours knocking back expensive fizz, laughing and swapping life stories. King didn't want to tempt fate, but he reckoned the date was going pretty well. Better than he could have imagined.

Shortly after eight o'clock, the hikers downed their pints and left. By now the place was almost empty. An old man with a golden retriever sat alone, sipping his bitter and watching the world go by. A pair of younger blokes watched Newcastle and Everton play out a turgid nil-nil draw on the big-screen TV.

A middle-aged couple sat at the bar, a thickly built man with a shaven head and heavily tattooed arms and a blonde-haired woman with the same general build. They were chatting away to the lazy-eyed barmaid. Every so often the couple would slide off their stools, snatch up their cigarette packets and lighters and pop outside for a smoke.

Helina drained her prosecco glass, set it down and turned to face King, giving him a front-row view of her cleavage. Soft fingers gently stroked the nape of his neck. She licked her lips.

Said, in a whisper, 'Can I let you in on a little secret?'

King nodded slowly, head swimming with booze.

'Of course, Helina,' he said. 'You can tell me anything.'

She leaned in closer. King could feel her hot breath kissing his cheek. The strawberry scent of her hair carried the promise of hot sex. Her voice dropped a note.

'I'm wet for you,' she said. 'Very wet.'

King felt his breath hitch in his throat. Helina glanced round, making sure no one was watching them. Then she let her arm fall to his belt. Delicate fingers brushed lightly against his crotch.

King hardened. With a great effort he managed to compose himself.

'We can go back to my place, if you want?'

'I'd really like that,' Helina said. 'But there's only one problem.'

'What's that?'

'I want you right now, big boy.'

The bulge in King's pants swelled.

Her hand moved away from his belt. She laced her arms round his neck and pulled him closer, kissing him. King felt her soft tongue in his mouth, the shape of her breasts pressing against his chest.

Sweet Jesus. He was rock-hard.

The Viagra pills were working a treat.

Helina slowly drew back from him and rose to her feet. She gestured for King to get up.

'We'll catch the ferry back to yours in a bit,' she said. She paused to bite her lip. 'First, I need to give you your present.'

King looked up at her.

'Present?' he repeated.

Helina laughed. 'Don't look so concerned. It's just a little surprise. You're going to *love* it. I promise.' She canted her head to one side, gentle eyes searching his face. 'You like surprises, don't you?'

King nodded. He really did. Especially when they came in the shape of a randy Estonian redhead with a tight-as-fuck body.

'Well,' she whispered. 'What are you waiting for?'

King had never been a big drinker, but as he levered himself up from the armchair he realised that he was pissed. Not just tipsy, but four-bottles-of-fizz drunk. A strange fuzziness had settled over his brain.

Helina beamed a smile at him so bright it could have powered a cannabis farm. King followed her across the bar, past the formal dining room. Briefly he wondered where they were going. Then Helina stopped in front of the restroom door. She pointed towards the corridor leading to the rear car park.

'Wait for me out there,' she said. 'I'm going to freshen up. Then I'll come and give you your present.'

Helina gave him another long kiss, then turned on her heels and disappeared through the door leading into the women's bathroom. King carried on towards the rear exit. A dirty thought penetrated the drunken fog clouding his mind.

So that was it. Helina wanted to shag him in the car park. Or at the very least a blowjob. King wasn't an exhibitionist. Not his kind of thing. But even with his head swimming with booze, he knew a good offer when he saw one. No way was he turning this one down.

He approached the door leading to the car park. A few hours ago, he had hoped for nothing more than a kiss at the end of their date, maybe with the promise of more to come if he played his cards right. Now he was about to get a blowjob, or more, from the woman of his dreams. In a matter of hours his luck had completely flipped.

He stepped through the door. Emerged onto a tarmacked car park roughly the size of a tennis court, enclosed on two sides by ivy-smothered brick walls. To the south, twenty metres away, was an access road leading to the main road. Beyond that, a clump of woodland. Security lights glowed like signal beacons in the darkness, floodlighting the potholed blacktop. From the beer garden on the other side of the eastern wall, King heard the hubbub of drunken laughter.

The car park was deserted. No one in sight. No CCTV cameras either, King noted as he looked round. A couple of vehicles occupied the spots reserved for staff on the left side of the lot. A Ford Focus polka-dotted with bird shit and a knackered grey Peugeot 207.

Further away, King spotted a third vehicle parked on the grass verge on the other side of the access road. A dark grey panel van with tinted side windows and a satellite dish mounted on the roof. Vanlifers, King supposed. Digital nomads touring the south coast in modified commercial wagons. Fitted out with sinks, cookers, fridge freezers, beds, water tanks, Wi-Fi. There were loads of them around Rame these days, blocking traffic, parking on narrow country roads to avoid paying the daily rates at the caravan sites.

King scanned his surroundings, looking for a good spot for a quick knee-tremble. He didn't want the tattooed smokers at the bar popping outside and interrupting their fun. He spotted a wheelie bin to his right, overflowing with bin bags and glass bottles. That was no good, but next to it he noticed a wooden log store with a gap behind it, wide enough to admit two people. Empty beer kegs and vape sticks littered the ground; the air carried the fetid stench of piss and rotten food. Hardly the most romantic spot. But on the plus side it was secluded, and dark. They would be hidden from view of anyone in the main car park area.

King stepped away from the log store and retraced his steps towards the back door. He wondered if Helina had always been into public sex. Was it a fetish, something that she would expect from him on a regular basis? Or had she made an exception for tonight?

He decided he didn't give a shit either way. He was about to get some with an incredibly beautiful woman. Only thing that truly mattered, when you got right down to it.

King was about to experience the greatest shag of his life.

That was when he heard the noise.

It started as a faint shrilling. A continuous hum that seemed, at first, to come from somewhere in the distance. Except it wasn't, King realised. The sound was coming from inside his head.

The noise quickly grew louder, swelled to a high-pitched drilling. A sharp pain flared between his temples, scraped like fingernails down the sides of his skull.

King suddenly felt nauseous. He screwed his eyes shut, clamped his hands over his ears in a futile effort to block out the sound.

The shrilling was impossibly loud now. He called out to Helina for help. Could barely hear himself above the screaming in his ears. He felt feverish. Like a bout of flu, but a billion times worse. Pain shot through his jaw, stabbed at the backs of his pupils.

He wondered if it was the Viagra he'd purchased online. Maybe it was a dodgy batch. Some sort of Chinese knock-off containing all kinds of weird shit. Or maybe someone had spiked his drink.

Then King felt a hot and sticky substance on his face. He pawed at his lips. Glanced down at his hand. Blood lacquered his fingers. Lots of it. Gushing out of his nostrils, his ears.

His mouth.

What the fuck . . . ?

King reached into his jeans pocket. Trembling fingers extracted his personal phone. Through the vicious pressure building inside his head he realised that the screen was blank. Had he turned it off earlier? He couldn't remember. He tried switching the device on. Got nothing.

Dead. His phone was dead.

King staggered towards the door. He was feeling dizzy now. He stumbled forwards, lost his balance, crashed against the wheelie bin. Bottles fell free from the overspill, shattered into fragments on the ground. He braced his arm against the bin, stopped himself from falling over.

The door flung open, and for a moment King thought Helina had come out to help him. Then he recognised the two figures emerging from the pub. The middle-aged couple he'd seen at the bar. The blonde woman and her shaven-headed partner. The guy with the meaty arms. King stumbled towards them, grabbed hold of the woman with outstretched arms and pleaded for help.

'Fuck's sake! Watch it, you pissed cunt,' the man seethed.

King ignored him and directed his pleas at the woman. Sweat trickled down his back, pasted his shirt to his skin.

'Please,' he gasped. 'You've got to help me. Please . . .'

The blonde woman stood staring him, mouth agape with a mixture of horror and confusion.

King tried to speak again. Realised he was foaming at the mouth. Then his stomach convulsed. Something bitter surged in his throat. He bent forward and vomited blood on the ground. The woman shrieked in terror.

The tattooed meat-head jerked back in disgust. As if someone had just told him that King had contracted Ebola.

'Jesus!' he shouted. 'Jesus, what the fuck . . .'

King hawked and spat, gasping for breath. He looked down at the pool of blood at his feet. Spotted a couple of teeth. His molars, he realised.

Christ, his molars had fallen out.

What the shitting hell is happening to me?

Blood trickled out of the corners of his eyes, traced veins down his cheeks. More of his teeth broke loose. King tasted blood in his mouth. He didn't know what the fuck was going on, but he was sure of one thing.

This isn't a batch of dodgy Viagra. Or a spiked drink.

No fucking way.

He wondered where Helina had gone.

King vomited again. Then his legs gave way beneath him, and he slumped to the floor, spasming violently.

He was dimly aware of the blonde-haired woman running back inside, shouting for help, calling for someone to call an ambulance. Moments later more people came bursting outside. The two young blokes who had been watching the footy. The barmaid.

By now King could no longer feel his arms or legs. As if someone had injected him with novocaine. The piercing noise in his ears had settled into an unremitting hum. Blood crowded in at the edges of his vision. He became vaguely aware of the barmaid dropping to a knee beside him, placing a hand on his shoulder.

'They're on the way, love,' she said. Her voice sounded small and distant, dampened by the blood oozing out of King's ears. 'Don't worry. The ambulance will be here soon. It'll be okay.'

He wanted to tell the barmaid that she was wrong. Things weren't going to be okay. King knew that. But he could no longer move his lips. Or any other part of his body. Everything had gone numb. He was scared now. Very scared. He voided his bladder; warm piss trickled down his legs. The pain inside his head was excruciating. Like someone had taken a blowtorch to his scalp.

King's world turned red.

Then black.

Two

London. The next day, 05.49 hours

David Hawkins, the one-time hero of the SAS, had been staring at the pills when his phone buzzed.

He kept a stash of them on his bedside table. Blister packs of sertraline, sleeping meds. Codeine for the pain in his left knee. His own miniature pharmacy. Hawkins had been lying in bed with a pounding hangover, counting the pills and thinking. He thought about swallowing them. Washing them down with a bottle of Jim Beam. He wondered whether that would be enough to do the trick. Put an end to everything.

Surrender to the darkness.

Pull the plug on his shitty existence.

Two or three times a week, Hawkins went through the same thought process. Usually after a night of solitary drinking. He'd pass out drunk on the bed. Slide gently into oblivion. The next morning the black mood would smother him. Like a shroud. It would whisper in his ear, telling him that he could never move past what had happened. That he could never forget the memory of that day on the hills six years ago.

The image of Jacob's body.

So end it, Davey boy, the voice would tell him softly. *Put a stop to the nightmares.*

Why go on any longer?

On the good mornings, Hawkins had the strength to resist the voice. Force it back into the box in his mind. He'd get up, go to work. Pretend to be a fully functioning member of society.

But on the bad days, the voice refused to be silenced. It would be there, murmuring in his ear. Telling him that all he needed to do was take his own life, and the pain would end. The grief that he had been carrying round with him, the loneliness, the images that haunted him daily.

All of it would be gone.

Hawkins had never given in, of course. He was a warrior. Fighting was in his blood. Even when the war was against his own damaged soul. But on those occasions the sheer effort of facing the new day overwhelmed him. Even the smallest act – getting out of bed, washing and dressing, going to work – seemed as exhausting as the prospect of a long march on the Brecon Beacons during Selection.

Lately, Hawkins had been suffering more bad days than good.

He had tried reaching out for help in the past. He'd seen enough Regiment lifers lose the battle with depression to know that no good could come from ignoring the symptoms and hoping it would go away. The equivalent of hunkering down in your foxhole instead of confronting the enemy.

So Hawkins had acknowledged his problem. He'd approached his doctor. Told him about the despair that stalked him. Shadowed his every move. How the alienation of his new life in London had made things worse. How his twenty-two-year-old daughter never returned his calls. How he would sometimes wait to cross the road and imagine hurling himself in front of onrushing traffic. His mangled body going under the wheels of a bus.

In death, at least, he would no longer have to carry round the guilt he'd shouldered for the past six years. The pain. The memory of Jacob's lifeless body.

Hawkins had unloaded all of his darkest fears on the doctor, with one exception. He hadn't mentioned the memory that haunted his life.

The frozen corpse lying on the hillside, nestled amid the snow-blanketed gorse and heather. Sugar-white frost dappling Jacob's beard and eyebrows. The strange bluish-grey colour of his skin.

Hawkins knew that there were some things you had to keep to yourself, because they were too painful to vocalise.

That image was one of them.

The doctor had listened sympathetically as Hawkins described his failed attempts at therapy. The suicidal thoughts that suddenly seized hold of him, like fingers around the throat. How nothing seemed to alleviate his depression. Then he had prescribed Hawkins a daily dose of anti-depressants. Fifty milligrams of sertraline.

The drugs had worked, at least for a while. Stabilised Hawkins. He no longer experienced the despairing lows, the sense of impending doom that had plagued him in the past. The irrational fear that the sky was about to fall in on his world. Neither did Hawkins feel any great sense of joy, though he had few reasons to celebrate the turns his life had taken since he'd quit Hereford.

But the pills couldn't block out the memory of Jacob's body.

Nightmares Hawkins could deal with. Christ, he'd suffered plenty of those in his time. But this was different. The image visited Hawkins during the day. Snuck up on him when he least expected it. Sometimes he would be sitting in a meeting, and it would flash across his face for a millisecond. Like a subliminal message. The ghost of it imprinted on his vision. Then the voice would start up again.

You want to get rid of this, don't you, Davey boy?
Then you know what you have to do.
End it.
Once and for all.

Eventually, Hawkins had gone back to the drink. The one thing that he could rely on. Booze didn't stop Hawkins from seeing Jacob's face – nothing could do that – but it did take the edge off. Dialled down the raw intensity of the memory. Made it manageable.

He knew self-medicating was a bad idea but told himself that he had no other choice. It was the bottle, or death.

Each day, after leaving work at DeepSpear's head office in St James's, Hawkins would return to the company-owned studio apartment on the fifth floor of a block on Kensington High Street. He'd sit alone on the sofa, the lights switched out while he worked his way through a bottle of Jim Beam. Then he'd collapse on the bed.

Rinse and repeat.

London was not good for his health. Hawkins knew that. The solitude. Too much time to think. Too many evenings spent alone with nothing but his dark thoughts and cheap bourbon for company. But the job at least gave him a steady income. Kept his mind occupied. Stopped his thoughts from drifting back to the corpse. Allowed him to keep up his monthly payments to his ex-wife.

Hawkins had landed the gig a year ago. After a decade dedicated to 22 SAS, fighting at the tip of the military spear, he had finally turned his back on Hereford. Walked out on all he'd ever known. Which had been surprisingly easy. A lot of lads struggled when they left the Regiment. Spent their careers being told they were the best of the fucking best. Then they got out and realised they had been living in a bubble. On Civvy Street, no one gave two shits about you.

Hawkins had avoided that pitfall. He'd never thrown his weight around. Never allowed his ego to get in the way of getting the job done. A humble kid from Wearside, he was grateful for the opportunities the Regiment had given him. He felt an obligation to repay that debt, by working to become the best version of himself.

He had been surprised to find that not all of the Blades felt the same way. There were some lads who were more interested in being part of the in-crowd at Hereford. They went out on the piss together. Formed tight cliques. Looked out for one another. Bullied and belittled those outside the group.

Hawkins had shown no interest in that side of things. He wasn't tribal. Never had been. He detested bullies. Preferred his own company to bantering with the lads.

But not being part of the crowd came with its own problems. Because when trouble came knocking, Hawkins had no friends in the unit. No one who had his back.

A mistake, in hindsight. One that had ultimately cost him his career.

He had one ally. That guy had argued his case with the head shed, but in the end it hadn't been enough. Banished from Hereford, Hawkins had served a few years in Regimental exile before handing in his chips.

Now he lived alone and worked as Head of Security at Deep-Spear Defence Industries. A mid-level position. Fifty grand a year, plus company benefits and pension. Health insurance. Steady work. The best he could have hoped for, under the circumstances. But spirit-crushingly dull.

Hawkins spent half his time sitting behind a desk, writing reports, pulling together presentations, hacking his way through emails. The rest of the time he was on the road, travelling to meetings at DeepSpear's other sites around the UK: Hull, Clyde, Bristol. A bunch of other places. Routine security inspections. Checking padlocks, replacing broken CCTV cameras, drawing up risk assessments. Overnight stays in three-star hotels with anonymous décor and bland coffee.

The most boring job he'd done before joining the army was working on an assembly line at a car plant in Sunderland. His new gig was almost as mind-numbing. No risk, no thrills. The biggest danger he faced was bad eyesight from staring at a screen for too long. That, or going out of his mind with boredom.

Not the future he had imagined for himself. Better than a punch to the kidneys, maybe. But for a former SAS man, there could be no bleaker fate.

The tiny voice at the back of his mind piped up again.

Time to face facts, pal.

You're a sad ex-soldier. Your family wants nothing to do with you. Forty-three, but you might as well be a hundred given the way your colleagues look at you. Like something that walked out of the Stone Age.

What the fuck have you got to live for?

Why keep going on?

Zoe, Hawkins told himself.

I have to keep going for Zoe.

In the end, the drinking had destroyed Hawkins's marriage. Collateral damage in the wake of the catastrophe on the Brecon Beacons. One evening, after a heavy session of solo boozing, Hawkins had returned to an empty home, a scrawled note on the kitchen table. Michelle's handwriting.

I'm sorry, David. I can't do this anymore.

Hawkins didn't blame her for walking out on him. Would probably have done the same thing, in her position. In the divorce that followed he decided not to fight her. He didn't want to poison the well. But his relationship with Zoe had suffered. She had blamed him for the break-up. Understandable, in a way. There has to be villain in every story.

Hawkins had considered explaining why they had separated. The losing battle he had been fighting against his demons. But in the end, he figured he should spare Zoe that trauma. She had enough problems in life. She didn't need her father to add to them with his own grief. Instead, he allowed his daughter to drift away from him.

Maybe it's for the best, the voice had said.

Look at all the damage you've caused. The pain you've inflicted on those around you. Everything you touch turns to shit. Maybe Zoe's better off without you.

Since then Hawkins had tried to patch things up with her. Mostly after he'd necked a few double measures of Jim. But the flurries of late-night messages had gone unanswered, and it had been eight months since he'd last heard from Zoe. After his last attempt to reach out to her, Zoe had ghosted him. Blocked him from her social media. He had no idea where she was living, what was going on in her life, whether she had a boyfriend. Knew nothing about her life.

Despite everything, he clung to the faint hope that Zoe would come back into his life one day. The one thing that kept him going.

That was why Hawkins limped on. Zoe was why he showed up for work, pretended to enjoy the banter of his colleagues. Why he returned to his flat each evening, instead of throwing himself in front of a bus.

Christ, he missed her like hell.

Sometimes, late at night, three sheets to the wind, Hawkins would flick through the photo library on his phone. Zoe in her school uniform for the first time. Family holidays. Christmas at the in-laws'. He thought he might give anything to hear her laugh one more time, to see her brilliant smile.

Hawkins's phone rang again. The vibration echoed loudly inside his skull. Pain flared viciously between his temples. As if someone was drilling directly into his cranium.

Hawkins reached for the handset, knocked over a pack of paracetamol, an empty bottle of whisky and some other bits of rubbish on the bedside table. He wondered if Zoe was calling him.

Maybe she's read my messages, telling her how sorry I am. How much I miss her, Hawkins thought.

He frowned at the screen.

Not his daughter.

His boss.

Tom Gracey was the Global Director of Security at DeepSpear Industries. Global Chief Dickhead, as Hawkins preferred to think of him. Civilian born and bred, privately educated, Home Counties parents and the silvery accent to match. First-class degree from UCL, an MA in Security Studies at St Andrews. Not posh, but a rung or two below. Worse, in some ways. Intent on clawing his way up the greasy pole, fluent in corporate-management bullshit. A company man to the bone.

Gracey looked down his nose at Hawkins. Regarded him as dumb muscle and made fun of him in team meetings, humiliating him in front of his junior colleagues. Called him a dinosaur to his face.

Hawkins hated his guts.

But Gracey calling him was a rare event. Like an extinction-level asteroid hitting the earth, or the trains running on time in Britain.

Which begged a question.

Why the fuck is he bothering me at this hour?

Hawkins figured that there had been some colossal balls-up at one of DeepSpear's sites. A security malfunction over in Bristol, maybe, or campaigners from the Campaign for Nuclear Disarmament staging a protest outside the docks at Faslane. A group of hairy-arsed lefties waving placards.

Hawkins briefly considered ignoring the call. Sleep off the hangover. He'd call in sick later.

Tempting.

The phone buzzed a third time.

Shit.

Hawkins hack-coughed, clearing his throat, then swiped to answer. He clamped the phone to his ear.

'David, thank Christ,' Gracey said in his plummy voice. 'Where the hell are you?'

'Home,' Hawkins said. 'I'm at home.'

Like any normal person at 5.50 in the morning, he was tempted to add.

Gracey snorted. The noise came down the line like a rattlesnake hiss.

'For God's sake. Haven't you seen my messages? I've been trying to get hold of you for the past hour.'

Hawkins considered telling his boss to go fuck himself. Decided against it. Channelled his inner Zen Master instead and waited for Gracey to go on.

'Listen. You need to come into the office. Now. We've got a problem.'

Hawkins wondered if he was in trouble. Maybe someone had seen him turning up pissed at work and grassed him up to senior management. Gracey would relish the chance to make an example of Hawkins. Humiliate him again. The guy had been angling to sack Hawkins from the moment he'd joined the company in the spring.

'What's going on?' Hawkins asked.

Gracey said, 'I can't say. Not on the phone. All I can tell you is that we have a situation. It's serious, and we don't have much time. There's going to be a briefing this morning. We'll get into the weeds of it then.'

Gracey had an irritating habit of talking in the lingo of corporate management execs. Another reason why Hawkins despised him.

He said, 'When?'

'Seven o'clock. Secure room on the fourth floor. Bring your go-bag with you.'

The line went dead.

Go-bag, thought Hawkins.

Which could mean only one thing. He was being sent somewhere.

Hawkins listened to the dead air for a beat and regarded the pills. He took the voice that had been telling him to end his life and put it back in the box. Closed the lid on it, turned the lock. Took the key out. Visualised every step. The way he always did when the voice brought him to the brink.

Then he took a deep breath and prepared to face the day.

Three

Cadmon House looked like it had been standing since the days of the French Revolution. It occupied one corner of King Street in the heart of St James's, a gleaming five-storey behemoth dressed in Portland stone, opposite an Indian restaurant and a dark-windowed wine bar. Spitting distance from the stuffy private members' clubs and the imposing corporate offices based around St James's Square. What tourists imagined London looked like, before they debussed from the plane and found themselves in a dilapidated airport terminal in Luton.

The building blended in perfectly with its surroundings. There was nothing to suggest the company's interests. No business logo, no corporate slogan. Just a small brass plaque above the glass doors with 'CADMON HOUSE' engraved on it in elegant lettering. It looked more like a gentlemen's club than the headquarters of a cutting-edge defence contractor. The anonymity was deliberate. Like hiding in plain sight. DeepSpear provided clients with everything from cyber security to advanced drones and robots. The kind of people who valued discretion.

Hawkins had a company car but he preferred to walk the three miles to the office. He found it helped to clear his head, and keep himself somewhat trim. A few minutes before seven o'clock he crossed the street and beat a path towards the entrance, the hangover reduced to a faint throbbing at the back of his skull. He'd scrubbed up in a hurry after the crack-of-dawn summons from Gracey. A cold shower, followed by a handful of Nurofen washed down with two mugs of industrial-strength black coffee. Something to take the edge off the pain.

As he swept through the entrance Hawkins wondered again if he was in the shit. He'd racked his brains, thinking of any recent incident that might have landed him in hot water. Couldn't think of any. And there was the fact that Gracey had told him to bring in his go-bag. Which suggested a trip to one of DeepSpear's regional offices, rather than a slap on the wrist.

Hawkins slapped his security pass against the entry reader, stepped into a marble-floored lobby the approximate size of the Colosseum. A reedy white-haired bloke in a cheap suit sat in the waiting area, reading a paperback thriller. Hawkins recognised him as the CEO's personal chauffeur. Two receptionists sat behind a desk the size of a cruise ship, tapping away on keyboards.

Hawkins nodded curtly at the on-duty guard and made for the turnstile barriers. Swiped his pass. The glass gates hummed softly open; he made for the bank of lifts at the far end and rode the next one to the fourth floor. Whereupon he emerged to a grey-carpeted open-plan space, the walls decorated with photographic murals depicting DeepSpear's great success stories down the years. The company's first drone on a test flight over the Nevada desert. Another photograph showed a robotic dog clambering over rubble in a warzone.

The office was almost empty at this hour, except for a few employees sitting at their workstations, ear buds blocking out background chatter. Hawkins breezed past them and headed straight for the secure room on the other side of the floor. Which was essentially a soundproofed space fitted out with advanced signal-jamming equipment. Somewhere DeepSpear's senior personnel could hold sensitive internal discussions without fear of anyone listening in. Only those with the top level of clearance were permitted inside.

Hawkins tapped his card against the reader below the door lock, wrenched the chrome handle and stepped into a blandly furnished room dominated by an oval-shaped conference table in dark oak encircled by a series of executive chairs. Like the Round Table minus the knights. There was a fifty-inch TV mounted on the back wall, a few artificial plants and bookshelves lined the room. A light above the door glowed green, indicating that it was currently unlocked.

Hawkins had attended several meetings in this room since he'd joined DeepSpear. Discussing the schedule for testing a new type of underwater drone, or the talking through the details of a weapon system being sold to a foreign partner. Anything considered top-secret.

Two figures sat at the table. Tom Gracey was dressed, as usual, in a Jermyn Street three-piece suit over a silk shirt. A Breitling titanium watch with a face as big as a roulette wheel gleamed on his left wrist. His butter-smooth skin suggested a lengthy morning regimen with expensive grooming products. He had a cyclist's physique, gaunt-cheeked and angular, sculpted by long rides in the Surrey Hills. Atop it sat the world's most punchable face. He greeted Hawkins with a brisk pump of his hairy maw.

'David, good man,' Gracey said with fake chumminess. 'Thanks for coming in. You know Alex, of course. She'll be working with you on this one.'

He indicated the third person in the room. Alex Millar. DeepSpear's newly appointed Head of Cyber Security. Hawkins had been briefly introduced to her when she'd first taken up her role several months ago. He didn't really know her, although they had attended many of the same meetings, and there was a natural overlap between their fields of responsibility. Hawkins tended to avoid the tech crowd. Not his scene. He knew about people. Weapons. Killing. The old ways of warfare. The new stuff – hacking into national grids, stealing data, disinformation – that was a mystery to him. Up there with drill music and the appeal of cosy crime.

Millar smiled awkwardly as she shook his hand. She looked tense, Hawkins noticed. He wondered why.

'All right, lass,' he said. 'How's tricks?'

Millar gave him an icy look. 'Excuse me?'

At his side Gracey coughed and said, 'My apologies, Alex. I'm afraid David is rather – antiquated in some of his views.'

'Shit,' Hawkins muttered. 'Sorry, ah—'

'Alex,' Millar said. 'How about you just call me Alex.'

She spoke with a distinctive Midlands drawl. Brummie, maybe, thought Hawkins. Or Nottingham. Somewhere in that ballpark.

'Right,' he said. 'Alex. Sorry.'

Hawkins looked her up and down. He'd never really paid Millar much notice before, but now she was standing in front of him, he took in her appearance properly. Short brown hair framed soft almond-shaped eyes; thin lips smiled faintly beneath a button nose. She wore a plain blouse under a dark blazer. Pencil skirt and penny loafers. The dress of someone who didn't have time to fuss endlessly in front of a mirror but knew how to look good anyway. The kind of hard-won attraction shaped by the training ground and life experience.

Which wasn't surprising. Hawkins had heard on the office grapevine that Millar had been attached to 18 Signals some years ago before she'd joined DeepSpear. They were the Sigs guys who worked alongside UKSF. Best in the business. Shit-hot at comms and cyber warfare. Since Millar had landed the job at DeepSpear she had quickly earned a reputation as a straight talker. Not someone afraid of calling people out or dishing out bollockings when the situation called for it.

'Have a seat, David,' Gracey said, closing the door.

Hawkins dumped his go-bag next to the door, dropped himself into a high-backed chair that looked like it had been ripped from a spaceship cockpit. Whatever the reason for the meeting, Hawkins reassured himself that he wasn't in trouble. Definitely not a bollocking. The presence of Millar at the briefing confirmed that much.

And told him something else. The crisis Gracey had mentioned required the input and skillsets of both the Head of Security and the company's Cyber-Security Chief. Which meant it had to be something big.

Bigger than a security glitch. Bigger than a few protestors outside a nuclear submarine site.

Gracey leaned forward and laced his fingers together, signalling the beginning of the briefing.

'Let's get down to brass tacks,' he began. 'I'll keep this short. We're against the clock here, and there's a lot of ground to cover. Alex has already been briefed but I've asked her to sit in on this thing in case you have any questions. I know cyber isn't exactly your bailiwick, David.'

Gracey chuckled at his own risible joke. Hawkins stared back, teeth gritted.

'First things first,' Gracey went on. 'I very much hope this goes without saying, but what we're about to discuss doesn't leave this room under any circumstances. This is an extremely sensitive situation, and it needs to stay in-house before we operationalise. Are we clear?'

'Just tell us what the fuck's going on,' Hawkins said, impatiently.

Gracey gave him a look that could cut through ten inches of steel. Then he said, 'Yesterday evening, one of our employees working at the Devonport office died in unusual circumstances.'

That caught Hawkins's attention. He swapped a puzzled look with Millar.

'Unusual how?' he asked.

'We're not quite sure at the moment,' Gracey replied. 'There are a lot of blanks in the narrative, and we're still trying to establish the facts. What we do know is that at around eight o'clock last night a DeepSpear engineer named Matthew King collapsed outside a pub in Cremyll, across the Sound from Plymouth. Unverified reports on social media claim King was found collapsed in the car park, foaming at the mouth and vomiting blood. At nine o'clock he was taken to Derriford hospital by air ambulance. Pronounced dead on arrival.'

'Jesus. What the fuck happened?'

'Cause of death is currently unknown. The police obviously aren't sharing any details with us, other than the bare facts. Time and location of death, victim's identity and so on. They're doing a full autopsy and toxicology report, naturally.'

Hawkins narrowed his eyes to points. 'You think his death is suspicious?'

'I'm just telling you how it is.' Gracey spread his hands. 'King was a healthy guy. Thirty-four, keen amateur runner and cyclist. Then one evening he drops dead in a pub car park.'

'History of substance abuse? Secret coke habit?'

Gracey shook his head firmly. 'Nothing like that. Clean bill of health at his last company medical. Colleagues say he wasn't the type to dabble in drugs. We can't say for sure until the autopsy is in. But on the balance of probability, I'd say we're looking at foul play.'

A thought scratched at the nape of Hawkins's neck. 'What was your man King doing at the pub?'

'It appears,' Gracey said, 'he had gone there to meet a woman. Looks like she fled the scene shortly before the air ambulance arrived. It's likely she's involved.'

'I'd say it's more than fucking likely. It's a nailed-on certainty.'

Gracey merely shrugged.

'Who was she?' Hawkins asked.

'We don't know. The police are still trying to establish her identity.'

'Have they got any idea what happened?'

'Right now, the working theory is that King was poisoned.'

Hawkins said, 'Makes sense. Why else would a healthy bloke in his thirties suddenly kick the bucket?'

'There's more,' said Gracey. 'King is the second employee at Plymouth to have died in the past month.'

Hawkins squished his eyebrows. 'Who's the other?'

'King's manager. Chap by the name of Steve Rideout. He died three weeks ago, while out on his morning run near his home in

Saltash. At the time, his death didn't raise any red flags. Rideout was in his late fifties, family history of heart disease. He'd been on statins for several years. High blood pressure. Stress. All the signs pointed to a massive heart attack. That was the coroner's verdict.'

'But now you think the deaths are linked?' Hawkins asked.

Gracey said, 'We're talking about two workers dying in the space of less than a month. Both based at the same location, and on the same team. The odds of that being a coincidence are vanishingly rare. Like finding a Geordie with more than two brain cells.'

Hawkins glowered at him.

'Plus,' Gracey added, 'there's the breach at Devonport.'

Hawkins frowned heavily. 'What breach?'

Gracey tipped his head at Millar. Who turned to Hawkins and said, 'Four months ago, there was a serious cyber incident at Devonport. The network was compromised by foreign agents.'

'So what?' Hawkins said. 'I bet those systems get attacked all the time.'

Millar shook her head. 'This was different. Most hacks are stopped before they can get into the system. The people behind this one, they managed to penetrate the defences.'

Gracey said, 'Management is naturally keen to keep a tight lid on the incident.'

'Why?'

'Reputational risk. The Faslane contract.'

Hawkins nodded slowly. He'd heard the news shortly after he'd joined DeepSpear. A joint announcement with the MoD. DeepSpear had won the lucrative contract for the management of the naval base at Faslane and the nearby nuclear warhead storage site at Coulport. A major deal, worth potentially billions of pounds. A potential game-changer for a startup firm less than twenty years old.

'You want the incident to stay buried, you mean,' Hawkins said.

Gracey said, 'We're no different to any other large organisation that's been hacked. No one wants to admit to it, for obvious reasons.'

'How did they get in?'

Millar shifted her weight and said, 'A senior executive's login credentials were published on the dark web. We don't know how that happened. But it's an increasingly common tactic. Instead of trying to hack into a network, you just get hold of someone's password.'

Gracey said, 'We want to know if there's a link between the deaths and the earlier attack. Anything that might come out in the wash, so to speak. You can imagine the embarrassment if this becomes public knowledge. Demands from ministers to revisit the terms of agreement, that sort of thing. You know what those Whitehall types are like. Any excuse to save the taxpayer a few quid.'

Hawkins turned to Millar and said, 'Did the hackers get their hands on anything classified?'

'Thankfully, no,' she replied in her strong Midlands twang. 'We managed to detect the breach before they could destroy or steal any sensitive material. But we recognised the tactics. Without getting too technical, the hackers used a very specific approach. One that we recognised from previous incidents. Sort of like their MO. We're confident it was the work of the Russians. Specifically, Unit 29155.'

'Who the fuck are they?'

'It's a secret intelligence cell,' Gracey explained. 'Within the GRU.'

GRU, thought Hawkins. *Main Intelligence Directorate.*

Everyone at Hereford knew about the GRU. Russia's foreign military intelligence service. Had their own armed wing of Spetsnaz operators.

Millar said, 'Unit 29155 is a small group of experienced operators, tasked with disrupting the Kremlin's enemies by any means possible. They specialise in everything from industrial sabotage to assassinations. They're the ones behind the Salisbury poisonings. Two years ago, the same unit launched a massive cyber campaign against Ukraine on the eve of the invasion, targeting the country's critical infrastructure. The electricity grid, hospitals, schools, government systems. The scale of the attack was unprecedented.'

'So we have two dead employees,' Gracey said, 'and a cyber-attack at their workplace, likely carried out by a covert unit within Russian intelligence.'

Something occurred to Hawkins. A question that had been bothering him since the start of the briefing. 'What kind of work was King doing down at Plymouth?'

'He was attached to the team working on the autonomous torpedo programme. Devonport has hundreds of people working on it. King was part of the project management team. Therefore fully vetted. Highest level of security clearance. A cog in the wheel, so to speak. But an important one.'

Hawkins had heard of the project. The Makara programme, they called it. Named after a sea creature in Hindu mythology. A joint partnership with the MoD. Whitehall was playing catch-up after decades of military stagnation. A nuclear-powered torpedo that could be launched from a conventional submarine, able to move undetected through hostile waters, operating for long periods, and capable of carrying nuclear warheads. Everything else about the venture was shrouded in secrecy. Only a handful of people at the very top knew the full details of what was being developed by the Makara team.

Hawkins had been told by a colleague that Nish Varma, Deep-Spear's CEO, had high hopes for the torpedo, the first of several new weapons being designed in collaboration with the British government. Hawkins wasn't so sure. He'd seen plenty of swanky presentations in the past. Guys in suits giving it the hard sell. Brand new weapon platforms that were going to change the face of battle. Most of them had been consigned to the dustbin.

He said, 'Is there any indication that King's death is somehow related to his work?'

'Honestly, we don't know. Had King been selling secrets to the woman he'd met at the pub? Did he give information to her? Was she blackmailing him? Did he owe money to the wrong people? Right now, we're in the dark. Which is why I need you two to go down to Plymouth. Find out what's really going on.'

'What for? Sounds like the local plod are already on the case. They'll be over it like flies over shit.'

Gracey flapped a hand dismissively. 'Forget the police investigation. It'll go nowhere.'

'You can't guarantee that.'

'Actually, we can.'

Gracey stared meaningfully at Hawkins.

He said, 'We've instructed management at Plymouth to tell the police that King was a low-level maintenance worker. Fixing pipes and ducting, that sort of thing. His co-workers have been told not to say anything about the nature of their work. That should throw the investigators off the scent.'

Hawkins stared at him aghast. 'That's interfering with a criminal investigation.'

Gracey shrugged. 'It's in our best interests to keep this situation in-house.'

'Besides,' Millar cut in, 'if the Russians are involved, we need to think very carefully about who we can trust.'

'Meaning?'

'We have information that the GRU has been ramping up its activities in the UK in recent months. Engaging in what we call sub-threshold warfare.'

'In layman's terms,' Gracey said, 'the Russians are testing us, using foreign agents to probe our defences for weak points. Sticking drones over RAF bases. Getting merchant vessels to slice underwater cables with their anchors. Using criminal gangs to do their dirty work, killing anyone who tries to expose the Kremlin's lies. All of that and more. We're talking about a concerted attempt to undermine national security both in the UK and elsewhere. The GRU,' Gracey added, 'is a big part of this new type of warfare.'

Millar said, 'Part of the GRU's mandate is to recruit officers within the Met and the National Crime Agency.'

'Why would they do that?' asked Hawkins. 'It's not as if them lot have access to top-secret info.'

'No, but they can access information on suspects. Locations of safe houses. The identities of people living in witness protection. They can tamper with evidence. Forewarn Russia's UK-based assets if they come under investigation.'

Gracey said, 'The local constabulary won't have the expertise to handle King's death. They'll look to on-ramp national partners. Cross-pollinate skillsets. Which means Met or NCA involvement. Which means there's a chance some of the investigators may be in the pocket of the Russian security services.'

'And if the Russians are somehow involved,' Millar put in, 'they could use their influence with the Met to get them to forestall the investigation. Give the Kremlin time to cover their tracks.'

Hawkins scratched his cheek and considered. He'd met a few blokes in the Met during his time on the SP Team. They were always banging on about their crap salary. At least some of them, he assumed, were corruptible. Therefore potentially vulnerable to foreign influence. Moreover, Hawkins reflected, the Kremlin could buy them on the cheap. Less time-consuming and costly than trying to recruit a double agent inside Five or Six.

Gracey continued, 'It's crucial that we stop the police from poking around on this one. Could be dangerous for us. For Whitehall, too.'

'What about the dead bloke's family?' asked Hawkins. 'His friends? Do they know what's going on?'

Gracey gave a quick shake of his head. 'King wasn't exactly sociable. Parents live in a village a few miles outside Aberystwyth. He has an older brother in Leeds but as we understand it they weren't close and rarely spoke. We're sending someone from HR to speak with them. Ask not to make any public statements as it'll only fuel speculation.'

'They might not cooperate.'

'I very much doubt that. There's a very generous financial offer on the table in return for their cooperation. A life-changing sum. The Kings,' Gracey added pointedly, 'are not rich people.'

Hawkins said, 'What do you want us to do?'

'The police are going to want to seize King's laptop. You need to get down to Plymouth immediately. Liaise with the local security manager and get hold of his computer. Search it for any incriminating information before the police show up and confiscate it.'

'How can you be sure that he left his laptop at work? Might be at his digs, for all we know.'

Gracey shook his head. 'The engineers aren't allowed to take their work devices home with them. Company policy. King will have left it at his desk. You can count on it.'

'Get the Head of Security at Plymouth to deal with it, then. Save the company a few quid on travel expenses.'

'That's not going to cut it for me. We need you both on-site. Given the nature of his job, King's laptop will contain some extremely sensitive information. The kind we'd prefer to stay confidential. This task is too high-level to leave to some junior colleague down on the south coast.' Gracey ran a hand over his bald dome. 'Anyway, there's a second reason we need you down at Plymouth.'

'What's that?'

'We need you to find out what really happened to King. Poke around, ask questions, but for God's sake do it quietly.'

'What for? So you lot can hide it from the police?' Hawkins asked sarkily.

Gracey shot him a glare so ice-cold Wim Hof could have bathed in it.

'This isn't about the police,' he replied tersely. 'We need to get in front of this thing. Anticipate any problems so we can control the narrative before it ends up controlling us. That means finding out the truth about King, and Rideout, and if they're related to the cyber-attack. Once we have the full picture, we can decide on next steps. Do we go on the offensive, or do we need to circle the wagons? How much do we share with our security partners? And so on.'

'It's possible, too,' Millar interposed, 'that there might be information on King's laptop about the woman he met in Cremyll. That might help us to identify her. Or track her down.'

'Waste of time,' Hawkins responded. 'If she's implicated in his death, she'll be long gone.'

Gracey said, 'You may well be right. Either way, we need to know what's really going on down there.'

'We'll do our best to avoid the police,' said Hawkins. 'But I can't make any promises. One of the investigators might be switched on. They might wonder what we're doing down there in the first place.'

'That can't be helped. Just make sure there's nothing that could come back to haunt us down the line. Any problems with them, let me know. I'll take it upstairs to Nish.'

Nish Varma, thought Hawkins.

DeepSpear's CEO and founder.

Out of the many thousands of employees at DeepSpear, only a handful of people could confidently refer to Varma by his first name. Gracey was one of them. A stark reminder of his proximity to power.

Hawkins said, 'What about management at Plymouth? Do they know we're coming down?'

'We've updated them. Just don't expect the red-carpet treatment when you get there. They're running around like headless chickens. Got their hands full at the minute, trying to keep a lid on the rumours about King.'

Gracey stole a glance at his watch. A less-than-subtle hint that the meeting was over.

'You'll report directly to me,' he continued. 'I expect a full update tomorrow. Understood?'

'Fine.'

'One more thing.'

Gracey leaned forward. Stared evenly at Hawkins and Millar in turn.

'You are not to discuss this situation with anyone else in the building,' he continued. 'That goes for both of you. Any problems, you come to me. We're trying to keep this situation contained as far as possible. Last thing we need is to loop in more people.'

'I get it.' Hawkins held up his hands in mock surrender. 'The company image. Reputation. All of that. We'll be careful.'

'Just so we understand each other.' Gracey nodded curtly and stood up. 'Any more questions? No? Then I suggest you get a move on. You leave at once.'

Four

They rolled out of Cadmon House nine minutes later. Grabbed their go-bags, exited the secure room and took the stairs to the underground garage. Millar followed Hawkins as he swept through the fire door and marched towards the Mercedes-Benz GLE SUV in his allocated parking space a short distance away. One of the perks of the job, Hawkins reflected. One of the few. Eighty thousand pounds of luxury vehicle and leather interior. Almost made the mind-numbing meetings and two-hour Power-Point presentations worth it.

Almost.

He stowed both go-bags in the boot and slid behind the wheel, with Millar riding shotgun. Hawkins dumped his phone face-up on the console charging mat. Thumbed the START-STOP button. The engine roared into life. He worked the infotainment screen, opened the navigation app and punched in the address for Deep-Spear's Plymouth office. The computer crunched the numbers at hyper-speed. Came up with a route that would take them west out of the city, past Reading and towards Bristol. Then a straight downward run through Exeter and Dartmoor. The less direct option, on the face of things. But quicker than the other routes, apparently. A distance of two hundred and forty miles. Hawkins resigned himself to five long hours on the road.

He steered out of the garage, arrowed the Merc up the ramp and hung a right onto St James's Street. Joined the traffic slow-chuntering west along Piccadilly. Eight o'clock on a Monday morning. London was dusting off its Sunday cobwebs. Putting the weekend in the rear-view. Commuters thronged the roads. Lycra-clad cyclists. Helmeted motorbikers buzzing around with brightly coloured food delivery boxes, backpacked workers jogging to work for reasons that eluded Hawkins. Idiots weaving through traffic on e-scooters and hire bicycles. The whole universe in a mad rush to be somewhere else, five minutes ago. Hawkins was grateful for the chance to leave London for a couple of days. Too long in the capital and he started to feel like an alien living among a colony of coked-up ants.

Millar said, 'We should head straight to Devonport. No rest stops on the way. We don't want the police beating us there because of a weak bladder.'

Hawkins said, 'You really think there's something incriminating on King's laptop?'

'I think,' said Millar, 'that getting our hands on that computer is our best chance of finding out what happened to him.'

'Assuming he left a trail. He might have deleted everything.'

Millar smiled in faint amusement. Like a kid hearing a grandparent describe the world before the internet.

She said, 'Data can almost always be scraped. First rule of cyber security. Even when you think you've deleted something, chances are it's still going to be floating around somewhere in the cloud. All the websites you've ever visited, all the porn you've looked at, the passwords you've saved. Everything.'

Hawkins said, 'Then how do you destroy the evidence?'

'You don't. Not without considerable time, and technical expertise.'

'Could King have done it?'

'In theory. But he had no reason to cover his tracks.'

'Unless he was selling secrets to the enemy.'

Millar gave him a sharp look. 'Do you think that's what he was doing?'

Hawkins shrugged his broad shoulders. 'It's the most likely explanation. Why else would he go to meet that woman in Cremyll? Other than the obvious.'

'The obvious?' Millar repeated.

Hawkins nodded. 'She might have promised him the ride of his life.'

He grinned. Millar did a thing with her eyes as if to say, *Men*. Hawkins put his serious face back on and continued.

'Here's what I think happened. Your man King went to the meet to sell information to this woman. Either that, or he was being forced to hand it over. Blackmailed or whatever. He gets there, delivers the package. She spikes his drink. Bumps him off to make sure there's nothing that might lead back to her. Then legs it straight to the airport.'

Millar looked away and thought for a beat. 'I don't think it's that simple. From what Gracey told us, King wasn't the traitorous type. Model employee. No skeletons in the closet. No bad habits.'

'Unless you count being a paranoid loner.'

'He was an engineer. Half his workmates are probably classified as paranoid loners. Doesn't mean he was flogging secrets to the enemy.'

'Maybe there was a side to him his colleagues didn't know about. Maybe he had a gambling problem. Or he might have owed money to the wrong people. Someone like King, with his tech skills, would know how to hide that stuff from his muckers.'

'*Tech skills?*'

'Expertise. Computer knowledge. Whatever you want to call it. You get my point.'

Millar said, 'You're forgetting about the death of King's boss.'

'Rideout? What about him?'

'Let's pretend for a moment that King was supplying information to the Russians. Why would they go after his boss as well?'

'Rideout might have got wind of what King was up to. Maybe King panicked when he found out and spilled his guts to his handler.'

'How does that fit in with the cyber incident at Devonport?'

'I don't have a clue, mate. That's your bag, not mine.'

Millar chewed on her bottom lip. She said, 'Gracey thinks they're linked.'

'He also thinks the sun shines out of his arse.'

'But he's right about the timing. The cyber-attack, then the two deaths a few months later. It looks suspicious.'

Hawkins thought for a moment and said, 'How easy is it to hack into our networks?'

'It's not. Laying the groundwork for an operation on that scale takes a lot of planning. We're not talking about a spotty teenager in a basement, breaking into the Pentagon between sessions on his PlayStation. Why?'

Hawkins shrugged. 'I'm just wondering why the Russians would go to the effort of trying to breach the network if they already had a man on the inside.'

'Maybe they didn't. Maybe the hack was their first approach, and when that didn't work, they turned to King. Or it could have been a misdirection attack.'

'You mean someone broke into the system to divert our attention from somewhere else?'

Millar nodded and said, 'We thought we were being smart when we detected the breach. But maybe the Russians *wanted* to be found out. Make sure we weren't focused on some other part of the system. As in, a human asset.'

They drove on. Skated past the southern fringes of Hyde Park, bowled west through Knightsbridge. Following the voice directions on the map as they snaked through Hammersmith, under banks of dishwater-grey cloud. By the time they hit Chiswick Hawkins's hangover had come back with a vengeance. He could feel it stabbing at his temporal lobes.

Then he glanced in the rear-view and saw the face.

Jacob was sitting in the back seat. Eyes popped wide, meeting Hawkins's gaze in the mirror. Pale lips stretched into a grimace.

Screaming silently.

The pounding inside Hawkins's head worsened.

He gripped the wheel. Refocused his attention on the road. But when he looked up at the rear-view the face was still there.

Christ, he thought.

We've only just started the mission, and I'm already hanging out of my arse.

Hawkins was sweating heavily as they joined the traffic-snarl outside Heathrow. He wondered how the fuck he was going to get through the rest of the day and considered pulling into the next rest stop. Rush inside, grab a bottle of whisky from one of the shops. Disappear into the toilets and help himself to a quick hit. Not much. Just something to take the edge off. The only way he could get rid of the image.

Then he looked again in the mirror, and the face had gone.

He felt a twinge of relief. But it would come back, he knew. It always did.

A while later the rain struck. Needle-like drops drummed against the windscreen. Suburban England streamed past, rain-sodden and beaten down. Mosaic of charity shops and vape stores, fried chicken joints and dilapidated housing estates. Concrete multi-storeys loomed like Aztec temples over garishly lit retail parks. The collapse of civilisation in slow-motion.

No wonder our enemies are getting bolder, he thought to himself. *Look at the state of us. They can smell blood.*

Past Slough they settled in for the long run west towards Bristol. A ninety-mile stretch of rain-slicked blacktop. Boring as fuck, but Hawkins was happy to do it. He had sometimes driven twenty-four hours straight in the Regiment without stopping for so much as a piss break. Something to do with his programming. Life in the SAS taught you to focus on a single task to the exclusion of all else. Empty your mind of all the unnecessary shit. Concentrate on the thing right in front of you.

Millar spent a chunk of time on her phone during the journey. Reading through emails, firing off responses on a bunch of different messaging apps. After a while she put her handset to sleep and said, 'Gracey told me you're ex-Hereford.'

Something clicked inside Hawkins's head.

So that's what the two of them were discussing before I showed up at the briefing, he thought. He wondered what else Gracey had told her. Whether she already knew about Jacob.

'Aye,' Hawkins answered tersely. 'That's right. Cashed in my chips a year ago.'

'I don't remember hearing your name when I was posted with 18 Sigs.'

'You wouldn't have done. I haven't graced the camp in a while.'

He didn't explain further. He had no desire to fill in the gaps in his origin story. Especially with someone he'd only met a couple of hours ago. In his head, he wanted to get the job done and go home. Pull the curtains, pour a fresh slug of Jim B. Drink himself into a stupor. Black out. Escape Jacob's dead face, if only for a few hours. Bonding with a woman young enough to be his daughter wasn't on the agenda.

Millar didn't take the hint.

'So Gracey was right, then,' she said.

'About what?'

'He said you left under a cloud.'

'That's one way of putting it.'

'What happened?'

'Nothing much,' he lied. 'Just the usual Hereford politics.' He moved on before she could grill him further. 'I spent a couple of years down at St Athan, training up the lads in 1 Para. Survival School. Then two more years up at Manchester working as a permanent staff instructor with the TA squadron. Bone appointments.'

'Bone?' Millar grooved her brow into a slight frown.

'It means shite,' Hawkins explained. 'It was the head shed's way of forcing me out. They knew I wouldn't stand it up there, not for long. Two years of sitting behind a desk, drinking tea. Lonely as fuck.'

'So what did you do?'

'I got my head down. Enrolled on an MA in Security Management at Manchester University. Couple of years later, got myself a qualification. First in my family to graduate.'

'Do you miss it? The Regiment?'

Hawkins stared out of the rain-lashed windscreen. 'Not really. Some of the lads I know, they'll end up spending the rest of their lives in Hereford. Swinging the lamp with the remnants from their intake. That was never going to be me, though.'

'Why not?'

'I wasn't part of the in-crowd. Bantering. Going out on the lash. All of that.'

'You make it sound like you're glad to be out of there.'

'I am, more or less. Apart from when you lot start droning on about the cyber stuff. Dropping in all of them buzzwords. Gives me a bloody headache. Might as well be talking Chinese.'

Millar chuckled. Hawkins scrunched up his face.

'What's so funny?'

'My dad says the same thing,' Millar replied. 'Next thing you'll be reminiscing about the good old days and telling me how much a pint used to cost.'

Hawkins glanced briefly at her, eyes wide with feigned horror. 'Jesus, man. Give us a break. I'm not that fucking ancient. Not yet.'

They both shared an easy laugh, lightening the atmosphere in the Merc. Then they lapsed back into silence as they shuttled along the motorway, the wipers working overtime as the cars in front churned up a continual spray of dirty rain-haze. They were nearing Swindon now. The navigation app put them a hundred and fifty miles from their destination. Another three hours on the road.

A long way to go yet.

Hawkins had no real interest in getting to know Millar. They were two people at radically different points in their lives. She had the summit in front of her; there was nothing in front of Hawkins but slow decline. Probably she could smell the failure coming off him in waves. At work they called him the Homeless Pilgrim, on account of his scruffy appearance, the sure sign of a man who had long ago given up caring what the rest of the world thought about him.

But he felt he ought to feign a passing interest in Millar. *We're spending the next few days together.*

May as well try to get along.

'What about you?' he asked. 'How long did you serve with 18 Sigs?'

'Couple of years. I know what you mean about the in-crowd. Two years in Hereford was long enough for me. After that, it started to feel like a bit of a meat market. I couldn't see myself staying there long term. Too many egos. Regiment men throwing their weight around, behaving as if they were living legends. Not my kind of scene.'

'And then what? You went straight to work for the big companies?'

'Not straight away. Actually, I did consider training as a teacher.'

'What changed your mind?'

'Hereford. I'd just spent a few years looking after a bunch of children. Couldn't face more of the same.'

Hawkins's chest heaved up and down as he laughed. 'Fair point.'

'After I left the army I bounced around for a while on the Circuit. That wasn't for me either. Then I heard about a job going at one of the security contractors. I decided to go for it. Turned out to be the best decision I ever made. Worked my way up to head of cyber security before DeepSpear approached me.'

'You enjoy it?'

'I do. You?'

'About as much as a vasectomy,' Hawkins said. 'This job was never part of the plan for me. It's not where I imagined myself ten years ago.'

'You should be grateful. At your age, you're lucky you've got any work at all.'

'Thanks. Really. Big compliment, that.'

Millar rolled her eyes at him. 'You know what I mean. There are plenty of guys on the Circuit fighting over the handful of private gigs on offer. The pay's not what it used to be on those contracts, either. They'd peel their eyelids off for your job.'

'A few more years and they can have it. I'll have died of boredom by then.'

'I find the work interesting,' Millar said. 'It suits my mindset. And I'm good at it. I was always interested in technology as a kid. Me and my brothers, we'd spend our evenings building computers from discarded hard drives and CPUs, or playing video games. Not what you'd describe as a normal childhood for a girl.'

'Live to my age, and you'll realise there's no such thing as normal.'

Millar laughed. 'I don't doubt it.' She fell silent and gazed out of the side window.

'What's your plan?' she went on. 'If this isn't what you want to be doing with your life, you must have some other goal.'

'Haven't a clue. I ain't looked that far ahead.'

Which was a lie, Hawkins knew.

He had no personal ambition beyond getting through the day. Then the next one. His only aim in life was to provide for his daughter. That was why Hawkins ignored the voice. Why he kept going despite the loneliness and the drinking, the image he could never banish from his memory. Each month he deposited a slice of his salary into a savings account for Zoe. He had few outgoings, after all. The company covered the rent and bills on his flat. He ate little, rarely went out, shopped at the local Tesco Metro. Had no expensive tastes or habits.

The last time he'd spoken to Zoe, she had mentioned opening an art gallery in Eastbourne to display some of her linocuts. The next logical step in her career. Hawkins figured he'd carry on until he could give her a decent lump sum. Enough to cover the costs of the gallery and a deposit for a place of her own. Then he'd retreat from the world. Tactical withdrawal. Move to some tiny village back in Northumberland and drink himself to death.

Better than struggling on. Better than living with the torment. Sometimes you just had to admit you couldn't beat a thing.

One last effort.

For Zoe.

First we get to Plymouth, Hawkins reminded himself.

Find out who killed King and his boss.

And why.

They looped round Bristol and continued south on the M5. His hangover finally eased somewhere around the Mendips, reduced to a light kneading at the sides of his head. Hawkins turned his mind back to the puzzle of King's death. A healthy guy with no pre-existing medical conditions walks into a bar, and a few hours later he drops dead.

Vomiting blood. Foaming at the mouth.

What had happened?

What could do that to a man?

The working theory is that King was poisoned, Gracey had said.

Poison, Hawkins knew, was the weapon of choice for the Kremlin intelligence services. Then there was the attempted hack several months ago, likely carried out by the GRU. Unit 29155. The same people behind the Salisbury attack. Novichok. Nerve agents stored in perfume bottles.

Slow, agonising deaths.

Russia's fingerprints are all over this thing.

But why had they killed King? What had he been selling to them behind the backs of his colleagues? Who was the woman he'd met with in Cremyll? And how did the death of a talented young engineer and his line manager connect with a failed attempt to break into the Devonport network? What had the Russians been after?

I don't know, Hawkins thought.

But one way or another, we're going to find out.

Five

They hit Plymouth two hours later. Rode the Devon Expressway south past Exeter at a good clip, the Merc low-humming as they glided round the fringes of Dartmoor, approaching the city from the east. Traffic was light. Twelve o'clock on a wet Monday in early September. The sweet spot between the end of the summer and freshers' week. Everybody had gone home except for the hardcore surfers.

Millar said, 'What's the plan, once we arrive?'

Hawkins said, 'First of all, we'll get hold of King's laptop. You work your magic on it before we do the handover to the plod while I meet with the security manager. Get updated on the situation.'

'And then what?'

'We'll figure that out later. First rule of any op. The plan changes as soon as it goes noisy. You don't think any further than the next step. That's when mistakes happen.'

'Is that what they teach you at Hereford?'

Hawkins spread his lips into a grin. 'Some of us might act like kids, but we're not all idiots.' He added, seriously, 'We worry about what's in front of us. The Regiment way.'

'For someone who says he doesn't miss Hereford, you talk about it an awful lot.'

Hawkins glanced at her with raised eyebrows. 'Christ, they weren't wrong about you, were they?'

Millar snapped her gaze towards him. 'Who's "they"?'

'People at the office. They said you were a straight talker. Blunt as an old axe, man.'

'I grew up in a big household,' Millar replied matter-of-factly. 'Four brothers and a sister in a three-bed terrace in Hyson Green.

Dad spent half his time at the bookies and the rest down his local while our mum worked three jobs to put food on the table. You grow up in that environment, you become allergic to bullshit.'

It had stopped raining. Sunlight speared through the gaps in the tissue-shred clouds, reflected off puddles the size of oil spills. They followed the satnav directions past the city centre, then took the A-road leading towards the naval district.

'Do you know the manager down here?' asked Millar.

Hawkins shook his head. 'The last bloke quit a couple of months back. I've not visited since then. But whoever the new guy is, he's been slack. They've had two dead employees in the space of a month, on the back of a large-scale hack. He's got some fucking explaining to do.'

They zigzagged their way down suburban roads lined with dilapidated Victorian terraces, before cutting south on a route parallel with the naval dockyard. An old stone wall topped with barbed wire shielded the port from the landward side, the roofs of the maintenance sheds, warehouses and doss blocks just about visible above it. A massive operation. Three miles of dry docks, basins and wharves. Thousands of personnel working round the clock to maintain Britain's navy. Impressive, in a way. But also madness. Billions of pounds spent on the upkeep of an out-of-date fleet, at a time when Britain's enemies were gaining in strength on every front. The typical Whitehall approach. Frittering away money to fight yesterday's wars. Huge sums lavished on ego-massaging aircraft carriers. Politicians who cared more about making statements than giving the men on the ground the kit they needed to get the job done.

Millar returned her attention to her phone. Dashing off texts, then pausing to read the replies from the other party. Something made her smile. After several exchanges Hawkins nodded at the screen.

'Who are you messaging?'

'No one,' she said, evasively. 'Just a friend.'

'A bloke?'

Millar laughed. 'Something like that.'

She wrote a final message, put her phone away.

Four minutes later they turned onto Duke Street and approached the entrance to the DeepSpear facility. Which was essentially a sentry booth and a pair of barrier arms fronting an opening in the wire-topped wall. Warning signs decorated the worn stonework either side of the gate, threatening would-be trespassers. A handful of men and women in hi-vis jackets and dark trousers milled about near the booth. Beyond it, across the car park, stood the main site office. A futuristic building, six storeys of curved glass surrounded by an ocean of gleaming new tarmac and neatly trimmed lawns. DeepSpear's logo riveted to the top floor of the building, like a giant fridge magnet.

Hawkins eased to a halt in front of the arm barrier. Left the engine ticking. Waited. One of the hi-vis gang caught sight of the wagon and plodded over. A shaven-headed guy with the thickset build of a bricklayer. He stopped beside the driver-side window while Hawkins buzzed down the glass, reached into his jacket pocket and produced his DeepSpear security pass. Handed it to the guard, along with Millar's ID. The guy scrutinised them, brow heavily puckered. As if he'd never seen laminated plastic before.

'We're from London,' Hawkins said. 'We're expected,' he added, remembering that Gracey said he had called ahead to Devonport prior to their departure.

We've updated them. Just don't expect the red-carpet treatment when you get there.

The guard made a big show of studying his clipboard. Putting on a performance of official thoroughness, matching their passes to the names on the list. Then he moved away, spoke into his comms unit. There was a brief back-and-forth with the person on the other end before the guard strolled back over. He passed the ID cards to Hawkins. Nodded.

'Through you go, sir. They're waiting for you in reception.'

He stepped back. The barrier arm lifted skyward. Hawkins nosed the Merc over the ramp, steered round to the half-empty car park. Most of the spots closest to the entrance had been taken, so he wedged the wagon in a free space a few rows further back. Cut the engine and debussed.

A sharp wind gusted in from the coast, rifling through Hawkins's hair as he dropped down to the rain-greased tarmac. He stretched his legs and looked round, taking in the scene. Threat assessment. No sign of any police vehicles in the vicinity. Which could be good news, or bad. Either they hadn't arrived yet, or they had already scooped up King's company hardware and fucked off.

And if they have, thought Hawkins, *it's game over for us.*

He locked the Merc, circled round to join Millar in front of the grille. They marched towards the building entrance, passed a series of abstract sculptures, stepped through the automatic doors, into a wide reception area.

A figure in an ill-fitting suit approached them from the central stairwell, a grey lanyard garlanding his thick neck. Hawkins recognised the man from his last trip to the facility. Keith Cleland. Managing Director at Devonport. A shapeless Glaswegian in his early fifties with hair the colour of dirty linen and bead-shaped eyes pressed deep into the fleshy folds of his face. The kind of guy who'd look crap in a three-piece from Jermyn Street. Cleland was DeepSpear's seniormost man at Plymouth. Top of the operational ladder. A former engineer who'd traded the shop floor for the slow death of management.

Cleland extended his arm towards Hawkins.

'David, good to see you again. How are you?'

'Fine, mate,' Hawkins said.

'Good, good.'

Cleland looked nervous. Worried about the optics, Hawkins supposed, and his future job prospects. Two people had died on his watch, and he'd already had the embarrassment of a network breach. None of which would reflect well on him. Therefore Cleland would be desperate to assist their investigation. Earn himself some brownie points with head office.

Hawkins introduced him to Millar. Cleland shook her hand and said, 'Sorry for dragging you both down here like this. I told Gracey we could take care of it in-house, but he insisted on bringing you guys in. You know what he's like.'

'Aye. We do.' Hawkins furrowed his brow and said, 'Where's your security manager? We were told he'd RV with us here.'

Cleland shook his head. 'John's not around right now.'

'I can see that. I'm asking why.'

'He's on his lunch break. He'll be back later.'

'That's not fucking good enough. He shouldn't be on a break. He should be here right now, getting to grips with the situation.'

'That's what I told him, more or less.'

'What did he say?'

'He just said he had some important errands to run. Said it couldn't wait.'

'I'll need to have a word with him when he's back,' Hawkins said, biting back on his rage. 'He's gone AWOL in the middle of a crisis. That's a sackable offence, that.'

Millar said, 'Any word from the police?'

Cleland shook his head quickly. 'Not since this morning, no.'

'When did you speak to them?'

'Around ten o'clock. Told us they would be sending a team round to search the premises and seize evidence before lunchtime.'

'What did you tell them?'

'The truth. I said that this is a restricted area, that only vetted staff are permitted on-site, visitors need to go through the security checks beforehand, and if a load of police rocked up with their blue lights flashing our friends at Whitehall would hit the roof. Took them a while, but they eventually saw the light. Agreed to delay their visit until the end of the working day. Minimise the disruption to our work. They won't get here before six o'clock this evening.'

'That was good work,' Hawkins said. 'Gives us a bit more time.'

'Did they say anything else?' asked Millar.

Cleland said, 'They asked for a list of everyone King worked with. I told them it'd take a while to get that information. Delaying tactics.'

Millar said, 'Where's the laptop now?'

'At his desk on the third floor. That's where King worked. I've sealed the whole floor off and deactivated every member of staff's access card. No one can gain access to that floor except myself and our security manager.'

Millar said, 'We should get to work. Can you show us King's workstation? We've wasted enough time already.'

Hawkins smiled to himself. He was beginning to understand why Millar had earned such a ferocious reputation since joining DeepSpear. In some ways she reminded him of his daughter. Zoe was also a straight shooter. Had the same lack of patience with excuse-makers and inertia. A useful quality, in certain situations. But also with the potential to create friction and rub people the wrong way. Like a mortar used indiscriminately to attack a target. Hawkins decided to keep a close eye on her.

Cleland led them past the staff restaurant, crossed to the lift lobby and took the next cab to the third floor. Thirty seconds later they emerged to a blandly furnished corridor lined with pot plants and landscape paintings. Stairwell to their left. At the far end a secure door led through to the engineering team. There was a keyless entry reader mounted to the left of the doorframe, and a sign on the wall next to it. 'AUTHORISED PERSONNEL ONLY'.

Cleland tapped the card attached to his lanyard against the reader. The lock beeped, bolts clacked, then Cleland wrenched open the door, and Hawkins and Millar followed him into an open-plan workspace that looked nearly identical to the layout at St James's. The same humourless décor and glass-partitioned meeting rooms. Except the floor was deserted. No muted din of ringing phones or fingers tapping on keyboards. No low-level office chatter.

'What are the guys on this floor working on?' he asked.

'A number of projects at any one time,' answered Cleland. 'Some, like King, are on the team overseeing the autonomous torpedo programme. Others are working on naval drones, lasers. Our guys are working on a lot of exciting stuff.'

The main door locked behind them while Cleland worked the light switch. Ceiling panels flickered on, broadcasting stark white rays across the empty workspace. Cleland thigh-chafed his way across the floor, Millar and Hawkins tailing close behind, until they stopped in front of a desk in the far corner.

'Well,' Cleland said, 'this is it. This is where King worked.'

Hawkins ran his eyes over the workstation. It was clean. Tidy. Sterile. No hint of the occupant's personality. There was a lever-armed desk lamp and an A4-sized diary planner, a pencil holder filled with red biros, pencils, a pair of scissors and a ruler, elastic bands. A mobile desk pedestal crouched underneath the table; a sliding fabric divider provided a small degree of privacy from the desk on the other side.

Then Hawkins noticed something else.

'Where's the laptop?' Millar asked.

Cleland stared dumbly at the beechwood desk, as if by focusing on it he could magic the computer into existence.

'I – I don't know,' he stammered. 'It should be here . . .'

Millar lifted her gaze to the director. She wore an expression of professional contempt.

'You mean to tell me you're in charge down here, and you don't know where King kept his laptop?'

Cleland's mouth moved, but no words came out. He looked round the floor, frown lines etched into his doughy face, rubbing the nape of his neck. Like a stressed father searching for a screaming kid's favourite toy.

Hawkins said, 'Was the laptop here when you sealed off the floor?'

'I think so,' Cleland responded.

'Think doesn't exist in my line of work, mate. Was it here? Yes or no?'

'I mean, I didn't actually *check*,' Cleland corrected himself. He added, defensively, 'I just assumed it would be here.'

'Has anyone else been up here this morning?'

Cleland gave a firm shake of his head. 'No one. It's been out of bounds all morning. We've disabled every employee's access card for this floor. Only ones that work are the universal cards.'

'How many people have those?'

'Just me and the security manager. No one else can get inside.'

'What about the weekend? Anyone drop in out of hours?'

'I already asked the guards to check the logbook. In case King had been in the office. There are no entries for those dates. No one's been in here since Friday afternoon.'

'So where the fuck is the laptop?' Hawkins growled.

Cleland didn't answer, because he couldn't.

Millar said, 'Where did King usually keep it?'

Cleland swept a hand towards the desk. 'Right there. Same as everyone else.'

'Could he have taken it out of the office? Maybe he was on a tight deadline and took it home to work on late one night?'

'They're not allowed. Company policy. We're very strict on that stuff.'

'Doesn't mean the rules don't get broken from time to time. There are people at head office who have been caught using their work emails for personal use.'

'I don't doubt it. But King wouldn't have done that. That's not like him at all.'

A tiny groove formed above Millar's brow. Then she knelt down beside King's desk pedestal and tried the top drawer.

Locked.

'Do you have the keys for this thing?' she asked Cleland.

He rummaged around in his trouser pocket, fished out a bunch of keys, dropped to a knee beside Millar. Tried several of them in the lock before he hit paydirt on the fifth attempt. He twisted the key to the right, stood up and stepped back, giving Millar room as she began searching through the drawers.

She worked sequentially, starting at the top and working her way down. Looked underneath papers, folders, instruction manuals, the usual office-clutter of elastic bands, paper clips, Post-it notes, spare chargers.

But no laptop.

'Shit,' Hawkins said.

Millar slammed the drawers shut, the groove on her brow deepening. 'Did anyone else use this station? Was it hot-desked?' she asked Cleland.

'What the fuck does that mean?' Hawkins cut in.

Cleland said, 'It means you don't have your own desk. You book one out as and when you need it. Saves space. More efficient, too. But no,' he continued, addressing Millar. 'We haven't introduced hot-desking on this floor yet. No one sat here apart from King.'

Millar said, 'Can you get IT to remotely locate the device?'

They waited while Cleland made a call to the IT manager. After a short exchange he hung up and said, 'No luck. Looks like King disabled the feature on his laptop.'

'Why would he do that?' Hawkins wondered.

'Multiple reasons,' said Millar. 'King might have wanted to stop anyone stealing the laptop. Or he might have worried that someone would try to access it remotely and do a full disk wipe. Erase the contents at the click of a mouse.'

'But if he's disabled that function, how are we supposed to find it? It could be bloody anywhere.'

Millar said, 'You need to put yourself in King's shoes. You're worried about someone finding your work computer. Why? Because you have something incriminating stored on the drive. But where can you hide it? You can't take it out of the office, because that's against the rules. And your flat isn't safe. Anyone could break in while you're not home. King didn't have any close friends or family. No one he could trust to keep his laptop safe.

'That leaves the office. Which makes sense, if you think about it. Safest location available to him. Plenty of cameras and security guards. No one can get access to this place without passing through multiple layers of security. It's got to be here.'

Hawkins pointed towards the desk on the other side of King's divider. 'Who sits there?'

'Petar Vitanov,' Cleland responded. 'One of our senior engineers. One of our best.'

'Vitanov?' Hawkins arched an eyebrow. 'I'm guessing that's not English.'

'No. Petar is Bulgarian.'

'Do you get a lot of foreigners working here?'

'We cast a very wide net. But no one gets to work here without being thoroughly vetted by Whitehall beforehand. As you well know.'

'Is Vitanov in today?'

'Afraid not. He called in sick first thing. Nasty bug doing the rounds. Why?'

'I'd like to speak with him. The guy spent his working day four feet from King. Maybe he picked up on something. He might have noticed King acting weird. Or overheard a conversation on the phone. Anything that could help us figure out what happened.'

Cleland said, 'I'll drop him an email, ask him to come in. But I really don't see how that will help. They weren't close.'

'Who *was* King mates with?'

Cleland shook his head. 'Nobody.'

'He must have had one or two friends here.'

'Not as far as I'm aware. King was a dictionary-definition loner. Very talented, knew his stuff inside out, but he didn't socialise.'

'Is that normal, for this place?'

'You get the quiet ones, for sure. Guys who would rather be solving problems than talking about the football results. But there was more to it than that with King. He had a bit of a reputation, you see.'

'Reputation?' Hawkins repeated.

Cleland gave a slight nod. 'He could be arrogant. Thought he was better than everyone else. And he was invested in his conspiracy theories. People here considered him a bit of an oddball. That didn't exactly endear him to his colleagues.' Cleland made a half-hearted shrug. 'That's my reading of the situation. Others may tell it differently.'

'Anyone here have a beef with him?'

'Not to my knowledge.' Cleland crinkled his brow. 'Wait. You don't *seriously* think he was murdered by one of his colleagues?'

'Right now,' Hawkins said, 'we're not ruling anything in or out. Not until we get hold of that laptop.'

Millar wasn't listening. She stood staring at the pedestal. Head cocked to one side.

Thinking.

'Is that the same model as King's laptop?' She pointed towards the device resting on Vitanov's desk. An ultra-thin computer finished in black. Expensive looking, thought Hawkins. Better than the nine-pound brick he had been issued with at St James's.

Cleland nodded. 'All the guys here were issued with new computers a few months ago. Why?'

Millar said nothing. She knelt back down beside the pedestal. Eased the top drawer out a short way and reached down the sides, running her fingers along the metal slide tracks until she located the release levers. She disengaged both levers at the same time. Gently pulled on the drawer, lifting it out.

Hawkins watched her quizzically.

'Fuck are you doing?' he asked.

Millar still didn't reply. She upended the drawer, emptied the contents onto King's desk. Checked the underside and the back panel. Then returned to the pedestal and took out the middle drawer. She went through the same process. Emptied everything, flipped the drawer over, inspected the bottom and rear sides. Cursed again.

Millar turned her attention to the third drawer. The last one. Also the biggest. About twice the height of the two other drawers. She prised it free from the glide rails. Set it down. Hauled out a thick wedge of printed documents, dumped them on the desk beside the rest of the clutter. Upturned the drawer.

Hawkins dropped his eyes to the underside of the base panel. So did Cleland, and Millar.

All three of them were looking at the same thing. A slick-looking computer roughly the dimensions of an A4 envelope, held in place by a couple of strips of industrial duct tape.

King's work laptop.

'Jackpot,' she said.

Six

Millar ripped off the duct tape and scooped up the laptop. Cleland stared at her, frown lines deep as grave-pits carved into his brow.

'How did you know King hid it under his drawer?' he wondered.

She said, 'I didn't. I just looked at it from the perspective of a paranoid engineer. Once you Google Earth the problem, there aren't many hiding places that work for someone with that mindset.' She half-smiled. 'But I also got lucky.'

Millar flipped open the laptop and did a quick visual inspection of the device. Looking for signs of damage, Hawkins presumed.

She said, 'I'm going to need a newly formatted laptop. The exact same model as this one, if possible. Plus a set of chargers and admin access to your enterprise system.'

'What are you going to do?' Hawkins asked.

She said, 'We'll do a crawl-through of the files on King's laptop. Any classified information will be transferred to a new drive partition, so it's separate from the rest of the data. Once that's done, we'll upload the unrestricted information to the clean laptop and hand that over to the police.'

Hawkins stared at her. 'You're talking about tampering with evidence. That's fucking illegal.'

'If you want to get into it, then technically, yes. But we also have a duty to make sure that top-secret information doesn't accidentally fall into the wrong hands. That's a matter of national security.'

'Why bother transferring the data to another laptop, though? Why not just delete the high-level stuff and hand over the original to the police?'

'Too risky. There's a chance that we might miss something. A hidden folder, or a secret area of the drive. Even if we do get rid of everything, there are ways of retrieving that erased data. Our best bet is to silo the classified material in a separate partition, transfer the non-sensitive files to a clean new device. Keep the original.'

'She's right,' Cleland cut in. 'That laptop will have some extremely top-secret material on it. Whitehall would go ballistic if anything leaked. We have to take precautions.'

Hawkins looked at Millar steadily. 'Are you sure the police won't be able to tell the difference?'

'One hundred per cent,' she replied confidently. 'Trust me, they won't suspect a thing.'

'Let's bloody hope not. Otherwise we'll be in deep shit.'

Millar said, 'Before we do anything, we'll need to get the laptop sheep-dipped.'

'What the fuck is a sheep-dip?'

'Exactly what the term suggests,' Millar said. 'You use a dedicated device to screen external portable media for viruses before they have an opportunity to infect the network.'

'What for?' Cleland asked. 'I'm telling you, that laptop hasn't left the building. It's not been on any other network. It's clean.'

'So you say. But we've got a dead engineer, and a lot of unanswered questions. There's no way of knowing for sure what's on that drive. King might have broken the rules and logged onto an external system. He could have inadvertently downloaded malware onto that thing. Or brought something into the office and installed it on the laptop to deter anyone who tried to access his files. We start messing around with it, we could end up destroying the entire system.'

Hawkins said, 'How are you going to break into it without King's password?'

Millar said, 'We don't need it. Once I've got administrative access, I can reset his password and get into his files. But that's the easy part. There's a chance that King might have installed additional security features. That's when it starts getting tricky.'

'What kind of features?'

Cleland said, 'There are programs that can encrypt sections of a drive, or even the whole computer. Accessible only by entering the specific recovery key. Without the key all you get is gibberish.'

'If King's done that, how are you supposed to break in?' asked Hawkins.

'Ordinarily, you can't,' Millar said. 'Those features are specifically designed to be unbreakable. If you lose the key, you need to manually wipe the entire device. Like a factory reset on your phone. Everything gets erased. But we have ways of getting around that.'

'How so?'

'There are programs we've acquired from the US and Israel, and some other places. Programs that can penetrate even the most secure device. Strictly speaking, they're illegal, and using them means breaking multiple national laws. But in extreme cases it's our only option.'

Hawkins rubbed his brow. He felt tired. A combination of the long drive and listening to a lot of technical jargon.

'How long is all of this going to take?'

'Hard to say,' Millar responded. 'I need a couple of hours at least. Longer, maybe. It depends on whether King has manually encrypted the drive, the app he's used, what data he's secured. A lot of variables.'

Hawkins glanced at his G-Shock. 13.49 hours. Millar wouldn't be finished until four o'clock. Two hours before the police were due to arrive. He straightened up. Cocked his chin at Cleland.

Said, 'How far is the crime scene from here?'

'Half an hour or so. You have to drive down and catch the ferry from Admiral's Hard to Cremyll. Boat runs every fifteen minutes. A couple of quid each way. Cash only. White Horse Tavern, that's the name of the pub on the other side. Where King collapsed. But you're wasting your time.'

'What do you mean?'

'The police won't let you inside the pub. It's cordoned off, mate.'

'How do you know that?' Millar cut in.

'One of the guys in facilities management lives over in Cremyll. He's been keeping an eye on the site for us all morning. Says the pub's been designated as a crime scene. Police all over the place.'

'What about the surrounding area?' asked Hawkins.

'Open, as far as I know. It's just the pub that's off-limits.'

Hawkins exchanged a knowing glance with Millar. He turned to Cleland and said, 'I'd still like to do a quick recce. Get a mark-one eyeball on the place. It might help.'

Cleland looked at him intently. 'What do you think happened to him?'

'That's what we're trying to figure out. When we have information to share with you, we'll let you know.'

'Of course.' Cleland held up his hands. 'Anything else I can help you with right now, guys?'

'We're fine, mate,' said Hawkins.

'Right you are.' Cleland stood up straight and nodded at Millar. 'I'll go and get your equipment sorted out. Give us two minutes.'

He nodded again and strode back across the floor, steering his portly frame between the desks. Millar unlocked her phone, read a new chat message. A teasing smile spread across her lips. The male friend, Hawkins guessed. She put her phone screen-down on the desk and said to Hawkins, 'At least he seems eager to help.' Tipping her head at Cleland.

Hawkins grunted. 'Don't get fooled. He's acting out of self-interest. He's pissed off with how his security manager has handled the situation and now he's worried he might be facing the sack. He knows his best bet is to cooperate with us. Hope that we put in a good word with Gracey when we get back.'

'He could be right, you know,' Millar said quietly. 'About the crime scene visit being a waste of time. The police will have already gone through it with a fine-tooth comb. What can you possibly hope to find?'

Hawkins said, 'You give the plod too much credit. There's always the chance they might have overlooked something. Besides, we know about the Russia angle. The GRU. Those guys don't. That gives us an edge.'

'All the same, I'd prefer it if you stayed put. What if the police show up here while you're gone?'

'They won't. Cleland said they'd agreed not to show up before the end of the working day, remember? Six o'clock. I'll be back well before then.

'The only thing you need to worry about is making sure that no fucker will be able to tell that new laptop from the original.'

Millar stared levelly at him.

'Do you still think it was a poison that killed King?' she asked.

'How else could they have done it?'

'I don't know. But the police are clearly having second thoughts. If they really suspected a chemical weapons attack, they would have isolated the whole area around the pub. No one would get within two miles of that place. They'd be worried about contamination.'

'There's a lot about this situation that doesn't add up. Let's just hope there's something helpful on that laptop.'

'Bound to be,' Millar insisted. 'Otherwise, why would King have gone to the effort of hiding it from his colleagues?'

'Better get to work, then,' Hawkins said. 'Because as it stands, we're in the fucking dark.'

Seven

Hawkins hammered the release button and exited the secure area on the third floor. He took the stairs back down to the lobby, bypassed the corporate flunkies and geeks milling around the reception area and emerged to the greyness of a Monday afternoon in Plymouth. A light drizzle hung like a dirty veil across the car park. He remembered reading somewhere that the Scots had more than four hundred words to describe snow, and he wondered if the English ought to have the same number of terms for rain.

As he started across the rain-specked blacktop, making for the Merc, he noticed a figure behind the wheel of a muddied Jeep Grand Cherokee parked twenty metres away. Hawkins couldn't be sure – the windscreen and side windows were spattered with dirt, partially obscuring his view – but the driver seemed to be asleep. At two o'clock on a Monday afternoon. An employee, he figured, catching forty winks on company time.

Hawkins clenched his jaw in disgust. This was a shoddy environment. Employees breaking company rules by taking home their work laptops. Dossing in their cars. People dying in suspicious circumstances. Once Hawkins got hold of the security manager he was going to give him the mother of all tongue-lashings.

One he won't forget in a hurry.

Hawkins folded himself behind the wheel of the Merc GLE and punched in the details for the ferry crossing to Cremyll. Then he pointed the wagon out of the car park, rolled through the exit barrier and cantered west through Devonport for half a mile, past rows of soulless new-build apartment blocks and housing estates, the strips of vacant storefronts interspersed with tattoo parlours and nail bars and charity shops. Tableau of modern Britain. Across the bridge Hawkins hooked a right and rumbled down a narrow one-way street flanked by quaint Victorian terraces and vape stores.

The satnav directed him to a car park on Strand Street. Hawkins squeezed the Merc into a space between a couple of oversized SUVs. He debussed, marched north, made a left turn at the Bunch of Grapes pub and stopped beside the crossing point.

While he waited for the next ferry he tried to put himself in the shoes of King's assassins. He sketched out a scenario in his head. King selling secrets to a Russian contact, then getting cold feet about the arrangement. Or making unrealistic demands. The Kremlin ordering its assets to liquidate King. Operational details would have been left to the guys on the ground. If they were pros they would have done a thorough recce of the area beforehand. Get eyes on the target's place of work, his home. Surveillance duty. Stick a couple of people on King. Get them to tail as he went about his daily routine. His commute. Jogging or cycling routes. What coffee shops or restaurants he liked to visit. What was known in the trade as pattern of life.

Then he got out of the killers' heads and looked at it from King's perspective. Building a picture in his head, brick by brick. He visualised the last hours of King's life. Leaving his apartment on a pleasant Sunday afternoon. Strolling up to the slipway. Boarding the boat to Cremyll.

The ferry stop was located at the end of a narrow one-way street. There was a greasy spoon at Hawkins's one o'clock, a pair of tables outside. At his three o'clock, twenty-five metres away, the run-down boozer.

Whoever had targeted King would have likely positioned someone near the slipway, ready to verify that the target was en route to Cremyll. Hawkins ruled out the Bunch of Grapes as an observation point. No outdoor seating, net curtains pulled across the windows. A strictly local joint, Hawkins guessed. Not the kind of place a stranger could go and sit with a pint without the regulars getting in his business. The Russians would have either set up an OP at the café, or in a car parked a short way up the street, with direct line of sight to the boarding point for the ferry. With a second team in position at the landing spot in Cremyll. Watching the slipway. Waiting for the target to arrive.

Hawkins dug out his personal phone and checked his messages. Zoe still hadn't replied to him. He thought about dropping her a casual text. Ask how things were, check that she was okay. He immediately rejected the idea. Recalled what Michelle had told him when they'd last spoken a month ago. Over coffee he'd asked about Zoe. About the radio silence. The way she'd turned on him after the divorce with a ferocity that had surprised both of them.

Leave it, Michelle had told him.

Give her space, David.

Let her process.

He considered ducking into the pub for a quick livener. A couple of double slugs of Bushmills. Enough to keep the image of Jacob's face at bay for a while longer. Then the ferry approached. It stopped beside the slipway, a deck-hand looped a frayed rope round the mooring post. Then the passengers climbed aboard. Hawkins paid the return fare, parked himself on a paint-blistered bench. Sat back and enjoyed the ride.

The boat reached Cornish soil ten minutes later. Hawkins climbed over the gunwale and trudged up the concrete ramp, the wind tugging at his jacket as he took in his surroundings. Ferry ticket office to his immediate left. Drop-off point at his twelve o'clock. Further inland, thirty metres away, stood the White Horse Tavern.

A forensics tent had been erected in front of the pub. Police cordon tape sealed off the beer garden. A pair of bobbies stood guard in front of the taped-off area. Behind them, three figures in scene-of-crimes suits, face masks and bright blue overshoes shuffled around the perimeter of the pub, occasionally stopping to bag and label scraps of evidence. No attempt had been made to seal off the wider area beyond the White Horse, Hawkins noted. Just like Cleland had told him.

Whoever had decided on the location for the hit had chosen well, Hawkins realised. The peninsula attracted a lot of tourists. People would be coming and going all day, especially at the weekend. The killers could have dressed like ramblers, and no one would have paid them the slightest attention. Plus they had multiple escape routes. They could have left on the ferry, or escaped by car, crossing over the Tamar bridge.

Hawkins crossed the road, circumnavigated the cordon and the bored-looking constables. He paced around the outside of the pub, careful not to venture too close to the tape. Didn't want to accidentally expose himself to traces of a Russian nerve agent. Although the police had seemingly ruled out a poisoning, Hawkins wasn't so sure.

A thirty-four-year-old man with no history of substance abuse goes to meet a woman at a pub on a Sunday afternoon. Six hours later, he's found in the car park by his fellow drinkers.

Foaming at the mouth.

Vomiting blood.

Not a gun, thought Hawkins. Or a knife. Poisoning remained the most likely explanation, in his opinion. The police had initially reached the same conclusion until something had made them change their minds. Results of the toxicology report, probably. But that didn't prove anything. The Russians might have used a new type of chemical weapon to murder King. One that wouldn't show up on a blood test.

Except there were several holes in that theory. First, why lure King to a public place in order to kill him? Why not smear the front door of his apartment with the poison, or catch him at some other moment in private, away from any potential eyewitnesses?

Unless the chemical had to be ingested in order to take effect, Hawkins thought to himself. Which would explain why the woman had lured King to the pub. So she could spike his drink, then leg it before the guy started spewing blood.

That line of thinking led him to hole number two. According to Gracey, the victim had spent six hours at the pub with the woman before he had collapsed. Why wait so long to administer the poison? Could it take that long for a nerve agent to take effect in the body? Hawkins wasn't a scientist, but it seemed improbable.

The third hole in the theory bothered him the most. The targets of Russian attacks were typically ex-spies. Double agents. Traitors to the motherland. Why would the GRU assassinate a middling British engineer?

I don't know, thought Hawkins.

But something's wrong with this picture.

He looped round to the southern side of the pub, walked on for fifty metres, stopped and scanned the ground immediately beyond the White Horse. A footpath ran towards the carpet-smooth lawns of the country park a hundred metres away. Shingle beach to the east.

To the west a single-lane access road led to the car park behind the pub. A strip of cordon tape dangled loosely from the sign at the edge of the road. Hawkins supposed that some sharp-eyed officer had sealed it off the previous night. Back when they had believed they were dealing with a poisoning. Then the narrative had changed, the threat level had been reduced and the road had been reopened.

He started down the stretch of potholed tarmac, continued west for twenty-five metres before he halted again. At his right lay the pub car park. Ahead of him the access road carried on for another twenty metres until it terminated at a bank of concrete domestic garages, the ground piled high with bits of rubbish. To his left, directly opposite the car park, an overgrown grass verge bordered a patch of dense woodland. A pair of tyre tracks had been gouged into the mud.

Hawkins ran his eyes over the car park. The entrance had been sealed off, but a quick visual inspection confirmed that there was no CCTV in the area. No domestic or commercial properties overlooking the lot, either. Therefore, no chance of anyone getting caught on a neighbouring doorbell camera. Whoever had targeted King had deliberately lured him outside, away from any witnesses who might capture the attack on their phones. With a getaway vehicle probably waiting close by, so the killers could escape as soon as King had been dropped. They wouldn't want to hang around Cremyll longer than necessary. A four-person team. At the minimum. One to watch the ferry at Devonport, another person with eyes on the target at Cremyll. The woman, plus a getaway driver.

A complex operation, requiring serious resources. Financing, intelligence. Preparation. Not something run by a couple of amateur crooks, or a lone wolf, but the work of an organisation with deep experience in carrying out attacks on foreign soil.

Such as the GRU.

Hawkins walked up and down the access road, scanning the ground. Looking for anything out of the ordinary. There was always a chance the killers got careless when bugging out of Cremyll.

He checked the space around the garages, the plastic bins. Looked under the parked cars. Found nothing of interest. Just broken glass, vape sticks, discarded takeaway cartons. He paced back down the access road, approached the wooded area directly opposite the car park. Leafy boughs overhung a grassy patch choked with nettles and weeds. A muddied bridleway snaked between the clumps of ancient trees, led towards a decrepit cottage at the far end of the track.

Hawkins stopped.

Something had caught his eye.

He marched over to the tyre tracks scored into the mud at the side of the access road. The tracks were new, Hawkins noted, with clearly defined edges not yet eroded by the British weather. Next to them, scattered in the dirt, Hawkins had spotted a pile of cigarette butts. He counted thirteen of them in total. More than half a pack. Which suggested the smoker had lingered at that spot for some time.

Hawkins dropped to his haunches and picked up one of the filter tips. It was still dry. Therefore smoked after the heavy downpour the previous Saturday. He cast the tab aside and scanned the ground around him. Three or four paces away, half-buried among the tangle of weeds, he found what he was looking for: a crumpled cigarette packet. He plucked the packet out of the undergrowth. It was a brand Hawkins had never heard of. Cream-coloured design with the letters 'DS' stamped in large capitals over a yellow anchor. Above it, a deep-blue band with 'Durres Special' printed across it in a stark white font.

Hawkins looked back towards the car park. A distance of no more than fifteen metres from the grass verge to the rear exit. A thought began to take shape.

He glanced round to make sure no one was watching him, stuffed the packet into his jacket pocket. Then he stood up, walked back down the access road and retraced his steps to the slipway. Checked his G-Shock. 15.43. By the time he returned to DeepSpear's offices Millar should have almost finished creating the sanitised version of King's laptop.

And then we'll find out what the fuck is going on.

* * *

Hawkins caught the four o'clock ferry back across the river. He returned to the car park on Strand Street, hopped into the Merc, rolled out of the lot, pointed west down Admiral's Hard and followed the satnav directions back to the Devonport office. Past the yachting specialists, the car dealerships flogging luxury SUVs on credit and the oriental supermarkets.

Six minutes later he reached the barrier outside the DeepSpear office. Hawkins flashed his ID at the thick-necked bloke manning the sentry booth, veered round to the staff car park and nosed the

Merc into the space he'd vacated two and a half hours ago. He climbed out of the wagon, started towards the main building.

Then he stopped in his tracks.

Off to his left, twenty metres away, the driver was still sitting behind the wheel of the mud-spattered Jeep. The same one Hawkins had noticed when he'd bugged out of the office earlier that afternoon. At the time he'd assumed it was a DeepSpear employee sneaking in a power nap. But that had been a whole two and a half hours ago.

Which got him thinking.

If it's not a worker slacking off, who is it? And what the fuck are they doing hanging around an office car park?

Are we being watched?

Hawkins frowned.

It wasn't an outlandish idea. If the Russians were behind King's death, they'd want to keep an eye on the investigation. Make sure their tracks were fully covered. They might have other sources inside DeepSpear, Hawkins realised. Kremlin agents who were at risk of being exposed by the company's investigation into King.

Or it could be entirely innocent. A lazy bastard sleeping off a killer hangover.

Only one way to find out.

Hawkins walked over to the Jeep, quickening his stride. The front windscreen was caked in dirt and mud, making it difficult to pick out the details of the driver. Whoever it was, Hawkins was determined to wring the truth out of them.

He was four or five paces from the side window when he caught sight of the face behind the grimy glass.

And froze.

Hawkins recognised the guy dossing in the wagon.

Found himself staring at the face of a ghost.

Eight

The ghost was in his mid-fifties, with silver hair and eyebrows that slanted down towards his brow like a pair of pinball flippers, giving him a permanent scowl. He had an outdoorsy face, lean and hard-edged, with flared nostrils and lips so thin you could string a piano with them. There was a Z-shaped scar on his right cheek, and a savage glint behind the cold grey eyes. He looked like the kind of bloke who would smile at you one moment and cut your throat the next, and he wouldn't give a damn either way.

Hawkins stood dumbfounded.

He hadn't seen the ghost's face in seven long years. It had suffered some wear and tear since then. But Hawkins recognised him all the same. Every Regiment warrior knew about John Bald, the former legend of 22 SAS. Hereford's prodigal son, and later its most infamous pariah. A brilliant soldier who had gone over to the dark side after leaving the unit.

Rumours followed John Bald around like viruses around a Chinese wet market. Hawkins had heard the stories about him from the few Blades he'd stayed in touch with. Second-hand whispers of Bald doing Six's dirty work. Enriching himself in the narcotics trade.

Arms dealing. Murder.

All of which prompted a question.

What the fuck is Bald doing here?

Hawkins stopped beside the window. Rapped his knuckles against the glass, jolting the figure out of his slumber.

'Yeah, yeah. Wait a fucking mo,' Bald croaked in a thick Scottish brogue.

Hawkins waited. Bald hack-coughed, pitched his seat fully upright. Empty bottles clinked in the footwell. The window buzzed down. Bald poked his head out of the opening, squinted hard in the grey daylight. Looked up at Hawkins.

Grinned.

'Geordie Hawkins. Christ. Long fucking time, son.'

'Jock . . .'

Hawkins stared at the interior of the Jeep in disgust. Red Bull cans and fast-food containers littered the front passenger seat. Empty vodka bottles and coffee cups. Newspapers, takeaway menus, plastic shopping bags. All kinds of junk. He swivelled his gaze back to the craggy figure in front of him. Bald. Hereford's spirit animal. Reduced to living like an alcoholic.

'What are you doing here?' Hawkins demanded.

'The fuck does it look like?' He pointed at the DeepSpear offices. 'I work here, Geordie. Security.'

Hawkins stared at him in disbelief.

'You're the Head of Security?'

Bald grinned again. 'In the flesh, pal.'

He hawked and spat out of the window. Phlegm splattered the tarmac a few inches from Hawkins's Timberlands.

'No one told me you'd found a job here,' Hawkins answered lamely.

Bald laughed. 'Yeah, well. Now you know.'

Hawkins frowned at his old mucker. He privately wondered why Gracey hadn't mentioned anything about Bald's appointment back at the King Street briefing. Probably the guy hadn't been aware of the connection between Hawkins and Bald. DeepSpear employed a lot of people. More than a few of them had worked in the UKSF community in one capacity or another. Sometimes they knew each other from their past lives, sometimes they didn't. Most likely Gracey had figured it wasn't worth mentioning.

'How long?' Hawkins asked. 'Since you started here?'

'Couple of months. Probation period. Boring as fuck, though. Don't know how you stand it.'

He didn't seem surprised to see Hawkins. When he pointed this out, Bald chuckled and said, 'I heard you were on the company payroll. Gracey sent us a message. Told us he was sending you and some cyber nerd down here to look into that situation with the engineer.'

'That's right. So what the fuck are you doing in your car?'

'Hangover, Geordie. Bloody killer. Thought I'd catch some shut-eye before you showed up. Must have overslept.'

Hawkins thought back to the last time he'd laid eyes on Bald. Seven years ago, but it felt more like seven lifetimes. Back when Hawkins still believed he had a future in the Regiment. Bald had been an occasional presence at Hereford; he had been reportedly attached to the Revolutionary Warfare Wing, the covert unit within the SAS that worked closely with Six. Only the best Blades were chosen for that posting. Operators trained to a very high level, tasked with providing the manpower for black ops. Men who could be trusted absolutely to do the business, no matter what.

Then, suddenly, he had dropped off the radar.

Two years later Hawkins had heard through a mutual friend that Bald had put his soldiering behind him. Ditched life on the Circuit to become manager of a bed-and-breakfast on the Isle of Islay. Since then, there had been no news.

As if he had vanished into thin air.

The intervening years had not been kind to Bald. There was something frayed about him, Hawkins noted. He looked worn away at the edges. Ground down by life. The swept-back hair was thinner; the cheeks were gaunt. His jaw visibly sagged. His eyes, once a cold blue, had faded to a dull grey. But there was still a hard gleam in them, simmering below the surface. Waiting to explode.

Bald unfolded himself from the Jeep. He stretched and coughed to clear his lungs. Looked Hawkins up and down.

'Fuck me, Geordie. You look like a pile of reheated shit.'

'I could say the same thing about you, mate.'

'This is temporary,' said Bald. 'Few days off the sauce and I'll be fit as fuck again. But from where I'm standing, you've really let yourself go. Too many liquid lunches.'

Hawkins didn't want to admit that he'd spent most of the past year drinking alone in his flat. Least of all to Bald. He moved the conversation on.

'How much do you know about King?' he asked.

'Only what Gracey told us this morning. Said the guy expired in a pub last night. There's stuff on social about him bleeding out of his mouth and ears. Is that right?'

Bald's eyes narrowed to points. Hawkins evaded the question. Gracey's warning ringing in his ears.

You are not to discuss this situation with anyone else in the building. We're trying to keep this situation contained.

Hawkins said, 'We should get inside, mate. Come on.'

He updated Bald as they walked towards the main building. Gave him the condensed version of events. Gracey's orders to wipe any classified material from King's computer before the cops showed up. How Millar planned to hack into the dead engineer's laptop, scraping anything they'd want to keep from the police, then transfer the harmless data to an identical-looking clone device.

He left out the stuff about the Russian cyber-attack. The suspected link between the deaths of King and Rideout. The working theory about the GRU's involvement.

'Smart move to keep the plod in the dark,' Bald said. 'Always a good idea, in my book.'

Hawkins said, 'If we're found out, we'll get done for obstructing a police investigation.'

'Better hope that lass knows what she's doing, then.'

'I know.'

'Is she fit?' Bald asked. He grinned slyly.

Hawkins glared at him. 'Piss off, Jock.'

As they crossed the reception, Hawkins wondered what had happened to his old mate. John Bald, once the pride of Hereford. A first-rate warrior. He'd once vowed to make his millions when he left the Regiment. Now he was a shabbily dressed security guard in Plymouth, probably earning thirty grand a year at most. A guy on the downward slope of life, accelerating at full speed towards the gutter.

People are probably saying the same things about you, Davey boy. You're not all that different from Jock.

Hawkins knew he was in a shit state. But seeing Bald hungover, sleeping in his filthy car, was a reminder of the fate that awaited him if he failed to push back against his demons.

You can't go on like this forever, the voice told him. *Relying on a steady stream of medication and booze to get you through the day.*

Keep this up, and then you'll end up like Jock Bald.

'What were you doing?' Hawkins asked. 'Before you landed this gig?'

'This and that,' Bald replied vaguely.

Hawkins wasn't sure if he could trust Bald. He knew the guy would have been thoroughly vetted before landing the job. But equally, Bald had a dark reputation. If even half the stories about him were true, he'd been caught up in some dodgy shit since quitting Hereford. Was it possible that he had been taking backhanders from the Russians? It seemed unlikely, but you never really knew where you stood with Bald.

Hawkins decided to probe a little deeper. 'Last I heard, you were living up in the Hebrides.'

'That was years ago, Geordie. Ancient history.'

'Why'd you move up there?'

'Couple of ex-Reg lads at H stiffed me on a business deal. Took my hard-earned wedge and did a runner. Had enough of that fucking place, so I tried making a go of it back home. Got myself a little hotel on Islay. Thought that was me. Early retirement. Make my nut from all of them Yanks coming over on distillery tours.'

'What happened?'

'Life, Geordie. Life.'

'What do you mean?'

'Never go into the hospitality trade. That's my advice. It's a fucking minefield, the money's shite, and you'll spend your life dealing with complaints from entitled wankers.'

Hawkins chuckled. 'You didn't stick it out, then?'

'For a while. Then I sold off the business for pennies. Went back on the Circuit. Spent a few years bouncing around before the work dried up and I had to pack it in. When I came back home, I had fuck all going on, Geordie. No one would give us a job. Them bastards at Hereford blackballed us.'

'How did you land this job, then?'

'An old mate owed me a favour. Told me he'd heard about an opening at Plymouth and offered to put in a good word for me with the top brass. Hey fucking presto, here I am.'

Hawkins nodded but said nothing. A soft ping announced the arrival of the next cab. The lift doors hushed open. Hawkins stabbed the button for the third floor.

'What about you?' asked Bald. 'What's the craic?'

'There isn't much to say, Jock.'

'That's not what I heard.'

Hawkins's jaw tightened. He said nothing.

'I heard,' Bald carried on, 'that you ran into some trouble of your own a few years back. The head shed forced you out of Hereford. Banished you to some crap posting with the TA.'

'Something like that,' Hawkins muttered.

To his relief they reached the third floor before Bald could quiz him any further. They tramped down the corridor, Bald touched his universal entry card against the reader, the secure door unlocked. Bald pulled it open, gestured for Hawkins to enter ahead of him.

'Ladies first.'

'Twat.'

They crossed the secure area, passing the banks of deserted desks and the breakout areas as they made for King's workstation. They found Millar seated in the dead engineer's chair, hunched over the laptop. A second identical-looking laptop beside it. Cables and external drives were strewn across the desk. At the sound of their approaching footsteps, Millar looked up from the screen.

Hawkins made the introductions. A dirty look spread across Bald's face as he sized up Millar.

'Did you find anything?' Hawkins asked her.

Millar said, 'I'll explain after I've finished the transfer. But I might have found something, yes.'

'If it's hardcore porn, I wouldn't worry,' Bald joked. 'Half the saddos on this floor are in full-time relationships with their right hands.'

He grinned.

Millar gave him a disapproving look and said to Hawkins, 'This isn't that. This is completely different. I don't know what it means yet, but it could be related to what happened to King.'

'How do you mean?'

She pursed her lips. Didn't want to elaborate. Hawkins understood her hesitation. Bald was a lowly local security manager. He wouldn't have the necessary clearance to discuss the case in detail. Hawkins was about to tell him to sod off when the secure door at the other end of the floor flew open and Cleland came barrelling through the doorway. He lumbered towards them from across the floor, panic stencilled on his mug. Sweat patches dappled his supersized work shirt. He glared at Bald.

'Where the hell have you been?' he asked. 'Never mind,' he added. He nodded at Millar and Hawkins in turn. 'They're here, guys.'

'Who?' asked Hawkins.

'The police. They're at the gates. Sentry just alerted us.'

'Shit,' Hawkins said between gritted teeth. 'They're early. They're not supposed to be here before six, for fuck's sake.'

'Maybe they got bored of waiting,' Bald said.

Millar said, 'We haven't finished the transfer yet. You need to stall them.'

'I can't,' Cleland replied in a strained tone. 'They told the guards they have a search warrant. They've got a right to enter and seize evidence. We can't obstruct them.'

Bald tipped his head at Millar and said, 'How long do you need to finish them transfers?'

'Fifteen minutes. No more than that.'

Hawkins hurried over to the window overlooking the company car park. Four storeys below, a silver Volvo XC90 and a police-liveried Volkswagen Touareg rolled through the barrier and headed towards the front of the building.

Hawkins spun away from the glass and inclined his head at Millar. 'Get that transfer done soon as you can. When you're finished, hide the cloned computer in that drawer. Same place you found King's laptop. Then get down to reception. Got it?'

Millar nodded.

'Downstairs,' he said to Bald. 'With me. Now.'

He broke into a jog with Hawkins, the two ex-Blades flying past the maze of desks, Cleland hurrying after them. Bald tapped the door release button, hustled down the corridor and dived into the lift with the others. Thirty seconds later they hit the ground floor. They stepped out of the cab just in time to see a pair of uniformed officers sweeping through the main entrance.

The officers were followed by a man and a woman, both dressed in cheap-looking civilian clothing. A dark-haired guy in a crumpled suit, and a woman in black trousers, a white shirt and a mid-length trench coat. They both looked to be in their late thirties or thereabouts. The guy was basketball-player tall. Around six-five, Hawkins guessed, with a lightly stubbled jaw. A slight paunch bulged beneath his work shirt. The woman was about nine or ten inches shorter, with thin features and straight hair the colour of straw.

Cleland intercepted the cops midway between the lifts and the reception desk. Hawkins was about to move after him when Bald grabbed hold of his arm and said, in an undertone, 'Stay here and hold them up, Geordie. I'll be right back.'

Hawkins looked at him quizzically. 'Where are you going?'

'Upstairs. Just wait here. Whatever you do, don't let them fuckers get past.'

'What's the plan?'

Bald didn't answer. He had already started up the stairs, clearing the treads at a quick jog. A few beats later he disappeared from view. Hawkins took in a breath and marched briskly over to the officers.

'Fellas,' he said, shaking their hands in turn. 'I'm David Hawkins, Head of Security at DeepSpear. What's going on?'

The straw-haired woman flashed her police warrant card and said in a thick Lincolnshire accent, 'I'm DCI Gregory. This is DI Kendall.' Indicating the pot-bellied guy stood at her side.

'As I was just explaining to your colleague,' Gregory continued, 'we have a signed warrant to seize and retain any electronic devices used by Matt King, under the Police and Criminal Evidence Act.'

Hawkins said, calmly, 'If you don't mind, I'd like to see a copy of that warrant.'

Kendall produced a typed document from her jacket. Thrust it at him. Hawkins knew what it would say, but he pretended to read through it slowly anyway. Buying himself time. Wasting precious seconds.

Cleland's phone buzzed. He peered at the glowing screen, made an apologetic face to the two detectives and wandered off to field the call. Hawkins passed the warrant back to Kendall and wondered how the fuck he was going to obstruct the coppers for fifteen minutes.

'You're from Lincolnshire?' he asked Gregory. She gave a slight nod. 'Not far from my patch, that. Tyne and Wear man myself. Gosforth born and bred.'

Gregory looked unimpressed.

'We need that laptop,' she said. 'Now.'

'No worries. It's upstairs, guys. We'll take you up there in a moment. Before we go up, is there anything you can tell me about the case? Anything I can relay back to London?'

He directed the question at Gregory. The DCI. The more senior of the two officers. Therefore, more likely to be privy to information than the bloke in the crap suit.

She said, flatly, 'The investigation is ongoing. Once we're able to share further details, we'll let you know.'

'I appreciate that. I really do.' Hawkins inched closer and went on in an undertone, 'Look, between you and me, I'm getting it from all sides on this one. You know how it is. I've got the bloke's family asking questions, and there's media speculation, too.'

'Refer them to us,' said Kendall. 'We'll deal with them.'

'It's not just outsiders. My bosses are pressing me for answers. Anything you could tell me – anything at all, you'd be doing us a huge favour.'

'Like I said, we can't reveal the details of an investigation.'

'But you must have some idea of what's going on.' Hawkins pointed to the warrant. 'You wouldn't have got a judge to sign off on that unless you had reasonable grounds to suspect foul play.'

Kendall said nothing. Hawkins continued, playing the role of the harassed middle manager.

'Look, I'm just trying to do my job. Same as you. We've got mothers in the office, pregnant women. People with disabilities. Do I need to be worried about them? Should I be sending them all home?'

Gregory said, 'All I can tell you is that it looks like King suffered bleeding in the brain. We won't know more until a full post-mortem has been carried out. But your colleagues aren't in any danger.'

Hawkins guessed about four minutes had passed since they had left Millar on the third floor. Which meant she would need another ten or eleven minutes to finish the data transfer to the clean laptop. In his peripheral vision he saw Cleland pacing up and down beside the reception desk, talking furtively on his phone.

Hawkins stole a glance at the stairs. Wondered where the fuck Bald had gone.

Maybe he's sodded off.

Left us to deal with this mess while he sits in his Jeep necking voddie. That'd be just like Jock.

Hawkins knew one thing for sure. If the police found Millar tampering with King's laptop, they'd be in a world of shit. Destruction of evidence. A serious crime.

'You're legally obliged to comply with the warrant,' Kendall reminded him. 'We need that laptop, mate.'

Hawkins had run out of questions. He briefly considered starting a fight. Flooring Kendall with a sharp blow to the jaw. Satisfying, from a personal point of view. With a high chance of landing him in jail. But Hawkins was out of ideas. He had do something. Stop them from going upstairs and walking in on Millar cloning King's computer.

That was when the fire alarm shrieked.

Nine

For a moment no one moved. Kendall and Gregory glanced at one another in puzzlement, as if wondering what they should do next. *What's the protocol for a fire alarm going off in the middle of a search-and-seize?* Then Cleland got off his phone call and shouted at the top of his voice, 'Everyone out of the building! Head to your designated assembly points!'

The handful of people in reception stopped what they were doing and headed for the entrance, moving without any great urgency or panic, accustomed to the routine annoyance of a fire safety drill. They were swiftly joined by the two receptionists and the security guard. More people trickled out of the canteen, office workers and catering staff. Then a great crowd came rushing down the stairs from the upper floors. They surged past Gregory and Kendall, and the uniformed officers, and then Hawkins was ushering them outside, joining the throng of employees spilling out across the car park.

Those members of staff trained as fire wardens corralled their teams towards the assembly point. Cleland directed Hawkins and the police officers to a spot at the side of the main group. Within two or three minutes the bulk of the workers had filed out of the building. Hawkins looked round, but he couldn't see Bald or Millar anywhere.

Minutes passed.

The alarm kept screaming.

People mingled and waited.

Hawkins heard the usual mixture of gossip. People speculating about whether the fire was real or a spontaneous drill, or some sort of fault with the alarms. Others vented their frustration at this unexpected interruption to their busy schedule. A few more sneaked in a quick vape or tapped out messages on their phones.

Kendall and Gregory stood on the fringes of the crowd with Hawkins, looking increasingly frustrated. They'd anticipated a swift operation. Arrive at DeepSpear's office, execute the warrant, seize the laptop, bug out. A quick job. Or rather, it should have been. Instead they found themselves waiting in the car park with three hundred employees. Powerless to do anything until they had the all-clear to go back inside.

'How much longer is this going to take?' Gregory demanded.

Hawkins sensed her patience wearing thin.

'Shouldn't be long now,' Cleland said. 'The wardens just need to do a headcount, make sure no one has been left inside. Bear with us, guys.'

Gregory glowered at Hawkins and looked away. Probably she suspected that the alarm had been deliberately triggered to delay them. But there was nothing she could do to prove that, Hawkins reassured himself. She could only stand there and wait, like everybody else.

Thirty seconds later, Bald trotted out of the building, moving at the tail-end of a group of stragglers clutching folders and backpacks. Hawkins left the officers beside Cleland and met his old mucker at the edge of the crowd.

'What's going on?' he said in a low growl. 'Where's Alex?'

'Upstairs. Doing the transfer. She'll be done in a few minutes.'

'This was your handiwork?' Hawkins gestured towards the crowd.

Bald grinned. 'There's an emergency alarm in the men's room on the first floor. Only way of stopping Sherlock and Watson over there.'

'What about Millar?'

'What about her?'

'She needs to get off that floor once she's done. It's supposed to be off-limits to all staff.'

'All sorted, Geordie. Once she's completed the transfer she'll head downstairs. The entry door will lock automatically behind her. She'll hide out in the toilets on one of the lower floors. Wait it out until one of us lets her know the coast is clear.'

Hawkins said, 'This is fucking dicey, mate. We're a cunt hair away from getting caught red-handed.'

'Stop panicking, you daft prick. Everything's under control. I'm taking care of it.'

'That's what worries me.'

Bald shot him a flinty stare. 'You should be thanking me for saving your sad arse. If it hadn't been for me them coppers would have caught your mate in the act by now.'

Three more minutes passed.

Then another.

Hawkins glanced at his watch. 17.12. Fourteen minutes since the police had rocked up at the office. He tapped out a short message to Millar on his phone. All OK? Hit send and waited for a response.

A few paces away Cleland kept the officers busy. Reassuring the detectives, chummying up to them. 'Yes, we'll be back inside shortly, guys. Any moment now, I'm sure. Sorry again, but it's protocol...'

A minute later one of the fire wardens picked their way through the crowd and consulted with Cleland. The headcount had been completed. Everyone had been accounted for, apparently. Hawkins was relieved that he and Millar hadn't bothered to sign in on arrival.

Then the alarm died, Cleland got the thumbs-up from the facilities chief and the wardens began slowly herding the staff back into the building. Hawkins joined the crowd shuffling towards the entrance, like spectators flocking into a football stadium ahead of the big match. He checked his phone again. Still nothing from Millar. Sixteen minutes had passed. Enough time for her to complete the swap and get off that floor. He hoped.

And if she hasn't?
Then we're shafted.

They were passing into the reception now. Hawkins crossed the floor, Bald in the vanguard and Cleland at his six. Gregory, Kendall and the two uniformed officers bringing up the rear. Ahead of him people were heading back upstairs, their chatter punctuated by shouts from the wardens to move along in an orderly fashion. Others peeled off in groups and made for the canteen.

Hawkins started to worry. If the detectives found Millar at King's desk, they were bound to realise something was up.

Five seconds later, he received a new message. A thumbs-up from Millar. Hawkins allowed himself to breathe a sigh of relief. He slowed his stride as he typed out a response.

Where are you now?

He sent the message. The three dots danced at the bottom of the screen as Millar wrote back. Then a second message popped up.

Toilets. First floor.

Is it all done? Hawkins asked.
Millar replied with another thumbs-up emoticon.
Good, Hawkins replied. Wait there.
He put his phone away and grabbed Cleland by the arm.
'A word, mate.'
The director apologised to Gregory, muttered something about a problem with the fire safety drill and left the police waiting by the stairs. Hawkins took him to one side and glanced over his shoulder, making sure the officers were out of earshot before he spoke.
'Millar's done the swap,' he said quietly. 'She'll have left the clone in the same place King hid the original. Take the cops up there

and act like you've got no clue where King might have stashed the hardware. Let them turn his workspace upside down if they want to. They can give themselves a nice pat on the back when they find the computer. They won't give you any more trouble.'

Cleland gave him a look. 'Aren't you going to deal with them?'

Hawkins shook his head. 'I need to talk with Millar. Is there a secure location somewhere in this building? Somewhere we can chat in private?'

Cleland said, 'There's a meeting room on the first floor. All the standard soundproofing and jamming equipment. You can use that. John will show you where it is.'

He waved Bald over and said, sternly, 'Take David up to the secure room. He needs to consult with Millar. I'll deal with our friends from the police.'

'Roger that.'

'John?'

'Aye?'

'We'll be having words later, you and me.'

Cleland about-turned and walked back over to the detectives. 'Fucking twat,' Bald muttered under his breath.

He started climbing the stairs at a quick clip, forcing his way past the slower-moving members of staff, Hawkins hurrying after him. On the first floor he followed Bald down a short corridor and through an unlocked entry door leading into an open workspace laid out almost identical to the engineering department two floors up.

Bald led Hawkins across the floor and stopped in front of a meeting room in the far corner. He swiped his access card against the electronic reader and ushered Hawkins into a rectangular-shaped room with a conference table surrounded by a dozen sleek chairs. In the centre of the table a smart projector pointed at a tripod-mounted screen against the back wall. Shelves displayed neatly arranged rows of books on military history, along with several copies of a biography of DeepSpear's founder, Nish Varma.

Bald gestured for Hawkins to take a seat. Then he left to retrieve Millar. Three minutes later the door snicked open again and Millar entered, clutching King's original laptop. She pulled up a pew beside Hawkins, set the device down on the table, flipped it open. Bald lingered in the doorway.

'What's going on? Some sort of sneaky-beaky shit?'

Hawkins gritted his teeth and said, 'Fuck off, Jock.'

'Bollocks. I'm in charge of security here. You should be filling me in. King was my responsibility.'

'Not anymore. This is a head office issue now. Well above your level of clearance, mate. We can't discuss it with you. Do us both a favour and stop sticking your bloody nose in.'

Bald's expression darkened. 'Fuck off, Geordie. I just saved your bacon back there.'

'I'll buy you a box of Quality Street. Now leave us.'

Bald stormed out of the meeting room, pulled the door shut behind him. Millar waited for the security light above the doorframe to flash red.

She said, 'I'm not sure I like your friend much.'

'Jock?' Hawkins laughed drily. 'He's not a mate. He doesn't understand the meaning of the word. In his world you're either the person holding the knife, or the guy getting stabbed in the throat.'

'Do you trust him?'

'About as far as I could spit a brick.' Hawkins nodded at the laptop. 'What did you find?'

'I said I *might* have found something. Equally it might be nothing at all.'

'How do you mean?'

'It's probably easier to show you. Look.'

Millar powered up the laptop and entered a series of commands on the boot screen. The desktop populated with icons and folders over a wallpaper photo of King posing beside a prototype torpedo.

Millar traced her index finger across the trackpad, clicked open an email app.

A new window popped up on the screen. Long list of folders running down the left-hand sidebar and a larger panel to the right displaying the messages in King's inbox.

Millar clicked on an arrow next to the Sent Items folder, revealing a column of sub-folders. She rested the cursor over one of the last items under the Sent Items heading. A sub-folder labelled 'Enterprise Delivery Management'.

'What am I supposed to be looking at?' asked Hawkins.

'This folder,' Millar said. 'It's an acronym.'

Hawkins shook his head. 'I don't follow.'

'EDM is the name of a cult software developer from the early Nineties. A bunch of guys based in south Wales. Elite Dreams Multimedia. They were at the cutting edge of graphics and software engineering at the time. Every British kid who owned a computer in the Nineties has heard of them. A lot of big names in the industry cut their teeth at the company. King choosing that name for a folder is sort of like an in-joke.'

'That's your idea of humour?' Hawkins gave a sad shake of his head. 'Jesus, you geeks are a barrel of laughs.'

'Don't you see? King deliberately created a folder with a name that only someone with knowledge of the British video game scene would recognise. To anyone else, it just looks like an ordinary folder.'

'Why would he do that?'

'To hide sensitive messages. Ones that King didn't want anyone else to read.'

'What's inside that folder?'

'That's the problem. I don't know.'

Hawkins looked at her. Waited for Millar to explain.

She said, 'I was right about King adding layers of security to the system. He protected the drive with military-grade encryption. You can't access it without entering the recovery key.'

93

'But you got in.'

'Right. Because we have specialist software. The same one used by various governments.'

'So what's the problem?'

'King added a second layer of security to this folder.' Millar tapped a finger against the EDM folder icon. 'I can't open or view the messages without the relevant key. What's known as double encryption.'

Hawkins gave her a look. 'Can you translate that into English?'

Millar rolled her eyes and said, 'Ordinarily, someone will encrypt either the whole drive, or a specific partition. You have to enter the assigned key or password before you can access the encrypted data. But King has added another layer of encryption on top of that to specific files. In this case, a sub-folder under Sent Items. It's like adding a second lock to a bank vault. Or putting a vault within a vault.'

'Why the fuck would he do that?'

'It's not an efficient system. More passwords to remember. More keys. You have to jump through more hoops to access the data. Whatever is in this folder, King must have been very worried that someone else might get hold of it.'

'Can't you hack into that sub-folder?'

Millar shook her head. 'It's an extremely complex algorithm. A different one from the main encryption. I'd need more time. Could take days.'

'But if we can't read the emails, what makes you think this folder has got anything to do with what happened to King?'

Millar said, 'It took some work, but I've been able to access the metadata. That's basically information about the data.'

'And?'

'There are only seven messages inside the EDM folder. Six of them are between King and Rideout. His late manager.'

'What about the seventh?'

'It's an email from King to Nish Varma. Sent two days before his murder.'

'Fuck me.' Hawkins lifted his eyes from the screen to Millar, his brow heavily furrowed. 'King was emailing the CEO directly?'

Millar nodded tersely and said, 'At first I couldn't believe it too. So I went away and checked the employee database, just to be sure. There's only one Nishant Varma across the whole company.'

'Why would he be emailing the big boss?'

'Without being able to view the message content, it's impossible to know. But I was able to scrape something else from the metadata. The subject for the email.'

'What was it?'

'Just one word: *Bulgarians*. Followed by a pair of exclamation marks.'

'What does that mean?'

Millar said, carefully, 'Earlier, when we were searching for the laptop, Cleland mentioned something about a Bulgarian working on the same team as King.'

Hawkins cast his mind back three hours. Before the arrival of the police. Before he'd found Bald sleeping off a hangover in the company car park.

'Petar Vitanov,' he said.

One of our senior engineers, Cleland had said.

Unease percolated into Hawkins's guts.

'Do you think Vitanov is somehow connected?' he asked.

'He has to be,' Millar said. 'The guy sat two feet away from King. Who then writes an email to Varma concerning some Bulgarians shortly before his death. That's too much of a coincidence.'

'But how?'

'I don't know.'

'What about the emails between King and Rideout?'

'Nothing. Subject field is blank on all six messages.'

Hawkins felt a sharp pang of frustration. Nothing about King's death was clear-cut; they had only tantalising fragments of the whole, scraps of information. Part of him yearned for the clarity of his old life in the Regiment. Kicking in doors, raiding strongholds. Lifting bad guys. A world without the grey uncertainty of the civilian world. Go through this door, or that one. Drop your enemy or get dropped yourself.

Life or death.

Black and white.

He said, 'How many Bulgarians work at DeepSpear?'

Millar said, 'I have no idea. We'd have to look into it. But it has to involve multiple persons. King wrote *Bulgarians*. Plural. We're dealing with more than one individual.'

Hawkins sat back in his chair, arms folded across his chest. Cycled through the questions in his head. He considered the most obvious question first. King had been a mid-level engineer. One of many at DeepSpear. A guy on the lower rungs of the corporate ladder, emailing the CEO of a major disruptor in the defence industry. Varma wouldn't have known him. Probably didn't even know that King existed. He wasn't the kind of leader who donned a hard hat and visited the shop floor, shaking hands with the rank-and-file. His world was international summits, sit-downs with tech bros, sipping Krug on his private yacht in the French Riviera. A completely different universe.

King wouldn't have reached out to him unless he had a damn good reason.

Which led Hawkins to the second question. Who were the other Bulgarians King had been referring to in his email?

We cast a very wide net, Cleland had said.

Millar said, 'We know one thing from the metadata.'

'What's that?'

'The exclamation marks at the end of the subject field. That tells us King was jumpy. He was clearly panicked about something. Panicked, and desperate enough to try to get Varma's attention.'

'Whatever is in that email,' said Hawkins, 'it's got to be serious. We're talking about engineer bypassing his line managers and going straight to the big boss. That kind of behaviour puts people's noses out of joint.'

'And King was careful to cover his tracks. Hence the double encryption. He must have been worried that someone would find out about his correspondence with Varma and Rideout. Someone with the ability to break through the outer encryption layer.'

Hawkins scratched his cheek as he thought back to their conversation with Cleland earlier that afternoon. Then he snatched up his phone and typed out a new email.

Millar said, 'Who are you messaging?'

'Cleland,' he replied. 'Telling him to get someone to pop round to Vitanov's home straight away.'

Millar stared at him. 'You think Vitanov is planning to skip town?'

'If he hasn't done so already. Tenner says he's not sitting at home with a mug of Lemsip, feeling sorry for himself.'

'Assuming you're right, he's not the only one involved. Because of the plural.'

Hawkins considered, then said, 'We should tell Cleland to find out if any of Vitanov's Bulgarian co-workers have called in sick today. This thing is getting bigger by the minute.'

'How do you mean?'

Hawkins fished out the cigarette packet he'd retrieved from the wooded area opposite the pub car park, dumped it on the table.

'I found this in the car park at Cremyll,' he said.

Millar picked up the packet and studied it.

'Cigarettes,' she said. 'So what?'

'Not just any ciggies. See here.'

He pointed to the logo. The initials 'DS' superimposed over the anchor graphic. 'DURRES SPECIALS' stamped above it.

'Durres,' he went on, 'is a place near the capital of Albania.'

'This isn't the time for a geography lesson, David.'

'Listen. These are domestic Albanian smokes. Not the kind you can find at your local Tesco. Someone was puffing away on these in the last day or two, in a partially concealed area facing the car park. I checked and there's an unobstructed line of sight to the spot where King died.'

Millar said, doubtfully, 'We don't know that this is linked in any way, though. It could just as easily have been some random Albanian sleeping rough in the woods.'

Hawkins shook his head. 'The smoker got through a whole pack in the same spot. That means he – or she – was standing there for some time. Several hours or more.'

'What are you saying?'

'I think whoever killed King set up an OP – observation point – in a semi-concealed position. Perhaps sitting in a vehicle to avoid drawing attention. They waited there until King stepped outside the pub, then killed him. Either using a poison that can't be detected through regular tests, or some other weapon that doesn't leave a trace.'

'But how could they be certain of luring King into the car park? They must have known he'd arrived there on foot.'

'I don't know.' Hawkins paused. 'And there's another problem with that theory. With every theory we've come up with so far, in fact.'

'What's that?'

'We still don't have the faintest fucking idea how King's killers carried out the hit.'

Millar said nothing.

Hawkins said, 'We should have a word with Varma. Question him about the email. Ask him what the fuck's going on.'

'That might not be helpful. What if he denies knowing anything about it? Someone like him must get thousands of emails a day. Maybe it went into his junk.'

Hawkins conceded the point. 'Is there some faster way of breaking into that second vault? Do we have the hardware in London?'

Millar considered, then shook her head. 'The only people who have that sort of capability are the folks at the Doughnut.'

The Doughnut, thought Hawkins.

Officially known as GCHQ. Government Communications Headquarters at Cheltenham, though everyone referred to it as the Doughnut, because of the uncanny resemblance when viewed from above. Home to the nation's most talented coders and cyber experts. Or rather, the ones who hadn't gone to make their millions with the gods of Silicon Valley.

'I have a contact over there,' Millar said. 'A friend. I could try reaching out to her. See if she could help us.'

'Could they break that second key?'

'I'd bet my house on it, if I owned one. They have access to resources on a scale that we simply don't. More storage. More processing power. More everything.'

'How long would it take?'

'I don't know. I'd have to ask my friend. But the sooner we get it to her, the quicker she could get it done.'

Hawkins made a rough calculation. Cheltenham. A distance of approximately a hundred and fifty miles. A three-hour drive. They wouldn't make it there until gone eight o'clock.

'Will she be on shift this evening?' he asked. He knew that GCHQ operated round the clock, with teams working eight-hour shifts on rotation.

'Don't think so. She's got a kid. I think she does regular office hours.'

His phone jolted with a new email. He hard-stared at the screen to unlock it and tapped open the message. 'It's Cleland. The police are finishing up. He's sending Bald over to Vitanov's home now. An address in Efford. He'll let us know soon as Jock reports back.'

'What do we do now?'

'Now,' said Hawkins, 'we wait. If our luck's in, we can isolate Vitanov before he has a chance to get away.'

Then we can get some fucking answers.

Ten

They passed their time in the secure room. Millar grabbed a pair of coffees from the canteen and reached out to her contact at the Doughnut. Hawkins sent another message to Cleland, asking him to find out how many Bulgarians were employed at the Devonport office, in what capacity, and whether any more of them had failed to show up for work. Along with the names of any Albanians they had on the payroll. Then he sat back and reviewed what they knew so far.

Which wasn't much, Hawkins reflected. They had a dead engineer, a report that he had suffered bleeding in the brain. They had an email addressed to Varma, mentioning some unspecified Bulgarians. A cigarette packet. Hardly a mountain of evidence. They had nothing that indicated how King had been killed, or why. Or the identities of the bastards behind the attack.

Hawkins felt sure that the answers lay with Vitanov and his fellow Bulgarians.

Find them, Hawkins reassured himself, *and we can start cracking skulls. One of them is bound to spill their guts.*

Twenty-eight minutes later, Cleland knocked and entered the room. Hawkins looked up at him expectantly. Didn't like the expression plastered on the director's face.

'I've heard back from John,' Cleland said. 'He's just on his way back from Vitanov's address now.'

'Aye,' Hawkins said. 'And?'

'All the lights are off. Curtains drawn. No one answered the door, and Petar's car was missing from the front drive. An Amazon package has been left outside since yesterday afternoon.'

'Does anyone else live at the property?'

Cleland shook his head. 'Vitanov lived alone. No family, no girlfriend. But a neighbour says they saw him leaving on Sunday night. Around ten o'clock in the evening. The neighbour is sure of the time, because that's when they put their bins out.'

Hawkins and Millar looked at one another. 'That's two hours after King collapsed in the pub car park,' said Millar.

'Did Vitanov say where he was going?' Hawkins asked.

Cleland said, 'He mentioned something about a work trip, apparently.'

'A blatant lie.'

'Yes.' Cleland paused. 'The neighbour said something else. Claimed that Vitanov wasn't his usual talkative self. Like he was in a big hurry to be somewhere.'

'Shit.' Hawkins thumped a fist on the arm of his chair.

Cleland said, 'I've got the information you asked for. About the Bulgarians we employ. There are eighteen in total.'

He read out an email on his phone.

'Four in engineering, including Petar Vitanov. Five in catering, four in IT. The rest are scattered across various departments. Legal and what-have-you.'

Hawkins said, 'What about Albanians?'

'None. Our HR director thinks one or two of the cleaners might be Albanian nationals, but they work for an external contractor, so that information isn't on our systems. We're waiting on that.'

'Any of the Bulgarians call in sick today?'

Cleland nodded. 'We've got three confirmed absences: Simeon Bachev, Valentin Petkov and Anita Nedeva. Also an IT network engineer by the name of Denis Yordanov. He hasn't checked in with his manager, so they're not sure what's going on there yet.

'None of them,' Cleland added, 'are answering their phones.'

'We should send people round to those addresses right away,' Millar said.

'One step ahead of you,' Cleland responded. 'I've notified our security guards. They're on their way as we speak.'

'Waste of time,' said Hawkins. 'They won't find anything. If Vitanov has legged it, the others will have done the same.'

Cleland stared at him with narrowed eyes. 'Do you want to tell me what the hell is going on?'

'Later, maybe,' Hawkins said. 'What happened with the police?'

Cleland talked them through the scene. A play-by-play account. The police had turned King's workspace upside down searching for his computer. Slashed open his chair seat, gutted his desk, dumped the contents of the drawers on the floor. It had taken them a little while, but eventually they had discovered the cloned laptop. The officers had been pleased with their find, Cleland reported. Patted themselves on the back, like pirates finding buried treasure. Photographs had been taken, forms completed. Details logged. Kendall had bagged up the hardware, while Gregory had given Cleland a receipt for the item, along with instructions on how to reclaim it once the investigation had closed.

'Did they suspect any tampering? Anything like that?'

Cleland thought for a beat. 'I don't think so. They were pissed off about the fire alarm, but I told them the system had been glitchy lately. They seemed to buy it.'

'Then we're in the clear,' Millar said.

'Not yet. We've got to hope them officers don't find anything fishy on that cloned computer,' Hawkins reminded her. 'Anything that makes them realise we've duped them.'

Millar shot him a fierce look. 'They won't.'

Hawkins skated his gaze back to Cleland and said, 'Let us know when you've heard back from the other guards. I'll give you a shout if we need anything else.'

Cleland left the room. Minutes passed. Then Millar's phone lit up with a message from her friend at GCHQ. She had agreed to take a look at King's laptop, Millar said; she had already left the office but promised to tackle it first thing in the morning.

'Are you sure we should be giving her the laptop in the first place? We've gone to a fucking lot of effort stopping the police from getting hold of it. Now we're giving it up.'

'That's different. I don't trust the police.'

'But you trust your friend?'

'With my life. Besides, we don't have a choice. Either we do this, or we waste a lot more time trying to break into that folder at our end. It could take us potentially days to find out what's in there.'

Hawkins checked his watch. Unease percolated into his guts. 17.48. Nearly twenty hours since Vitanov had done a runner. Almost certainly with the other four absent Bulgarians. The trail would already be running cold. By now they could be on a plane, bound for somewhere that didn't have an extradition treaty with Britain.

He said, 'I still think we should talk to Varma.'

Millar pulled a frown. 'Gracey told us to report directly to him.'

'Gracey says a lot of things. I generally find it's a healthy policy to ignore anything that comes out of his mouth.'

'I'm serious, David.'

'So am I. This situation is bigger than just Gracey now. We've got multiple potential Kremlin agents on the run. Varma needs to know what's going on here. And we need to get his side of the story. About the emails from King. Find out what he knows.'

Millar said, 'If we're going to do that, we need to head back to London. Fix a meeting and speak with him in person. We can't do this over the phone or email.'

'Why not?'

'Our enemies have ways of breaking into even the most secure networks.'

'The Russians, you mean?'

'Among others. The only completely secure way of talking to Varma is face-to-face.'

'Fine. I'll check in with his EAs. One of them must know if he's free.'

'I'll make the call. It's better coming from me.'

'Why?'

'I know Nish. You don't. Varma won't give you the time of day.'

'What are you going to tell them?'

'We need to be upfront. Those assistants are Varma's gatekeepers. No one gets to sit down with him without a very good reason. That's assuming he's even in town tomorrow. For all we know he might be sunning himself in Tuscany.'

Hawkins rubbed his temple. 'Keep it simple. Just say we want to speak with him about Matt King, and it's urgent. That should get his attention.'

Millar unlocked her phone and drafted a message to one of Varma's assistants, fingers moving nimbly over the glass. She sent the message. Waited. A minute passed. Then another.

On three minutes her phone trembled. Millar frowned at the screen. 'The assistant says Varma is in King Street tomorrow, but he's extremely busy. Back-to-back meetings. Best she can offer is a thirty-minute window.'

'When?'

'Ten o'clock.'

'Tell her we'll meet him then.' Hawkins thought for a beat. 'Book the secure room. This isn't the sort of chat we should be having in Varma's office.'

'What about King's laptop? Someone will need to run it up to Cheltenham.'

'One of Cleland's people can do that. Or better yet, we can get Jock to run it up there. Give him something to do, other than getting shitfaced and sleeping on the job.'

'He doesn't strike me as someone who likes courier duty.'

'He won't have a choice. You outrank him. We both do.'

Millar gave him a long searching look. 'Do you think Varma has something to hide?'

'I don't know. But King sent him an email, and a short time later he wound up dead. Now it's looking like a bunch of Bulgarians have gone on the run. That doesn't fill me with confidence.

'Either way, we need to get some answers. No one ever won a battle sitting on their arse.'

'Is that another SAS motto?'

Hawkins smiled sadly. 'No. Just something my brother liked to say.'

'I didn't know you had a brother.'

An image flickered across his line of sight. A face frozen in the agonising moment of death.

Hawkins felt his stomach muscles tighten. His palms began to sweat.

'David? Are you okay?'

He shut his eyes. Opened them.

The image vanished again.

He abruptly stood up. He felt a compulsion to leave the room – the building – before the vision returned.

'Come on,' he said. 'Let's get moving. We've got a long road trip ahead of us.'

Eleven

Millar shut down King's laptop while Hawkins dashed off a message to Cleland, asking him to meet them in reception. Then they exited the secure room and cantered down the stairs to the ground floor. Two minutes later, Cleland and Bald emerged from one of the lifts. Hawkins led them over to a quiet corner of the lobby.

'We're heading back up to London,' he said. 'Any word on them other Bulgarians?'

Bald said, 'My lads are checking the addresses at the moment. Petkov's place is definitely empty. Same story as Vitanov's gaff. Lights switched off, car's missing, phone is turned off. Lad in the flat next door reckons Petkov left in a hurry on Sunday evening. Around ten o'clock. Now, do you want to tell us what the fuck this is about?'

Hawkins gave a stern shake of his head. 'Top-level security clearance only. You know the rules, Jock.'

'If there's something dodgy going on around here, we need to know about it.'

'Not my decision, mate. You have a problem, take it up with Gracey.'

Hawkins ignored the glowering look from Bald and turned to Cleland. He said, 'We'll be on our way. Any further questions, we'll let you know.'

'What about the police?'

'They shouldn't bother you anymore. Any problems, point them in our direction.'

'Can I open up the third floor again?'

'Don't see why not. It'll be good for staff morale. Make people think things are getting back to normal. No one wants to turn up for work next to a crime scene.'

'Better clear away King's possessions, first,' Millar put in. 'In case we need to check anything else with you. Dump everything in a box and store it somewhere safe.'

'Got it. Anything else, guys?'

Hawkins smiled to himself. He could smell the anxiety coming off Cleland in waves. The fear that his career was hanging by the barest of threads. He would be fretting about Gracey, and the report Hawkins and Millar would make once they got back to London.

'I need just a word with Jock,' said Hawkins. 'Alone.'

'Of course.' Cleland glanced slantindicular at the old Scottish soldier. 'I'll leave you lads to it. Meet me upstairs once you're done, John. My office.'

'Rog, boss.'

Cleland wheeled round and recrossed the reception floor and took the next lift. Then Millar indicated the laptop and said to Bald, 'We need you to run this thing up to the Doughnut. There are certain files that we can't access without their help.'

'When?'

'Tomorrow morning. A friend of mine works there. She's agreed to look at King's computer. Personal favour.'

'Why can't you do it?'

Hawkins said, 'We need to get back up to London this evening.'

'This is important,' Millar pointed out. 'It may help us figure out who killed King, and why. You'd be really helping us out.'

'I'm not your bloody errand boy, for fuck's sake,' Bald fumed.

'We're not asking nicely, mate,' Hawkins said, pulling rank. 'We're telling you to get it done.'

Bald glared at him but stayed silent.

Millar said, 'My friend will be at her desk at eight o'clock tomorrow morning. I'll send you her contact details. You'll be expected. Message us once you've made the delivery.'

She left the laptop with Bald and started towards the front entrance. Hawkins watched her go and then rounded on Bald, placing a hand on the latter's shoulder. Looked him hard in the eye.

'Notify me,' he said, 'when that thing gets delivered tomorrow.'

Bald wrinkled his nose in contempt. He said, 'This is a piss-take. Get someone else to ferry it up there. I'm more use to you down here, Geordie.'

'How's that?'

Bald scoped out the lobby, making sure no one was listening in. 'Look, those Bulgarians, they're tight. Stick together. I see them all the time, hanging out in the same places. In each other's pockets, that mob.'

'So what?'

'There's a restaurant on Cornwall Street. Bulgarian joint. Vitosha. Vitanov and that lot are there all the time, stuffing their faces and getting pissed on foreign lager.'

'And you know this how?'

'It's all them fuckers ever talk about. Vitanov is always telling everyone how good the food is at the place, how he gets a special discount because he's best mates with the owner.'

'I don't see how that helps us.'

'Let me go over there. Rough up the owner. Shake a few trees, like.'

'No,' Hawkins said. 'Absolutely not.'

'Why not?'

Hawkins made a face. 'Do I really have to explain how it would look if we beat up a load of foreign nationals just because they happen to come from the same country as the suspects?'

'Geordie, that restaurant manager is shifty. He knows something.'

'I don't care what you think. Just focus on getting that laptop up to GCHQ. Make sure you don't screw this one up.'

'What the fuck is that supposed to mean?'

'You've lost your edge, Jock. This situation happened on your watch.'

Bald's jaw visibly tensed. 'Bullshit.'

He took a step forward. Moving into Hawkins's personal space.

'If I hadn't dug you out of a hole with that fire alarm,' he went on, 'you would have ended up in serious fucking trouble with the police. You and that new friend of yours. So don't give me any fucking lectures about losing my edge. *Mate*.'

Hawkins stared darkly at the Scot. 'I've still got what it takes.'

'Yeah?' Bald gave an ugly laugh. 'Could have fooled me. Look at you, for fuck's sake. I know an alcoholic when I see one. You're on the booze. Big time.'

'That's rich, coming from you. Biggest pisshead in the Regiment.'

'Aye, but I can handle it. Iron stomach, me. Scottish genes. You're a sad drinker. Stuck in the past, feeling sorry for himself.'

A hot flame of anger flared up inside Hawkins's chest. 'You don't know what you're talking about,' he replied, lamely.

Bald said, 'I used to respect you as an operator. You might have been a cunt – but you were a cunt who knew how to soldier. Now you're just tragic. A sad prick sitting behind a Civvy Street desk, playing detective.'

'Watch yourself, Jock,' Hawkins growled. 'Keep this up, and I'll have you binned before the month is out.'

Bald's face hardened like cement. 'Is that a threat?'

'Take it as a friendly warning. Start doing your job properly, or I won't protect you.'

Bald stared at him but said nothing. Then he turned his back on Hawkins and stamped up the stairs, carrying King's laptop. Hawkins watched him go, hands clenched into tight fists, the rage still sweeping through his veins. Bald's words burning in his ears.

You're just tragic.

A sad prick sitting behind a Civvy Street desk.

Hawkins spun away and marched swiftly towards Millar. She stood in front of the entrance, frowning hard at a message on her phone.

'Bloke trouble?' Hawkins asked.

Millar said, 'None of your business.'

'It is,' Hawkins replied, 'if you're not fully focused on the job. I need your mind on this thing, not stressed about your relationship.'

Millar sighed and said, 'It's nothing. Really. I'm supposed to meet someone tonight. I won't make it back in time. They're not taking it very well. I won't bore you with the details.'

'As long as it doesn't get in the way of the job.'

'It won't.' She nodded in the direction Bald had gone. 'What's the matter with him?'

'Jock? Nothing,' he said. 'Just an old Blade who needs to get his head back in the game.'

Me and him both.

Millar canted her head to one side and gave him a long look. 'Is there something in the water at Hereford? None of you seem to walk out of the gates as healthy well-adjusted males.'

Hawkins laughed. 'You may have a point.'

* * *

They steered out of the DeepSpear facility and tooled north-east in moderate early-evening traffic. Shortly after seven o'clock they stopped for fuel at a service station outside Exeter. They loaded up on disgusting coffee, salty pre-packaged junk and filled the tank with a hundred pounds of unleaded. Fifteen minutes later they were bombing along the motorway when Millar's phone hummed with an incoming email. She opened it, skim-read the text, her face faintly illuminated by the bluish glow of the screen.

'It's Cleland. He says they can't reach any of the Bulgarians. They're not at their homes and their phones are turned off.'

'Any indication of where they might have gone? Any of them have any friends or family we can question?'

She typed out the message. Dashed it off and got a speedy reply from Cleland.

'The Bulgarians were all unmarried, no kids. At least not in this country. But the IT guy, Yordanov, had a house-mate. A student at the local uni. He was at home at the time and let Cleland's people search his room. They found Yordanov's passport in his bedside table.'

'Doesn't mean a thing,' Hawkins said. 'If they're working for the Kremlin, they'll be relying on fake passports to get out of the country.'

They reached the drab outskirts of London a few minutes before eleven o'clock. Millar said that her contact at Cheltenham would reach out to them the next day, as soon as she had gained access to the hidden folder. She couldn't say for sure until she had the laptop in front of her, but the friend reckoned she'd need a few hours to get it done.

She gave Hawkins an address in Paddington. Half an hour later he pulled up outside a cookie-cutter block of flats overlooking Paddington canal. Millar rested a hand on the chrome door handle and paused.

She said, 'We should talk things through tomorrow morning, when we're both fresh. Discuss strategy for the meeting with Varma. This might be our only shot at quizzing him.'

Hawkins nodded and said, 'Where do you want to meet?'

'There's a greasy spoon near Charing Cross. Pete's Café. Meet there at nine o'clock. We can walk to the office afterwards.'

Hawkins drew his head back in surprise. 'Greasy spoon?'

'Yes. Is there a problem?'

'You don't look like the kind of person who enjoys a full English.'

Millar smiled teasingly. 'There are a lot of things you don't know about me,' she said.

She tugged open the door and stepped out into the cigarette glow of a London night. Hawkins fired the engine, pulled away, steered down a couple of secondary roads. He hung a right and pointed the Merc due west on the Bayswater Road. Heading back in the direction of his flat.

Back to the whisky, and the pills. The solitude.

Alone that night, in the darkness of his bedroom, he thought back to that day on the hills. He remembered the barren slope in winter, exposed to the icy wind. Gorse thorns braided in fresh snow. Yellow flowers pocking the whiteness. Pale sunlight gleaming faintly behind salt-grey clouds.

But mostly he remembered the brutal cold. A cold like nothing he had ever known before. How it felt as if it was slowly skinning you alive, hacking away at every scrap of exposed flesh.

He thought about the face, too. The one he could never forget.

Jacob staring up at him.

Accusing him.

What have you done?

How could you let this happen?

Hawkins threw more whisky down his throat. He drank until he had drowned out the voice. Until the face disappeared – and the darkness had closed its fingers around him, and the pain had been numbed – and then, at last, he fell into the sweet embrace of oblivion.

Twelve

London. The next day.

Hawkins rose early. Doused his broken body in the shower, knocked back his pills and enough black coffee to fill a forty-five-gallon drum. At dead-on eight o'clock he received a message from Bald, reporting successful delivery of the laptop to the contact at Cheltenham. Which was immediately followed by a message from Millar confirming the same.

A few minutes later Hawkins folded himself into the front of the Merc and pointed it through traffic-clogged central London, the speedometer needle rarely climbing above the twenty-per-hour mark. He dumped the wagon in the parking garage beneath DeepSpear's head office on King Street, took the pedestrian exit to ground level and strolled through the tattered grandeur of St James's towards Charing Cross.

Hawkins composed his thoughts during his walk. He found it helpful to think on the move. A habit he'd picked up during his time in the Regiment. When you had a sixty-kilometre march ahead of you on the Brecon Beacons and every muscle in your body was screaming at you to stop, you could either surrender to that voice or move past it. Direct your mind elsewhere. Distract your brain from the hurt you were feeling.

He focused on Varma. Specifically, the email he had received from King days before the engineer's murder. A bunch of questions jumped out at him. Foremost among them: why had King gone directly to the CEO with his concerns, instead of his superiors at Devonport? Had King feared that Cleland, or whoever else he reported to down there, wouldn't take him seriously? Or – worse – that he couldn't trust them?

Whatever had been troubling him, King must have been reasonably confident that he could get Varma's attention. Otherwise why go to the effort of emailing him? But that puzzled Hawkins. He assumed Varma received thousands of messages in his inbox each day. A daily avalanche. Someone in his position, with his workload, was unlikely to pay attention to a message from some junior engineer. But for some reason King felt he would get a fair hearing from DeepSpear's CEO.

Why?

What did Varma know?

By the time he had reached St Martin-in-the-Fields, Hawkins had formed a rough plan in his head. They would sit down with Varma, brief him on the details of King's death. Talk him through their findings from their visit to Plymouth. The Albanian cigarette packet found opposite the pub car park. The information the detectives had shared about King suffering from a bleeding in the brain. King hiding his work laptop in the desk pedestal. Getting GCHQ's help to break into the encrypted folder.

But they wouldn't tell him about the email King had sent to Varma.

Not at first.

We'll lay out the rest of it. Gauge his reaction.

See if he volunteers the information.

That decision resolved another question drumming away at the back of Hawkins's mind. He had been wondering whether to share their findings with Gracey. But Gracey was a corporate stooge. He prized loyalty to the badge above all else. If they told him what they knew, he would go straight to Varma, forewarning him. Giving the latter time to prepare his story. Better to keep Gracey in the dark for now. Then lay the trap for Varma.

Hawkins walked north past Charing Cross station and paced down Chandos Place. He found the greasy spoon midway along the street. An old-school relic with a green-tiled frontage, half-height curtains drawn across the windows and a painted sign above the door, peeling away like a picked scab.

He glanced at his watch as he approached the door. 08.45. He was early. Another leftover habit from his Hereford days. Years of living and working in an environment that placed great emphasis on personal discipline. Especially when it came to timekeeping. On an op, even a delay of a few seconds could mean the difference between life and death. Between success and failure. Hawkins had carried that attitude through to his life on Civvy Street.

A doorbell *ta-tinged* as Hawkins stepped inside, barely audible above the din of chatting customers, the waitresses shouting orders to the kitchen staff across rows of Formica tables.

Hawkins stopped just inside the doorway and scanned the café. Searching for Millar.

Then he saw her.

She was sitting at a table in the far corner, ten metres away from the entrance. A cup of coffee and a plate of half-eaten scrambled eggs and smashed avocado in front of her. She wasn't alone. Another woman sat opposite, holding hands with Millar. Fingers laced together.

Hawkins shifted his attention to the other woman.

And did a triple-take.

He found himself looking at a face he hadn't seen in eight months.

Zoe.

She hadn't spotted Hawkins yet. Mainly because she seemed fully absorbed in her conversation with Millar. They were laughing and smiling in a way that implied the two of them were more than just friends.

A lot fucking more.

Hawkins stood stock-still, struggling to process the scene in front of him. He felt like someone had smashed him in the face with a kettle bell. Then the shock calcified, and he felt only a cold, hard anger at seeing his daughter enjoying someone else's company.

Not just anyone else. Someone he actually knew.

The doorbell pealed behind him. A couple of labourers in hi-vis jackets and work boots, reeking of cheap fags and talking in thick Eastern European accents, barged past Hawkins, making for the counter. One of them bumped into a waitress carrying a stack of greasy plates, knocking her off-balance. The plates tumbled to the floor and shattered. An argument broke out between the waitress and the Eastern Europeans. Zoe broke off from her conversation and looked towards the commotion near the door.

Then she saw her father.

Their eyes met for no more than a second or two. Her demeanour instantly shifted. She went stiff and pale. The smile dropped so quickly from her face Hawkins half-expected it to hit the table with a jarring thud. Millar looked in the same direction and caught sight of Hawkins. She said something to Zoe, but they were too far away for him to catch the words.

Zoe shook her head vigorously. She snatched her hands back from Millar.

Hawkins took a step towards their table. Behind him the waitress was still shouting at the labourers.

'Sweetheart,' he said, gently. 'Love, how are you . . . ?'

Zoe didn't answer. Something like contempt flashed in her wide green eyes. She said something else to Millar. Then she shot to her feet, chair legs scraping against the scuffed vinyl as she grabbed her leather jacket and pushed her way towards the exit at the back of the café.

Hawkins started to follow her. 'Love, please. I just want to talk.'

'Leave me alone,' Zoe snapped, loud enough to attract attention from the other customers. 'I mean it.'

Hawkins stopped in his tracks. Knew it would be pointless to go after her. A middle-aged man pestering a young woman in the middle of London was not a good look. He could only look on, choked with despair, as she disappeared through the back door into a litter-strewn side street. Then the door slammed shut, and Zoe was gone.

Hawkins shook himself out of his stupor. He turned towards the table. Millar sat staring hard at her plate, as if she was searching for meaning in her cold eggs. Either that, or she really didn't want to meet Hawkins's angry gaze.

He paced over to the table. The sadness he'd felt a few moments earlier incinerated by the rage stirring in his chest.

'What the fuck is going on?' he demanded.

Millar said nothing. Kept her head lowered.

'Alex?'

Millar drew in a deep breath, taking a moment to decide how to respond. 'It's not how it looks,' she said.

'Isn't it? Because from where I'm standing it looks like you're in a fucking relationship with my daughter.'

Millar lifted her head and met his cold stare. She wore a defiant expression. 'Before you say something you might regret, you really need to calm down.'

'Don't tell me what to do,' Hawkins said, struggling to control his anger. 'How long has this been going on?'

'Sit down, David.' Millar added in a low voice, 'You're making a scene.'

Hawkins snorted and dropped into the empty chair. The seat was still warm. 'Answer the fucking question.'

'A few months,' Millar said, quietly. 'We've been together for a few months. Since the convention in Birmingham.'

Hawkins tried to retrieve a vague memory from the depths of his mind. He remembered Millar travelling up there for a cyber-security conference. All the major firms had been invited, along with the usual collection of AI start-ups, tech bros and Whitehall lifers.

Millar said, 'She was working as an assistant for another company. A temp job. They had her working the stall, doing the sales pitch stuff.'

'I didn't even know Zoe was there,' he said, thickly.

'She was behind on rent and needed money, and she hadn't sold any of her artwork in months. She went to one of your old friends from Hereford, some guy who works for a boutique security firm in Mayfair. Asked if he could get her a job for the summer.'

'Jesus. Why didn't Zoe come to me? If she was hard up I could have helped her out.'

Millar shrugged. 'She didn't want your help, I guess.'

The waitress came over, interrupting their chat. Hawkins ordered a black coffee, waited for her to leave them in peace.

'Did you know she was my daughter? When you met her, I mean . . .'

Millar shook her head determinedly. 'No. Zoe goes by her mother's maiden name these days, although I guess you already know that. And she never talked about you. Didn't even mention you at first.'

The words pierced his heart. To be ignored: somehow, that seemed worse than being despised. As if his daughter had cancelled him out of existence.

Christ, he needed a drink.

'When did you find out? That Zoe was my daughter?'

'About a month back. We had one of those stupid little arguments late one night. She wouldn't meet me at the office. Flat-out refused to meet anywhere nearby. I asked her why. It seemed so irrational. I was jealous, you know. I thought she might have dated someone in the office, and I didn't like how that made me feel. Then she came out and told me the truth, and how things stood between the two of you.'

'What happened then?'

'I said it was time to stop hiding from you. That we should tell you the truth. Come clean about everything. Zoe refused. She insisted it wasn't a good idea.'

'Why?'

'I got the impression that she's afraid of you.'

The dagger twisted deeper in his heart.

'I'm her father, for Chrissakes. Not a fucking monster.'

'You have every right to be pissed off,' she said. 'But you have to understand. I'm only trying to protect Zoe. I don't want to see her get hurt.'

'Bollocks. You're running around with my daughter behind my back. All you care about is getting her in the sack.'

Millar gave him a frosty look.

'You're angry. I can see that. So I'm going to ignore that last comment. But I'm not going to be used as a human punchbag. You want to blame someone, try looking in the mirror.'

Hawkins felt the anger drain from his body. Clarity of thinking slowly returned. He realised that directing his rage towards Millar was counter-productive. If anything, that would only turn Zoe against him even more.

Something else struck him too.

'Yesterday,' he said. 'When you said you were messaging some bloke—'

Millar nodded. 'That was Zoe. We had made plans to meet up last night. I had to make up some elaborate excuse about why I couldn't make it.'

'Why?'

'If I told her I'd spent the day with you, she would have flipped out. She hates the fact we work in the same building. More than once she's threatened to end things unless I leave my job.'

'You should have told me. She's my daughter, for fuck's sake.'

'I know. But I had my reasons.'

'Such as what?'

'I'd given Zoe my word, for one thing. Plus, I wanted to get to know you better. Find out what kind of a person you are. See if Zoe was right to want you out of her life.'

'And?'

Millar bit her lip and considered. 'I haven't decided yet.'

'Did she tell you why we fell out?'

Millar sighed wearily and folded her arms. 'She just said that your divorce was messy and you're not a nice person to be around when you're on the drink. That you've done some things she's not proud of. She said the divorce wasn't the first time someone close to you got hurt.'

The waitress brought over a cup of steaming hot coffee. Hawkins stared at his callused hands.

'Is that true?' Millar said after the waitress had moved away. 'About someone else getting hurt?'

'What difference does it make? You'll take her side, whatever I say.'

'I just want to know the truth. There's something between the two of you. I can sense it.'

'Ask Zoe.'

'I've tried. Believe me. Whenever I put the question to her, she just clams up and says she doesn't want to talk about it.'

'Can you at least tell me where she's living? What she's doing with herself?' He spread his hands. 'I've been shut out of her life. Ain't got a clue what she's up to these days.'

'She's selling a few things online. Linocuts, mostly. The money comes in dribs and drabs.' Millar pursed her lips. 'She's thinking about moving to the countryside. Has this dream about living in a cottage in Somerset.'

Hawkins smiled to himself. 'Her mother's parents are from that way. We used to take her there in the summer holidays.'

'Must have been some good memories. She talks about it a lot.'

'A long commute for you.'

Millar nodded. 'And I'm not sure I'm ready to leave London behind.'

An unspoken truce descended over them. They moved on to safer territory and talked through the plan for the meeting with Varma. Hawkins laid out his idea to share everything with Varma. except the discovery of the email King had sent him.

'What makes you think Varma has something to hide?' Millar asked.

'Just an instinct.'

'An instinct?' Millar looked sceptical.

'Call it a Regimental sixth sense. You don't survive at Hereford without it. If you'd spent your military career looking round corners instead of sitting in front of a computer, you'd know what I mean.'

'We don't need soldiers to look round corners. Not anymore. We have drones that can do that.'

'Maybe. But a drone can't smell fear. A drone doesn't have a gut feeling for when something doesn't look right.'

'Give it time. Twenty years from now we'll all be out of a job.'

Hawkins said, 'Any word from your contact at the Doughnut yet?'

'She dropped me a line half an hour ago. She's in the office now and working on the drive.'

'Any idea how long it'll take to get into that hidden folder?'

'It's too early to say.'

'Doesn't sound promising.'

'My friend knows it's urgent. She won't let us down.'

'I've heard that one before.' Hawkins snorted his contempt. 'It's a mistake to rely on the tech. What if your mate can't break the encryption?'

'She'll get into it. She always does.'

'We should be throwing our energy into tracking down the Bulgarians. Manhunt. That's a better use of our time.'

Hawkins beckoned to the waitress, making the universal sign for the bill.

He said, 'I was wrong to snap at you earlier. You didn't deserve that.'

Millar shrugged but said nothing.

'I – I just want to put things right,' he went on. 'Between me and Zoe.'

'Honestly,' said Millar, 'I don't know if that's possible. But whatever way she goes, you need to let her get there in her own time. She won't be pushed. I'm sure you know that.'

Hawkins smiled sadly. 'Her mother always said Zoe knows what she wants. Strong-minded, that one.' He hesitated. 'She's right not to be proud of me, though. That much I agree with. I've done some – some bad things.'

'What do you mean?'

He didn't reply. Mostly because he could see Jacob's face again. He had spotted it past Millar's shoulder. Staring at him through the grime-flecked window. The deadened eyes and frozen lips. The snow-flecked jaw. The skin tinged a deathly blue.

He clamped his eyes tightly shut. When he popped them open again, the face had vanished.

'Forget it,' he said. 'It's nothing.'

'Doesn't sound like nothing.'

'I said drop it,' Hawkins said sharply. 'I'll tell you another time. We need to get to the meeting. Come on.'

The waitress sauntered over with her card machine. Hawkins dug out a sheaf of notes from his leather wallet and slapped them on the table. Millar watched him in surprise.

'You still pay in cash?' she asked.

'Old school, lass. That's me.'

'There's old, and there's prehistoric. You're dangerously close to the second camp.'

Hawkins left the change and stood up. Millar looked evenly at him. 'Did you always know? About Zoe being gay?'

'She never formally came out to us, if that's what you mean. But I had my suspicions. We both did.'

'Such as what?'

'Certain little things. The way she behaved, or something she'd say. The lack of boyfriends. When you're a parent, you just know your kids.'

Millar pursed her lips. 'Is this going to be a problem between us?'

'Which bit, exactly? You shagging my grown daughter behind my back, or the fact you bat for the other team?'

'You know which one.'

'No,' Hawkins responded plainly. 'No problem at all.'

Millar searched his face closely. 'You're not just saying that, in case I take offence?'

'I might look ancient to you, but that doesn't make me a complete dinosaur.' Hawkins smiled again. 'You never know. I might not be such a monster after all.'

'We'll see.'

Thirteen

They walked back to the office, took the same route Hawkins had taken to the café earlier that morning. Swept through the entrance to the King Street HQ fourteen minutes later. Dead-on schedule. Varma's chauffeur was still there, slumped in a velvet armchair, engrossed in another paperback. Hawkins tipped his head at the plump security guard, crossed the lobby with Millar and rode the lift to the fourth floor. The doors shushed open; they marched down the corridor and beat a path to the secure room. Millar unlocked the door, Hawkins followed her inside, and then they seated themselves at one end of the conference table.

Millar checked her phone. 'Varma's EA. Varma sends his apologies but he's running a few minutes late. He'll be down shortly.'

Hawkins nodded and wondered if that was true. Or maybe it was just a power thing. Establishing dominance. He'd heard Putin did the same thing. Foreign dignitaries had sometimes been left waiting for hours for a meeting with the big man.

Millar exchanged messages with her contact at GCHQ, getting updates on the latter's progress with King's laptop; Hawkins flicked through a defence industry magazine someone had left on the conference table.

Three minutes passed. Then the door swung open, and Nish Varma barrelled into the secure room, a huge figure, broad-shouldered and brimming with can-do energy and determination. Hawkins and Millar stood up to greet him. Varma shook her hand and glanced cursorily at Hawkins.

'Alex. Sorry to keep you waiting,' Varma said, his voice carrying the faint trace of his upbringing in South London. 'Journalists. Bane of my existence.'

'It's fine, really,' Millar said.

'How's your dad, by the way? Feeling better, I hope?'

'He's on the mend, though he's pissing my mum off. You'd think a triple bypass would make him slow down a bit. Not Dad.'

'I can imagine.'

Varma relaxed his features into an easy smile. Hawkins had never met him in person, had only ever seen him in passing. But he'd heard the legendary stories about DeepSpear's founder and CEO. The superhuman drive – and the cunning – that had transformed DeepSpear from a little-known startup into the darling of the defence industry. One of the few British success stories in an era of managed decline.

Varma swivelled his gaze towards Hawkins. Looked him up and down, like a butcher assessing a cut of meat. 'And you are?'

'Hawkins, sir. Head of Security.'

'You can ditch the "sir", David. You're not in the military anymore. Just call me Nish. All right?'

'Yes, sir.'

'Hawkins.' Varma scrunched up his face as he searched his memory. 'You're ex-SAS, aren't you?'

'That's right,' Hawkins said.

He took in Varma's appearance. He was dressed in his trademark plain white tee under a dark-blue jacket, stonewashed jeans and a pair of Timberland desert boots. He had a bullish look about him, with his shaven head and thick neck. The hands were meaty, the legs as wide as Nelson's Column. Like a rugby prop gone to seed, or a nightclub bouncer. Thin lips curled up at the corner, ready to break out into a cheeky grin. But there was a steely glimmer in the eyes. He had the look of a man who could switch between easy charm and cold ruthlessness without missing a beat.

Varma seated himself at the head of the table and said, 'Let's get down to it, shall we? Tom briefed me on the situation yesterday morning. That business with the young engineer. So tragic. Why did you need to see me so urgently?'

Hawkins glanced at Millar. Giving her the floor. They had agreed on the way over that she would do most of the talking. Partly because she could talk confidently about the technical side of things, and Hawkins couldn't. But also because she knew Varma. And how to speak to him.

Millar crossed her legs and said, 'I hope you understand this wasn't something we could do over the phone, Nish. It's a highly sensitive issue.'

'I'm listening. What's the story?'

Millar walked him through their discoveries, describing how they found King's laptop. The race to clone before the police got hold of it. Hawkins's recce of the crime scene. The cigarette packet he'd found. The realisation that Vitanov and four other Bulgarians had gone off the grid. The military-grade encryption King had used to protect his drive. The second recovery key he'd added to his Sent Items folder.

Varma listened intently. Hawkins studied his face, waiting to see if he'd volunteer the information about the email from King. But the confession never came. He didn't say a thing.

'What you mean to say,' Varma said after Millar had finished, 'is that you don't have a clue who murdered King yet, or why. That's what you're telling me, isn't it?'

'That's correct,' Millar replied.

'Please tell me you have a plan.'

Hawkins said, 'We need to track the missing Bulgarians. Before the trail runs cold. They're connected somehow to what happened to King in the car park.'

'Do you have any idea where they might have gone?'

Hawkins shook his head. 'We should start by searching their home addresses. Question their colleagues. Someone is bound to know something. But we need to move fast. Every minute we waste here risks the trail going cold.'

Millar said, 'You're looking at this through the wrong lens. The trail's not with the Bulgarians. It's with the laptop.'

'Which is where, exactly?' Varma asked.

'With a friend. At the Doughnut,' she explained. 'They're working on the decryption as we speak.'

Varma's face tightened. Anger glinted in the eyes; the lips pressed into a hard line. For the first time, Hawkins got a glimpse of the other side of Varma's personality. The man who had terrified and bullied those who dared to stand in his way.

'I didn't give you permission to do that,' he said.

Millar said, 'I had to make a judgement call on the spot. There wasn't time to go through all the proper channels.'

'Be that as it may, you're in breach of contract. I could fire you for that. I've definitely fired people for less.'

'Nish, we needed to get King's email decrypted as fast as possible. This is a live investigation. Time is of the essence. If we had done it in-house, there's no telling how long it might take.'

'This friend of yours. Can we trust them?'

'We go back a long way. She's on the level. You have my word on that.'

'It's not your word that concerns me. What's to stop her running to her mates in Whitehall and sharing a load of highly classified material with them? They might be poring over it right now.'

'She wouldn't do that. I trust her.'

'Then she must be very special. In my experience it's a mistake to trust anyone with a government email address.'

Varma gave her a long hard stare. Then he continued.

'What do we know about the folder King encrypted?'

'It's a series of messages,' Millar replied. She darted a glance at Hawkins, sticking to the lines they'd agreed on before the meeting. 'Several of them. That's all we know.'

'No attachments, anything like that?'

'Not as far as I'm aware.'

'I see.' Varma frowned. 'What about the woman? The one who met King at the pub in Cremyll?'

Millar said, 'There's been no sign of her, as far as we know. The police are searching for her, but it looks like she's vanished into thin air.'

'The woman is a dead end,' Hawkins asserted. 'She'll have gone underground. Waste of time trying to look for her.'

'What did the police tell you? Do they have any suspects?' asked Varma.

Hawkins said, 'They didn't mention anything to us on that front. I got the impression they're struggling to get their heads around it. It looks like they've ruled out poison. But they've got no answers.'

'Same as us, then.'

Hawkins shrugged.

'You're a military man,' Varma said. What do *you* think happened?'

'In my book, it's a poisoning all day long.'

'Even though the police think otherwise?'

'It could be some sort of new nerve agent. Sprayed in the victim's face, perhaps. It's been done before. The North Koreans have used the same method in the past.'

Varma nodded. 'I remember the story. Kim Jong Un's half-brother. The guy who was murdered at Kuala Lumpur airport.'

'That's the one.'

'As I recall, in that particular case the assassins used VX. The police found traces of poison in his body.'

'That's right.'

'But as far as we know, the police haven't discovered anything on King, or in the vicinity of the pub. Anything that points to exposure to a nerve agent?'

'Not yet,' Hawkins pointed out. 'We're still waiting for the results of the autopsy. That might throw something up.'

Millar said, 'It's not a poisoning. The police wouldn't have opened up the area around the crime scene unless they were absolutely sure the area was safe.'

Varma murmured his assent. 'Agreed. Even the police aren't that incompetent.'

Hawkins persisted with his argument. 'Just because they haven't found something, doesn't mean it ain't there. The Malaysians found traces of poison because the North Koreans used an old-school weapon. They're behind the curve. The Russians are much better at this shit. They've got stockpiles of nerve agents they developed at the back end of the Cold War. Other types of Novichok. Ones we don't know about.'

Varma said, 'You may well be right. But I fail to see how that helps us find the Bulgarians. If they're involved, locating them won't be as easy as you seem to think. They've planned this whole thing in detail. Logical to assume they'll have taken steps to cover their tracks.' He directed his gaze at Millar. 'How long will your friend need to break the encryption?'

'Another hour. Give her that long. If she can't get into the folder, for whatever reason, we'll go with David's plan.'

Before Varma could reply there was a gentle double-rap on the door. Millar got up and opened it. A button-nosed woman in a pencil skirt stood in the doorway.

'Your ten-thirty is waiting for you, Mr Varma,' she announced.

'Right. Of course.'

Varma stood up.

'Let's hold off making a decision until we hear back from Cheltenham,' he said. 'Now, if you'll excuse me, I'm due to meet with our new junior minister for the armed forces. He's got some big plans, apparently.' Varma smirked. 'Same old story. I'll meet you back here once I'm done.'

He strode powerfully out of the room and followed the assistant down the hallway. Millar closed the door behind him. Hawkins stood up and lapped round the conference table, stretching his legs. Too much sitting down in the past twenty-four hours. Meetings and long car journeys.

'What do you think?' Millar asked.

Hawkins stroked his jaw and said, 'If Varma is worried about that business with the email, he's doing a bloody good job of hiding it.'

'Either that, or he really doesn't know.'

'He knows,' replied Hawkins. 'That's for fucking sure. I'd bet my right bollock on it.'

'So why didn't he say anything?'

'Maybe he's trying to buy himself some time. It doesn't look good, does it? The CEO of a major company gets an email from an engineer who gets killed a few days later, and he keeps quiet about it. He'll be thinking about damage limitation. Getting his excuses in. Could be any number of reasons.'

'There's another explanation,' Millar said.

'What's that?'

'He's concerned about how this will play with Whitehall. He wasn't happy when I told him I'd given the laptop to GCHQ.'

'That's putting it mildly.' Hawkins grunted. 'Better hope that friend of yours cracks the code soon. If she hasn't done it by the time he comes back, we'll have to confront Varma ourselves.'

'It won't come to that,' Millar insisted. 'We'll have those emails opened before the hour's up.'

Hawkins grunted. 'This is a waste of bloody time. We should be on the ground in Plymouth, rooting out them Bulgarians. Old school. That's the way to do it.'

'Is that your solution to everything? Violence?'

'Sometimes it's the only way.'

Fourteen

Minutes ticked by. Millar popped downstairs for coffees, came back and checked her phone more often than a teenage influencer. Waiting for further updates from the Doughnut. Hawkins sipped his Americano and scanned the latest news on his phone. A couple of articles had been placed on local sites covering Plymouth and the surrounding community, documenting the bare bones of the King case. A thirty-four-year-old male had been taken ill at the White Horse Tavern in Cremyll on Sunday evening and rushed to hospital, where he had been pronounced dead. The police were appealing for witnesses to come forward.

Elsewhere it was the same old shit. Strikes on the trains. Floods. Another council had been declared bankrupt. An oil tanker linked to Russia had damaged an undersea power cable in the Baltic Sea, causing widespread blackouts in Estonia. Growth forecasts had been downgraded again.

A minor item further down the list caught Hawkins's eye. NATO leaders were meeting in Berlin to discuss plans to support Ukraine in the coming months, in light of a statement from the favourite to win the US presidential election, vowing to withdraw all financial and military support for Kyiv on his first day in office.

The article claimed that there were deep divisions between the various countries on how to respond. The hawks, led by the British PM, were determined to continue propping up Ukraine with money and hardware. Others were less enthusiastic: Italy, Spain, the Slovaks. The Hungarian Prime Minister had renewed his calls to negotiate a peace with Moscow, though no one took him seriously. The journalist seemed confident that a deal would eventually be struck, with Britain and Germany footing most of the bill. All agreed that a Kremlin victory was unthinkable.

A few minutes after eleven o'clock, the door clicked open. Varma swaggered back into the room.

'Any news?' he asked. Directing the question at Millar. Hawkins thought he detected a slight strain in the guy's voice.

'Almost there,' Millar said without looking up from her phone. 'My contact is sending across a link to download the contents of the encrypted folder. Should be with me any minute.'

Varma nodded and reseated himself at the head of the conference table. Everyone in the room waiting for the files to download to Millar's phone. Thirty seconds later she sat upright and peered at the screen, face puckered into a heavy frown.

'Got it,' she said, a surge of excitement in her voice. 'I can see the emails now. All seven of them. Exported in PDF format.'

Hawkins said, 'What do they say?'

'There are four separate messages addressed to Rideout from King. The first one was sent six weeks ago. King is telling Rideout he has concerns about some of his colleagues. He's asking for a meeting.

'The next three messages to Rideout are much briefer. Two or three lines. Again with the meeting request. In the third email King explains that it's a matter of utmost urgency. The last one is dated four days before Rideout's death. King is threatening to go over Rideout's head unless he acts at once. The tone is increasingly desperate. He sounds panicked.'

'How did Rideout respond?'

'The first reply is quite long. Four paragraphs. He seems to be taking it seriously. The second one is much shorter. Rideout is basically explaining that he's looking into the allegations, but he can't take any action without clear proof of wrongdoing. There's no reply to King's third and fourth emails.'

'Does he describe the allegations in any of those messages?' Hawkins asked.

'Doesn't look like it. From the tone I'd say these emails are part of a broader conversation in real life. Rideout seems to know what King is talking about. Or who.'

Varma sat rigid, watching Millar closely as she scanned the correspondence. He looked uneasy, thought Hawkins. Anxious.

He wondered about that.

He said, 'What about the seventh email?'

'I'm just getting to that,' answered Millar. 'It's dated last Friday afternoon. A long email.' She paused as she lifted her eyes to Varma. 'It's addressed to you, Nish.'

Varma stayed quiet.

'What does it say?' asked Hawkins.

Millar read the email aloud in a stilted tone.

'Dear Mr Varma.

'My apologies for contacting you out of the blue. I am fully aware that there is an established protocol for raising security concerns in-house, but in this case it simply can't wait. The truth of the matter is that there's a critical situation unfolding at Devonport, one you absolutely need to know about, and I am afraid that unless we act at once it might be too late to stop it.

'I am one of the project managers assigned to the Makara Project. Until recently I reported to Steve Rideout, team engineering leader for the same programme. As you are no doubt aware, Steve tragically died while out jogging three weeks ago.

'Six weeks ago, on Monday 29th July, at around 6.30 p.m., I was working at my desk when I heard voices coming from a top-secret area on our floor. The area in question houses the workstations storing highly classified information on our torpedo programme. Only a small number of staff are permitted to access these stations. As most of my colleagues had already left the office for the evening I naturally became suspicious and went to investigate.

'I discovered two engineers looking around the top-secret area: Simeon Bachev and a female colleague, Anita Nedeva. These

individuals are not part of the Makara team, nor do they have the necessary clearance to use these workstations.

'When I asked them what they were doing, they became defensive and said they got lost while searching for the design department. Since they had only joined the company recently, I took their explanation at face value, pointed them in the right direction and thought no more of it.

'Three days later, while working at a station in the same restricted area, I noticed two other employees sneaking about: Petar Vitanov and Valentin Petkov. Again, I was working late. No one else was present at the time. They did not see me, and although I could overhear them, they were talking in a foreign language and I could not understand what was being said. They left a short time later.

'Following this incident, I approached my line manager, Steve Rideout, and shared my concerns with him. He seemed doubtful but agreed to look into the matter. At the same time I decided to keep a close eye on the Bulgarians.

'On Thursday 8th August, I discovered Anita Nedeva hanging around the top-secret area. The following Monday, at 5 p.m., I noticed an IT network engineer, Denis Yordanov, at the same workstation. Yordanov also has no authority to access top-secret material.

'Yordanov had his back to me, so I did not have a clear view, but I am fairly sure that he had connected his phone to the aforementioned workstation. However, before I could confirm this Yordanov turned round and caught sight of me. From the look in his eyes I could tell that he knew I had been watching him, and that I suspected he was up to no good. I left in a hurry, and Yordanov did not raise the incident again.

'Since Steve's death I have tried repeatedly to flag this issue with senior Devonport personnel, but all such attempts have been dismissed out of hand. It is my firm belief that the Bulgarians are not to be trusted and are engaged in an act of corporate espionage.

'I trust that you will take the appropriate measures. If not then I will be left with no alternative but to go public with this information. I have no desire to embarrass yourself or the company but I hope you will understand that this is an issue of national security and the matter simply cannot be ignored any longer.

'I look forward to hearing from you in due course.

'Sincerely, Matt King.

'PS This email will self-delete after twenty-four hours. Now that the Bulgarians are onto me, I cannot take any chances. To contact me, please message me on Signal. Search for my phone number and you'll find my account.'

Millar looked up from her phone screen. Varma stared at a point on the back wall, lost in thought.

'That's it,' Millar said. 'That's the end of the email. There's nothing else in the folder.'

Hawkins shot an accusing look at Varma.

'You knew about the threat,' he growled. 'All this time, we were running around Plymouth like a couple of headless chickens, and you bloody knew.'

'Don't be ridiculous, man. Do you know how many emails I receive each day? Thousands. Christ, I don't even get to read the majority of them. My assistant reads them first.'

'But this isn't some bog-standard message. This is a detailed warning from one of your engineers, about espionage going on inside your own company. Why wouldn't your assistant bring it to your attention?'

'I don't know. You'd have to ask her.'

'We should bear in mind,' Millar put in, 'that King had a reputation among his colleagues. That's what Cleland said, remember? A paranoid loner and a conspiracy theorist.'

'Then that's probably what happened,' Varma asserted. 'My assistant must have assumed it was another rambling message from an unhinged employee and screened it out.'

'But she wouldn't know about King's paranoia.'

A trace of irritation crept into Varma's voice. He held up his hands in a pose of mock surrender. 'Look, I don't know what to tell you. All I know, is that email never crossed my desk. If it did, I would have acted on it.'

Impossible to tell whether the guy was telling the truth, thought Hawkins. He showed no hint of embarrassment at being caught out in a lie. But Hawkins guessed someone in Varma's position would be physically incapable of shame.

'I just don't see how your assistant could have read this email and decided that it wasn't worth sharing with you,' he said.

Varma threw up his arms in exasperation. 'Look, we can either sit here and waste time pointing fingers, or we can focus on getting to the bottom of this thing. What's it going to be?'

Millar said, 'We can be sure of one thing from this email.'

'What's that?' asked Hawkins.

'Whoever was responsible for King's death also murdered Rideout. Because of what he knew.'

'But the coroner concluded that Steve died of a heart attack,' said Varma.

'True,' Millar said. 'But based on what we know, the Bulgarians, or whoever they're working for, killed King using some new kind of weapon. A new nerve agent, or something else. It's possible that they employed the same method to eliminate King's boss.'

'Someone's cleaning house,' Hawkins said quietly.

'Before we do anything,' said Varma, 'we need to establish cause of death. We need to know what we're up against here. What technology they're using. Who's behind the attacks.'

'It's the Russians,' Hawkins said. 'Has to be them lot.'

'I suspect you're right, but we need more concrete evidence. That means finding out the results of King's autopsy.'

'Good luck with that. Last time I spoke to the plod, they hadn't done the post-mortem yet. Also, why would they share the results with us? We've got nothing to offer them in exchange.'

'I might be able to find out.'

'How?'

Varma said, 'There's an old friend of mine at the Met. Assistant Commissioner Terry Powell. He's in overall charge of specialist operations. Worked here for a spell, back in the good old days. I could ask him. Call in a favour.'

'Would he give that information up?'

'I'd hope so. We're still on good terms. I'm sure I could persuade him to talk off the record.'

Millar automatically tensed.

She said, 'I don't know. Can we really trust him?'

'Oh, I think so. I'm the one paying him.'

He smiled broadly. Hawkins remembered what Millar had told him about corruption within the Met. Russian bribery and blackmail. Sub-threshold warfare.

The GRU's mandate is to recruit officers within the Met and the National Crime Agency.

But that worked both ways. The officers open to blackmail from Moscow had a price. Loyalty could always be bought, as long as you had pockets deep enough to pay for it. And Varma's pockets were deeper than most.

They waited while Varma put in a call to the Assistant Commissioner. Millar recrossed her legs and checked her phone. Hawkins mentally reviewed their findings. At least he now understood why King had hidden the emails on his laptop, rather than simply deleting them. Because he needed evidence, in the event that he decided to go public. The computer had been his backup plan. And the email confirmed that the Bulgarians had been stealing secrets; that King had found out what was going on; and that he had been killed before he could spill his guts.

But they had no lead on the Bulgarians' whereabouts, and Hawkins doubted whether the Assistant Commissioner would share that information with Varma. Even corruptible police had their red lines. He cursed himself for agreeing to Millar's plan to head back to London rather than staying on in Plymouth to search for Vitanov and the others.

Right now, we should be tearing apart the Bulgarians' homes, grilling their friends and colleagues and searching their personal devices for any clues as to their whereabouts.

Instead we're sitting in an office, making bloody calls.

Not for the first time, Hawkins felt singularly useless.

The person on the other end of the line answered. Varma leaned back in his chair and chatted casually to the gruff-sounding voice. Powell. The special operations chief. In the pay of one of the most powerful businessmen in the country. The conversation was brief and to the point. One minute of phoney chit-chat, then the calling in of the favour. Varma offered a bonus if Powell could get the autopsy results to them within the hour. There was some gentle pushback from the senior officer, no doubt an attempt to salvage some shred of dignity from the transaction. Then the call ended.

'Powell says he can help us,' Varma said. 'He'll send on the report. Shouldn't take long.' He made a sly smile. 'Money is a powerful motivation in the lives of small men. Most important lesson I ever learned.'

'We still need to figure out what the Bulgarians were stealing,' Millar said. 'Presumably it's something to do with the Makara programme, based on King's email. But what?'

Just then Hawkins's phone shook urgently. He pulled out his handset, eyeballed the screen. Incoming call. From a mobile number he didn't recognise. He swiped to answer anyway.

'Hello?'

There was no reply. At first Hawkins assumed it was a scammer. Any moment now, someone called Rohit would come on the line, telling him they were calling from his bank and needed his details and security answers to unfreeze his account.

Then he heard a series of muffled noises. Several of them. The soft padding of footsteps across a carpeted floor. Faint drone of road traffic. In the background a woman whimpered tearfully. A male voice, closer to the phone, spoke in what sounded like an Eastern European accent. Hawkins couldn't understand him, but it sounded like he was begging with someone.

Pleading.

He heard something else, too. A second male voice, low and menacing. One he recognised instantly.

Jock Bald, talking in his distinctive Scottish burr, telling someone to shut the fuck up.

'Jock? Are you there?' Hawkins said.

Still no reply.

On the other end of the line, came a bubbling noise, like a pan of water coming to the boil.

Then the man screamed.

Fifteen

Hawkins listened to the scream for a long beat. The colour plunging from his face, a cold sensation spreading across the nape of his neck. Millar and Varma were both staring at him inquisitively. Wondering what the hell was going on.

Me too, thought Hawkins.

Me fucking too.

For a moment he sat frozen and continued to listen to the man's agonised cries, punctuated by a sharp hissing noise. Somewhere further away, the woman shrieked hysterically.

Dread seeped into Hawkins's guts. He wondered if Bald had lost his mind. *Jock's finally snapped*, he thought. *He's gone on a killing spree.*

Then he remembered what Bald had said to him back at Devonport. Moments before they'd left the facility.

There's a restaurant on Cornwall Street.

Bulgarian joint. Vitosha.

The manager will know something.

'Jock?' Hawkins shouted down the line. 'Jock, for fuck's sake!'

The hissing stopped.

Then there was a muted rustling noise, interspersed with dull thuds and whooshes, the tearful moaning of the other man, the faintly audible cries from the woman.

'Geordie?' Bald's voice came down the line obsidian-sharp. 'That you, mate?'

'What the fuck's going on?' Hawkins fumed.

'Sorry. Phone was in me back pocket. Must have arse-dialled you by accident.'

Hawkins fought to contain his rage. A losing battle. 'Where are you?'

'Vitosha. The Bulgarian gaff.'

Hawkins felt his stomach drop into his balls.

The man wailed in agony.

Millar and Varma were still staring at him.

'Had to be done,' Bald said. 'I'm only doing what we should have done yesterday. Getting some answers.'

'Jesus Christ, no.'

'David, what's happening?' Millar asked. Her eyes were wide with anxiety.

Hawkins ignored her. On the other end of the line, Bald laughed drily.

'You always were a goody-two-shoes, Geordie. Play it by the book. Should engrave that on your fucking headstone. But it won't get us results. Not this time.'

Hawkins bit back on his rage.

'What have you done, Jock?' he hissed.

Had to ask the question, though he already knew the answer.

'Nothing, mate. Just having a friendly chat with the owner in his kitchen. His wife's tied up front of house. They won't be serving up any kebabs for a while, if you know what I mean.'

'You can't do this. Listen to me, we're not in the Regiment anymore. You're breaking the law, for Chrissakes.'

Millar leaned towards him. 'That's Bald, isn't it? What's he doing?'

She looked queasily at Hawkins, waiting for a response. At her side, Varma's expression became severe and tight-lipped. Hawkins ignored them both. He focused on Bald's voice. On the call. On the soft snivelling of the woman, and the cries of her husband. The owner of the Bulgarian restaurant.

'Stop getting in a flap, son,' Bald replied angrily. 'All I've done is slap the owner about a bit and stick his right hand in the deep-fat fryer. Shred a few nerve endings. He won't be having any hand-shandies for a while, but he'll survive.'

'This isn't right.'

'Fuck off. One of us had to do something to locate them Bulgarians. What are you doing to find 'em, eh? Tell me that? Sitting on your arse in some office, scratching your balls? At least I'm being proactive.'

'You're torturing a civvy, for fuck's sake.'

'Do you have a better idea?'

'There are other ways. We can search their homes . . .'

'Bollocks. It'll take too long. This needed to be done. Only way to find out where the Bulgarians have gone.'

Hawkins tried another line of argument. 'He might not be part of it. The owner.'

Bald chuckled drily. 'This scumbag is besties with Vitanov. He's in on it, mate. Mark my words. I'll call you when I've finished grilling him.'

He said something to the restaurant owner. 'Right, sunshine. You gonna talk, or am I gonna cook your other hand?'

The owner screamed.

Then the line cut out.

'Jock? You there?' Hawkins said.

No reply.

Three bars.

Not a crap reception, he realised.

Bald had killed the call.

Hawkins felt sick.

Varma said, 'What's going on?'

Hawkins didn't reply. He brought up the recent call list on his phone, tapped on the most recent number. It rang and rang. Nobody picked up. After six rings it went through to a boilerplate voicemail message.

He tried again.

Voicemail.

Fuck.

'David, what is it?' Millar asked impatiently.

Hawkins tried the same number a third time, got the same response. He wrote a short message to Bald. CALL ME BACK. NOW. Pinged it across and then filled in Varma and Millar. Told them what Bald had done, and why.

'We've got to stop him,' Hawkins said. 'We need to alert Cleland right this minute. Get someone over to that restaurant before Jock makes the situation even worse.'

Varma held up his palm. 'Now hold on. Let's not rush into anything, shall we? This situation may work to our advantage.'

Hawkins was speechless. He stared at Varma, his mouth hanging open.

'As things stand,' Varma carried on, 'we can plausibly deny knowledge of your friend's plan. There are the call logs, of course, but we can arrange for those to be scrubbed. Did you know about his intentions?'

Hawkins said, 'He told me about it yesterday. The restaurant. Wanted to go over there and start cracking skulls. I told him not to do that, under any circumstances.'

'And he ignored you. Which means we have valid grounds for dismissal without compensation. That's all to the good. Now, did anyone else witness this conversation?'

Hawkins tried to quell the frantic pounding in his chest. 'No,' he said. 'It was just the two of us.'

'Do you think he'd kill either of them?'

Hawkins shook his head quickly. 'Not even Jock would go that far.'

'Then we're in the clear. If he manages to extract valuable information from the restaurant owner, that's to our benefit. If it gets messy, or it turns out to be a dead end, we'll tip off the police and claim that Bald acted off his own bat. A rogue employee. We can throw him to the wolves.' Varma spread his hands. 'It's a free hit.'

Hawkins bristled with anger. 'He's torturing someone, for fuck's sake.'

'I don't agree with his methods, of course. But your friend is right in one regard. We have no other potential leads on the whereabouts of Vitanov and his mates. This line of inquiry may be our best hope of locating them. Our only one, as a matter of fact.'

'Bald will deny acting alone. He'll say we knew.'

'No doubt he will. But it'll be our word against his. I know who I'd believe, if I was a copper.'

'This isn't right. It's illegal.'

Varma said, 'There are bigger things at stake than your conscience. Two of our people have been murdered, and it looks like the Bulgarians have stolen classified information from Devonport. Information that our enemies would dearly love to get their hands on. This is now a national security issue.'

'Tip off Whitehall, then. Bring them on board.'

'That's not an option at this moment. If we raise the alarm, it'll cause panic. People will wonder how on earth we allowed top-secret information to be stolen from one of our sites. It could jeopardise our other business arrangements.'

'Nish is right,' Millar interjected. 'We don't have any other choice. We should keep this thing contained.'

'This can't come as a huge surprise to you, surely,' Varma said. 'You must have encountered similar situations in the SAS, if those news reports are even remotely accurate.'

Hawkins started to protest further, then clamped his mouth shut. Varma's willingness to look the other way had shocked him. But maybe it shouldn't have done. The sharks who swam in Civvy Street could be just as ruthless as any Regiment operator. Sometimes even more so.

They waited. Hawkins kept trying Bald and got his voicemail. He visualised the scene at Vitosha. Smell of deep-fried flesh in the air. The owner screaming as hot cooking oil shredded the nerves in his right hand. Bald would have secured the woman first. Drawn the curtains, checked the restaurant for bods, cleared it. Flipped round the 'CLOSED' sign on the front door.

Just having a friendly chat with the owner in his kitchen.

On nine minutes, Hawkins's phone vibrated. He peered at the screen.

Bald.

He answered.

'Jock?'

'You owe me a fucking apology,' Bald said, between ragged intakes of breath. 'I was right. Nikolay. The owner. He's working with them lot. The Bulgarians.'

'He fessed up?'

'Not at first. Had to threaten to shove his ugly mug in the fryer. That's when he started pissing himself. Fessed up to providing the Bulgarians with money, documents. All sorts.'

The tightness banding round Hawkins's chest tensed a little more. 'Where are they now?'

'Liverpool,' said Bald. 'They're in Liverpool.'

Which blindsided Hawkins. He had assumed the Bulgarians would have already bugged out of the country. A whole thirty-seven hours had passed since they had left Plymouth in a hurry.

'All of them?' Hawkins asked.

'That's what the owner says, aye.'

'Where, exactly?'

'A car wash near Princes Dock. Run by an Albanian by the name of Medon Abrashi.'

'Why the fuck would they go there?'

'It's a front business. Abrashi and his brothers are members of an organised crime network. Drugs, mainly. Coming in across the Irish Sea. They launder the proceeds through the car wash and a host of other local businesses. Nikolay says Abrashi is the next link in the chain of command. Says the Bulgarians have been given orders to go up there and lie low while the people above them sort out their extraction.'

'What people?'

'Nikolay doesn't know. Which is probably the truth. The guy's low-level. Bottom of the criminal ladder. They wouldn't loop him into any of that stuff.'

'What did he tell you?'

'Says he got a call from Abrashi on Sunday evening. Bloke sounded nervous. Told him there had been a change of plan. Vitanov and his mates were summoned to the restaurant and given clean passports and driving licences, plus five grand in cash and an RV at a lay-by a couple of miles outside Taunton. A van was supposed to pick them up there. The Bulgarians had orders to dump their rides at the lay-by and pile into the Transit van for the onward journey north.'

Hawkins said, 'We should send someone up to that RV in Taunton. See if the Bulgarians' wagons are there.'

'One step ahead of you, Geordie. Got a lad on his way up there now. I'm willing to bet he'll find a pair of abandoned vehicles, burnt out or doused in chemicals to cover their tracks.'

'Does Nikolay know when the extraction is due to happen?'

'It's scheduled for tonight, he says. Waterborne exfil. Says that's all he knows.'

Which made sense, Hawkins thought to himself. Containment. Oldest rule in the military book. Practised by all the great generals in history. Don't tell your subordinates more than absolutely necessary. The fewer people knew about your plans, the lower the chances of your enemies finding out.

He said, 'How do we know Nikolay isn't bullshitting us?'

'Crossed my mind too,' Bald replied. 'So I got the fucker to open up his phone. He's got a WhatsApp from an unknown number. Dated Sunday evening. Eleven o'clock. A picture of a car wash, and a caption in Albanian or some foreign-looking language. I'll send it on to your tech genius. She might be able to verify it.'

Hawkins said, 'Stay where you are. I need to brief the others. I'll call you back.'

He ended the call. Relayed what he knew to Varma and Millar. Told them everything as quickly as he could, without skipping the important details. The clock was ticking now. Every second they spent in the secure room was another second pissed away.

In the next instant Millar's phone hummed with the arrival of a forwarded attachment. Hawkins peered over her shoulder at the screen. He was looking at a photograph of a drab car wash set in a shabby industrial estate. Row of waxed sports cars in the background, along with buckets, sponges and pressure-washers, a small office set to one side. A blue-painted metal fence separated the wash from the muddle of dreary warehouses and office buildings to the rear.

'What are you doing with that?' Hawkins asked.

'Reverse image search,' Millar said. 'It'll tell us where this photo was taken, or near enough to verify the owner's story.'

Hawkins looked on as she saved the snap to a local folder on her phone. She opened a new browser tab and punched in a web address. The home page for an AI-powered reverse image search filled the screen. Millar tapped the upload option, selected the saved photo and hit 'Search'. Then waited for the results to come in.

'It's a match,' she said a few moments later. 'According to the AI software this is a view of the Ultimate Shine Hand Wash on Westlake Street. Ninety-seven per cent confidence. The owner's telling the truth.'

Hawkins said, 'We need to run up there immediately. Before the Bulgarians can give us the slip.'

'I'll inform Powell,' Varma suggested. 'We could flood that car wash with police within the hour.'

'No,' Hawkins responded. 'We can't trust them.'

'He's right, Millar put in. 'Powell's on our side, but the people below him are an unknown quantity. All it takes is for one of them to be on the Russians' payroll and we're screwed.'

'I could alert my old crew in the Regiment,' Hawkins said, 'or we could notify the security services and get them to handle it. But either way, we've got a problem.'

'What's that?' asked Varma.

'Once the Bulgarians are arrested, they're in the system. They'll be lawyered up, and we won't be able to find out what they've stolen from us, or who they're working for.'

'What do you suggest?'

'Let me and Jock at them. We can sort the Bulgarians out ourselves.'

Ever since the investigation had begun, Hawkins had been drifting. He felt irrelevant. Found himself operating in a world he didn't recognise. Knowing about recovery keys and hidden folders was more valued as a skillset than being able to drop an enemy or sweep through a stronghold. Now he sensed his chance to get back in the game.

Isolate the Bulgarians.
Stop them from getting away.

Varma looked at him evenly and said, 'Are you sure you can catch them?'

'If we hurry, we've got a chance,' Hawkins said. 'But we've got to leave right fucking now.'

Something like grim determination settled over Varma's face. 'You'd better tell your friend in Plymouth about the plan, then.'

Hawkins nodded approvingly. His respect for Varma had just gone up several notches. The guy was decisive. A risk-taker. Not a shirker. There was none of the hand-wringing or indecisiveness Hawkins had come to expect from Civvy Street lifers. Say what you wanted about the bloke, he had a pair of balls on him.

Hawkins got back on the blower. Bald answered on the second ring.

'Well?'

'The photo is a match,' Hawkins said, hurriedly. 'They're definitely at that car wash, or in the immediate vicinity. We're heading up there now. How soon can you leave?'

'Soon as I'm finished here, son.'

'Wrap it up and get on the road. We'll send you the details for an RV and meet you en route.'

'Just like old fucking times, eh?' Bald chuckled.

'What about Nikolay and his wife?'

An important point, Hawkins knew. They couldn't let the couple go free. Out of the question. They would go straight to the Albanians. Forewarn them.

Bald said, coolly, 'There's a walk-in freezer at the back of the restaurant. No inside door latch. I could keep them on ice for a while. Buy us enough time to get up to Scouse-land.'

'Do it,' Hawkins said. 'Message us once you're on the road.'

Hawkins ended the call. Rose to his feet, adrenaline pulsing in his veins. His mind racing ahead of him. He was already mapping out the next few hours in his head. The race up to Liverpool. Locating the car wash. Cornering Abrashi and whatever henchmen he had at the car wash. Lifting the Bulgarians and subjecting them to a hard interrogation.

Then Millar said, 'I'm coming too.'

'No,' Hawkins insisted. 'No fucking way.'

'It's non-negotiable. I need to be there when the Bulgarians are questioned,' Millar argued. 'You can do the heavy lifting, but when it comes to the interrogation you're going to need someone who knows about the tech.'

'Me and Jock can wheedle the truth out of them.'

Millar shook her head forcefully. 'This is my world, not yours. You and Bald don't have a cyber bone in your bodies. You're going to need me.'

'I agree,' Varma said. 'Clearly this thing doesn't stop with the Bulgarians. They've hacked into a highly classified network and stolen God-knows-what on behalf of someone else. Besides, they might well have hidden the stolen data somewhere. Alex will know where to look for it. How to retrieve it and so on.'

'It could get ugly up there,' Hawkins warned. 'Rough stuff.'

'I'm a big girl. I can handle myself.'

Varma stood up ramrod straight. Nodded at Hawkins and Millar in turn. 'Get moving, both of you. Keep me updated.'

Hawkins nodded back. 'The autopsy results—'

'I'll let you know the moment I have them. Just promise me one thing.'

'What's that?'

'Make sure you stop those Bulgarians. Don't let the bastards get away. Whatever it takes, guys. Just get the job done.'

Sixteen

They up-ramped out of the basement garage in the Mercedes-Benz GLE, the satnav taking them on the same westward bearing they had followed the day before to Plymouth. Down Brompton Road, slicing through Chiswick and Hammersmith. Noon-time in London. Light sheered in through the windscreen, blinding Hawkins. He flipped down the sun visor, kept one eye on the road and the other on the infotainment display. A little under two hundred and twenty miles to their destination. Journey time of four hours thirty minutes, the satnav estimated. Which seemed slow, until you factored in congested British roads. An ETA of 16.30 hours.

Exfil is scheduled for tonight, the restaurant owner had told Bald.

It's going to be fucking close, Hawkins thought.

Millar alternated between watching the road and checking her phone, right foot nervously hammering against the floor mat. Waiting for the information on King's autopsy to flow through from Varma. Her laptop on the back seat, along with a set of magnetic power banks in case they needed to recharge their handsets on the go. Plus specialist equipment to help break into any electronic devices the Albanians might be carrying with them.

After twenty minutes on the road her phone buzzed with a succession of incoming messages.

'Varma?' asked Hawkins, hopefully.

Millar said, 'No. More photographs from Bald. The restaurant. Framed pictures on the wall. Groups of diners posing for the camera.' She reverse-pinched the screen, zoomed in on a face in one of the pictures. 'One of them looks like Petar Vitanov. I don't recognise the others.'

'Anything else?'

'Shots of the back office. Looks like a hoarder's dream. Junk everywhere. Boxes of files. Computer drives. Specialist equipment, too. Ethernet multi-tools, IMSI devices. A treasure trove of stuff.'

'What the fuck are they?'

'Multi-tools are basically portable hacking gadgets. IMSIs are mobile phone interceptors. They're very expensive. Some of them cost tens of thousands of pounds.'

'Not the kind of crap a restaurant owner would have lying around his office, then.'

'Definitely not,' Millar said.

'Get Varma to have a look at them snaps of the other diners. He might know someone at Five or Six who can ID them. And tell him to find out everything he can about Abrashi and his gang. We need to know what we're dealing with here. His mate at the Met might be able to fill us in.'

Millar got to work. Fingers moving in a blur as she fired off messages to Varma. She checked her email for the seven millionth time and said, 'Update from Bald. He's on the A38. Nearing Exeter.'

Hawkins nodded his approval. Bald was making good progress. He had a greater distance to cover, but south of Bristol there were no speed cameras, so he could claw back some time on the first leg of the journey. The guy was probably tearing along in the fast lane at that very moment.

'Tell him to pull into the northbound services at Stafford, between junctions fourteen and fifteen,' he said. 'We'll link up with him in the car park and continue north. We'll get there for about three o'clock. Reckon he'll get there not long after.'

Millar punched out a reply and said, 'How do you think the Bulgarians are planning to escape?'

Hawkins had been considering the problem from the moment they had left DeepSpear's headquarters on King Street. Looking at it from different angles.

Waterborne exfil, the restaurant owner had told Bald. Which could mean any number of things.

'Best bet is that they'll piggy-back on the drug smuggling route,' he said. 'Make the crossing from the docks across the Irish Sea. Land in a cove, or a small fishing port and get a flight out of Dublin. Or maybe hitch a ride on a fishing trawler at Wexford. All sorts of exit points available to them.'

'Why not take a commercial ferry instead?'

'Too risky. They'll be worried about beefed-up security. Border force officers demanding to see their passports. But I know one thing.'

'What's that?'

'As soon as the Bulgarians reach Irish waters, it's finished. We won't be able to lay a glove on them. Legally, they'll be out of bounds. They'll know that, too.'

'How would we get to them then?'

'We'd have to leave it to the bods in the Foreign Office to sort out. At that point, it's game over. All we can do is get to that car wash as quickly as possible. Grab the Bulgarians while they're still on dry land.'

Millar chewed on a thought. 'Something I don't understand. Why would they bother to kill King,' she said, 'if they were planning to skip town anyway?'

'That bothered me too,' said Hawkins. 'Maybe they're not the only ones involved in this thing. What if there are other assets in play? Ones we don't know about, but who might have been compromised if they left King alive?'

'But why go to the effort of a waterborne extraction once they'd liquidated him? Why not jump on a flight out of the country instead?'

Hawkins said, 'Look at it from their perspective. Killing King is a hugely risky move. You're guaranteed to draw instant heat from the police, maybe the security services.'

'So?'

'The Bulgarians would have expected the authorities to tighten security at every major airport and ferry terminal as soon as they learned of King's murder. They probably figured they had no choice but to go underground and find some other way out of the country.'

'That still doesn't explain why they didn't leave on the Sunday night. They could have been in the air a couple of hours after the attack. Before anyone could connect them to the murder.'

'But the Bulgarians couldn't know that. Not for sure. We're talking about the elimination of a senior engineer attached to the torpedo project. Someone with access to highly classified information. They had to work on the assumption that the alarm would have been raised very fast, presumably while King's body was still warm.'

'Except it didn't turn out that way. Because we downplayed King's importance.'

Hawkins nodded. 'Gracey's orders.'

We've instructed management at Plymouth to tell the police that King was a low-level maintenance worker.

Fixing pipes and ducting, that sort of thing.

'What do you think they were doing at Devonport?' asked Millar.

'Stealing secrets. Either to sell on the black market, or to pass on to their handler. That's got to be it. Why else would they be hanging around a classified area on-site?'

'But why? Who would want that information?'

'One of the usual suspects. We've got plenty of enemies in the world.'

'Is this the point where you mansplain geopolitics?'

'I'm just telling you how it is. There are loads of people who'd peel off their eyelids to get hold of that int.'

'I'm not so sure that's true. Think about it. The Russians have got their own torpedo programme. It was in the news a while back. Something called the Poseidon. Nuclear-armed autonomous missiles. Why would Moscow be interested in getting their hands on our own torpedo project?'

'No clue,' Hawkins retorted. 'But one thing's for sure. This is much bigger than a few shady Bulgarians and a local criminal network. We're dealing with a large organisation, with deep pockets, the ability to execute two clean kills and coordinate a waterborne exfil.'

'You think it's the GRU?'

'I'd say it's more than likely, aye.'

They lapsed into silence as they glided along the M4. Speeding past the tattered outskirts of West London. Jumble of smog-blackened terraces and crumbling high-rises hedging both sides of the dual carriageway. After a while Millar spoke up again.

'Do you think Varma was lying,' she said, 'when he claimed he didn't know about King's email?'

'Definitely,' Hawkins responded. 'He knew about it. One hundred fucking per cent. He looked put out when you told him about handing over the computer to Cheltenham. Like he was worried he'd get into trouble with Whitehall, if they realised he'd failed to respond to King's allegations.'

'But why lie about it?'

'He's embarrassed. He gets an email from an employee, warning him that several of his co-workers are stealing secrets, and he dismisses it out of hand. Makes him look negligent.'

'It might be worse than that.'

Hawkins gave her a sidelong glance. 'How do you mean?'

'What if Varma knew about the problems, but chose to ignore them anyway? Sweep them under the carpet to protect the company's reputation? It wouldn't be the first time DeepSpear had done that.'

Hawkins thought back to the original briefing with Gracey nineteen lifetimes ago. The big contract to manage the naval base at Faslane and the nuclear warhead facilities at Coulport. Worth several billion pounds to the company's bottom line.

Reputational risk.

'You may be right,' he said after a pause. 'Varma and his cronies would throw us under the bus if it meant avoiding a corporate clusterfuck. But we can't worry about that now. Leave the political smoke-and-mirrors to them bastards. Let's focus on our job. Only thing we can do.'

They continued clockwise on the North Orbital past Heathrow, took the slip road at Pinewood Studios and dismounted to the M40. The indistinct zone where suburban London sprawl melted into drab Home Counties new towns. Whereupon the traffic began to thin out. Hawkins stamped his foot to the floor, the Merc purred satisfyingly, engine burning, the speedometer clocking above eighty per as they bulleted north-west, heading in the direction of Oxford and Birmingham.

They were coasting through the fringes of Beaconsfield when Millar's phone trilled again. She opened a new email attachment. Squinted at the screen, fingers tracing slowly up and down the glass.

'What is it?' asked Hawkins.

'It's a copy of King's autopsy report,' Millar said. 'Varma got hold of it from Powell a few minutes ago.'

She fell quiet again as she hastily scanned the report. A frown played out on her face.

'Well?' Hawkins asked.

Millar said, tersely, 'It's not a bleed in the brain. That's not how King died.'

'What, then?'

Millar scrolled back up through the document. Frown lines deepening as she re-read it. Like she was trying to interpret an optical illusion that had gone viral. Hawkins waited for her to continue.

'The report says that King suffered catastrophic internal organ failure,' Millar said. 'Traumatic brain injury. Massive internal haemorrhaging. Rupturing of the ear membranes. Corneal perforations. Compression of the lungs. Severe damage to the blood-brain barrier and nerve tissue. All his major organs had been liquified. Death would have occurred within a minute or two.'

'What the fuck would cause that to happen?'

'Definitely not a nerve agent.'

'Some sort of virus?'

Millar ignored the question.

'There's more,' she said. 'According to the first responders, four witnesses in the pub reported hearing a sharp piercing sound for several seconds at around the time of the attack. One person collapsed and said he felt as if his head was going to explode. The others experienced severe spells of dizziness and nausea. Loss of teeth. All four were subsequently taken to hospital for further observation.'

She looked up at Hawkins. Her complexion was bone-white, and there was a look on Millar's face he didn't like. One he had never seen before. A look of fear.

'This wasn't a virus,' she went on. 'There's only one kind of weapon that could have done this, and it's not any kind of chemical. I think King was killed by a DEW. What's known as a directed-energy weapon.'

Hawkins drew his head back. DEWs. The name rang a bell.

'I've heard of them,' he said. 'There were rumours the Yanks used something similar in Afghanistan for a spell.'

'Active Denial System,' Millar said with a nod. 'Designed to disperse crowds by firing a burst of electromagnetic rays at a non-lethal frequency. Anyone caught in its path feels like they're standing in front of a furnace and moves on. Or that was the idea. But it was a clunky system, too power-hungry and unreliable to be an effective deterrent.'

That drew a puzzled look from Hawkins. 'Wait. You're saying the Bulgarians used one of them things to murder King?'

'Not quite.'

Millar stared out of the windscreen. Ahead of them, a ribbon of dark grey cloud fringed the horizon, threatening rain.

'Have you ever heard of Havana Syndrome?' she asked.

Hawkins shook his head. 'The fuck is that?'

'A few years ago, staff at the US embassy in Cuba began experiencing a range of mysterious symptoms. People suffered from dizzy spells, vertigo, headaches. Some heard a painful ringing sound in their ears. Others developed insomnia and memory loss.

'Over time, it became apparent that there were similar cases at other US embassies around the world. Cambodia, Vietnam, Colombia, going back several years. We're talking about thousands of employees. Some diplomats were so badly affected they had to retire.

'At the time, no one knew what might be making all these people fall ill. Experts put forward all sorts of theories. And the intelligence agencies were quick to deny any suggestion of a deliberate attack. But one possible explanation is that a hostile power was deliberately targeting US embassy employees with some kind of new directed-energy weapon, firing ultrasonic or microwave energy pulses from a portable device.

'There are rumours that Unit 29155,' Millar added, 'has been working on DEWs for years.'

Which made Hawkins jolt upright. Unit 29155. The secret intelligence cell within the GRU. Russia's foreign military intelligence service. The people behind the Salisbury poisonings and the attempted breach at Devonport.

'Fuck me, those guys get about. Is there anything they're not involved in?'

'It's not just the Russians,' Millar pointed out. 'China has been investing heavily in this field, testing devices capable of using different kinds of directed energy to disrupt or disable enemy comms and hardware. But here's the thing. The same technology can also be used to target the human brain. What we call neuroweapons. In theory they could be used to disable enemy soldiers, beam speech into someone's head or control their minds. Or even kill them.'

'Sounds like a load of bollocks to me. Science fiction stuff.'

'There are some major technical hurdles to creating a lethal DEW,' Millar admitted. 'Such a weapon would need a huge amount of power. But given the sums of money our enemies have committed in research, it's possible they've made a breakthrough.'

Hawkins gripped the wheel tightly and processed what Millar had just told him. 'So you're saying that our enemies have got weapons capable of turning your insides into soup?'

'Either the Russians, or the Chinese. In this case, the smart money's on Russia. They've been doing this research for longer. Stretching back to the early decades of the Cold War.'

'How would that kind of weapon even work?'

'You're asking the wrong person. If this is a DEW, then we're dealing with technology more advanced than anything we've produced in the West. Anything that has been made public, at least. But if Moscow has the ability to attack embassy staff in Havana, it's not a great leap to imagine them developing lethal neuroweapons.'

Hawkins thought back to the pub in Cremyll. The cigarette butts deposited around the wooded area facing the car park. 'Could that sort of device be concealed in a van or a car? Maybe in a satellite dish?'

'Theoretically, yes. It would need to be small enough to be transportable. With the ability to precisely take out a target without causing widespread damage to the surrounding area.'

A problem chiselled away at Hawkins. 'Let's say that this weapon exists, and the Russians are the ones who've developed it. Why would they use it to kill King? Why not simply give him the double-tap treatment instead? Or kill him at the office? Much easier.'

'The same reason the Kremlin has used nerve agents in the past,' Millar said. 'They're sending a message to their enemies abroad by making their deaths as slow and agonising as possible. "This is what happens to those who betray us." Plus it'll confuse the criminal investigation.'

'How's that?'

'The police won't know about the existence of DEWs. They'll be scratching their heads for a while yet, trying to figure out how King died, and who killed him. That'll buy time for the Bulgarians to flee the country.'

Hawkins stared at the road ahead. *We're dealing with some seriously powerful enemies*, he realised.

This thing is getting bigger by the minute.

He thought back to the mission. They were breaking the cardinal rule of Reg ops. Going on a mission half-cocked. That was when mistakes happened. They had no idea how many Albanians they were up against. He presumed at least some of them were packing heat.

And we haven't got a pea shooter between us.

The voice inside Hawkins's head started up again. Goading him.

Why are you doing this?

What are you trying to prove?

He tried to shut it out and thought about the next few hours. He sketched out a rough plan in his head. Once they had RV'd with Bald they would do their planning. Assess the target location. Study maps and street views. Layout of the car wash and immediate vicinity. Look at entry and exit points. Then they would move in on the Albanians. Disable any threats, find Abrashi and interrogate him.

Find out where the Bulgarians were hiding.

As they continued north Bald regularly updated them with his progress to the west. After ninety minutes on the road he was closing on Bristol. Half an hour later he messaged again, letting them know that he had passed Gloucester and was approaching Worcester. Which put him about two hours from Stafford services. Approximately twenty minutes behind Hawkins and Millar on the M40.

At two o'clock they hit Solihull and the satnav reckoned they were less than an hour from the rest stop. Two-and-a-half hours from the car wash on Westlake Street.

They were getting closer.

When he'd walked out of Hereford Hawkins had felt an overwhelming sense of relief. He'd been glad to wash his hands of the place, after everything those fuckers had done to him. *Good bloody riddance.* But he had been telling himself a lie. He understood that now. Soldiering was his life. Without it, he was rootless.

You're just fucking tragic, Bald had told him.

A sad prick sitting behind a Civvy Street desk.

Those words had cut deep – because they were true. In his darker moments Hawkins knew that he had lost something vital after Jacob's death. The qualities that had moulded him into a first-class Blade, fighting at the tip of the spear, had been blunted by the years of heavy drinking, the prescription meds and the bouts of insomnia. Until the one thing that had given him a sense of purpose in life had been ripped away from him.

Hawkins had tried to move on. Put his old life at Hereford behind him. Refused to accept the idea that he would end up on the scrapheap like so many other retired SAS men. He'd worked hard to reinvent himself as a fully functioning member of Civvy Street. But it had been a wasted effort. The pages of history were turning once more, and Hawkins was on the wrong side. No one wanted a trained killer these days. Instead of starting over, he had found himself yearning for his old life as a warrior. Now he was going back to what he did best.

Fighting.

Killing.

They had been silent for a while when Millar said, carefully, 'Are you sure you're up to this?'

'What's that supposed to mean?'

She looked at him with flat eyes. 'I know you've been on the drink. It's an open secret at the office. Everyone talks about it. This morning, I could smell the whisky on your breath. And yesterday, when the police showed up, your friend Bald had to bail you out.'

'You don't need to worry about me,' Hawkins said testily. 'I can perform.'

'That's not what Zoe says.'

Hawkins briefly glared at her but kept his mouth shut. Tried to suppress the anger brewing in his chest.

'We're about to go into a potentially hostile environment,' Millar continued. 'And Zoe tells me you're a fuck-up. No offence, but I don't want to find myself in a situation where I'm putting my life in the hands of someone who hasn't got their shit together.'

Hawkins gritted his teeth so hard his jaw hurt. He saw Jacob's face again. Sitting in the rear of the Merc. Bluish skin. His eyes locked shut. Lips twisted in agony. Whispering to Hawkins.

Look at me, David.

Look at what you've done.

'Zoe blames me for the divorce,' he said at last. 'She's right. That's on me. I fucked that one up. But that's not the whole story.'

I've done some bad things.

Millar didn't say anything. Letting Hawkins tell the story in his own good time. He continued, 'Jacob always looked up to me, even when we were kids. Don't know why. Our old man was hardly ever around, so maybe that had something to do with it. He was usually down the pub, getting pissed or getting into fights.

'When I joined the army, Jacob decided that was what he wanted to do with his life as well. He worked as a scaffolder for a few years after leaving school. Did a few other jobs before he joined the Paras. Did well in his unit. Showed a lot of promise. After three years I told him he should consider applying for Selection. He was a top-class soldier. He wasn't sure, but I persuaded him to give it a shot.

'He trained hard for a solid year before Selection started. Put the work in. Clocking up the miles on the hills, swims and bike rides every day. He passed the first tests on the Hills Phase. Made it through to Test Week.

'Final exercise of the week was the Long Drag. Sixty-five kilometres with a fifty-five-pound bergen, rifle and water. The forecast was bad. Freezing cold, heavy rain, wind. Someone told me later there was a heated debate among the Directing Staff about whether they should go ahead with the exercise. Opinions were aired. The general consensus was that it should be postponed.

'The chief instructor at the time was a bloke called Carl Edwards. Nasty little bastard. What we call a retread. He'd failed Selection first time, made it through by the skin of his teeth on his second attempt. That reputation followed him around the camp like a bad smell. When he joined Training Wing he saw his chance for revenge. He bullied the students. Treated them like shit. Especially the most promising ones.

'At the meeting Edwards stood up in front of everyone and said that if the students couldn't deal with a bit of wind and rain, then they didn't deserve to wear the winged dagger beret. I know for a fact that some of the other instructors disagreed with Edwards, but they were too afraid of him to speak up. Bottom line, that exercise should never have been allowed to take place.

'The weather rapidly deteriorated that night. Blizzard conditions. Fucking horrid. One of the instructors told me it was the worst he'd ever seen it on the mountains. Horrible wind and snow. Visibility was so poor you couldn't see further than two or three paces in front of you. Some of the students began to really struggle, but Edwards refused to call it off.

'All candidates have to wear tracking devices on Selection these days. Makes it easier to geo-locate them if they get lost or need urgent medical treatment. Towards dawn, one of the staff noticed that Jacob's dot hadn't moved for a while. He pointed this out to Edwards, but the guy didn't want to know. Said Jacob was probably sitting on his arse and didn't need help. That was bullshit. He knew my brother was in trouble, and the bastard did nothing.

'The guy in charge of comms that day began to worry. He reached out to the instructor at the nearest checkpoint, gave them the location for Jacob's GPS tracker and asked them to go and take a look.

'Forty-five minutes later they found Jacob sprawled on the hillside, his clothes soaked through. He was slipping in and out of consciousness. Severe hypothermia. The instructor did his best to help, but the nearest medics were several miles away and there was no way they could get an air ambulance up there until the weather had cleared. By then it was too late. Jacob died on that hillside.

'I was down at the camp at the time. The Squadron Sergeant Major came looking for us and told me what had happened. I rushed over there. Jacob had been airlifted to hospital by then. There was a big crowd around the starting point. Police were taking statements, questioning the instructors and candidates. I found Edwards. Demanded to know what had happened. He just laughed in my face and said Selection was the survival of the fittest, and if Jacob hadn't been a fucking loser he wouldn't be dead.

'Something snapped inside me. I dropped the cunt. Pummelled him. Would probably have beaten him to death if the other lads hadn't pulled me away.

'Edwards should have kept his mouth shut after that. Taken his punishment on the chin. But he didn't. He went running to the head shed and made an official complaint. He lost the respect of the other lads when he did that.

'Of course, the top brass had to be seen to take action. I thought they were going to sack me, but one of the Ruperts took a stand and spoke up in my defence. Tom Redpath. Good lad. One of the best guys I ever served under. He said if I was RTU'd the Regiment would be losing a fine soldier, that he would have done the same thing if he was in my boots.'

'Sounds like this Redpath guy really admired you.'

'I wouldn't put it like that. It was a mutual respect thing. We used to go out on ops together in Iraq. Battling ISIS. We were always first ones through the door, breaching compounds. Tom didn't have to do that. He could have been a rear echelon motherfucker, but he wanted to lead from the front. That took a lot of courage.'

'What happened then? After the hearing?'

'The Regiment didn't sack me, but they did the next best thing. Banishment. Put me on shit postings, well away from Hereford. Away from Edwards.'

'The bone appointments,' Millar said, recalling their earlier conversation.

Hawkins nodded. 'When they sent me up to Manchester, I knew that was it for me. They were never going to give me a commission, not while Edwards was still in the building.

'That was when I started seeing Jacob's face. Dying. Alone on that hillside. My kid brother. I drank a lot. Too much. Got into stupid rows at home with Zoe's mum. Jacob's wife had been pregnant at the time. She blamed me for his death and shut me out. Then my marriage broke down.

'The divorce was hard on Zoe. Her whole life was turned upside down. She went from a nice family house to living in a grim mid-terrace in a rough part of Hereford. Started at a new school and lost all her mates. I should have been there for her, but I had too much shit in my head. I let her down, big time. That's on me, that. No one to blame but myself.

'One night I got pissed, got into the car and drove around for a while. I was thinking about driving into a fucking tree. Stamp on the accelerator and end it all. I came *this* close to killing myself. Probably would have ended up dead, sooner or later. But I was lucky.'

'How so?'

'Redpath. He took an interest in me. Felt sorry for me on some level, I guess. He knew Edwards was a bully and told me to stop wasting my time. That I should enrol on a master's course. Get a qualification. "Don't let those bastards win," he told us.'

'Good advice.'

Hawkins nodded. 'Wasn't the only thing Redpath did for me. He helped me land this job, after I left the army. He'd heard on the Regiment grapevine about me handing my card in and said he'd put me forward for a job. He didn't have to do that. But he warned me that I'd have to learn how to live all over again. That things were very different on Civvy Street. He was right about that. Right about a lot of things.'

'Didn't the top brass take action against Edwards? After what he'd done?'

Hawkins gave a mirthless laugh. 'Not a chance. The Regiment wanted to avoid another public scandal. The inquiry was a stitch-up. Edwards and his cronies got their ducks in a row, and the bosses went along with it. But I know the truth. Hypothermia didn't kill my brother. Carl fucking Edwards did.'

Millar was quiet for a spell. Then she said, 'You shouldn't be so hard on yourself. You can't hold yourself responsible.'

Hawkins made a noise in his throat. 'Don't you see? It was my fault Jacob was on the hills in the first place. If I hadn't planted that idea in his head, he probably wouldn't have applied for Selection, and he'd still be alive today. Now he's dead, my career is in the fucking gutter and I've got a daughter who won't even return my calls.'

Millar gave him a withering look and said, 'You need to crawl out of your own headspace. Look at it from Zoe's point of view. Why would she want a relationship with someone who's constantly let her down? Who spends his downtime getting drunk and feeling sorry for himself?'

'Bloody hell. Don't hold back, will you?'

'If you're looking for someone to put an arm round you and listen to your problems, you're talking to the wrong person.

Download a therapy app instead. Talk to a chatbot about your mental health. But if you really want to patch things up with Zoe, you need to show her you've changed. Prove that you're not the same person who wrecked her childhood.'

'How am I supposed to do that, when she won't even speak to me?'

'I don't know. Maybe I can persuade her to meet you for coffee after this. The three of us can have an honest chat. Start over.'

'I'd like that,' said Hawkins. 'But we've got to survive the day first.'

Seventeen

They pulled into the services at Stafford fifty-five minutes later. 15.03. Ninety minutes from Liverpool, according to the Merc's built-in satnav. Ninety minutes from the car wash, and a bunch of Albanian criminals.

Hawkins followed the signs to the petrol station, put a full tank in the wagon and steered back round to the main services car park. He pulled up outside the Holiday Inn, opposite a litter-strewn outdoor seating area. Away from the throng of families lumbering out of the food court, sucking on vapes or stuffing their faces with ultra-processed fast-food, waddling back over to their oversized tanks.

Hawkins sent a message to Bald, updating him on their arrival and their precise location. Then he ducked inside the deli with Millar. They bought energy bars, pre-packed sandwiches, snacks and bottles of water. Refuelling while they still had the chance. Millar took the magnetic power banks from her bag, slapped one on the back of Hawkins's phone, fixed the second bank to her device, topping up the depleted batteries.

Hawkins pounded down a second protein bar and glanced at the dash clock. Clenched his jaw in frustration.

15.21.

Where the fuck is Jock Bald?

Has he let us down this time?

'Any word from Varma on Abrashi and his mates?' he asked Millar.

'Not yet,' Millar said. 'Nish has reached out to his Met contact for information about the gang. He's also sent the photographs of the diners at the restaurant to a friend at Thames House for identification. Still waiting to hear back on both scores.'

'Tell him to hurry up. We need that int before we hit Liverpool.'

Nine minutes later, a silver Jeep Grand Cherokee speared into the car park and eased to a halt two metres behind the Merc. Bald clambered out of the vehicle and hustled over to the Merc. Millar switched to the back seat while Bald scooched into the shotgun seat. Hawkins gunned the engine, followed the service exit signs and rejoined the traffic catapulting north along the motorway. The sat-nav had added another twenty minutes to their ETA. Traffic jams on the M6 between Knutsford and Warrington. They wouldn't reach Liverpool until nearly five o'clock.

Bald said, 'What's the plan for hitting the car wash?'

Hawkins said, 'We'll throw on our work lanyards and claim to be agents from Customs and Excise. Demand to speak with the manager. That should get their attention. They'll think it's to do with immigration. I bet most of the guys who work there are in the country illegally. Should buy us time to assess the situation, deal with any threats and get Abrashi to start talking.'

'What if any of them are packing heat?' Bald asked.

'It's a front business. They're not going to be pressure-washing your car with a nine-milli pistol jammed down their pants.'

'Maybe not. Different story for the guys on the boats, though. Them lads are at the sharp end of the operation. They'll want some hardware for that trip across the Irish Sea. If that was me, I wouldn't feel comfortable without a shotgun and a few assault rifles. Minimum.'

Hawkins said, 'No point worrying about that. Let's make sure we stay alert when we approach the car wash. Stay sharp and react to the situation.'

Rumbling north in the Merc with Bald and Millar, planning a mission, preparing to take down some very bad people, Hawkins felt alive for the first time in many months.

He felt ready.

I won't screw this one up. No way.

They carried on past Crewe, dropped down to thirty miles per as they hit dense traffic north of Sandbach, and then Millar announced that she had a new message from Varma.

'He's heard back from Powell,' she said. 'Information coming through now on the Albanians.'

Hawkins said, 'What's the craic?'

'Medon Abrashi is a member of the Jashari crime clan.'

Bald said, 'I've heard of them. They're major players.'

'Biggest criminal group in Europe, according to Varma's contact. Big enough to be listed on the FTSE 100. Billions of pounds in turnover. Network that stretches from Ireland to Belgium and Turkey. Mostly running coke and meth. But also women and guns. A whole load of other stuff.'

'Any int specifically on Abrashi himself?'

'He runs the car wash with a brother. Arlind Abrashi. They're both listed as directors of the business on Companies House. The same individuals are linked to dozens of other companies based in the local area. Massage parlours, takeaways, hairdressers, body shops. All registered to the same address in St Helens.'

'They're lieutenants,' Hawkins opined. 'The Abrashi brothers. Middle-managers. Paid to keep the foot soldiers in line, make sure no one helps themselves to a five-finger discount on the product.'

Millar said, 'Why would Albanian criminals help Vitanov and his friends?'

'They're both in the pay of the Russians. The Bulgarians and the Albanians. The Kremlin is running the op.'

Bald collapsed his face into a heavy frown. 'How do you figure that, mate?'

Hawkins pursed his lips. 'I can't say. You don't have the clearance.'

'Don't give me that bollocks. I'm putting my neck on the line, Geordie. You need to fill me in.'

'He's right,' Millar said. 'We should tell him what's going on.'

Hawkins laid it out for Bald as they ticked along the motorway. The report on King's injuries. Havana Syndrome. Directed-energy weapons capable of liquifying a person's vitals. The possible involvement of the GRU. King's email to Varma days before his murder, revealing a conspiracy by Vitanov and the other Bulgarians to steal secrets from the Devonport site.

Bald puffed his cheeks and exhaled. 'Christ. I had a hunch those Bulgarians weren't to be trusted, but I never had them down as Russian agents.'

Hawkins gave him a withering look. 'If you had your suspicions, why didn't you go to Cleland?'

'And say what? I've got a bad feeling about some of the foreigns? How do you think that would've gone down with them lot in HR? They'd have fast-tracked us on to an anti-racism course. Fuck that for a laugh.'

Hawkins grudgingly admitted that he had a point.

Bald said, 'Do you have any proof that Vitanov and the others are working for the Kremlin?'

'Not yet,' Hawkins replied. 'But all the signs are strongly pointing in that direction. There's the attempted breach, which has the fingerprints of the GRU all over it. The attack on King, potentially using a DEW. The use of the Albanians is another red flag.'

'How's that?'

'The Russian security services,' said Hawkins, 'have got previous for cooperating with criminal gangs. Supplying them with hardware, manpower, money. They do whatever Moscow tells them to do. Espionage. Extortion. Murder. Some of those thugs sit in the Duma these days.'

'But we've still got no clue what the Bulgarians have stolen from Plymouth?' asked Bald.

'Not yet. It may be linked to the Makara programme. Or it may be something else entirely.'

'Whatever it is,' Millar said, 'they've gone to a lot of effort to steal it. An operation this big, takes a huge amount of time and money and planning. The Russians wouldn't have given the green light unless they thought it was worth the investment.'

Hawkins unscrewed the cap on his bottled water, took a long gulp. He thought back over what they knew so far. The findings King had shared in his email to Varma. The Bulgarians hanging around the top-secret area on the third floor of the Devonport office. Their interest in the workstations that held sensitive information on the autonomous torpedo programme. King's claim that he had seen Denis Yordanov plugging his phone into one of the computers.

Corporate espionage.

Bald said, 'If Abrashi and his mates are involved in gun smuggling, they'll definitely have access to weaponry.'

Hawkins nodded. 'We'll have to proceed carefully. Eyes in the backs of our heads on this one.'

Bald grinned. 'This is gonna be like the good old days, Geordie. Flying by the seat of our pants. Going in, kicking down doors. Getting it fucking done, mate.'

'Did they have guns in your day? I thought it was just sticks and stones back then.'

'Cheeky cunt.'

The two ex-soldiers laughed. Hawkins had never really known Bald at Hereford. Bald had been coming to the end of his long career when Hawkins had first passed Selection. But he had deep respect for the guy as a fellow warrior. A living legend of the Regiment. Hero of the rebel siege in Sierra Leone. A guy who'd done the business in Iraq, Afghanistan and a ton of other shithole places.

But he also envied Bald. Hated to admit it, but it was true. Bald wasn't the kind of bloke who felt sorry for himself or wanted to talk about his feelings with a therapist. The exact opposite of Hawkins.

He was a man of iron self-confidence. Had turned his mind into a fucking fortress. Made himself bulletproof.

As they closed in on their destination Millar worked away in the back seat. More information was flowing through from Varma. His contact at Thames House had reported back to him on the pictures Bald had sent on. The framed photographs from the restaurant.

A few of the diners had been positively identified as senior members of the Jashari crime clan, Millar said. Several others were Bulgarian nationals employed elsewhere in the UK. A plasterer based in Enfield. The manager of a nail salon in Edgware. The owner of a boxing gym in Hackney Wick. A hotel worker in Bournemouth. Civilians, potentially. Guilty of nothing more than sitting next to a known criminal, perhaps. Or something much darker. Russian agents. A nationwide network of Kremlin sleepers. Operating in deep cover.

Varma had agreed to provide Five with any further information on the Bulgarians, Millar added. The guy was going into damage limitation mode, Hawkins realised. He'd been caught withholding vital information from Whitehall. Helping to expose a Bulgarian spy network would earn him some much-needed credit in the Whitehall bank. He certainly wasn't helping out of a burning sense of patriotism.

They pulled into the next rest stop. Millar took the wheel, while Hawkins and Bald scudded round to the back seat so they could get eyes on the int sent through from Varma. Hawkins flipped open Millar's laptop and familiarised himself with the photographs of the suspects. The images of the Abrashi brothers Five had on file. Plus the employee shots of Petar Vitanov and the other missing Bulgarians. Then Hawkins punched in the address for the car wash on Google Maps. They studied entry and exit points. Dead ground. Surrounding buildings. Distances to the nearest police stations. Quickest routes from the car wash to the docks.

They kept their plan stupid-simple. What was known in the trade as an Immediate Action drill. Nothing overly complex or sophisticated. The tactical equivalent of walking up to a bully in a bar and smashing him in the face.

'We'll have to get in and out of there as fast as possible,' said Bald. 'I'm willing to bet that Abrashi and his muckers aren't the only paid-up members of the Jashari network in the city. We need to be well clear of that place before the balloon goes up.'

'Bear in mind this is a legitimate business,' Millar chipped in. 'What happens if a customer shows up looking for a premium wax while you're busy roughing up the manager?'

Hawkins said, 'We'll demand to speak to Abrashi in private. Those guys always have a front office. If he thinks he's about to get deported he won't want that discussion to happen in front of his employees. Once we're out of sight we'll get to work on him.'

Bald scratched his stubbled jaw and considered. 'Let's assume this op goes hunky-dory and Abrashi spills his guts. What's the next step?'

'We'll locate the Bulgarians and interrogate them. It'll have to be on-site. Wherever they're hiding. We can't transport five Bulgarians.'

Millar said, 'Five against three. Not great odds.'

'We've faced worse in the Regiment.'

'Much fucking worse,' said Bald.

Hawkins said, 'We'll have to notify Varma. Once we've questioned Vitanov and the others. Get him to liaise with Scotland Yard.'

Bald looked round at him. 'What for?'

'The Bulgarians will need to be arrested and processed. I'm just thinking about it from their point of view. They'll want to tick boxes. Make sure everything is done by the book in case it goes to trial.'

'It won't,' said Millar, confidently. 'Not a chance. White-hall wouldn't want the embarrassment of a Bulgarian spy network infiltrating the Makara programme. Varma wouldn't want that either. Most likely Vitanov and the others will be quietly deported.'

Hawkins said, 'We're getting ahead of ourselves. We need to focus on stopping the Bulgarians first. That's the big target. If they get away, everything else is fucked.'

At four thirty they turned off the M62 and headed north through Huyton. Half an hour to their destination. A thirteen-mile journey, tracing a rough horseshoe around the centre of Liverpool. A more circuitous route, but faster according to the satnav. They were getting closer now. Hawkins felt the adrenaline juicing his bloodstream as they closed in on their prey.

They carried on for six miles, took the slip road past Knowsley. Bowled south-west past Gillmoss, Croxteth, Norris Green. Fume-choked postwar housing crowded the roadsides, interrupted by gigantic retail parks and rundown shop parades. Hawkins had seen army camps with more soul.

Millar hung a right on Queens Drive, made a series of quick turns and headed west on Bedford Road, the satnav directing them through Bootle. Less than a mile to their destination now. She hooked a left onto Stanley Road and continued south, staying well under the speed limit as they passed eyesore terraces, boarded-up storefronts and tattered convenience shops. Crumbling civic institutions plastered with fly posters. Chinese takeaways and betting shops. Blackened shells of vacant pubs, reclaimed by the weeds. A world clinging on by the skin of its teeth.

After half a mile Millar dropped her speed to fifteen per and turned down a deserted road lined with construction sites and derelict buildings screened by security fencing. Hawkins saw hoardings covered with graffiti. Mattresses and broken bits of furniture dumped on the roadside. Several units had faded 'FOR SALE' boards. Others had simply been abandoned to nature.

Millar rolled west for two hundred metres, and then they saw the car wash. It occupied the corner of a crossroad junction, on the fringes of a sprawling industrial estate due north of the main road. An A-road ran north to south, leading past the entrance to the car wash. Immediately east of the business Hawkins noticed a scrapyard enclosed behind a rusted metal fence, a handful of caravans and shipping containers amid the rubbish. There was a shabby café opposite with the lights turned off. Closed for the day, Hawkins guessed.

Bald pointed to the café and said, 'This is fine. Pull up here. We'll debus and approach on foot.'

Millar nosed the Merc to a halt outside the café. Directly opposite the scrapyard to the north. Hawkins slipped on his DeepSpear lanyard and security pass. Bald did the same.

'Looks quiet,' Millar noted. 'Can't imagine they get a lot of customers down this way.'

'It's a front,' Hawkins reminded her. 'They're not running the business to make a pile of cash. They just need it to clean the drug money through the company accounts. And HMRC isn't about to pay a visit to this neighbourhood any time soon.'

'Let's fucking do this,' Bald said.

Millar said, 'What about me?'

Hawkins thrust a hand between the front seats. 'Give me your phone,' he said.

Millar passed it back to him. Hawkins copied over a number from his own handset. Saved it to her device as 'TR'.

'Stay here,' he said, handing the phone back to Millar. 'Keep the engine ticking in case we need to make a quick getaway. We'll call you once we've isolated Abrashi. If we're not back in ten minutes, call this number.'

'Who is it?'

'Tom Redpath. My old Rupert. He's Director Special Forces these days. Top of the tree in Whitehall.'

Millar tipped her head to one side. 'You have the mobile number for DSF?'

Hawkins said, 'We still keep in touch. Meet up for beers now and then. If we're in trouble, reach out and tell Redpath what's happened. He'll know what to do.'

Millar nodded uneasily. 'Be careful.'

'Tell that to the Albanians. They're the ones who messed with the SAS. Big fucking no-no, that.'

Hawkins flashed her a reassuring smile. Then he popped open the passenger door and stepped outside.

Eighteen

Hawkins emerged to the cool of the early evening. Cloud-mottled sky, pale disc of September sun beginning its slow descent towards the horizon. A light breeze feathered across the street, carrying the first hint of autumn. He joined Bald at the front of the Merc. Behind them Millar kept the engine ticking over. Fumes misted out of the rear exhaust.

Hawkins looked round, orientating himself. They were in the old industrial heart of Bootle. Canada Dock roughly half a mile due west. City centre about two miles to the south. No pedestrians, few cars. Which was to be expected. All the businesses in the area were trade-focused: warehouses, delivery depots, commercial sign shops. The major housing developments were situated further east, on the other side of the train tracks. That was good, Hawkins thought. Less chance of someone witnessing their confrontation with the Albanians and calling the cops.

They paced west for fifty metres, hit the crossroads and tacked north, manoeuvring towards the car wash entrance facing the A-road. The place wasn't hard to miss. A pair of brightly coloured feather flags signposted the entrance, along with a sign displaying a menu of prices, in ascending order, a tacky name listed next to each one. Luxury, premium, prestige, gold star, elite.

Bald and Hawkins continued north for fifteen metres before they stopped outside the car wash and quickly assessed the situation. There was a tennis-court-sized patch of wet tarmac at the front of the business, backing onto a steel-framed workshop. A weathered sign above the entrance promised an unbeatable price for tyre fittings. A recent expansion, Hawkins figured. Someone in management spying a gap in the market for cheap tyre changes.

Next to the workshop stood a single-storey brick-built reception. A garish vinyl banner hung above the windows: 'ULTIMATE SHINE HAND CAR WASH. THE BEST WASH IN LIVERPOOL!'

A portly man and woman sat on plastic chairs outside the reception while they waited for their ride to be valeted. Three workers toiled away nearby, scrubbing down a Range Rover Sport on the forecourt. Humans living below the poverty line, slaving away to clean eighty thousand pounds of luxury SUV. Globalisation in action.

'Come on, Jock,' Hawkins said.

A stench of fermented soap water and industrial cleaning products hung in the air as they made for the reception. One of the guys scrubbing down the Range Rover caught sight of them and whistled to a co-worker. A skinny youth in a hoodie, emptying a bucket of soapy water into a drain. The kid set down the bucket and hurried over to Bald and Hawkins. He looked to be in his late teens or early twenties, thought Hawkins, with cropped dark hair and a bumfluff moustache. His hands were blistered from handling various chemicals.

'Wash, boss? Wax?' he asked in a guttural accent.

Hawkins waved his security card at the youth and hoped to fuck he couldn't read. He said, 'Customs and Excise. We need to speak to your boss. Is he around?'

The kid spread his hands in a helpless gesture and smiled an apology. He pointed to the three guys working on the Range Rover. 'Wash, boss? Cleaning? Wax and shine?'

'Fuck's sake,' Bald muttered under his breath. 'This twat doesn't have a bloody clue what we're saying.'

Hawkins tried again. Pointed to his card. 'Immigration,' he said, loudly and slowly. 'We're from immigration.'

The youth understood. His eyes went as wide as medallions. The smile replaced by a look of fear. He turned and made for the reception building, beckoned Hawkins and Bald to follow him.

'This way. Please,' he said in mangled English.

They crossed the forecourt, stepped past the couple fixated on their phones, followed the skinny kid into the workshop. A BMW 5 Series rested over a vehicle pit in the middle of the bay. Hawkins saw a bunch of garage equipment around the place. Tyre changers, fuel cans, oil drain pans and chain blocks. Wheel play detectors. Air compressors. Stacks of car tyres. A heavy-duty workbench to one side of the bay was strewn with filthy rags and a variety of tools. Pliers, grease guns, ratchets, an impact wrench. Cable ties. Foreign rap music thumped furiously out of a Makita site radio.

A side door led from the workshop to the reception. Skinny pushed open the door and gestured for Hawkins and Bald to enter. They stepped into a dingy back office, the walls garlanded with faded posters of Italian sports cars and topless women. Like any British garage would have looked, before the world went woke. There was clutter everywhere, Hawkins noted. Boxes of cleaning products. Stacks of fliers advertising the car wash and tyre fitting service.

Two guys sat behind the counter. A greasy-looking fucker in a wife-beater vest and baseball cap, and a stocky bloke with a man-bun and a trimmed beard, a gold chain thick as a garden hose hanging round his neck. Behind them, a separate door led to the rear of the site.

The two figures scrutinised Bald and Hawkins as they marched over to the counter. Hawkins recognised both men from the photos Varma had forwarded on from his friends at MI5. The guy with the man-bun and the gold chain was Medon Abrashi. The scrawny bloke dressed in the wife-beater was Medon's brother, Arlind. The latter stared suspiciously at Hawkins, small eyes buried in a mound of pitted flesh.

The skinny youth jabbered something to Medon in his native tongue. The Albanian grunted a terse response. Skinny hurriedly backtracked out of the office, while Medon reset his gaze on the two ex-Blades. Dark pupils peered out from beneath heavily lidded eyes.

The door slammed behind Skinny.

'Medon Abrashi?' Hawkins asked.

'Fuck wants to know?'

'Customs and Excise. We have some questions for you.'

Medon scoffed. 'Bullshit. You got ID?'

Hawkins stepped forwards, flashed his security pass at Medon. The latter leaned across the counter to take a closer look. Confusion spread across his features. Thin eyebrows angled sharply downwards.

'What the fuck, you're not—'

He didn't get to finish the sentence. Hawkins grabbed hold of the Albanian by his man-bun and slammed his face down against the counter-top surface, mashing all the fragile bones in the nasal region. Like getting punched in the face by a Ukrainian heavyweight.

Medon made a guttural groan of pain as he stumbled backwards, blood gushing in jets out of his nostrils, streaming down his chin, staining his bared teeth.

Then several things happened all at once.

Medon fell away, pawing at his face, as if trying to reassemble his busted nose. Hawkins spied a movement at his two o'clock. He snapped round. Saw Arlind snatching up a wrench from behind the desk, sweeping towards him from around the side of the counter, swinging and shouting wildly. Aiming at his skull.

Bald reacted first. Faster than Hawkins. The older man. Therefore slower, from a physical point of view. Muscles degraded by age and years of drinking to excess. But balanced by his experience, and something else. The innate ability to harness his emotions.

Civilians invariably assumed soldiering was about violence, but that was only half of the equation. The other fifty per cent came from control of body – and mind. Learning how to master the emotional self. Not something you could achieve in the gym, or by running up and down the hills, but through years of elite soldiering.

Arlind was working from the other direction. Letting his emotions take control of the situation. Surrendering the decision-making process to the limbic part of his brain.

The scrawny Albanian swivelled towards Bald. Right arm raised, shaping to execute a downward-chop. Getting his attack in first. A sound idea, in theory. Arlind probably regarded the Scot as the more immediate threat. But also the easier one to deal with. A grey-haired man with decades of hard living engraved on his weatherbeaten face. A logical assumption.

Then Bald kicked out at a low angle, striking his opponent's kneecap, and he tore that assumption to shreds. The first rule of warfare. Attack your enemy where he least expects it. The blow disabled Arlind, knocking him momentarily off balance. Robbing him of forward momentum. All of his efforts suddenly had to go into staying upright. He wasn't laser-focused on his enemy.

Bald moved into the Albanian's personal space in the next half-second, clobbered him with a series of rapid-fire digs to the face. The blows weren't powerful enough to knock him out, but they didn't need to be. Bald just needed to disorientate the guy. Scramble his circuitry. Stop him from having time to think and reorganise.

Arlind threw up his arms to shield himself. At which point Bald shifted to the Albanian's right, bent slightly at the knees and unloaded a meaty right hook, socking the other man in the kidneys. Arlind gasped in shock and agony. He dropped like a bad habit, landed on his back and lay writhing on the carpet.

Bald side-footed the wrench out of reach. Nodded at Hawkins.

'Grab the impact wrench, Geordie,' he said. Taking charge of the situation.

Hawkins ducked out of the office. Two of the workers were still cleaning out the interior of the Range Rover; the third guy was pressure-washing a Volkswagen Tiguan that had pulled up behind it on the forecourt. None of them appeared to have noticed the struggle going on in the reception. They were too busy with the next customers, and the pressure-washer would have drowned out the sounds of the fight.

Hawkins rushed over to the workbench. He grabbed a pair of cable ties and the cordless wrench. A half-inch impact socket had been attached to the wrench. The sort of thing used to unscrew wheel nuts or lugs. A specialist tool. More powerful than a bog-standard hammer drill, owing to its high torque. But they weren't going to be using it to replace a punctured tyre today.

He darted back into the office just in time to see Bald dragging Medon Abrashi round from the counter. The Albanian made a nasal moan of pain. Arlind was still sprawled on the floor, coughing and groaning.

Hawkins handed Bald one of the cable ties, then he set the impact wrench down on the counter, dropped to a knee beside Arlind. Rolled the guy onto his stomach, yanked his arms behind his back. Looped the nylon cable around his wrists and cinched it blood-cuttingly tight. The zip-ties were heavy-duty. Strong enough to secure a damaged engine shield or a radiator hose. The Albanians wouldn't be snapping out of them any time soon.

Bald finished binding Medon Abrashi's hands together. Stretched to his full height and cocked his chin at Hawkins.

'Let's get these cunts talking.'

Bald paced over to the counter. Picked up the impact wrench. Hawkins peeked out of the window at the forecourt. The three workers were still dealing with customers. But any minute now one of them might come over to confer with management. Some of them, at least, would be unlikely to put up a fight for their boss. The guys who were there under coercion. Like serfs toiling for the lord of the manor. They wouldn't be loyal to the Abrashi brothers. Given the chance, they would probably try to escape.

But Hawkins figured there might be one or two enforcers among the crew. Subordinates trusted to manage the shop when the Abrashi brothers were away. If one of them realised what was happening, they might send for reinforcements.

There was no time to fuck around trying to crack Medon and his sibling.

We need answers.

Right this minute.

Bald moved round to Arlind. Rolled the guy onto his back. Wielding the impact wrench in his right hand. He glanced up at Hawkins.

'Watch that door, Geordie. Anyone approaches, deal with them.'

'Roger that.'

Bald flicked the button on the left side of the wrench, rotated the chuck round to the hammer setting and depressed the trigger, testing it. The impact socket vibrated menacingly. Arlind stared at the wrench, eyes popped wide with terror. Sweat dappled his forehead. Bald knelt down beside him, clamped his left hand firmly around the man's jaw. The Albanian began trembling.

'No, please,' he begged. 'Shit, no . . .'

The man rocked from side to side in desperation. Bald shoved the socket into his mouth and squeezed the trigger. Arlind screamed as the wrench jarred violently, knocking out his teeth. Turning his gums to mush.

After six or seven seconds Bald released the trigger, and pulled the wrench out. Blood and gooey bits of tissue clung to the nut socket. Arlind lay sobbing and moaning, blood leaking out of his ruined mouth. He coughed and spat out bone fragments. White shards gleamed amid the blood puddling around him.

A metre away, Medon Abrashi thrashed futilely against his restraints, neck veins bulging like tensed ropes.

'You're a fucking dead man. Both you bitches. I'm gonna cut you up. You don't know who the fuck you're messing with.'

Bald stood up and calmly padded round to Medon. He towered over the car wash manager, impact wrench in his right hand. Blood dripping from the socket. Behind him, Arlind Abrashi made a strange mumbling noise.

'Where are the Bulgarians?' Bald demanded.

Medon Abrashi twisted his features into a scowl. 'Don't know what the fuck you're talking about.'

'Tell me,' Bald said, 'or you'll be drinking soup for the rest of your shitty life. Like your brother here. Last chance.'

Medon hesitated. Panicked eyes looked across at his brother. At Arlind Abrashi's messed-up face. The blood and shattered bits of tooth. Furious calculations were being made inside the Albanian's head. Odds evaluated. Options assessed. Horrific pain, versus the penalty for giving up the Bulgarians. Which one was worse?

'Fuck it, then,' Bald said.

He took another step towards the car wash manager. Ready to shatter his teeth into tiny fragments.

'No, wait!' Medon Abrashi cried.

'Start talking,' Bald said. 'Now.'

Hawkins glanced through the window. He guessed they had been in the office for no more than ninety seconds. Outside an orange Kia Sportage had pulled up on the forecourt. The driver had his window down, arm extended, tapping a bank card against a point-of-sale reader held by one of the car wash attendants. Skinny was chatting to another crew member. Pair of them sucking on cigarettes.

No one was paying any attention to the goings-on in the office. Yet.

Medon said, 'They're out back. The caravans. In the scrapyard. It's where we keep the workers.'

'Which one?'

Medon paused while he glanced at his brother. Arlind was weeping hysterically, face smooshed against the frayed carpet. Bald started up the impact wrench again. Moved closer to Medon.

'The grey caravan,' he replied quickly. 'Next to the skip. They're waiting in there. We're supposed to take them on the boat. When we make the trade.'

'What trade?'

'There's a shipment coming in tonight. Cocaine. On a trawler. From our people across the sea. We take the shipment, they take the Bulgarians. That's the arrangement. All I fucking know, man.'

Bald stood up and stepped back from Medon Abrashi. Tossed the impact wrench aside.

'Come on,' he said to Hawkins. 'Chop fucking chop.'

They hooked round the counter, left the Abrashi brothers bound up on the floor behind them and crashed through the rear door.

They emerged to a sprawling yard, half the size of a standard football pitch. Fifty metres long and about the same wide. A patchwork of weed-choked concrete enclosed on three sides by a metal fence topped with security wire. Piles of junk to their left: oil drums, discarded bits of electrical equipment, white goods, mounds of worn-out car tyres. A rusted gate at the far end of the yard led out to a one-way side street running from south to north. The gate was open, Hawkins realised. A white panel van had parked outside the yard. A Volkswagen Crafter with a colourful logo splashed down the side of the vehicle. A cartoon drawing of a cod and a shipwrecked vessel, next to the company name in bright blue lettering: 'BAY WRECK FISHING ADVENTURES'.

To their right, Hawkins spied a cluster of caravans and shipping containers. Accommodation for the car wash employees. He'd heard the stories of criminal gangs bringing over illegal immigrants and keeping them in slave-like conditions. Eight or ten blokes to a caravan. Filthy digs. No heating. Rats everywhere. Forced to work seven days a week for a pittance. Families threatened with violence if they tried to leave or alert the police. A good model for the business owners. Steady profits. But unending misery for the poor bastards working under them.

They sprinted towards a grey-painted caravan ten metres away. There was a skip next to it, filled with rubble and black bin bags, and a Portakabin out front. Broken furniture littered the ground outside. A coffee table missing a leg, a pair of armchairs with soiled foam cushions. Calor gas cylinders. Net curtains were drawn across the windows.

Hawkins chopped his stride, surging towards the caravan, running ahead of Bald. Gripped by a compulsive desire to capture the Bulgarians. A desire to win for once in his sorry life. The front door was slightly ajar. Hawkins grabbed the handle, yanked it fully open.

Then he charged inside.

Nineteen

Hawkins burst into a squalid living space. Shit everywhere. Clothes hung from wires strung like fairy lights above the dining table. Electric heater plugged into a kitchen socket in a feeble attempt to warm up the interior. Every surface was buried under a heap of rubbish. Hawkins saw a lot of empty soft drink cans, overflowing ashtrays, dirty plates and plastic shopping bags. Crappy old TV in the corner. Microwave cooker on a side table. The vile stench of mould, sweat and cheap cigarettes hung in the air.

No sign of the Bulgarians.

His phone vibrated in his jeans pocket. Hawkins ignored it and tacked to his right. Which brought him face-to-face with a closed door. He pushed through the door, eyes sweeping across his arcs. Ready to tackle any threats that might be waiting for him on the other side.

He plunged into the sleeping area where the slaves dossed between shifts on the forecourt. Four bunks, two arranged either side of a central aisle. Bin bags stuffed full of laundry littered the floor. Crumpled duvets on stain-covered beds. More shopping bags. Crushed beer cans. Half-empty vodka bottles, a cheap-as-shit brand Hawkins had never heard of. Toilet rolls racked along the window. Toothbrushes and phone chargers.

But no Bulgarians.

Nobody at all.

The caravan was empty.

Bald had stopped behind him, looked round with flared nostrils at the mess. 'Where the fuck are they?'

For a cold second Hawkins wondered if Medon Abrashi had bullshitted them. Sent them to the wrong caravan on purpose. Then his phone whirred again in his pocket.

Hawkins fished it out.

Millar.

Millar was calling him.

He answered.

'David, you need to get out here,' she said, breathlessly. 'Right this minute. They're leaving.'

Hawkins stood very still. Something cold snaked down his spine.

'Where?' he asked.

'I'm watching them now,' Millar said, voice taut with urgency. 'They're on the side street behind the scrapyard. Jumping into the back of a white panel van. It's definitely them. Hurry.'

In the distance, a car engine throttled. Tyres screeched.

'Shit.'

Hawkins dropped the call. Whipped round and shouted at Bald, 'Fucking move, Jock! Go!'

Hawkins flew out of the caravan and swung round to the east. The open gate at the far end of the scrapyard. Leading to the side street. Forty metres from their position. Hawkins raced towards it. Bald at his six, breathing heavily.

As they neared the gate Hawkins heard the roar of another engine. Coming from his three o'clock. From the south. Getting louder. There was the shrilling of rubber against tarmac as the Merc wagon jerked to a standstill outside the gate. Side window buzzed down. Millar behind the wheel.

'Come on!' she called out. 'Get in!'

Bald and Hawkins broke into a sprint. They reached the car in a few more strides. Hawkins wrenched open the front passenger door, dived inside. At the same time, Bald launched himself into the back seat. Then Millar stamped on the accelerator and the Merc rocketed forwards.

'Which way did they go?' Hawkins asked.

'Left,' Millar said. 'Next turn. Onto Forsyth Street.'

She eased off the accelerator and shunted the wheel round to the left, making the same turn as the Crafter. As they straightened out, Hawkins caught sight of the van thirty metres to the west. At the far end of the road the Crafter hung another left, joining the A-road, heading south. In the next moment it disappeared from sight once more.

'How the fuck did they know we were coming for them?' Bald said, breathing hard.

Millar said, 'I don't think they did. They didn't seem to be leaving in a hurry. We were just unlucky.'

Two minutes, thought Hawkins bitterly.

If we had crashed into that caravan two minutes earlier, we would have nabbed the Bulgarians. Game over.

Millar dropped her speed at the T-junction, cut left and merged with the traffic bombing south on the two-lane A-road. The Crafter was four cars ahead of them, motoring along a few miles under the speed limit. Doing nothing to attract unwanted attention.

'Where are they going?' Millar asked.

Hawkins made a back-of-cigarette-packet calculation. He was thinking clearly now. For the first time in a long while, he wasn't distracted by thoughts of the bottle of whisky waiting for him at home or anxiously wondering when he'd see Jacob's face again. Every cell in his body was concentrated on the mission in front of him.

Hunt down the prey. Capture them.

Find out who they're working for.

What they stole from Devonport.

And why.

He said, 'Abrashi told us they're taking the Bulgarians on a boat to an off-shore drug deal. Which means it'll be a cross-deck job. Two-way transfer. Cocaine unloaded from the larger trawler onto the boat. With the Bulgarians going the other way. Somewhere in international waters, probably. Which is twelve nautical miles from the coast. They could be leaving from Liverpool marina. Or across the river from Birkenhead. Those are the most obvious departure points.'

'Might be further down the coast,' Millar speculated.

Hawkins shook his head. 'This is a major operation. Lots of moving parts. They've got to send out the Bulgarians. Successfully land the drugs. Take the product to the processing unit, get it cut before onward distribution to the street-level dealers. The Albanians will want to keep everything close to their home turf. Easier for them to control the situation. React to any problems. The embarkation point has got to be somewhere in this area.'

'Either way, we've got them now,' Bald said.

Hawkins sensed the determination in his mucker's voice. He felt the same way. The electric thumping in his veins. The adrenaline rush of the hunt.

He dropped his eyes to the infotainment screen. 17.29. Two hours before sunset. The Bulgarians must be planning a night crossing to Ireland. On a mid-sized fishing vessel, from Liverpool, a journey of maybe fourteen hours, depending on the conditions at sea, the ship's cruising speed and their destination on the other side. Dundalk, perhaps. Or Wexford.

They carried on south, Millar maintaining a steady distance from the Crafter.

'Doesn't look like they know they're being followed,' she observed. 'They're not running any counter-surveillance drills.'

'They'll know soon enough,' Hawkins said. 'Only a matter of time before someone finds the Abrashi brothers. When that happens, they'll put a call into their mates. Sound the alarm. The guys in the van will realise we're onto them then.'

'They're taking a big risk,' Millar said. 'Using a smuggling network to cross the sea. What if they get caught by the coast guard?'

Bald said, derisively, 'Ain't gonna happen. The Irish haven't got a navy worthy of the name. Can't patrol their own waters effectively. Why it's such a popular route for bringing over the coke. They won't get stopped. More chance of Hawkins pulling a decent-looking bird.'

Hawkins glared at the Scot in the rear-view mirror. He said to Millar, 'Just stick to that van. Whatever happens, don't let them out of sight.'

They tailed the Crafter as it made a right onto Sandhills Lane, then a quick left onto Regent Road, funnelling south. Docks on their right, industrial estates at their nine o'clock. Traffic was gradually building up, forcing Millar to weave between lanes as she fought to maintain a clear line of sight to the Crafter.

From his brief map study of the local area Hawkins knew that Liverpool marina was a couple of miles to the south, downstream from the swanky waterfront bars and restaurants around Royal Albert Dock.

'They're heading for the marina,' he said. 'That must be where they're going to board the boat.'

Bald said, 'What are the opening times for the lock down there?'

Millar said, 'Lock opens at five o'clock in the morning. Closes just before nine at night.'

'That's definitely it, then,' Hawkins said.

They continued on Regent Road for a mile and a half. Then the van slammed on the brakes and made a hard left onto Paisley Street.

Heading east instead of south.

'Shit,' Millar said.

'Where the fuck are they going?' Bald wondered. 'The marina's in the other direction.'

'They must have found the Abrashi brothers,' Hawkins said. 'They'll have warned the driver. Stay with them,' he added to Millar. 'Don't let the bastards out of sight.'

Millar put her foot to the pedal, the Merc's six-cylinder engine snarling as they sped after the van. She turned down Paisley, tracking the Crafter as it arrowed across a bustling main road and veered south.

Millar took the same route, navigating through the traffic, and joined the rightmost lane. The van was forty metres ahead of them now, clearing a chaotic intersection before it sped down a secondary road fringed with swish new apartment blocks and glass-fronted offices.

Millar raced across the intersection in pursuit of the Crafter, narrowly dodging a black-helmeted delivery driver on a scooter before she blasted down the secondary street. Hawkins gritted his teeth, willing them to close the gap with the Bulgarians.

Further ahead, the panel van swerved sharply to avoid ploughing into an SUV nudging out of a parking bay, then briefly skewed into the opposite lane before the driver straightened out again and raced on. The Merc was less than forty metres behind, slowly clawing back the distance to the enemy.

That was when Hawkins saw the blur. It came from their ten o'clock. A cobbled side street that fed into the one-way system. A delivery van pulled blindly out of the turn ahead of the Merc, cutting them up and forcing Millar to slam hard on the brakes. Hawkins lurched forward in his seat, stomach trampolining as the wagon jerked to a near-halt, front bumper inches from the rear of the delivery van.

The delivery van driver honked his horn. Fifty metres further ahead, the Crafter's brake lights flared. A moment later it turned down another side street.

'Shit. We're losing them,' Hawkins said.

Millar took evasive action. She mashed the accelerator, steered into the opposite lane, overtaking the delivery van. An onrushing Lycra-clad cyclist sheered to the right, avoiding the Merc and crashing into a bus shelter billboard in a tangle of limbs and metal.

A short way further along, a dark-haired woman with a pushchair had stepped out from behind a parked Volkswagen Touareg to cross the road. The woman stood frozen in horror as the Merc pelted towards them.

For a terrifying moment Hawkins thought they might knock down the mother and child, but then Millar cut back into the other lane at the last second, avoiding the pedestrians by mere inches. She slung the Merc down the same side road the Crafter had taken, drifting into the corner, rear end fishtailing. They sped east for a hundred metres, turned right onto a one-way street. Hawkins momentarily glimpsed the van ahead of them. Sixty metres to the south. Making another right turn.

Millar pointed the Merc in the same direction, bombing down the one-way street as fast as she dared. She briefly mounted the pavement to avoid a driver stepping out of his parked BMW, swerved back onto the road and straightened out, then hurtled towards the right turn the Crafter had taken. In the aerial map in his head Hawkins realised the Bulgarians were heading back in the general direction of the marina, taking a circuitous route in an effort to throw off their pursuers.

Millar nudged the Merc down the narrow side street, the front bumper smashing into a row of recycling bins left at the roadside, spilling jetsam of damp cardboard and plastic bottles in their wake. Then they were flying along, rushing past loading bays and piles of festering bin bags.

Fifty metres further east, the Crafter was lost from sight as it hung a hard left, rejoining the flow of traffic rumbling south.

Millar tapped the brakes as they neared the end of the side street. She shunted the wheel anti-clockwise, made a stomach-somersaulting left, cutting up an incoming MG and forcing the driver to emergency brake. Tyres shrilled. Lights flared. A car horn blared its mechanical note of fury. The MG driver shouted out of his window.

Millar ignored him and continued south on the main road, heading in the direction of the train station.

Then Hawkins looked ahead.

And felt an anvil drop into his guts.

The Crafter was gone.

Twenty-five metres away, the road terminated in a T-junction. Traffic breezed along Chapel Street in both directions. An imposing old exchange building dominated the other side of the road. Marble-clad façade, more columns than the Parthenon.

Bald said, 'Where the fuck have they gone?'

'Must have turned left or right,' Hawkins said.

'Obviously,' Millar said. 'But which way?'

They had stopped at the edge of the junction. At their rear, the MG honked its horn a second time.

Hawkins made a split-second calculation. Right would take the Crafter down Chapel Street in the westward direction of the docks. From there it was a straight run for a mile to the marina. Whereas a left turn would lead them down Tithebarn Street, on a general bearing towards the entrance to the Queensway Tunnel. The longest road tunnel in the country, Hawkins remembered reading somewhere. Running for two-plus miles under the river before resurfacing across the Mersey in Birkenhead.

A fifty-fifty decision. Like flipping a coin. Heads or tails.

Except if we call it wrong, we'll lose the Bulgarians, Hawkins thought. *And they'll escape with a bunch of classified military secrets.*

Which way would they go?

Would they head to Birkenhead? Hawkins asked himself. Or the marina? The latter was closer. Therefore less chance of the gangsters and their passengers getting intercepted.

The MG driver punched his horn a third time. An extended beep, lasting several seconds. Emphasising his rage.

'Right,' Hawkins said. 'They must have gone right. To the marina.'

Millar hit the accelerator, spun the wheel and pushed west down Chapel Street for two hundred metres, then left-turned onto the main road and continued south. Speedometer needle steadily climbing as they raced towards the marina less than a mile away. Docks on their right.

Hawkins stared dead ahead, tightly concentrated on the traffic in front of them, searching for any sign of the Crafter. He saw nothing but a jumble of lorries, buses, tank-sized SUVs and taxis.

'Where are they?' Millar wondered.

Hawkins said, 'Keep going. The marina's not far from here. We'll catch up with them there.'

'Assuming they've gone that way.'

'They must have done. Birkenhead is too far away. Fewer landing points for a boat.'

They rolled on past the waterside clutter of museums, chain hotels and luxury apartments. Departure point for the river cruises. Tourist central.

Hawkins kept scanning for the Crafter.

After five minutes they came off the main road and skated down Sefton Street. They were drawing near to the marina now. Moment of truth. Millar eased off the pedal, nudged the Merc right at the next set of lights and trundled down Mariners Wharf at ten miles per hour as they passed a stretch of new-build housing blocks. Hawkins and Bald looked round, running their eyes over the vehicles in the residential car parks.

Still no sign of the Crafter.

Millar followed the road as it wound counter-clockwise towards Coburg Wharf. At which point the view promptly opened up, revealing the calm grey expanse of the Mersey to the west. A mile away, on the far bank, a ferry had been moored for repairs in a dry dock. Behind it stood a maze of construction halls, cranes and workshops.

They crept towards a grassy knoll. Millar dropped her speed again as they passed around the edge of the marina, Hawkins and Bald still peering out at the rows of parked cars. Hawkins saw dozens of vessels moored along the gangways. Barges. Speedboats. Sailing yachts.

He stole a glance at the infotainment screen.

17.40.

Eight minutes since they had lost sight of the Crafter.

'Keep on this road,' Hawkins ordered. 'There's another dock to the south. Let's try that one next.'

They crawled on. Down South Ferry Quay, past the marine yard, the boat brokerage firms and chandlery, the smaller dock. Millar followed the road all the way to the end. Whereupon it terminated in a stone-paved turning circle ringed with parking bays.

The Crafter was nowhere to be seen.

'Head back up,' Hawkins said. 'We might have missed it.'

Millar rounded the circle and took a different route back up the marina, past the private roads and car parks outside the waterfront apartment buildings. They crossed north on South Ferry Quay, and Millar slowed down as they passed another block of quayside flats set behind a wrought-iron security gate. Hawkins visually checked the cars outside of each block. He saw plenty of upmarket SUVs and saloons. But no white panel vans.

They steered round Coburg Wharf. Headed towards the same grassy knoll they had passed a few minutes earlier.

17.43.

Eleven minutes since the Crafter had given them the slip.

'The wagon's not fucking here,' Bald said. 'We've lost them.'

'What now?' Millar asked.

Hawkins stared out of his side window beyond the wharf, mind working frantically. Thinking through scenarios. As he looked across the Mersey he noticed something on the far bank. What looked like a charter boat bobbing on the gentle waters beside a stone slipway, a short distance from the workshops and construction hall further upriver. A van had parked at the edge of the car park above the slipway, Hawkins noticed.

A white panel van.

Cartoon logo of a fish on the side.

'Stop,' he said quickly. 'Stop right now.'

'What is it?' Millar asked as she engaged the handbrake.

Hawkins didn't answer. He leapt out of the Merc, ran over to the railings. Faint breath of wind against his cheeks, carrying the sharp tang of seawater. He looked out across the river, straining his eyes in the late afternoon light. On the other bank a group of tiny figures scurried down the slipway towards the waiting motorboat. Hawkins counted seven of them. At this distance they were too far away to identify. Five Bulgarians, presumably accompanied by a couple of Albanian heavies. Dumb muscle. Junior officers in the Jashari clan. Tasked with escorting the Bulgarians to the cross-deck at sea before making the return voyage with the drugs.

Hawkins heard the pounding of boots on the pavement at his six as Bald and Millar rushed over to the safety railings. Millar stopped beside him. She looked on in despair at the scene across the river. Two of them were lugging jerry cans down from the Crafter and loading them on the motorboat.

'What are you waiting for?' she asked Hawkins. 'We need to get across there. Now. Before they get away.'

Hawkins stayed rooted to the spot, shaking his head. He'd already calculated the distances.

He said, 'It's too late. We'll never fucking make it. They've got a twelve-minute head-start on us. By the time we get across to that slipway, they'll be long gone.'

Millar shook her head in acute frustration. 'There must be something we can do . . .'

Hawkins gave no reply. He kept his eyes on the boat on the far side of the Mersey. He was trying to glean as much information as possible on the target. Any details that might give them an edge later on. It was a fairly small vessel, he noted. No more than six metres long, with a single cabin for the captain. Bright red paint down the side, name visible above the waterline in white lettering. The *Wirral Dancer*. He assumed that the goods being loaded onto the boat included rods and bait and other fishing equipment. In the unlikely event that they were stopped and searched at sea they could claim to be on a fishing trip.

Hawkins watched the enemy. The germ of a plan taking shape in his head.

Waterborne exfil.

We're supposed to take them on the boat, Medon Abrashi had said.

There's a shipment coming in tonight. Cocaine. On a trawler. From our people across the sea. We take the shipment, they take the Bulgarians. That's the deal.

Across the Mersey, the figures finished loading the goods and clambered aboard the *Wirral Dancer*. The motor fired up. One of the figures cast off the mooring rope. The boat edged away from the bank and struggled through the grey-brown waters, leaving a trail of churned water in her wake.

The motorboat picked up her speed. Engine burring, bows throwing up jets of foamy white spray as she clawed her way downriver. Towards the bay, and the Irish Sea.

Millar said, 'We should alert the coast guard. Get them to intercept the boat before it's too late.'

Hawkins said, 'If we do that, they'll end up in the system. We won't get a chance to question them before they lawyer up.'

'What choice do we have?' Millar waved a hand at the boat. 'They're getting away, for God's sake.'

Hawkins said, 'There might still be a way to catch them ourselves.'

Millar turned away from the railing. Stared at Hawkins expectantly.

'How?'

Hawkins unlocked his phone and scrolled through his pitifully short contacts list.

'What are you doing?' Millar asked.

'Getting help,' he replied.

Hawkins found the number he was looking for.

Dialled.

Twenty

The phone rang and rang. Hawkins stood at the railing, looking on as the *Wirral Dancer* planed through the water, slowly shrinking from view. The phone rang a fourth time. Then a fifth. Twenty seconds passed without anyone picking up at the other end. They felt like the longest seconds of his life.

He's not there.

He's not going to answer.

We're fucked.

The phone rang again.

Then Tom Redpath said, 'Geordie? That you, mate? What's up?'

He had a bluff Yorkshire accent, softened by long years spent living in the south. Backgrounded by the low hum of office noise. People chatting, the clack of keyboards, phones trilling.

Hawkins bypassed the pleasantries. 'Boss, listen. I really need your help.'

'Can it wait? I'm about to go into a meeting, Geordie.'

'Afraid not, Tom,' Hawkins replied flatly. He paused. 'This is a national security issue.'

Redpath must have detected the seriousness in his tone, because the Director Special Forces said, without hesitation, 'What's the problem?'

'I can't go into details. Not on the phone. We're in Liverpool. Me and a couple of others from DeepSpear. We've got a serious situation here, involving potential Russian sleepers. I'm going to need you to mobilise the lads in Manchester. The thirty-minute team.'

'Wait one,' Redpath said.

On the other end of the line Redpath muttered something inaudible to a colleague. An excuse, maybe. Followed by the muffled thump of footsteps on carpet. The other voices abruptly faded. Redpath came back on the line again and said, in a hushed tone, 'What exactly is going on, Geordie?'

'There's no time to explain. I need the SP Team to conduct a waterborne interdiction on suspected enemy agents, and it needs to happen within the next hour.'

'That's a bloody big ask, mate.'

'I know. But it's the only way to stop something terrible from happening.'

'You're going to need to give me more than that.'

Hawkins said, 'This is an unsecured line. I need you to take it on merit for now. I'll fill you in later.'

'It's not about me, Geordie. What you're asking for – I can't just make that happen. I'd need to get approval from the higher-ups. They'll want specifics before they give me the green light.'

Hawkins drew in a breath. Exhaled through gritted teeth.

'All I can tell you,' he said, 'is that this is an issue of national security. There's a fishing boat currently en route towards the Irish Sea for a cross-deck with another vessel. We need to intercept the crew and seize the cargo before they make it back to Irish waters.'

'What's the cargo?'

'Bulgarians. Possible sleeper agents.'

'Christ.' Redpath fell silent for a double-beat. Then he said, 'Are you absolutely sure about this, Geordie? If I'm going to go and bat for you, I need to know that this is a genuine threat.'

'I wouldn't be speaking to you now if it wasn't.'

Redpath sighed heavily. 'Very well. The police will need to be notified. Five and Six too. I can't do this without bringing other agencies into the picture, you understand. That'll take a while.'

'Just as long as the SP Team lads are the ones running the show.'

'Where's the boat now?'

'Target has just left Birkenhead. Slipway next to the big shipyard. Heading downriver as we speak.'

'Wait there,' said Redpath. 'Keep the line clear. I need to make a few calls. Run this thing past the people upstairs. I'll ring you back once I've got the ball rolling.'

'Thanks, boss.' Hawkins added, 'I'll owe you a pint of Landlord after this.'

Redpath gave a strained laugh. 'If I pull this one out of the hat, Geordie, you'll owe me a lot more than that, you tight bastard.'

He clicked off.

'Who was that?' Millar asked.

'Tom Redpath,' Hawkins said. 'The DSF. He's going to take the request up the ladder. Mobilise the northern response team. Group of Regiment lads based up near Manchester. Get them to board the choppers and catch the Bulgarians at sea.'

'Redpath has that authority?'

'Not quite. He'll need to go up the chain of command. Get someone to sign off on it. Arse-covering exercise.'

Millar looked at him. Head tipped to one side. Something like admiration glowed in her eyes. Hawkins had the sense she was starting to see him in a new light. Not the drunken loser who'd driven away his daughter. But a guy who commanded the respect of the DSF. One of the seniormost officials in Whitehall. Someone who could mobilise an SAS team with a few phone calls.

She said, 'Why isn't Redpath calling in the SBS? Waterborne ops are their speciality.'

Hawkins said, 'They'd have to travel up from Poole. The northern response team's much closer. They're on a thirty-minute standby, dressed in their assault kit, ready to go. They can be on one of the Blue Thunder choppers very quickly after getting the order.'

'Do you think Redpath will get permission?'

'Your guess is as good as mine. Whitehall is a minefield. People with their own agendas, stabbing each other in the back. But this is our best shot. Either we do it this way, or we let those bastards get away.'

Hawkins returned his gaze to the *Wirral Dancer*. Within a few minutes the motorboat had reduced to a faint speck on the horizon as it cleared round the mouth of the river.

17.57.

Ninety minutes until sunset.

Millar said, 'Let's assume Redpath comes through for us. Will your friends get here in time?'

Hawkins said, 'We know the Albanians are going to cross-deck somewhere at sea. Transfer the drugs to the fishing boat, stick the Bulgarians on the trawler. Which will then ferry them back to Irish waters.

'Territorial waters begin twelve nautical miles from the coastline. Could take them up to eight or nine hours to make that journey, depending on the speed of the trawler and the conditions at sea. Choppers are much faster. We should be able to close them before they get out of reach.'

'That's not our biggest problem,' Bald said. He pointed at the sky. 'In ninety minutes it'll be last light. Landing on a moving target, at sea, at night, is a fucking nightmare.'

'If that's what it takes, we'll have to do it. Long as we get at them before they reach Irish territory. We can't risk another Flagstaff incident.'

'Flagstaff?' Millar repeated. 'What's that?'

Bald said, 'Some Regiment lads were apprehended by the Garda when they crossed the land border to the Republic. This was donkey's years ago. Height of the Troubles. Caused a diplomatic shitstorm.'

'It won't come to that,' Hawkins replied with feeling. 'Tom won't let us down. He'll get that permission for the SP Team before it's too late.'

'Let's fucking hope so,' Bald replied. 'Because I ain't doing time in an Irish nick. Not how the John Bald story ends, that.'

Millar said, 'What if the Albanians transfer the Bulgarians to the other ship before the response team arrives?'

'She's got a good point,' Bald said.

Hawkins thought for a beat. He said, 'I'll message Redpath. Get someone in his office to liaise with the harbour master. They can track the fishing boat on radar.'

'That will mean notifying the police as well,' Millar pointed out. 'Standard emergency protocol. Which means the authorities will find out about the Bulgarians and the data theft from the Plymouth office. It'll all come out in the wash.'

Bald said, 'Can't be helped. Cat's out of the bag now anyway. In less than an hour's time this area is gonna be crawling with Blades and police.'

'Just as long as we get to the targets first,' Hawkins said.

He put in the call to Redpath. Who agreed to give the order to one of his junior staffers to make contact with the harbour master. Notify them of the situation and tell them to expect a call from Bald and Hawkins. Even if he couldn't get consent for the deployment of the SP Team, the authorities would want to keep eyes on the *Wirral Dancer*. Find out where they were going. Who else was involved in the smuggling network.

At the same time Millar made a call to Varma. Laying out the sequence of events since they had departed St James's that morning. Letting him know that the security services and police were about to become aware of the wider situation involving the Bulgarians and the plot to steal secrets from DeepSpear. Varma didn't sound happy. Hardly surprising. His plan to contain the goings-on at Devonport had gone to shit.

18.03.

Eight minutes since Hawkins had ended the call with Redpath.

He checked his phone once more. Prayed that Redpath hadn't encountered any roadblocks at his end. Which could happen. Redpath was a man of action, a brother warrior. If Hawkins said there was an immediate threat, Redpath would take his word for it. But the people above him were different. Policy wonks and political researchers. Technocrats. People who didn't sneeze without briefing journalists beforehand and consulting the polls. They might look less favourably on the violent seizure of five Bulgarian nationals on a fishing trawler.

It's not a done deal.

Not yet.

At 18.07, Hawkins got a message from one of Redpath's subordinates. The harbour master had been told to expect their call. The message included a phone number for the port authorities. Bald punched it into his smartphone and dialled. Identified himself and demanded to speak to the harbour master. He walked off several paces while he briefed the guy on the situation, gave him the details of the *Wirral Dancer*.

Four minutes later, Bald hung up. He walked back over to Millar and Hawkins.

'Well?' Hawkins asked.

'The harbour master's on the ball. He's ex-navy. Liaison officer. Told him the score. They're tracking the boat now. He'll let us know if it stops next to another vessel. Then we'll know they're making the swap.'

'What about the police authorities?'

'Local armed unit has been alerted. It'll take them a while to get their shit together. They'll deploy on the police launch.'

Hawkins said, 'Get a message to the harbour master. No one else is to intercept or board the target without our say-so. This is a UK SF op. Anyone else tries to be a hero, they'll be answerable to the DSF.'

Bald put in the call.

Millar's phone buzzed with an incoming text from Varma. Demanding to know if there was any news. Bald checked in with the harbour master, getting an update on the *Wirral Dancer*'s location, speed and course. At 18.17 he received confirmation that the police launch was being prepared to shove off from its base at Runcorn. The boat would make its way downriver, linking up with the armed police at a pre-designated RV at Pier Head before heading out to sea.

18.19.

Thirty minutes since the charter boat had left the slipway across the Mersey at Monks Ferry.

By now the *Wirral Dancer* had disappeared round the headland. Hawkins tried to ignore the anxiety pulling like a rope around his chest. He badly needed Redpath to come through for them in the next several minutes. Any longer, and by the time they managed to intercept the boat at sea it would be almost dark, and a difficult mission would become much more perilous.

Hawkins tried to quell the rising panic in his chest.

What's taking Redpath so long?

One minute later, Redpath called him back.

'We're on, Geordie,' he said. 'PM has called a Cobra meeting. I'm on my way there now. Lads at Manchester are getting ready to board the choppers as we speak.'

A slight sense of relief flowed through Hawkins's veins, tempered by the knowledge that the hardest miles were ahead of them.

But we're still in the game.

We're not beaten yet.

'Boss,' said Hawkins, 'we need to be on one of those choppers.'

'What for?'

'I can't say. Not openly. But something big is going to happen, and we need to find out what. We've got to get on that trawler as soon as possible.'

There was a long beat of silence. 'That's going to be tricky, Geordie. It's against protocol.'

'Trust me boss, we need to bin protocol today. We've got to question the Bulgarians before they're passed over to the cops.'

'Can't that wait until they're on dry land?'

'Won't work. We both know that they'll get the lawyers in as soon as the police take them into custody.'

'But you can't tell me what this is about?'

'It's big, that's all I can say. Much bigger than you can possibly imagine.'

There was another bout of silence on the other end of the line. Hawkins went on, 'There's no risk, Tom. I'm not asking you to stick a few civvies on a Reg op. This is me and Jock Bald. We know what we're doing.'

'What's your precise location?'

'We're at Coburg Wharf, opposite the canoe club.'

Redpath said, 'I can't make any promises, because it's not in my gift. But I'll reach out to the team. See if they're willing to ferry you to the target.'

'Thanks, boss.'

Redpath broke off again. Hawkins had expected some token resistance, but Redpath had always been willing to bend the rules if the situation called for it. Hawkins had seen that side of his character when they'd fought alongside one another in Iraq. Taking the war to ISIS. Cutting the head off the enemy snake. Against that kind of threat, you didn't get results unless you were willing to break the rules.

He turned to Bald. 'Get on the blower to the harbour master. Find out where that fucking launch is. If we can't get on the choppers, we'll have to hitch a ride with the police. Catch the bastards that way.'

'Roger.'

They waited while Bald contacted the harbour master. The former naval liaison officer. There was a short call and then Bald said, 'Police launch is on its way to Pier Head. RV is a six-minute drive from our position.'

'What's their ETA?' asked Hawkins.

'Launch will reach Pier Head just before seven o'clock.'

'That's it, then. That's our backup plan. If we can't get approval to ride on the chopper, we'll link up with the armed officers at the jetty and embark on that launch.'

They continued waiting. Counting down the seconds.

After six minutes Redpath called Hawkins back. There was a lot of background noise. He sounded like he was in traffic. On his way to the Cobra briefing, Hawkins supposed.

'All right, Geordie,' he said, 'you're going with the sniper team.'

'Where's the RV, boss?'

'An old business park half a mile due south of your position. Leechwood Business Centre. Get down there now. Sniper-team chopper will do a land-on in the car park and ferry you to the target. But one condition. You're not to take part in the assault. Once the deck's been cleared and all targets apprehended, you can drop down and question them.'

'Fine. What's their ETA?'

'Guys are on their way as we speak. They'll make the RV for 18.45.'

Hawkins glanced at his watch. 18.30. They had fifteen minutes to bundle back into the Merc and tear down to the RV at the business park.

Time to get moving.

He terminated the call. Gave the others the heads-up on the RV and said to Millar, 'Once you've dropped us at the RV, take the wagon and get up to Pier Head. It's a six-minute drive from this position. Police launch will make its way there to collect the armed officers en route to the target. I need you to get on that boat.'

Millar creased her brow. 'I'm not going on the chopper?'

'We need an interlink on that launch,' Hawkins replied bluntly. 'Someone who can coordinate with Varma and the authorities. That's got to be you.'

'I should come with you. I can handle myself.'

This isn't up for debate. Me and Jock have got experience of waterborne assaults. You don't. Besides, we need you to stay back in case the op goes south. Anything happens to us, it's down to you to stop that trawler from getting away. Get Varma to ruffle feathers. Raise hell. Call your friend at the Doughnut. Do whatever it takes but make sure those Bulgarians are arrested before they make it to Irish waters.'

'Do you think it could go wrong?'

'There's no such thing as an easy op in our world. Every mission is a calculated gamble. Nature of the beast.'

Millar stared at him with a grave expression. 'You don't have to do this.'

'Yeah,' Hawkins said, 'we do. It's this, or we let the bastards escape.'

She gave a grudging nod. Conceding defeat.

Hawkins spun away from the railing and started quick-walking back towards the Merc, Bald and Millar hastening after him. Hawkins climbed into the front passenger seat of the wagon. Bald folded himself into the back while Millar kickstarted the engine. Hawkins punched in the address for the Leechwood Business Centre. A four-minute drive from their current position.

Millar retraced their route down Mariners Wharf, bucketed onto the main road and bulleted south, burning rubber for half a mile. Slewed round to the right at the roundabout, taking the access road into the business park. Which looked deserted. A massive red 'FOR LEASE' sign had been slapped over the park directory.

Millar stuck to the access road as it hooked round to the rear of the site and pulled up at the edge of an empty car park. Long row of loading bays and ramps at the back of the buildings. Another set of industrial units to the south-west, fifty metres downwind from the car park.

Millar kept the engine running while Bald and Hawkins dropped out of the wagon. Hawkins slammed the side door shut, and then Millar sped back out of the business park, racing in the direction of Pier Head a mile to the north, and the RV with the police launch.

Bald fielded a call from the group harbour master. Hawkins felt a twinge of anxiety in his guts as he peered at his G-Shock again.

18.35.

Ten minutes until the chopper was due to pick them up.

Fifty-six minutes, he reminded himself.

By the time we're airborne the Bulgarians will have a fifty-six-minute head-start on us.

Bald wound up his phone call and said, 'Update from the harbour master. The *Wirral Dancer* has cut her engines. Another vessel has moved along her port side.'

Hawkins said, 'When?'

'Four minutes ago, he says.'

'They must be transferring the Bulgarians. Moving the coke in the other direction.'

'Looks like it.'

'What's the other vessel?'

'Fishing trawler. *Santana Perez*. Sailing under the Spanish flag. Departed from Youghal earlier today.'

'Current location?'

'Five nautical miles off the coast.'

'Tell the harbour master to keep an eye on that trawler. Let us know when it's on the move.'

Bald relayed the request to the harbour master. Looked up from his phone and frowned at the empty horizon.

'Where's that chopper?'

Hawkins didn't reply. He was thinking about the cross-deck taking place at that very moment, somewhere beyond the bay. The crews of the two vessels would be working to transfer the cocaine from *Santana Perez* to the *Wirral Dancer* as fast as possible. Either breaking up the bales into smaller units and manually loading them onto the deck of the fishing boat or using the trawler's deck crane to haul across the massive bundles, tightly wrapped in plastic to keep the product dry. Then five Bulgarians making the opposite journey, hopping aboard the trawler.

A swift operation. Seven or eight minutes, max.

He got a message through from Millar, confirming that she'd reached Pier Head. Armed officers were also on their way to the same RV. Anticipated arrival time of seven o'clock. At which point everyone would board the police launch and set off in pursuit of the Bulgarians.

They would have the advantage over *Santana Perez* in terms of raw speed, Hawkins knew. The new police launches were highly capable, designed to zip across the waves at high speed. Top-of-the-range engines and propulsion system. It wouldn't take long for the launch to catch up with the enemy.

He checked the time again.

18.42.

He lifted his gaze to the sky and looked towards the bank of clouds close to the rim of the horizon. Willing the SP Team lads to hurry up.

Minutes dragged by with agonising slowness. He started to worry that something had happened to the chopper en route from Manchester. Engine failure, or an accident. If the SP Team had run into trouble, they would have to regroup and send out another unit. By which time dusk would have encroached across the coast.

Then we'll be looking at a night-time assault, thought Hawkins. *On the Irish Sea. With a much greater chance of the mission going south.*

18.45.

Where the fuck are they?

What's taking them so long?

At 18.47 Bald received another update from the harbour master.

He said, '*Santana Perez* has just pulled away from the fishing boat. Heading back across the Irish Sea. Looks like the *Wirral Dancer* is returning towards Birkenhead.'

'Shit. They must have finished the transfer.'

'Port authorities will track the *Dancer* on its return journey. We'll have to send a team to arrest them when they land. Thing will be carrying a boatload of Class A drugs.'

'The police can deal with that. A cocaine haul is the least of our problems. We've got bigger fish to fry, mate.'

Another minute lapsed.

Then Hawkins heard the chopper.

Twenty-One

It started as a faint droning, somewhere in the distance. Hawkins looked round, eyes searching the sky in the fading light. Then he saw it. A dark shape emerging from the horizon, black against the setting sun. Rotor blades blurring, LED lights glowing on the wingtips. Approaching the business park from the north-east.

The noise grew to a thunderous crescendo as the helicopter neared, the distinctive *whump-whump* of the rotor blades audible above the mechanical roar of the engines. One of the Eurocopter Dauphins. Otherwise known as Blue Thunder, because they were painted to look like civilian choppers. One of several flown by the guys in 658 Squadron, used by the SAS Special Projects (SP) Team to rapidly respond to counter-terrorism incidents. Maximum speed of a hundred and ninety miles per hour, with a range of over five hundred miles.

As the chopper slowed over the car park, Hawkins's eyes were drawn to another Blue Thunder heli in the distance. Heading on the same course as the first chopper, but further back. The second aircraft would be carrying the assault team, Hawkins knew. Six guys, with orders to fast-rope down onto the trawler and secure the crew while the two-man sniper team provided top cover, putting down threats on the deck. A total of eight elite soldiers.

More than enough to take down a few Albanian smugglers.

Hawkins and Bald edged back as the chopper transporting the sniper team drew closer, rapidly dropping both speed and height. The helicopter hovered over the car park as the pilot checked his bearings, making sure he had a clear landing zone. Then it began its slow descent, weeds whipping under the downwash from the main rotor blades. The landing gears bumped against the tarmac. The chopper came to a temporary rest, engines still burning, rotors slicing through the air. The side door was already open. Bald and Hawkins ran forward and clambered aboard.

Two figures were sitting on the cabin floor. A bloke built like a bear and a second guy with the physique of a greyhound. The bear had a ginger beard and freckled cheeks; a pair of binos hung from his neck. The greyhound was the taller of the two. Narrow eyes studded a pocked face, either side of a bulbous nose with nostrils the size of the Large Hadron Collider. He was gripping a .50 cal sniper rifle.

Both men were decked out in all-black dry suits, designed to keep the wearer warm if they plunged into a body of open water. They both had inflatable life jackets, waist-holstered Glock 17 pistols and swept-back ballistic helmets with night-vision goggles strapped to the top. Ready to bring down if they needed to use them. The outlines of their plate armour were visible beneath their dry suits.

They looked ridiculously young, thought Hawkins. Mid-twenties or thereabouts. He didn't recognise either of them. Figured they were recently badged operators from another squadron. These lads were the sniper team for the waterborne assault. One guy operating the .50 cal, the other as the spotter. The two of them working in tandem, identifying targets, slotting them before the assault team dropped onto the deck. Overwatch duties.

The greyhound with the monstrous nose was the shooter; the ginger-bearded bear with the binos would function as the spotter. Hawkins approved of Greyhound's choice of weapon. With a .50 cal, firing from a mobile platform, you could misjudge a round, miss a target by a few inches, and the velocity of the bullet would still inflict serious damage. A direct hit would turn the enemy to relish.

The spotter pointed to a couple of spare headsets towards the back of the cabin, with wires connecting them to the chopper's on-board comms system. Hawkins grabbed one headset and handed the other to Bald. They slipped the noise-cancelling headphones over their ears, patching themselves into the SF STARSTRIKE system. An ultra-secure net, with multiple channels allowing for clear comms chat between different teams. One frequency for the teams on each helicopter. A second line linking the SF operators and the pilots on both choppers. A third channel for the armed police unit on the launch boat. With a fourth one for the bods in the Cobra briefing room in London.

Each soldier could jump onto a different channel at the press of a button, allowing them to quickly and effortlessly deliver information to the people who needed to know it, without gumming up the radios with endless chatter.

Foam windshields had been fitted to the boom mics on each headset, cutting out background noise. The only way the guys on board could make themselves heard over the drone of the turboshaft engines.

Bald and Hawkins strapped themselves into the canvas seats. Greyhound signalled to the pilot and co-pilot. Giving them the all-clear to take off again.

The engines screamed, blades thrumming as the helicopter gained height. Once they were well above the surrounding buildings the aircraft banked sharply to the right, then levelled out and pitched forward. Suddenly they were hurtling towards the coast. Towards the fishing trawler.

18.51. An hour until sundown.

The lead pilot had tuned into the SP Team line. 'Nine minutes to target.'

From the second chopper came another voice.

'Remember, guys, we have the go-ahead to proceed to target, but don't engage until we get the green light from DSF.'

The guy spoke with a broad Brummie accent. Hawkins didn't recognise the voice. 'Who's that?' he asked Greyhound, flipping the button to scroll through to the chopper's separate comms line.

'Matt Lavery. Team Leader.' Greyhound said. 'He's a top operator. Knows his shit.'

On the SP Team line, the pilot on the other heli confirmed that they were one minute behind the sniper team. The two birds were flying in a convoy formation. The snipers would move into position ahead of the second chopper, suppressing any threats on the trawler. Giving time for the assault team to fast-rope down to the deck.

Meanwhile Redpath would be listening in from the Cobra briefing room, waiting for key updates from the SP Team. Senior personnel from the Doughnut and Scotland Yard would be patched into the same line using a one-time code. The assault team would avoid talking on that line unless they had something important to say. Mission success, or failure. Otherwise they would stay off that channel and communicate amongst themselves. Too many voices would make it impossible for the head shed to follow what was happening on the ground.

Equally importantly, avoiding the Cobra line meant the assault team wouldn't have to put up with constant interference from the Whitehall suits. Nothing pissed off an operator more than a demand from a desk jockey for a situation update in the middle of a firefight.

Greyhound looked up at Hawkins. 'You lads are ex-Regiment?'

They were talking on the internal net now.

'B Squadron. I'm Hawkins. This is Jock Bald.'

'Never heard of either of yous,' said Greyhound. Looking at Bald. He spoke with a Mancunian accent. 'Fuck me, mate. When did you do Selection? The Stone Age?'

He grinned. Bald shot him a filthy look.

Hawkins said, 'Targets cross-decked a few minutes ago. They're now on *Santana Perez*. Fishing trawler. That's the ship we need to target.'

'We know, Granddad,' Bear, the spotter, replied. He sounded like he was from the West Country. Devon, maybe, or Wiltshire. 'We're in contact with the port authority. They're on top of it.'

Greyhound, the sniper, said, 'We've been briefed from London and the Doughnut. They've told us there are five high-value targets on that tub. Unknown number of X-rays. Is that correct?'

Hawkins said, 'That's right. We're looking at two X-rays, at a minimum, but you should expect more.'

'Anything else you can tell us?'

'The X-rays are Albanian drug smugglers,' Bald said. 'They've just unloaded a large quantity of cocaine. You can assume they're tooled up. Shotguns, at the bare minimum. Maybe a couple of AK-47s to ward off anyone who tries approaching them.'

'What about the HVTs? Are they likely to put up a fight?'

'Possibly, but they won't be armed,' Hawkins asserted. 'The HVTs are civilians. Four males and a female. They're not trained soldiers, and the Albanians wouldn't trust them with weapons anyway.'

'Basically, anyone with a gun,' Bald said, 'is a target.'

Hawkins said, 'The main thing is to arrest those HVTs. We need them alive, at all costs. They're one piece of a much bigger puzzle.'

Greyhound flashed a grin.

'Don't sweat it, fella. We'll capture them. Just make sure your colostomy bag doesn't fall off when we drop down to the deck, eh?'

Greyhound and Bear both laughed.

The police launch, Green One, had jumped onto the same channel as the SP Team. Informing the pilots that they had docked at Pier Head. Millar had embarked on the launch. Officers from the armed unit were five minutes from the jetty.

Things are going to plan.

The pilots on Blue One and Blue Two were relaying information on their respective positions. The harbour master hopped on and off the same frequency, providing updates on the course and speed of *Santana Perez*. From experience Hawkins knew that the guys on the assault team, riding on the second chopper, would be armed with suppressed Colt Canada C8 rifles as their primary weapons. The shorter version, with a ten-inch barrel and pistol grips mounted on the underside of the forestock. Chambered for the 5.56x45mm NATO round.

Serious firepower.

Once Greyhound and Bear had cleared the deck the assault team would fast-rope down to the vessel, neutralise any threats, secure the Bulgarians and then wait for the police launch to arrive and make formal arrests. There would be a short window of time between the successful clearance of the ship and the handover of the Bulgarians to the police. Between twenty and twenty-five minutes.

That's our chance to question them.

They crossed the point where the Mersey spilled out into the bay. Skimmed across the grey-brown waters of the Irish Sea. Air rushed in from the open side doors, adding to the noise in the cabin. The sea looked placid. Forecast was light rain and a gentle breeze, the harbour master said. Hawkins breathed a little easier. Nobody wanted to be conducting an op in the teeth of a violent squall.

Further away, he spied clusters of lights scattered across the city, apricot orange in the pre-dusk light. It seemed incredible to him that twelve hours ago he had woken up in a plush flat in central London.

The pilot on Blue One came onto the SP Team channel. 'Vessel is two nautical miles from our position. Get ready, lads.'

Greyhound and Bear got to work. Moving fluidly, with controlled speed and precision. Like an F1 pit team replacing a wheel. Greyhound fetched up his .50 cal rifle and tied it to a pair of webbing strops fixed to carabiners, creating a stable shooting platform, with the barrel pointing out of the left side door. He dropped to a prone firing position, peering through the sights.

Bear lay on his front beside his mucker and stared out through his binos. Ready to get eyes on the target as they closed with their prey.

'Four minutes out,' the pilot reported.

'Boss, do we have the green light to attack?' the sniper asked.

'Not yet,' came the reply from the Team Leader on Blue Two. Matt Lavery. The Brummie.

'We need that confirmation, boss,' the sniper replied.

'I know. Any moment now.'

Hawkins imagined the scene at the Cobra meeting. The senior-most officials in charge of national security. The Director General of MI5 would be there, probably the Metropolitan Police Commissioner, the Defence Secretary, the PM. Information would be flowing in from various sources. Cheltenham, Five, Scotland Yard. A whirlwind of activity. Arguments flowing back and forth.

Hawkins looked at Greyhound and Bear with a strange feeling. The passage of time. He remembered being in their position not so many years ago. Going into an op, excitement thrashing in your veins. Thinking you were bulletproof. Armed with limitless self-belief, trusting in your training and your own abilities to get you through.

But he felt something else too. A feeling of the baton being passed. Watching these guys take control of the situation, Hawkins suddenly felt very old.

These lads are sitting next to a pair of Hereford legends, and they don't give a good fuck about us, he realised.

He didn't blame them. Would have reacted the same way at their age.

Face it. You and Jock are yesterday's men.

The lead pilot was back on the SP Team line.

'One mile out. Two minutes to target.'

'Blue One, we have the green light,' said Lavery.

Greyhound and Bear patted each other on the back, giving each other the thumbs-up. At the same time more int came through from the harbour master, updating the two pilots on *Santana Perez*'s speed and course. Since the port authority couldn't provide the SP Team with a visual description of the trawler, they were directing the choppers towards a rough patch of water. A two-hundred-metre circle. The target would be the only vessel within that confined area, thereby eliminating the possibility of the SAS operators intercepting the wrong ship.

The police launch pilot patched into the SP Team channel again. 'This is Green One. We have left the jetty. Officers from the armed unit have embarked. Heading downriver now. Twenty-three minutes from the target.'

'Blue Two, two minutes out.'

'Blue One, one minute to target, lads,' the pilot said. 'Prepare to intercept.'

18.58.

The chopper changed direction as it swooped down towards its prey. They were thirty seconds from the trawler. Then fifteen. Ten. Then they were racing past it, pulling ahead of the target before the chopper veered sharply round, hovering two hundred metres in front of *Santana Perez*'s bows, a clear signal to the captain.

Stop the engine.

Through the cabin opening Hawkins could see the trawler steaming on through the water. It looked about twenty metres long, with a wheelhouse aft, a lifeboat stowed forward of it. Boat crane, winches and drums at the stern. From his vantage point he couldn't see anyone on the main deck.

'Target still moving,' the spotter said into his mic. Now bumping back onto the chopper's separate net. 'He's not going to stop. Bring us round to the starboard side. Boarding team prepare to land-on.'

The Eurocopter banked sharply and slewed round, drawing alongside *Santana Perez*, with the snipers facing the trawler. The pilots were matching the ship's speed, maintaining a distance of two hundred metres to the target, while the sniper and spotter prepared to drop any X-rays in sight. Bear was a picture of concentration as he scanned the deck through his binoculars, feeding information to Greyhound and relaying orders to the pilots.

'Left a bit, guys. Left a bit more . . . that's it.'

'Blue Two, thirty seconds out.'

'Any sign of the HVTs?' Hawkins asked the spotter.

'Negative. Can't see them.'

'They'll be hiding below deck,' Bald said. 'They're the most wanted people in the country. The Albanians will want to keep them out of sight.'

The .50 cal boomed twice as Greyhound put a couple of rounds into the vessel. A further warning to the captain. In case he hadn't taken the hint the first time. But also to send a message to the crew.

Surrender. Or you're going to be in a world of shit.

The trawler stubbornly continued cutting through the sea.

'Two X-rays,' Bear said. 'Coming out of the wheelhouse now. Both armed with AK-47s.'

He was talking plainly, as if reading out listings in a telephone directory. No hint of panic or nerves in his voice. Just a bloke doing his job.

In the same breath the spotter directed the sniper towards the first gunman. Greyhound stared down the sights, centring his aim on the target. Then he squeezed the trigger. The .50 cal jolted and boomed. The spent shell popped out of the ejector on the side of the receiver and tumbled across the cabin floor.

'Enemy down,' Bear reported.

Hawkins sat in his canvas seat, concentrating hard on the chatter between the pilots and the sniper team. Trying to build a picture in his head of the assault.

The lead pilot on Blue Two, speaking on the SP Team frequency, announced that they were almost on target. Once they were within five or six metres the pilot would give the signal, and the operators would fast-rope down to the foredeck.

Blue One would be maintaining a distance of two hundred metres from *Santana Perez*, matching the speed of the target vessel, while Greyhound and Bear worked as a well-oiled machine, walloping anyone who burst out of the wheelhouse brandishing a gun. Providing top cover to their muckers while they fast-roped down and cleared the ship.

Everything was going to plan. In a few minutes' time, the assaulters would be fanning out across the deck to drop any more Albanian smugglers and secure the Bulgarians. Then Bald and Hawkins would make the descent from their chopper to question them.

The pilot on the police launch spoke up again. They were no more than twenty minutes out.

Twenty minutes, thought Hawkins.

We're not gonna have much time to squeeze the truth out of the Bulgarians before they reach the ship.

Whatever they know, we'll have to get it out of them fast.

Bear was directing Greyhound a fraction to the left, guiding him to the next target beside the boat crane. The second gunman.

'Blue Two moving into position,' the pilot said.

They were moments away from dropping the assault team over the trawler. Once they landed, it would be game over for the Albanians, Hawkins knew. A handful of gang toughs packing AK-47s and shotguns wouldn't stand a chance against a six-man team of elite SF operators, supported by a well-drilled sniper team.

Then Hawkins heard a muffled burst of gunfire, and the mission went to shit.

Twenty-Two

Cabinet Office, 70 Whitehall, London 18.59

They called it Cobra, and the name was obviously intended to conjure an image of power and intelligence at the very apex of government. The seniormost officials in the land, brought together to deal with a national crisis, sitting in a room filled with cutting-edge technology and wall-to-wall computer screens.

The reality was very different, Nish Varma reflected as he gazed round the cramped briefing room. One of several located deep in the bowels of the Cabinet Office.

A few years ago, conscious of the fact that the facilities were seriously out of date, the previous government had commissioned a refurb of the rooms used to host high-level Cobra meetings. The refit had been farmed out to an external contractor. In the finest Whitehall tradition, the project had run millions of pounds over budget, suffering from the usual delays, corner-cutting and technical problems. The end result was a drab soundproofed room, with a couple of large screens mounted on the back wall. No interactive maps, no live feeds from Five, Six or GCHQ. No system capable of unifying the various emergency services on a single network. Video calls were made over a freely available social media app, subject to the usual lags and sudden drops in connection. The room wasn't even swept for bugs.

Government, Varma thought with barely disguised contempt. *The faces in Downing Street might change, but the attitude never does.*

Eight other people were seated around the polished oak table. Nine in total, including Varma himself. To his immediate right was Sylvia Reade, the Director General of MI5, a severe-looking woman in her mid-fifties with frameless spectacles and a wave of blow-dried blonde hair.

Next to her sat Clive Norwood, the Metropolitan Police Commissioner, a shaven-headed man with a thickset frame running to fat, and his second-in-command, Mahika Desai, a small woman with immaculate short black hair and candy-apple-red lips.

Directly opposite Varma was Crispin Perry-Jones, the current Defence Secretary. Late forties, dressed like a Victorian railway tycoon. A three-piece suit hung from his spindly frame. He wore his trademark felt bowler hat, bow tie and monocle. Varma half-expected him to break out the snuff and start talking about the German Question.

To the right of Perry-Jones sat Nigel Wilcox, the jowly Home Secretary, and Major-General Tom Redpath, the Director Special Forces. The youngest man in the room. Still in possession of a full head of hair, and the only one with any real-world combat experience.

Redpath wore a headset with a mic attachment, allowing him to listen in to the main STARSTRIKE channel. Getting occasional updates from the SAS Team Leader, the senior officials at Cheltenham and the Scotland Yard Counter-Terrorism Unit.

Beside Redpath was Sir Ian Neville, the Chief of the Defence Staff. A former army general with a beak-like nose, liver-spotted hands and a noticeable paunch from years of boozy lunches in private clubs.

The Prime Minister sat at the head of the table. He looked terrible, thought Varma. Like reheated shit. The guy had been in office for less than a year, but the strains of the job had already taken a severe toll on him. His once smooth, slender complexion was now puffy and drawn; he had put on a serious amount of weight, his fleshy torso threatening to burst out of his too-tight shirt. The brown hair was shot through with streaks of grey. He'd aged ten years in a few months.

These were the men and women charged with keeping Britain safe.

Redpath was coordinating the operation over the net, talking to the SP Team conducting the assault on *Santana Perez*, while he stared at the laptop in front of him. The eighty-inch screen behind the Prime Minister displayed a live map of shipping traffic in the Irish Sea. Everyone waited nervously for further news from Redpath. He was the interlink between the Cobra team and the SP Team. The only conduit for information. Or rather, the only one the other attendees knew about.

In fact, Varma had his own direct line to Alex Millar, currently aboard the police launch in pursuit of *Santana Perez*. He had given her explicit instructions before she'd departed from Pier Head.

Let me know once you've questioned the Bulgarians.
Talk to me and no one else.

Some people accused Varma of being a law unto himself. He'd read plenty of opinion pieces by legacy media hacks, accusing him of being a threat to British democracy. According to his critics, Varma wielded too much power for an unelected businessman. He was too rich, they said. The PM was in his pocket. They worried about his many contracts with the MoD, his control of vast sections of the British defence industry and his outsized influence on foreign policy, in Ukraine and elsewhere. They viewed with suspicion his close connections to the man likely to become the next US President and the gaggle of tech bros that formed his inner circle.

Partly their criticisms were born out of jealousy, Varma knew. They hated his success. How he had fought tooth and nail against the sclerotic British establishment, transforming his company from a humble start-up to one of the most powerful companies in the country. He had achieved this in the face of determined opposition, in a world dominated by old boys' networks, and the upper-class suspicion of anyone who was prepared to roll up their sleeves and get to work.

But there was more to it than that. Varma's critics suffered from a critical blind spot. A simple failure to understand that the world they had been born into no longer existed.

The scaffolding holding up democracy and its civic institutions was coming down. Lamentable, perhaps, but it was happening, and there was nothing anyone could do to stop it. The old ways of governing were dead. Politicians were no longer the most important people in the country. Varma, and others like him, were the new leaders. They called the shots. They provided the spaceships and satellites, the crypto currencies and AI systems, the supercomputers and robots needed to build a new society in the decades to come. Governments were merely along for the ride, passengers on a train they no longer controlled.

The people around Varma were the last of a dying breed.

And they don't even know it, he thought.

The Prime Minister listened anxiously as Redpath fed across information from the SP Team.

'Team Leader says Blue One has identified two X-rays on the boat,' Redpath said. He paused for a beat, then carried on. 'One target is down. Blue Two moving into position now.'

The Prime Minister sat with his hands resting on his thighs. Trying to control his nerves. Perry-Jones reclined in his chair, drummed his long, dainty fingers on the table. A picture of calmness. Sylvia Reade, the MI5 chief, stared hard at Redpath, waiting for further news. Commissioner Clive Norwood ran a hand over his bald pate. His deputy, Desai, stared at the blown-up image of the shipping traffic on one of the screens. The Chief of the Defence Staff, Sir Ian Neville, doodled idly on the margins of a briefing paper in front of him.

Redpath abruptly sat upright, a frown scarring his normally smooth expression.

'Shit,' he said. 'Blue Two, what's going on? Report, over.'

'What is it, Tom?' asked the Prime Minister.

Redpath said nothing. He was solely focused on the comms feed. Piecing together whatever was happening two hundred miles away. Then he looked up at the Prime Minister.

'We have a problem,' he said. 'Blue Two has been hit.'

* * *

Two hundred miles away, one minute before seven o'clock – a full three seconds after the distinctive crackle of an assault rifle had split the air – Hawkins heard Matt Lavery's voice on the SP Team line. The Brummie-accented Team Leader.

'Guys we've taken incoming fire. Repeat, we've been hit. We're losing power. Aborting. We need to get back to land before we go down.'

'Blue Two, this is Blue One,' the co-pilot said. 'What's happening?'

There was a pause before Lavery answered. 'Looks like we've taken a couple of rounds to the engine block. Peeling off towards land now.'

Hawkins clenched his fists as he listened to the mission going rapidly sideways. Piecing together the situation from the radio chatter. The second gunman had obviously peppered the Eurocopter with rounds from his AK-47. At a range of ten or twenty metres, a couple of 7.62x39mm bullets could damage the jet engine and hydraulics, forcing the pilots into evasive action. At that moment they would be limping back to terra firma, desperately trying to gain extra height in case they suffered a catastrophic engine failure.

At a low altitude, if the chopper went down before it reached land it would cream into the water at speed, shattering the rotor blades on impact and flipping the bird upside down. But if they had enough height the pilots could auto-rotate into a descent, using gravity to keep the propellers spinning round and allowing them to make a soft landing at sea.

The pilot on Blue Two came back onto the SP Team frequency, reaching out to the police launch.

'Green One, this is Blue Two. Returning to land via your position. Prepare for waterborne rescue. If we can't make it, you're going to have to lift us out of the drink.'

Blue One started veering away from the trawler, the pilots plotting a course back towards the coast. Standard operating procedure. With the loss of the main assault team, the mission would have to be aborted. Which meant *Santana Perez* would be free to steam on towards Irish territorial waters.

It would take a while to brief, equip and despatch a second SAS team to hunt down the vessel, Hawkins realised. Hours, possibly. They still had the armed police team, but they wouldn't conduct an assault by themselves. Not without SF lads leading the way.

Even then, there was no guarantee that the Bulgarians would still be on board by the time the authorities managed to capture the trawler. A grim thought had been scratching away at the back of his mind for the past few hours.

The Bulgarians are expendable.

They know too much.

There's a good chance the Albanians will kill them before they make it back to the Irish coast.

We can't let that happen.

We need to get on that trawler as soon as possible.

'Have you got a fast-rope system on board?' Hawkins shouted, switching to the internal comms for their chopper.

'Back of the chopper,' the lead pilot responded. 'Why?'

'Here's what we're going to do. Me and Jock will rig the system up. Get us over that target. We'll slide down to the deck, deal with them X-rays and secure the HVTs.'

'We can't do that. We don't have the clearance—'

'Sod the clearance,' Bald said as he joined Hawkins outside the cockpit. 'We're going in. There's no time to argue. Now stop whingeing and get us over that fucking tub.'

The pilot saw the fiery look on Bald's face. Decided against arguing further. He faced forward again, nodded at his co-pilot. The helicopter banked round to port, heading back in the direction of the trawler.

'Team Leader, this is Blue One. We're heading onto target,' Hawkins said, flipping back to the SP Team channel.

Bald grabbed the olive-green canvas bag stowed aft of the cabin. Ripped out the fast-rope. An intertwined nylon rope, two inches in diameter, eighteen metres long, terminating at one end in a heavy-duty 45mm carabiner. He grabbed the end of the rope, fixed it to the shackle attached to the end of the metal arm fitted to the starboard side of the airframe, opposite the sniper team platform. Bald tested the hook, while Hawkins turned to Bear. He said, 'Give us your Glocks, mate. Both of them.'

The younger man deholstered his semi-automatic pistol, passed it to Hawkins, along with the two spare seventeen-round clips from his belt. Hawkins shoved the Glock down the front of his jeans, stuffed the mags of nine-milli ammo into his pockets. Took the second Glock and clips from Greyhound and handed them over to Bald. He wedged the pistol against the elasticated waistband of his cargos, deposited the clips in his side pockets.

Hawkins jumped back onto the internal line. 'Start putting rounds down. Any more fuckers come out of that wheelhouse, make sure you slot them,' he said. 'Once you've dropped us, move back two hundred metres and keep looking for targets.'

Greyhound grinned. 'How about you tell me how to boil an egg while you're at it?'

Hawkins smiled grimly. It felt good to know that these guys had his back. Men as highly trained as he and Bald had been. Guys who took pride in their ability to soldier.

'Thirty seconds to target,' the lead pilot announced. 'Get ready.'

Bald and Hawkins tore off their wired headsets, snatched up the thick leather gauntlet gloves stored beside the fast-rope and pulled them over their hands to stop them from getting ripped to shreds during their descent. Then Hawkins positioned himself so that he was sitting on the small step extending from the port side of the helicopter. Rope bag on his knees. One end of it rigged up to the overhead arm.

They were nearly over *Santana Perez*. On the opposite side of the airframe Greyhound and Bear were putting down rounds at the cabin, forcing the Albanians to dive for cover. The pilots had positioned the bird at a forty-five-degree angle to the trawler, so that the sniper team could sweep for X-rays while Bald and Hawkins dropped to the foredeck.

Hawkins waited for the signal from the pilot. His mouth was dry, as it always was in the moments before an assault. He had been in this situation hundreds of times in the Regiment, preparing to breach a stronghold, or crash through a door, and he knew what to expect. How he would react.

He glanced at his mucker. Recognised the look of steely determination in Bald's eyes. He felt exactly the same way. He wasn't risking his neck because he cared about King, or whatever it was the Bulgarians had stolen from Devonport. He was driven by something more primal. The same reason he had joined the Regiment all those years ago, pushed his body beyond its physical and mental limits. Earned the right to wear the winged dagger beret.

He understood that evil existed in the world. Evil thrived, because other people were weak, or afraid, or they chose to look the other way for the sake of an easy life. Sometimes the bad guys even won. An ugly truth. But truth all the same.

Not this time, Hawkins told himself.

I'm not going to let the bastards win today.

'Go now!' the lead pilot shouted. 'Go now!'

Hawkins threw the canvas bag down. It landed on the deck eight metres below. He grabbed hold of the rope between his gauntlet-sheathed hands. Took a deep breath.

Then he dropped out of the chopper.

Twenty-Three

Hawkins flew down the rope in a rapid blur. Like shooting down a fireman's pole. His boots thudded against the foredeck. In the next two seconds Hawkins tore off his gauntlets, drew the Glock from his belt and pushed away from the rope bag, raising his pistol in the same fluid motion, Bald sliding down after him. As Hawkins looked up, orientating himself, he spotted the gunman with the AK-47 popping into view from behind the lifeboat, no more than six metres from his position.

Further away, two more figures were spilling out of the wheelhouse, gripping shotguns. Rushing forward to contest the hostile boarding. Hawkins wondered why these guys hadn't rushed out of the wheelhouse earlier. Guessed they must have been below deck when the first shots rang out. Guarding the Bulgarians, probably. Keeping an eye on the targets while their mates handled the ship. When they heard the rounds coming in they would have had a decision to make.

Do we stay here with the hostages, and let our mates handle the attack? Or join in the firefight?

Four X-rays, thought Hawkins. *At the minimum. Minus the target Greyhound had already dropped.*

Which left three Albanians, plus the captain and whoever else might be holed up in the wheelhouse or below deck.

Hawkins processed the situation quantum-fast, his sensory perception working overtime. The fucker with the AK was the nearest threat. He had his assault rifle raised, stock tight against his shoulder. Business end of the weapon trained on Hawkins's central mass. Even a poor shooter couldn't fail to hit a target from six metres away.

X-rays Two and Three, the shotgun twins, were four metres further back. The guy with the AK had a navy smock over grey trousers. The two men with the shotguns were dressed in oil skins. One guy had a hi-vis yellow fishing jacket. His mate wore the same kind of garment, but in garish orange. Standard clothing for a trawler crew. Smart move. The Albanians would want to look the part in case they got stopped on the return leg of their voyage.

The guy with the AK had levelled his weapon at Hawkins before the latter could bring his pistol to bear. An easy kill, the Albanian must have thought. In the next beat a booming shot split the air, clearly audible over the rumble of the diesel engine and the hiss of water running past the hull. The familiar noise of a .50 cal rifle letting rip.

Across the deck, six metres aft of Hawkins, the guy with the AK-47 jerked wildly as the round slapped into his chest. He toppled backwards, arms flailing. Like a wrestler getting floored by a well-executed clothesline.

The .50 cal on the heli thunder-cracked again. A second round winged the Albanian smuggler on the way down, blowing apart his face. A combination of hot lead, plus massive amounts of kinetic energy, atomising bone and brain matter. What was left of the gunman flopped to the deck in a tangle of slack limbs.

Two down, thought Hawkins.

Two to go.

Plus any other X-rays we don't know about.

Above them the spotter unhooked the carabiner from the arm shackle, detaching the rope from the airframe to avoid getting snagged on the boat crane or rigging. Always a risk when fast-roping down to a moving platform. The rope fell away and landed in a heap a few paces from Hawkins, and then the chopper began pulling back to a safe distance from the vessel, just out of the effective range of an AK-47. Once they were two hundred metres from the trawler the spotter would resume his duties beside the sniper, putting rounds down on any X-rays still breathing on the deck.

Three seconds since Hawkins had fast-roped out of the side of the Blue Thunder.

He looked towards the shotgun twins near the wheelhouse aft of the main deck. The guy in the bright orange fishing jacket was the closer of the two. Eight metres from Hawkins. Four metres forward from the cabin. The guy in the yellow jacket was a metre behind, moving more awkwardly across the deck. A newer member of the smuggling crew, yet to gain his sea legs.

Orange was bringing his shotgun up to shoulder height. Hawkins figured he had a second or two before the Albanian lined up the barrel with his body and let rip.

Four seconds after he'd dropped down from the chopper, Hawkins adjusted his aim slightly, centred the Glock on Orange's torso. A nice big target. He squeezed the trigger three times in quick succession. The Glock barked once, then twice more. The rounds struck Orange in a close grouping around his upper chest, perforating lungs and tissue, fucking up all his internal plumbing. The Albanian dropped limply to the deck.

Yellow abruptly froze. An instinctive thing. Not the result of a logical thought process. But an emotional response to the high-stress situation unfolding in front of him. He had just seen two of his mates die. He would be feeling terror, primarily, plus the fear that he would be next, and panic at the realisation that he was trapped on a ship, at sea, with a couple of hard-as-fuck old soldiers bearing down on him and no way out.

Yellow whipped round and scampered back towards the wheelhouse. Favouring self-preservation over the long odds of beating Bald and Hawkins in a firefight.

Hawkins had no time to properly line up a shot. He put a bead on the Albanian's back, squeezed off a couple of rounds.

Two nine-milli bullets spat out of the snout of the Glock. The first missed and landed wide, thwacking into the lifeboat. The second thumped into the frame of the wheelhouse, a moment after Yellow dived into the galley, the door slamming shut behind him.

Bald charged forward, sidestepping the blood pooling around Orange's rag-order corpse. Surging past Hawkins as he rushed towards the wheelhouse.

Behind them, the chopper had moved back two hundred metres from the ship. On board the heli, Bear would be scouring the deck for further targets, Greyhound beside him in a prone firing position, feathering the .50 trigger. Ready to give any other fuckers the good news.

Three X-rays down, Hawkins told himself. Chalking them up in his mind. Two dropped by the sniper, plus the guy he had just turned into a human sieve. Out of a total of four Albanians on board the ship.

That we know about.

Conceivably there might be more enemies lurking in the wheelhouse. Or below deck, guarding the Bulgarians.

Only one way of finding out.

He hurried after Bald. Both men were leaning hard on their years of experience to get them through the next few minutes. Drawing on their training and the thousands of stronghold clearance ops they had carried out between them in the Regiment.

By now Bald was almost at the door. Ready to breach it. They had no idea what might be waiting for them on the other side. Could be one bad guy, or six. Like rolling a dice. Which summed up the mindset of the SAS. A civilian would consider the odds and step away from the door. The Regiment warrior saw it differently. He didn't see the risk, only the prospect of glory.

Bald wrenched open the wheelhouse door and charged inside. A gamble. But also a calculated one. Because in any room-clearance scenario, the hunter had a built-in advantage over the prey. Millions of years of evolution and conditioning at work. Being hunted was a terrible place to be, from a psychological point of view. The prey had no idea when their aggressor would choose to attack. That gave Bald a small but vital edge.

The Albanian was a half-second slower to react than Bald. But half-second was all the wiry Scotsman needed. He was on the smuggler in a flash, hammering the bloke across the skull with the butt of his pistol. Yellow went flying backwards, spine crunching against the galley table, knocking tea mugs and cutlery to the floor.

Before he could recover Bald kicked away the shotgun, grabbed the Albanian by his jacket and hauled him to his feet. Blood gushed down his unshaven face.

Bald dragged him outside.

Manhandled him over to the gunwale.

The guy must have read Bald's intentions, because he started jabbering at him in his native Albanian. Sweat glossed his brow, glistening beneath the floodlights. His voice trembling as he pleaded with Bald.

He shouldn't have wasted his breath. Bald lifted the Albanian off his feet and tossed him overboard. The guy screamed as he plummeted into the freezing waters below. At night, in the Irish Sea, his chances of survival were nil. If the cold shock didn't kill him, the water filling his waders would drag him down within minutes.

Hawkins stared slack-jawed at his mate. 'Jesus, Jock.'

'Fuck him. Let's go and find the skipper.'

He raced up the steps leading up from the galley, Hawkins scrambling after him. They stormed into the bridge. Found a double-chinned bloke standing beside the controls, podgy arms either side of a mountainous belly. The skipper took one look at the two armed Brits crowding the doorway and instantly shot his hands into the air, like an American televangelist proclaiming a miracle. Around him were banks of monitors, control panels and gears. Maps and communications equipment. Compasses.

Hawkins trained his weapon at the skipper. The man's eyes were wide as frisbees. 'English? You speak English?'

The skipper nodded quickly. 'Please. Don't shoot.'

'Turn the fucking engine off,' Hawkins ordered.

The skipper worked levers and buttons. The noise from the engine room cut out. The ship began rolling from side to side, rising and dipping horribly on the swell. Bald reached out and braced himself against the pilot's seat to steady himself on his feet. Hawkins felt as if he was standing on a giant spinning top. He refocused his attention on the skipper.

'Where are the Bulgarians?' he demanded.

The guy indicated the steps with a wave of his fat hand. 'Fishroom.'

'Any more of your mates down there?'

'No.'

'If you're lying,' Hawkins said, shoving the Glock muzzle against his cheek, 'you'll join your mate overboard. We're not fucking about.'

The skipper gave a frantic shake of his head. 'It's the truth. There is – no one else. Just – the Bulgarians.'

Hawkins grabbed the ship's satphone and punched in a telephone number from an emergency directory tacked to the wall. The number for the port authority at Liverpool. He spoke briefly with the harbour master.

'We've secured the vessel,' Hawkins said. 'Repeat, we've secured the vessel. Pass the message on to the police launch. They're free to board on approach.'

He terminated the call, swung round and stepped towards the skipper. Invading his personal space.

'Stay here,' he said. 'Police are inbound as we speak, so there's no point trying to make a run for it.'

Hawkins pointed out of the window at the sky. At the helicopter hovering two hundred metres off to port.

'See that bird? There are two lads on board with eyes on you. Make a fucking move, and they'll riddle this wheelhouse with bullets. Understood?'

The skipper nodded again. His fleshy face wobbled like a plate of jelly.

Hawkins cocked his head at Bald. 'Let's crack on.'

The two ex-Blades gave their backs to the skipper and took the steps descending below deck. They hurried along, knowing that they had only a short time to question the suspects before the police launch reached *Santana Perez*. Twenty minutes, perhaps.

Or less.

A sickening stench of diesel fumes, cigarette smoke and fish guts greeted Hawkins as he swept through the rooms amidships, adding to the powerful feeling of nausea in his stomach, the pounding between his temples. He checked the bunks and head while Bald cleared the captain's quarters and the engine room. They found no Albanians. No smugglers packing assault rifles. No more crewmen.

They pushed on towards the fishroom located forward of the bilges.

Hawkins yanked open the door and swept inside. Boxes of fish covered with fresh ice had been pushed against one of the walls. Hosepipes snaked along the resin floor. There was an area for cleaning and sorting the catch, six-foot-high stacks of plastic buckets, a basin for scrubbing down between shifts, a couple of freezers, an ice machine. Next to it, a worktop for gutting and processing the fish.

Something else had recently been processed.

There was a bloodied, mangled torso on top of the workbench. Ragged stumps where the victim's hands, feet and head had been chopped off. One of the hands had been dumped in a basket. Ready to be taken above deck and thrown to the fish, Hawkins guessed.

Invisible fingers squeezed Hawkins, digging sharply into his stomach. Nausea prodded at the back of his throat. The thumping in his head worsened. He thought he might puke.

Four figures were sitting beside the stack of buckets. Three men and a woman. All dressed in civvies. They had been tied up, their arms braced behind their backs and plasticuffed at the wrists. Dirty rags stuffed into their mouths were held in place with strips of duct tape.

Two of the guys had evidently pissed themselves. Wet patches stained their crotches. Someone else had voided their bowels. Hawkins could smell the fetid odour of human faeces, mingling with the stench of gutted fish.

Bald pointed with his eyes at the carved-up lump of flesh on the workbench and said, 'Looks like we got here just in time. Bastards are covering their tracks.'

Hawkins nodded. Just as he had feared. No witnesses. The safer option, from the Kremlin's point of view. Eliminate the risk of someone gobbing off to the wrong person. Probably the Albanians would have been wiped out themselves, somewhere down the line.

'Which one speaks the best English?' he asked Bald.

The Scot nodded at a small man with a dimpled chin and a high forehead crowned with a nest of receding hair. Black eyes punctured his bony face.

'That's Vitanov,' Bald said. 'The one who sat opposite King. He used to chat about the football with one of the security guards on his fag breaks. Big Manchester United fan.'

Hawkins jammed his nine-milli pistol under his belt and paced over to Vitanov. He dropped down beside the Bulgarian, ripped the tape from his mouth and tore out the rag. Vitanov bowed his head, retching and coughing, trying to catch his breath. The guy reeked of piss, Hawkins noted. Piss, sweat and fear.

Vitanov started mumbling incoherently. Tears streamed down his face. Snot bubbled under his nostrils.

'They killed Denis,' he said. 'The bitches, they fucking killed him . . .'

Hawkins looked back past his shoulder at the slab of human meat on the workbench. The butchered remains of Denis Yordanov. The IT worker. He wouldn't be updating Windows anytime soon.

The Eurocopter thundered in the distance as it continued to circle *Santana Perez*, keeping a close eye on the skipper in the wheelhouse.

Hawkins clamped a hand on Vitanov's shoulder. Looked him hard in the eye and said, 'Start talking. Tell us what's going on.'

Vitanov made no reply. Around him, the three other Bulgarians were sobbing, their cries stifled by the gags in their mouths.

Hawkins said, 'We've seen the email from Matt King. We know you stole something from Plymouth. What was it?'

The Bulgarian shook his head weakly. Someone had slapped him around prior to trussing him up. His lips were swollen and purpled. Face covered in welts and bruises. Blood dribbled out of his mouth.

Hawkins went on.

'Talk, and we'll hand you over to the police. You'll spend the rest of your lives doing chokey, but it'll be a fucking holiday camp compared to what you'd get back home.'

He gestured with his free hand towards Bald.

'If you refuse, Jock here will take you up to the deck, roll you up in a fishing net and throw you overboard. Your choice, pal.'

Vitanov looked at him with wide-eyed panic. 'You're fucking crazy. I don't know shit, I swear.'

'Wasting our time, Geordie,' Bald interrupted. 'Let's kill this cunt. One of the others is bound to spill their guts.'

Hawkins started to haul the Bulgarian to his feet, while Bald fetched a bundle of spare nylon netting from the other side of the room.

'No,' Vitanov gasped. 'No, please! They said they would kill our families if we – if we told anyone.'

Hawkins froze. 'Who?'

Vitanov licked his lips. Glanced at the body of Yordanov. The IT worker. Or what was left of him. Hawkins could see the gears turning inside the engineer's head. Weighing up the options in front of him. Like a gambler who'd racked up heavy losses at the poker table, debating whether to go all in on the next hand.

'Tell us,' Hawkins growled. 'Now.'

The Bulgarian swallowed hard. Took in a deep draw of breath. 'Okay, okay. I talk. But, please, you have to help our families.'

'Talk first.'

Vitanov pursed his lips. Beside him, the woman was whimpering softly.

'They didn't give us a choice,' he began. 'You have to understand. They told us our families would die unless – unless we helped them.'

'Who?' Hawkins demanded. 'Who are you working for?'

'The Russians. I don't know who, exactly. The man who recruited us, he was another Bulgarian. Ivan Dimitrov. I was studying at the time. At Sofia Technical University. This was seven years ago.

'Dimitrov, he was one of my professors. He said he had a job opportunity for me. Important work. He took me to a house in Sliven, introduced me to another man. A Russian. He didn't give his name. He just told me he had friends in the intelligence services in Moscow, and they wanted to make me an offer. One I couldn't refuse.'

Vitanov broke down in tears.

'They told me I was going to continue my studies in England,' he sniffed. 'They promised good money to support my family. My parents, my sister. Her kids. A nice house for them by the Black Sea. In return, the Russian said I would have to provide him with information. Watching people. Finding out where they lived, their routines. Friends.

'The Russian told me if I didn't help, it would be very bad for my family. He wouldn't be able to guarantee their safety.

'Of course, I agreed. What else could I do?'

'Go on.'

'I applied to Bristol University. Did my postgraduate studies there. Engineering. After I finished, the Russians told me to apply for a job at DeepSpear. That was three years ago.'

Sleeper agents, thought Hawkins.

A tactic as old as warfare itself. Assets living in a hostile state, posing as regular citizens and supplying int to their masters. But repurposed for the twenty-first century. In the age of facial recognition software and social media it was impractical, and expensive, to train up and insert professional spies into a foreign country. Far easier and cheaper to recruit thousands of business professionals, tourists and academics and embed them as clean skins. Turning the West's seemingly endless thirst for skilled foreign labour against itself.

A Bulgarian living in Britain would be unlikely to attract the same attention as a Russian national. The unnamed Russian Vitanov had met was probably an interlink between the intelligence services and the sleepers. Another layer of deniability, allowing Moscow to pretend that the Bulgarians had nothing to do with them.

Hawkins wondered how far the network had spread. He thought back to the photographs Bald had spotted on the walls of the Bulgarian restaurant in Plymouth. The faces of the diners pictured alongside the owner and the Albanian crime bosses.

He thought about the plasterer in Enfield. The manager of the nail salon. The gym owner in Hackney.

There might be hundreds of them living here, he realised. *Hiding in plain sight. Paying their taxes, working office jobs, picking their kids up from school.*

And all the while they're doing the Kremlin's bidding.

Spying on Putin's enemies.

Stealing information.

'And your mates?' Hawkins asked, nodding at the three other Bulgarians. 'Were they all recruited the same way?'

Vitanov shook his head. 'Only Anita,' he said, tipping his chin at the woman. Hawkins remembered her name. Anita Nedeva.

'The others,' Vitanov carried on, 'the others were already working at DeepSpear at the time. We introduced them to Dimitrov. He told us to recruit them. Said there would be a bonus for every person we won over to the cause.'

'How many others?' Hawkins asked. 'How many in the country?'

'I don't know. They never told us. But the Russian said we were true heroes. He said there were others like us, working in Berlin, Madrid, Prague. Many other places. We were going to create a new world.'

Hawkins said, 'What did you steal from the servers in Plymouth?'

Vitanov pursed his lips. 'They wanted a file,' he replied. 'Those were our orders. Retrieve a classified document from the system. That's all they wanted. But it doesn't matter now.'

He dropped his head. Stared at the floor.

'What the fuck do you mean?' Hawkins snapped angrily.

Vitanov didn't reply for a beat. When he looked up, Hawkins saw a bitter smile playing out on his lips.

'Don't you see? It's too late. They're already on their way.'

'Who?'

'The strike team,' the Bulgarian replied. 'They're going to make their move tonight. And there's nothing you can do to stop them.'

Twenty-Four

Cabinet Office, 70 Whitehall, London. 19.03

In the dreary situation room, the Prime Minister permitted himself a slight smile of relief. On the wall-mounted screen, the live map of shipping traffic in the Irish Sea showed that *Santana Perez* had stopped nine nautical miles from the English coast. Five minutes after the Team Leader had reported that they had been forced to abort, Commissioner Clive Norwood had received a short message from the port authority in Liverpool. The two ex-SAS men attached to the mission had successfully boarded the trawler. All X-rays had been neutralised, the message stated. The vessel had been secured. Police launch was on its way and would reach the trawler at around 19.22. Armed officers would detain the suspects, return the boat to Liverpool and take the Bulgarians away for questioning.

Meanwhile the Team Leader on Blue Two had switched onto the main channel, the relief evident in his voice as he explained that they had made it back to land, touching down in a field up from Crosby Beach. All passengers on board were reported safe and sound.

Disaster had been averted.

The PM was already turning his mind to the positive PR dividend from the operation. After months of negative headlines, he had a golden chance to reframe the narrative. Project himself as a strong leader, capable of decisive action. That ought to play well with voters in Middle England. Finally, things were starting to look up for him. Perhaps he might win the next election after all.

Across the room, Varma was checking his phone. He had an update from Millar, travelling on the police launch *Nighthawk*.

She was using the boat's satphone to communicate with him. They were fifteen minutes from the trawler now, Millar said.

Varma dashed off a swift reply.

Make sure you're first off the boat, he wrote. *Find Hawkins and get me a full debrief ASAP. We need to know what the Bulgarians have been doing.*

The mood in the room had visibly lightened. The crisis was almost over. Fifteen minutes from now armed police would be rushing aboard *Santana Perez*, taking control of the situation. The SP Team would be stood down. The police would take the credit for the capture of the *Wirral Dancer*, her hold filled with bales of cocaine.

Moreover, the mission had only succeeded thanks to a couple of ex-SF men on the DeepSpear payroll. That would be helpful in future contact tenders. The Prime Minister would be indebted to Varma for averting the escape of a group of Russian spies.

Then the screen flickered.

The map of the shipping in the Irish Sea vanished.

In its place, a familiar dead-eyed face appeared on the screen.

'Good evening, gentlemen,' Vladimir Putin said.

Everyone had stopped talking. They looked towards the screen in stunned silence. Staring at the face of the Russian President, with his peculiar resemblance to a ventriloquist's dummy. The bloated face and waxy skin, the tiny blue eyes riveted deep into their sockets.

A triumphant smile crept out of the small mouth.

'What the hell is going on?' Crispin Perry-Jones snapped, looking round the room and speaking in his plummy public schoolboy tone. 'How has he managed to do that?'

'The Russians must have hacked into our network,' Reade said.

'For God's sakes!' Perry-Jones fumed. 'This is supposed to be a secure room.'

Varma considered explaining the limitations of the technology in the briefing room – how any competent hacker with the right tools could break into the network supplying information to the Cobra committee. A situation that was very much of the Defence Secretary's own making, since he had ensured that the contract for the upgrade of the rooms had gone to one of his chums. Varma decided not to bother.

'Someone turn that fucking thing off,' growled Sir Ian Neville, the Chief of the Defence Staff.

'I wouldn't do that, if I were you,' Putin said.

Neville froze. So did the other members of the committee. The Russian President took a moment, making sure he had their full attention.

He can see and hear us, Varma realised.

He must have taken control of the cameras and microphones in the room.

Putin looked directly at the camera. He was speaking from behind a desk. From somewhere inside the Kremlin, Varma presumed. Oak-panelled wall at his back. A Russian flag hung from a brass pole.

'Time is of the essence, so I will get straight to my point,' Putin said in heavily accented English. 'My people have discovered details of an imminent attack on British soil. This attack will take place very soon. Sooner than you think. You are about to suffer a terrible catastrophe. One beyond your darkest imagination.'

Varma sensed the temperature in the room drop to meat-locker cold.

'Will someone tell me what the fuck is going on?' Perry-Jones said in exasperation. 'Is this some bloody deepfake?'

'No fake,' Putin replied. 'I am speaking to you as a courtesy. There are lives at stake, minister. Many innocent lives. We are prepared to help you save them.'

'Why?' asked Sylvia Reade. 'Why would *you* help *us*, Mr President?'

'The people who are prepared to commit this outrage are not Russian citizens. They have no ties to Russia, or indeed our security services. Nonetheless we have reason to believe they will try to implicate us in their actions. Such things have happened before, as you must know. That could trigger unfortunate consequences. It is in both our interests to stop the attackers.'

'What are they planning, Mr President?'

The question came from Redpath. The coolest head in the room. Varma had been impressed with the DSF so far. He made a mental note to approach the guy once this was over. Make him an offer to join the team at DeepSpear.

Putin leaned back in his chair, hands palm-down on the desk.

'Before we discuss this situation further,' he said, 'I will need certain assurances.'

'Assurances?' Neville snorted contemptuously. 'You must be joking. This government doesn't make deals with tyrants.'

Putin stared tautly at the camera. Eyes so cold they looked like they had been cryogenically frozen.

The Prime Minister raised a hand, cutting off his Chief of the Defence Staff.

'Now, hold on a minute,' the PM said, voice tremoring as he addressed Putin directly. 'What *exactly* are you saying, Mr President?'

'Let me be brief, Prime Minister. I am willing to share with you the details from my intelligence service. But before that, I need you to do something for me in return.'

'And what might that be?'

'Issue a statement announcing the immediate withdrawal of all British military and financial support to the fascists in Ukraine.'

Sir Ian Neville spluttered. 'Out of the question. Bloody ridiculous.'

Putin remained stony-faced. 'We are ready to help you, Prime Minister, in spite of our many differences. It is only reasonable that you help us in exchange.'

The PM shook his head slowly. 'What you ask is impossible. Surely you can see that. Our partners in NATO would never agree to it.'

'That is your problem, not mine.'

'Perhaps there is something else we can offer you instead? We could possibly remove sanctions from some of your colleagues. Unfreeze their accounts . . .'

Putin said, 'I am not here to haggle over terms with you or anyone else. Accept, or refuse. Those are your options. But I suggest you make your decision quickly. As I said, there isn't much time until the attack begins.'

'Wait,' the PM said, anxiously. 'Can you at least tell us what they're going—'

The video feed cut out. The screen went black. The map of the Irish Sea filled the display again.

Silence hung over the room. Varma could feel it. An oppressive weight, like a physical thing. For several beats no one said a word. The Prime Minister stared at the screen, blinking rapidly, as if the enormity of the decision had caused his internal software to crash.

'My God,' he said at last.

'Well, I think it's perfectly clear what needs to be done,' said Perry-Jones.

The PM looked towards his Defence Secretary. 'Yes, Crispin?'

Perry-Jones paused while he removed his monocle, polished the lens with a silk handkerchief.

He said, 'Putin has checkmated us. There's no point denying reality. We'll simply have to agree to his ultimatum. We should draft a statement and put it out for immediate release.'

Norwood pulled a face like he'd just necked a glass of piss. 'Cave in to that murdering bastard? Have you lost your mind, man?'

'Malum consilium quod mutari non potest,' Perry-Jones intoned.

Norwood said, irritably, 'Speak English, for God's sake.'

'*A bad plan cannot be changed.* Consider what happens if we refuse Putin's demands. Something catastrophic will happen, if he is to be believed, and we have no idea what it is, or how bad it will be. And it will be too late to reverse our decision.'

'How do we know he isn't bluffing?' piped up Mahika Desai, the Deputy Commissioner.

'We don't,' Reade said brusquely. 'Of course, Putin has form for making empty threats, with regard to red lines and so forth. But are we really prepared to take that risk when it involves a possible attack on our own people?'

'I presume,' Norwood said, 'that this is related to our interception of the Bulgarians on that ship.'

'Potentially. Though I fail to see how a few foreign nationals are in a position to seriously threaten national security.'

'So maybe it's not them,' Desai said. 'Maybe the attack is taking place elsewhere.'

Sir Ian Neville nodded his agreement. 'I believe Putin said the attack would take place on *British soil*. Rather rules out anything happening at sea, don't you think?'

'Could be a dirty bomb,' Norwood said. 'Detonated in the capital somewhere. We've long worried about terrorists getting hold of materials for a dirty bomb from inside Russia.'

Neville appeared unconvinced. He turned to Reade.

'Did we ever find out who put those drones over the RAF base at Lakenheath?' he asked. 'Could be that someone is planning a missile attack on one of our airbases.'

Reade said, 'We believe the drones were the work of the Russians. One of the GRU units, or a proxy linked to them, at any rate. So it could be that. A rogue missile targeting one or more of our air bases. Or equally it might be related to the recent incidents in the North Sea and the Atlantic. Russian spy ships disguised as tankers. Mapping out all the submarine internet cabling, sabotaging energy pipelines. They might be sending a submersible drone to the seabed, or a diver team tasked with cutting the cables.'

'But Putin said the people behind the attack aren't Russian nationals,' Perry-Jones said. 'They've got no ties to Moscow. We're looking at rogue actors, not a Kremlin plot.'

'Putin said the same thing about the soldiers who seized Crimea,' Redpath pointed out. 'He might be pulling a similar stunt. Denying any involvement with the attackers whilst covertly supporting them.'

'Either way, we should check in with the national grid,' Norwood said. 'Air-traffic control at the major airports, the major banks. If this is a cyber-attack they'll have targeted critical infrastructure.'

Neville said, 'What makes you think this is a cyber-attack?'

'I'm just trying to cover all our bases. Besides, if this is really the work of a few rogue individuals, a hack is more likely than sticking a missile on an RAF base.'

The Prime Minister, who had been quiet throughout this discussion, rubbed his eyes and let out a deep sigh of frustration.

'So just to be clear – and correct me if I'm wrong – we don't have a clue who might be behind this attack, what the target is, or when it might happen. Have I got that right?'

There was an awkward silence before Reade said, 'That is correct, Prime Minister.'

'Good. I'm glad we've cleared that up. Fucking hell.'

The Prime Minister settled back into his chair, his face contorted with indecision. Varma felt a degree of sympathy for the man. He seemed a good egg, all things considered. Honest and decent. But he was hopelessly out of his depth, mocked by his critics in the press and his own party. His cheerful optimism had long ago given way to poorly concealed grouchiness; he gave the impression that he would be happier working in the mortgage department of a high street bank than running the country.

Not the man to rise to the occasion in a crisis, Varma reflected.

Commissioner Norwood said, 'Prime Minister, I still think we ought to make some calls. At the very least we might rule out some possible lines of attack.'

'There's no time,' Perry-Jones said. 'The clock is ticking, for God's sake. We should accept the futility of our position and agree to Putin's demands.'

'Is that suggestion in our best interest, or yours?'

The question came from Reade. She and Perry-Jones were rumoured to have butted heads during the latter's previous role as Foreign Secretary, before the latest reshuffle some months earlier.

'I'm not sure I care for your tone, Sylvia,' Perry-Jones said haughtily.

That prompted a chuckle from the Five chief. 'Oh, piss off, Crispin. You've never bothered to hide your admiration for Putin in the past, have you? Or your opposition to the war in Ukraine, come to think of it. This plays right into your hands.'

Perry-Jones affected a wounded look. 'Firstly, I resent your implication that I am somehow involved in whatever it is our enemies are planning against us.'

Reade began to protest. The Defence Secretary raised a hand.

'Let me finish, please,' he said. 'Second, I have always said that I am opposed to the war in Ukraine for the same reason as our friends in Washington. It is a grievous waste of money in support of a hopeless cause that cannot be won, and the continuation of the conflict enriches no one except the hawks and the arms manufacturers. Such criticism hardly qualifies me a Kremlin lickspittle.'

Reade regarded him with dismay. She looked past him, towards the Prime Minister. Going straight to the source. 'We can't bow to our enemies. It would look weak.'

'Our position *is* weak,' Perry-Jones said. 'Get your head out of the sand, for Christ's sake. We're at Putin's mercy.'

Norwood said, gravely, 'I'm afraid Crispin is right, Prime Minister. Without having any details of the attack, we have no way of preventing it.'

'There's another point to consider. If word of this gets out,' Perry-Jones said, looking towards the Prime Minister, 'and lives are lost as a result of this attack, it could be extremely damaging. For all of us.'

'As damaging as abandoning our commitments to Ukraine?' said Reade.

'Kyiv must look to herself.'

Perry-Jones flashed a smile so thin he could have rolled a cigarette with it.

'Let me ask you a question,' he added. 'Are you prepared to sacrifice the lives of hundreds, or even thousands, of British citizens, in order to maintain our support for a foreign regime? Do you think their families would agree with that stance?'

Perry-Jones looked towards the Prime Minister.

He said, 'This might be a blessing in disguise. The American President has publicly announced his intention to pull his support for the war. This is an opportunity, however unfortunate, to extricate ourselves from a disastrous conflict and ally ourselves with the incoming US administration.'

Varma stared hard at the Defence Secretary. A populist with strong views on NATO, the Trident programme and capital punishment, he had been appointed by the PM to appease the hardliners on the right of his party.

Most people took one look at Perry-Jones – at the bowler hat and the bow tie, the monocle and the speeches peppered with obscure Latin phrases – and dismissed him as an eccentric fop. Old-fashioned, but essentially harmless. Varma knew better. Perry-Jones was a dangerous man, in spite of his ludicrous image.

Reade said, 'We must hold firm, Prime Minister. Let me notify the Americans before we do anything. They may have picked something up at their end.'

The PM didn't reply. He stared at the table, long hands resting in his lap, lost in his thoughts.

19.20.

Twelve minutes since Putin had delivered his ultimatum.

The launch boat carrying Millar was minutes away from boarding *Santana Perez*. Varma wondered if Hawkins and the other fellow had managed to get the Bulgarians to talk yet.

'Prime Minister?' Reade said again.

The Prime Minister looked up. His face settled into a look of resolution.

'Get hold of Putin,' he said. 'Tell him I've made my decision.'

Twenty-Five

Two hundred miles away, in the stinking belly of *Santana Perez*, Hawkins felt the cold rolling in his guts. The blood rushed in his ears, dulling the low drone of the Eurocopter circling the trawler, the slosh of water lapping against the hull. The gagged cries of the Bulgarians.

Vitanov's words echoed inside his skull.

The strike team.

They're going to make their move tonight.

And there's nothing you can do to stop them.

'What's the plan?' Hawkins said.

Vitanov said nothing. The ship rocked heavily. Hawkins felt his stomach roll with another wave of seasickness. Nausea tightened like fingers around his throat, digging into his trachea. Constricting his airway.

'Tell me,' he demanded.

'Coulport,' the Bulgarian said. 'They're going to attack Coulport.'

Hawkins jerked his head back and reached deep into his memory. Coulport. The name sounded familiar.

Bald said, 'That's the site near Faslane. On the eastern shore of Loch Long. Where they store all of them nuclear warheads.'

Hawkins felt a chill on the back of his neck. He remembered now. The original briefing at St James's with Gracey. The contract DeepSpear had signed with Whitehall a few months earlier. Management of the MoD sites on the Clyde. The naval base at Faslane.

The nuclear storage site at Coulport.

'That place is top-secret,' Hawkins said. 'Heavily guarded. Cameras all over the place. There's no way a strike team could pull that off.'

Vitanov smirked and said, 'That's where you're wrong.'

'What do you mean?'

'There was a security review. In the summer. After the announcement about the contract with DeepSpear. The company sent a team up to assess the facilities at Coulport. They produced a document for their bosses. It contained everything they needed to know about the sites. Locations of admin buildings, barracks. Storage areas for the nukes. Where the engineers sleep. Security features. Photographs of employees. Rosters. Alarms and cameras. Every detail, right down to the model of keypad used for the doors to the underground bunkers.

'Our handler told us to get hold of that document. He said another team had tried to steal it remotely, but the breach had been discovered before they could retrieve the file. He needed someone to physically access the servers at Devonport. Find the files related to Coulport and steal them.'

Bald said, 'How the fuck did your handler know about the review?'

'He didn't say. I guessed they had another source in the company. Or in the MoD, you know? Someone who would have been told about the review, and where the documents were stored.'

Hawkins thought back to what Millar had said at the original briefing the previous day. The hack at Plymouth four months ago. The serious cyber incident.

The network was compromised by foreign agents.

Now he understood.

'The team would still have to deal with the guards,' he pointed out. 'They'd get cut to pieces before they made it through them gates.'

Vitanov laughed. 'Coulport is not as secure as you think. There's no anti-drone protection there. The MoD guards are paid to patrol the site, but they're understaffed and a lot of them are off sick. Basic security, but nothing you can't overcome with some heavy firepower.'

Bald said, 'Why attack that place? To steal some nukes?'

Vitanov shook his head. 'The team has orders to break into the storage bunkers. Under the hillside. Where the warheads are kept. They're going to rig them with explosives. Then they're going to blow them up.'

'That's a fucking suicide mission.'

'The others, they don't think so. They've been told the devices are on a timer. They think they've got thirty minutes to place the bombs and get away from the site. But they don't have that long. Nothing like. The bombs are rigged to go off after thirty seconds.'

Cold fear spread through Hawkins's chest. He wondered how many nukes were stored at Coulport. Two dozen? More? He had no idea. A lump of high-explosive wouldn't detonate the nuclear warhead, but any physical damage it caused would be secondary to the political fallout. An attack at Coulport, and the destruction of Britain's nuclear stockpile would cause an international humiliation.

He said, 'What's the end game?'

Vitanov said, 'I don't know. They don't share that kind of shit with us. We're foot soldiers. Just do what they tell us to do.'

'What do you know about the strike team?'

'Only what the handler told us. I haven't met them. They're coming over for this one job. In and out. Or that's what they think.'

'Must have a screw loose,' Hawkins said. 'Volunteering for that op.'

Vitanov said, 'They don't have a choice. They're ex-military. Special Forces. Guys with criminal records. What our handler told us, anyway. These guys, they've been given a choice. Do the job, and their families will be looked after. If they had refused, the Russians would have killed them all. That's the deal.'

'How many bods?'

'I don't know. No one told me.'

'Where are they holed up?'

'They didn't say, and I didn't ask. The Albanians took care of the logistics.'

'They'll have supplied the strike team with all the hardware, too,' Bald said. 'Easy enough to ship some weapons and explosives over from Ireland with the coke.'

Hawkins looked the Bulgarian hard in the eye. 'Give us specifics. Now. Otherwise, you and your mates are going down with the fish.'

Vitanov said, voice shaking with anxiety, 'All I know is they're going to attack tonight. Nine o'clock. That's what they said.'

'Who?'

'The Albanians.'

Hawkins searched the Bulgarian's face, looking for any sign of a tell. Found none. 'Are you sure?'

Vitanov managed a lame nod. 'I overheard Medon Abrashi. At the car wash. He was talking to the team leader on a video call. Said he had a message from Moscow. They had been given clearance for the operation. Orders to make their delivery tonight, he said. Nine o'clock. When the marines on guard duty swap shifts.'

'It's a good plan,' Hawkins said. 'Best time to mount any attack is when the guards change shifts.'

Bald said, 'They'll never make it past the marines. They'll go through the Bulgarians like a dose of salts through a dog.'

Vitanov said, 'No, they won't.'

'How do you mean?'

'There's a training exercise. Most of the marines are off-base. Only a few have been left behind to guard the grounds. Eight guys. The strike team have orders to take them out before proceeding to the bunkers. There,' Vitanov said. 'I've told you everything I know.'

Hawkins looked down at the G-Shock cinched around his wrist.

19.22.

Ninety-eight minutes until the attack was due to go down.

Bald said, 'We need to get a warning to them guards up at Coulport. Tell them to expect visitors. Hunker down until help can arrive.'

Vitanov said, 'That won't work.'

'Why the fuck not?' Hawkins asked.

'They've got a drone over the base. Signal blocker. Knocks out all ground communication systems in a five-hundred-metre radius. Radio frequencies, mobile phone masts. Abrashi was boasting about the technology. Said he wished he'd kept one for himself.'

Hawkins stood up, stepped away from the Bulgarian. Left him sitting in his piss-stained jeans. His brain was all over the place. As if someone had just punched him in the jaw. The enormity of what Vitanov had just told him was beginning to sink in.

Ninety-seven minutes to go.

Hawkins tried to descramble his mind. A hundred different thoughts were competing for airtime in there. He shut out the noise, focused on the most immediate problem. The way he had been trained to react in a crisis.

Take it one step at a time. Don't try to tackle the whole thing at once, or it will overwhelm you. And you'll be paralysed.

'How far is Coulport from here?' Bald asked.

Hawkins shrugged. 'Couple of hundred miles, as the crow flies. Maybe a bit more than that. Why?'

Before Bald could respond a chorus of noise reached them from above deck. Footsteps. Boots pounding on metal. Voices issuing stern commands.

The armed police.

They're here.

'Come on,' he said.

They spun away from the tied-up Bulgarians, made for the doorway. Hawkins ascended the steps to the galley ahead of Bald, fighting off the exhaustion deep in his bones. He was shagged out. Flagging badly. Running on an empty tank, the needle deep in the red zone, his foot hammered to the accelerator.

Hoping to fuck he wouldn't flame out.

They emerged from the wheelhouse to the main deck. A light rain slanted needle-like across the trawler, pulled along by the faint breath of wind sweeping down from the coast. Dusk rimmed the horizon. Out across the water columns of wind turbines stood silhouetted by the tangerine glow of the setting sun.

The police launch had drawn up along *Santana Perez* on her starboard side. A sleek-looking vessel, fifteen metres long, yellow and blue livery splashed across the lower section of the wheelhouse. Spotlights flared in the semi-gloom.

Half a dozen armed response officers fanned out across the deck. Two guys clad in black stormed into the wheelhouse to arrest the skipper. Two more stooped down to inspect the bodies of the three Albanian gunmen. Bald pulled the other officers to one side and pointed them in the direction of the fishroom. They disappeared through the door while Millar made a beeline straight for Hawkins and Bald, steadying herself as the ship lifted and dipped over the stirring waves.

'Where are the Bulgarians?' she asked, scanning the deck.

'Below deck,' Hawkins said. 'Tied up. They're not going anywhere.'

'Good job we landed when we did. Albanians were about to turn them fuckers into fish food,' Bald said.

'What happened with the second chopper?' Hawkins asked.

Millar said, 'The pilot made it to dry land. Wallasey Beach. Touched down a few minutes ago. Everyone's fine. No injuries. They're waiting to be picked up.'

'Thank fuck for that,' Bald said.

Millar turned to Hawkins. 'Did you speak with the Bulgarians?'

Hawkins gave a tired nod. Christ, he would give anything to sleep. Pull the curtains, switch off his phone, put his head down. Let someone else deal with the world's problems. Hadn't he crawled through enough shit in his life already?

'We had a friendly chat with Vitanov,' he said.

'What did he say?'

Hawkins told her.

'That's what they stole from Devonport,' he said. 'That classified review of the Coulport site. They needed access to the blueprints and layout, so the strike team knows which areas to target, the fastest route to the bunkers, where the guards doss. They're going to break in, blow the place up.'

'My God.'

Hawkins said, 'You need to get hold of Varma now. Tell him they need to warn the guys nearby at Faslane. Local plod. Anyone with a gun. All hands to the pumps. Man the barricades until we can send up reinforcements.'

Millar crimped her brow. 'I don't think that's a good idea.'

'Why not?'

'If what Vitanov says is true, and the Bulgarians really have deployed a drone capable of blocking out comms at Coulport, there's a chance it can listen to what's coming *into* the base as well. Soon as we raise the alarm, the Russians will realise we're onto them. And they'll bring forward the attack.'

'Vitanov might be bullshitting about the drones. Or the tech might be flawed. The Russians have got previous when it comes to dodgy kit.'

'Do you really want to test that theory?'

Bald said, 'Millar's right, Geordie. We can't piss about making calls. There's only one way we can stop them.'

'How?'

'We need to get back on that chopper. Land next to the grounded bird, have the lads cross-deck and get up to Coulport ourselves. Set up a defensive perimeter around the nuclear bunkers. Hold off the bastards until the cavalry rocks up.'

Hawkins said, 'If we're going to do that, we need to alert Redpath. Get a green light from the top.'

'No time. Do that and we'll put ourselves at the mercy of Whitehall bureaucracy. Those idiots at the Cobra committee love the sound of their own voices. They'll waste time debating what to do. If we're gonna do this, we've got to move *now*.'

'That's not procedure,' said Hawkins, shaking his head.

'Fuck procedure. We can call Redpath later. Once we've collected the assault team lads.'

'I'm with Bald,' Millar said. 'This is no time for doing things by the book, David.'

Hawkins glanced at his watch.

19.30.

Ninety minutes until the attack.

'Okay,' he said. 'Let's fucking do it.'

A grin spread across Bald's lips. Hawkins looked towards Millar, turned his weary mind to what needed to be done.

'Get hold of the pilots on Blue One,' he said. 'Tell them they've got three packages to be winched up. They need to move fast.'

'Three? You mean—'

Hawkins nodded. 'You're coming with us. We'll be going in blind, so you'll need to coordinate with Varma. Get hold of all information on the Coulport site while we're inbound. Blueprints, maps. Location of the nukes. Everything that was pulled together for that security review.'

'Varma should have all of that stuff. It'll be on file.'

'Get the pilot to contact the other chopper, too. Find out where they've landed and get the coordinates for the LZ. Make sure they don't move from their position. We'll head down there and collect them before we head north.'

Millar hastened round to the starboard side of the trawler. She scrabbled over the gunnel, landed on the deck of the catamaran, stepped into the wheelhouse cabin to get on the VHF unit.

'How did they know about the security review?' Bald asked as they waited.

Hawkins said, 'I've been asking myself the same question. That document would have been top-secret. Need-to-know. Senior management only. Well above Vitanov's pay-grade.'

Bald searched his mucker's face in the gloom. 'You think they have someone on the inside at DeepSpear?'

'That,' Hawkins said, 'or Whitehall.'

'Fuck. Should we tell Varma?'

'Not over the comms. It's an open line. I'll get Millar to send him a message on her satphone. Give him the heads-up.'

Bald stood grinning.

'Never thought I'd see the day,' he said. 'Bloody miracle.'

'What's that?'

'You, mate. You've grown a pair of balls at long last.'

'Jock bastard.'

They laughed, easing the tension they were both feeling in their bones, the nervous anticipation all elite professionals felt just before they headed out on a mission. The determination to perform.

Two hundred metres away, the Blue Thunder chopper swept towards *Santana Perez*, wingtip lights reflecting off the darkening water like a million knife points. Across the deck, a pair of armed officers marched the Bulgarians out of the galley, forcing them to sit on the exposed aft deck. Two more officers bundled the handcuffed skipper out of the wheelhouse.

The police would have a busy night ahead of them. The launch would have to remain alongside the trawler until a tug could be brought up to tow it back to the port. Once *Santana Perez* had been docked investigators could begin the arduous task of gathering evidence and processing the four Bulgarians and the Albanian skipper.

The chopper drew closer to the deck. Millar crossed back over from *Nighthawk* to the trawler and joined Hawkins and Bald as they hustled round to the bows. Moving well away from the tangle of masts, rigging and the boat crane aft of the cabin.

The Eurocopter hovered no more than seven or eight metres above the bows of *Santana Perez*. The spotter lowered a hydraulic winch cable to the ship's deck, with a hi-vis harness connected to the hoist hook at the end of the cable. An extension line linked a rescue strop to the main harness. Bald helped Millar seat herself in the harness bucket, checked she was secure. Looped the rescue strop under his armpits. Gave the thumbs-up to the crew.

The spotter operated the winch. The cable tensed, winching in Bald and Millar. Hoisting them up to the cabin. Whereupon the spotter gripped the handle on the main harness and pulled them inside.

The winch cable lowered again. This time Hawkins climbed into the harness. Felt his legs lifting off the deck, swinging freely as the cable reeled him in. Hands pulled him in from the cabin doorway. He crawled out of the canvas.

Bald handed him a spare headset, gave another one to Millar. Hawkins clamped it over his head, tapped the lead pilot on the shoulder.

'How far to the other chopper?' he asked.

'Eight miles,' the pilot replied. 'We'll get there in four minutes.' There was a moment of hesitation. 'Are you sure about this, mate? We've got no orders from Hereford to collect the lads.'

'Course I'm fucking sure. Get moving.'

The chopper climbed higher, pulling away from the deck. The pilots brought the bird round, then pitched forward, and suddenly they were skimming across the Irish Sea at speed. Heading towards the LZ. On the SP Team radio channel, Hawkins heard the lead pilot reaching out to the guys on the second helicopter. Even though the aircraft had been badly damaged the radio would still be functioning. The assaulters would have disembarked as a safety measure; the pilots would be maintaining radio contact with headquarters, waiting for news on their rescue.

'Blue Two, we're inbound in four minutes. Prepare for fast exchange. Assault team operators will cross-deck to Blue One. Confirm.'

'Confirmed,' came the swift reply from Blue Two's pilot. 'Assault team will be ready.'

'How are we looking for fuel?' Hawkins asked.

'She'll get us to Coulport. You've got no worries on that front. Looking at a flight time of seventy minutes to target.'

Hawkins did a back-of-ciggie-packet calculation. 19.39.

Eighty-one minutes until the strike team attacked Coulport.

Four minutes to reach the LZ.

They'd have to do a very fast turnaround once they landed. Two minutes to get all the SP Team guys on board before taking off again.

We'll get there with minutes to spare.

Cutting it bloody close.

They raced towards the mud flats and sand dunes fringing the Wirral coastline. Through the open side door Hawkins could see the darkness closing like a fist across the bay. Lights pricked the coastline. Somewhere out there, far to the north, a group of Bulgarian ex-Special Forces, following Kremlin orders, were preparing to strike at the very heart of Britain's nuclear deterrent.

He was thinking about what Vitanov had said. About the Bulgarians on the strike team. The bombs rigged to go off in thirty seconds.

They think they've got thirty minutes to place the bombs. But they don't have that long.

Nothing like.

He thought specifically about the end game. Why had the Russians targeted Britain's stockpile of nukes? What did they stand to gain? He found only one reason that made any kind of sense. To deliver a message to Britain. Revenge, for Westminster's staunch support of the Ukrainians.

This is what happens when you mess with us.

The language of the jungle. Oldest language in the world. The only one Putin and his cronies understood.

Hawkins war-gamed the consequences in his head. The destruction of the nukes would damage Britain's remaining shreds of credibility. Climate change activists would be outraged. The Scots would renew their calls for independence. The Americans would be incensed; almost certainly they would suspend military cooperation between the two countries.

But such an attack had to be deniable. Hence the thirty-second detonators. And the orders given to the Albanians to carve up Vitanov and the other sleeper agents. The Russians intended to cover their tracks. No voices. No paper trail, no smoking gun. Nothing to link them to the plot. Moscow would issue the usual denials about its involvement. The usual crew of useful idiots would believe them – but that was the point. By outsourcing the attack, the Russians could protest their innocence.

Now it's up to us to stop them.
Hit back. Send a message of our own in response.
We're not done yet.
We're not surrendering that easily.

After two minutes the pilot announced that he had sight of the second Eurocopter. Hawkins peered out of the cabin doorway as the pilots banked round and swooped down to the LZ.

The damaged bird had landed on a patch of levelled ground ten metres up from the sea wall. Half a dozen operators were kneeling three or four metres away from the chopper, tiny black figures barely visible in the dying light. The two pilots would stay behind with the helicopter, waiting for a rescue force to retrieve them.

The pilots brought Blue One down a short distance from the waiting assault team. They kept the engines burning and the blades turning, down-draught whipping up a cloud of dust and dirt around the fuselage. Bald and Hawkins flipped up the canvas chairs, making room for the extra passengers piling into the helicopter. Everyone moved with practised urgency, like a pit-stop team changing the wheels on a Formula One car.

Lavery, the Team Leader, was the last to jump aboard. He found a space in the cramped interior, spotted Hawkins among the faces in the cabin.

'I've seen you around the camp before,' he said.

Hawkins nodded. 'Used to be in B Squadron. Hawkins.'

Lavery's eyes popped wide with recognition. 'Fuck me. You're the fella who beat the bollocks out of Carl Edwards.'

'That's right. You're A Squadron, aren't you?'

'Yeah, that's me. Air Troop.' He tipped his head at Bald sitting a few paces away. 'Who's the old geezer?'

'Jock Bald. One of the Old and Bold. Don't piss him off.'

'You sure he's good for this op?'

'We might be coming up against an unknown number of bods. We're gonna need all the manpower we can get.'

'This is no place for an old fogey, mate.'

Bald, who had overheard the chat, gave the Team Leader a scolding look. 'Sit down and shut your fucking mouth. We're coming with you. Show you dickheads how medals are won.'

Hawkins shot Lavery an *I-told-you-so look*. Lavery caught sight of the savage glare on Bald's face and admitted defeat. He looked round, making sure his mates were safely aboard. Gave the all-clear to the pilots over the closed comms.

'We're ready. Let's fucking move.'

The Eurocopter took off immediately, climbing above the sand dunes and the grounded helicopter. The pilots veered round; the nose pitched forward and then they were bounding north, plotting a course for Coulport, two hundred-plus miles away. From landing to lift-off had taken less than two minutes. An expertly executed manoeuvre. Not for the first time, Hawkins was grateful for the skills of the guys from 658 Squadron. Some of the best pilots in the business. Capable of landing on a sixpence.

We might not be good at much else in this country, he thought. *Our industry has gone to shit, the government hasn't got two pennies to rub together. But we can still produce top-class pilots and killers.*

At his side, Lavery switched channels on his headset. Jumping onto the open line to the Cobra committee. Giving the sitrep to Redpath. The new mission to beat the Bulgarian strike team to Coulport.

19.47.

Seventy-three minutes before the attack went down.

Twenty-Six

Cabinet Office, 70 Whitehall, London. 19.48

In the Cobra briefing room, Varma sat watching the most shameful act in British political history unfold before him.

After a brief conversation with Putin, acceding to his demands, the Prime Minister had ordered his two closest aides to draft an official statement. Putin had insisted that Downing Street make a formal declaration before he would share details of the imminent attack. The PM's aides, sworn to secrecy, had drawn up a single page of text. Four short paragraphs announcing Britain's decision to immediately withdraw all military and economic aid to Kyiv.

Now the Prime Minister, Perry-Jones and Wilcox, the Home Secretary, crowded around the latter's laptop, poring over the latest version of the text. Making last-minute editorial changes, trying to make the announcement sound less like a spineless retreat from the world stage. *Like polishing a turd*, thought Varma contemptuously.

'Should we add a line emphasising our firm commitment to the peace and prosperity of the Ukrainian people?' Wilcox asked. 'I worry as it stands that it looks like we're throwing them under the bus.'

'That might irritate Putin,' Perry-Jones argued. 'But we might throw in something about our hopes for a glorious new era of peace and cooperation with Russia *and* Ukraine. Something like that.'

Varma had seen enough.

'This is a mistake, Prime Minister.'

That prompted a scathing look from Perry-Jones. 'Stick to your profit margins, man. Leave politics to the grown-ups in the room.'

'Says the man with the bowler hat and monocle.'

Perry-Jones smiled coldly. 'My dear fellow, you really shouldn't go around throwing cheap insults. You're very fortunate to be here, you know. Considering you hold no official position in His Majesty's government.'

Varma wasn't going to give up. 'Putin is like a bloodhound on the scent. He smells weakness. If we concede to him this time, it'll only make him bolder. He'll know he can bully us going forward.'

'The alternative is that we let a terrible attack take place on our watch. Is that what you want?'

'We should at least wait until we've heard back from my guys,' Varma suggested. 'They must have spoken with the Bulgarians by now. They might have information on the plot.'

'If that's the case, why haven't they contacted us?'

Varma gritted his teeth. The last communication they had received on the STARSTRIKE network was from the armed police leader several minutes earlier. Letting them know that they had successfully boarded *Santana Perez* and detained the Bulgarians and the ship's captain. Hawkins, Millar and the other fellow had departed on the helicopter shortly thereafter.

Since then, there had been no word from them.

Varma tried again.

'Prime Minister, I strongly encourage you to reconsider. If you do this, there's no going back. As soon as we pull our support the Germans and French will undoubtedly go the same way. They won't want to – indeed, can't – shoulder the burden alone. You're going to condemn Ukraine to vassalage and give Putin a free hand to invade Poland and the Baltic states without fear of future retaliation. Surely you must realise that?'

'The Ukrainians,' Perry-Jones pronounced snootily, 'have freeloaded off the backs of the British people for long enough. It is our duty to protect our country first and foremost. As you damn well know.'

'We also have a duty to our allies. When this statement is made public, we're going to surrender any remaining prestige on the world stage. We shall likely never recover it.'

The Prime Minister said, testily, 'I've made up my mind, Nish. We're doing this in order to save lives. If you disagree with my decision, then you are free to leave.'

Perry-Jones smiled gleefully. Varma slumped back in his chair. He had given it his best shot. And failed.

Redpath must have heard something over the STARSTRIKE channel, Varma noted. Because the DSF suddenly sat bolt upright, hand pressing the headphone closer to his ear. There was a short exchange with the person on the line lasting no more than two minutes. Terse, short responses. The other person did most of the talking.

Then Redpath turned to the Prime Minister and said, 'We've received an update from the SP Team Leader, sir.'

'Yes ... ?'

The PM had looked up from the laptop screen.

Redpath said, 'They're on Blue One, sir. The whole team. Currently heading north.' He glanced at Varma. 'Your people are with them. Hawkins and the two others.'

'Heading where?'

The question came from Perry-Jones.

'Coulport,' Redpath said. 'The nuclear warhead storage site for Faslane,' he added by way of explanation.

His words cut through the room like a machete.

'Coulport?' The Prime Minister shook his head. 'Why are they going there?'

'They're acting on intelligence from one of the HVTs, sir. The HVT claims that a Russian-sponsored strike team is going to breach Coulport and destroy the stockpile.'

Redpath briefed the others on what he'd been told by the Team Leader. The information Hawkins and Bald had gleaned from

Vitanov. The drones deployed to intercept communications around Coulport. The plan to strike during the change of guards at 21.00.

Sir Ian Neville rubbed his nose and said, gruffly, 'Putin. The bastard. He wasn't bluffing, then.'

'It appears not.' Redpath cleared his throat. 'The team is en route to Coulport now, Prime Minister. They're going to secure the bunkers. Put a defensive shield around them until help can arrive.'

Anger flashed on Perry-Jones's face. 'They've no orders to proceed to Coulport. Who the hell do they think they are?'

'They're acting on initiative, sir,' Redpath responded drily. 'It's what we train them to do in the Regiment.'

The Prime Minister said, 'Will they make it in time?'

Redpath was consulting the laptop in front of him. 'At their present course, they should reach the site shortly before nine o'clock. A few minutes before the attack is due to commence,' he added.

'Then there's still time to stop it.'

'Barely,' Perry-Jones said, wrinkling his nose. 'What if there's some unforeseen problem between now and then? That operation of yours on the sea almost went tits-up. The same thing could happen here.'

Reade brushed a stray hair behind her ear and said, 'Are there any other forces in the area we could call upon, Tom?'

'Nearest bases are Edinburgh barracks and Leuchars Station, near St Andrews,' Redpath answered. 'But it would take a while to organise and deploy a force from either location. There's the garrison at Faslane, of course. But the Team Leader has advised against notifying them.'

'On what grounds?' Perry-Jones asked.

'The drone being deployed by the enemy preliminary to the attack. There's a chance it may be monitoring communications coming into the immediate area. The Bulgarians may accelerate their plans if they realise that we're onto them.'

Perry-Jones looked indignant. '"May", "might". "Chance." This is all guesswork.'

'That's correct, sir. But the latest drone models Russia has been using in Ukraine have comms-intercepting capabilities. Natural to assume they'd use a similar model here.'

'Don't we have the ability to knock the damn thing out of the sky?' asked the Prime Minister.

'Not presently, sir. Drone counter-measures haven't been installed at Coulport yet. We had planned for it as part of last year's upgrades, but with the recent budget cuts—'

'Yes, yes.' Perry-Jones cut Redpath off with a curt wave of his hand. 'No need to get on your soapbox, Major-General. Neither the time nor the place for political point-scoring.'

Redpath said coolly, 'I'm merely stating the facts as they are.'

Perry-Jones glowered at him but kept his lips pressed firmly shut.

Reade said, 'Do we have any idea how many men are on this strike team?'

'Not at this moment, no,' Redpath said.

'But if you had to guess . . . ?'

'An attack of this scale and planning would require a sizeable attacking force in order to stand a chance of success. Twelve men at the minimum, I would say. Very possibly more than that.'

'What about the guards at Coulport? I'm assuming there is some sort of garrison based there.'

Redpath said, 'In theory, one of the squadrons from 43 Commando, Fleet Protection Group, is in charge of site security at Coulport. But they're currently fifty miles away, training up a section of Ukrainian marines. There's only a single Troop left behind, and they're under-strength. Plus a handful of MoD guards. Though, of course, they're not armed.'

The Prime Minister rubbed his brow. 'How many guards are on-site at this very minute? Can you tell me that?'

'Eight, sir.'

'To protect our entire stock of nuclear warheads?' Neville fumed. 'That's disgraceful. Who the hell signed off on that?'

'The Defence Secretary, sir,' Redpath said.

Perry-Jones squirmed in his chair. The Prime Minister glared at him as Redpath went on, addressing himself to the Defence Minister.

'If you recall, minister, you specifically requested using 43 Commando for the training package. At the time I told you that depriving Coulport of the bulk of its guards was dangerous, but you insisted it would not be a problem, since the men would only be away from Faslane for two weeks. Now it's coming back to haunt us.'

'For fuck's sake, Crispin,' the Prime Minister ranted.

Varma looked long and hard at the Defence Secretary.

Thinking.

'Perhaps we could approach Putin directly,' Wilcox suggested. 'Tell him we know he's behind it and demand that he calls his men off.'

'It'll never work,' Varma said dismissively. 'Putin will stick to his guns. Claim he knows nothing about the strike team. Even if he did promise to stop them, it could be a stalling tactic. We can't trust him.'

'I'd also advise against any negotiations,' Redpath said. 'If we try to bargain with Putin we'll be showing him our hand. He'll realise that we've got wind of his plans. My team will have lost the element of surprise.'

'Are we *sure* Putin is behind the attack?' Norwood asked. 'Why would he offer to provide us with details of the plot if he was involved in planning it?'

'The same reason,' Varma said, 'that he used troops with unmarked uniforms to take Crimea. His little green men. Soldiers posing as pro-Russian separatists. The Bulgarians are doing his bidding. Putin is using them to strong-arm us into agreeing to a deal that will throw Ukraine to the wolves and leave European security in tatters. At the same time, he gets to humiliate us. He's having his cake and eating it.'

'Personally, I find it hard to believe,' Perry-Jones said, 'that Putin is prepared to trigger a global war simply to make a point.'

'He's wrong-footed us in the past. We didn't think he would take Crimea, but he did. We didn't believe he would invade Ukraine, right up until the moment his men crossed the border. We can't make the same mistake again.'

'What if the Bulgarians have sold your men a pack of lies, to divert our attention from the real attack?'

Redpath said, 'I personally know the two former soldiers who questioned the HVT. They say he's telling the truth, and I trust them.'

Perry-Jones pulled a face and said, mockingly, 'Well, my dear friend, I don't know how you do things in the army, but in Whitehall we don't rush blindly into things on the say-so of a couple of old squaddies.'

Redpath ignored the cheap taunt and said to the Prime Minister, 'We had a saying in the SAS, sir. Always trust the man on the ground. If Hawkins is right,' he added, 'and I believe he is, we have a chance to foil the enemy.'

'We're not talking about green-lighting an attack,' Neville put in. 'The men will organise a defensive perimeter, secure the nukes and conduct a hard arrest of the suspects. The risk of it going noisy is quite low, and one worth taking, in my opinion.'

The Prime Minister ran a hand through his grey-tinged hair. 'I've heard enough. The time for bargaining with our enemies is over. The team will continue to Coulport. If the Bulgarians attack, we'll stop them in their tracks,' he said, striving for Churchill but succeeding only in sounding more wooden than normal.

Perry-Jones opened his mouth to protest. The PM said, 'I'm sorry, Crispin, but my decision is final. There will be no negotiations with Putin, or any member of the Russian government.'

'I suggest, Prime Minister,' Varma said, 'that you continue to string along Putin. Let him know you're still drafting a statement but hope to release it soon. Keep him in the dark about our plan.'

'Good idea, Nish.'

'We'll need to alert the SP Team at Hereford, too,' Redpath said. 'Get them on their choppers and up to Coulport. Our men on the ground will need reinforcements.'

'Get it done.'

Varma stared at the Prime Minister, struggling to believe what he was seeing. The amiable party man, suddenly developing a backbone.

Maybe we're not completely fucked, he thought.

Across the room Perry-Jones sat flat-lipped, simmering with silent fury. He stood up, stretching to his full height, and started towards the door.

'Where the devil d'you think you're going?' the Prime Minister demanded.

'Outside,' Perry-Jones replied tetchily. 'To smoke my pipe. If you need me, you shall know where to find me.'

He stormed out of the room, wearing a face like thunder.

No one else had noticed it, but Varma was aware that something monumental had happened that evening in the briefing room. He had won a signal victory over the establishment. Power was shifting away from the old elite. The hedge-fund managers and spin doctors, the ranks of the political technocracy. The world belonged to the billionaire geniuses now. Varma's people had uncovered the plot against Coulport. The Prime Minister had taken his side against Perry-Jones. In the battle for influence in Downing Street, he had vanquished his deadliest opponent.

From now on, Varma would be calling the shots.

But his efforts would count for nothing if they couldn't stop the attack, Varma reminded himself. Everything now hinged on the eight SAS operators and the three DeepSpear employees racing north.

He prayed that they would beat the Bulgarians to Coulport.

20.04.

Fifty-six minutes to go.

Twenty-Seven

The Eurocopter thundered on through the black night.

In the confines of the cabin, Hawkins briefed the others on the situation at Coulport. The credible intelligence gleaned from the Bulgarian sleepers, pointing to a Russian-backed strike team targeting the warheads. The training exercise involving the lads from the Fleet Protection Group, leaving them light on numbers on the ground. Eight marines and a few unarmed MoD guards. The plan to defend the bunkers until the cavalry rocked up.

At his side Bald chewed furiously on a wad of gum and stared grimly out of the door at the black landscape below, scattered with pockets of light. Millar traded messages with Varma over the helicopter's military-grade satellite communications system. State-of-the-art kit that enabled frictionless video calls, email, text messages and file downloads. The rest of the lads sat or knelt on the cabin floor, alone with their thoughts.

Matt Lavery, the Brummie Team Leader from A Squadron, got off the open channel to Whitehall and said, 'Update from the DSF. We've got the all-clear to head to target. Set up the defensive perimeter and make hard arrests of the suspects. But we'll need to notify DSF if it's about to get noisy. Get him to sign off and take control of the situation.'

'What's our current ETA?' Hawkins asked the lead pilot.

'Forty-seven minutes out.'

Hawkins did a very quick calculation.

We'll get there with a few minutes to spare, he thought.

Enough time to land and set up a defensive shield around the bunkers.

Aside from Lavery, he recognised a couple of faces among the assault team. Munro and Vale were good lads. Solid operators who had done the business in Iraq and Afghanistan. The other guys he didn't know. They looked incredibly young. Mid-twenties, or thereabouts. Hawkins had reached the age where he could no longer tell. He reminded himself that he had once been in their boots. Fresh out of Selection, full of enthusiasm, believing he was the best fucking soldier in the world.

Christ, that had been a long time ago.

After thirty minutes the lead pilot gave a short update. They were making good speed. He reckoned they would hit Coulport five or six minutes before nine o'clock. In the cabin, Millar filled in Varma on their progress. DeepSpear's CEO was sending through a steady flow of information on Coulport. Everything the company had on file about the base. The same information the sleepers had nicked from Devonport and passed on to the strike team.

The operators passed the time checking their kit and familiarising themselves with the environment, each man taking turns to study up-to-date satellite imagery on a rugged-cased tablet.

Hawkins found himself looking at a wedge-shaped parcel of land occupying the eastern side of a peninsula, with Loch Long to the west and the nuclear docks at Faslane two miles east, on the far side of Gare Loch.

Coulport itself was a mile across at its widest point and two miles from north to south. A maze of roads, car parks and structures, enclosed on all sides by a two-metre-high perimeter fence topped with barbed wire. Main entrance to the south. An outer entrance protected by a guardhouse and concrete Jersey barriers, and an inner gate a hundred metres further west, leading to a sprawl of admin buildings, barracks and offices. Stop bollards on the road to the north of the marines' dossing-up block, preventing unauthorised vehicles driving up to the nuke storage area. Large covered jetty on the eastern shore of Loch Long, for the loading and unloading of warheads.

Eight hundred metres east of the shoreline Hawkins identified the sixteen nuclear bunkers arranged in a snaking line from north to south on the slope of a forested hillside. Pond to the north, security fence beyond it. A vast structure, six hundred metres long and about as wide, built on an area of raised ground on the hillside. Running deep underground, Hawkins guessed. Billions of pounds and years of work to excavate the slopes. Blastproof doors guarded the entrance to each bunker. An access road ran parallel to the doors.

Almost immediately Hawkins realised that they had a problem. They had no idea which direction the Bulgarians were planning to attack from – or which bunker they were targeting.

Hawkins ruled out an attack from the eastern side. Too far away. Too much ground to cover. The Bulgarians would have to walk a mile to target, across open ground, giving the defenders plenty of time to prepare a defensive position. Which left the northern and southern approaches.

Any force attacking from the north could advance to the site unseen, moving through the forested areas and dead ground on both sides of the fence. The shortest distance between the fence and the nukes. Six hundred metres at most. But it also had drawbacks. The broken ground would slow the attackers down, delaying their arrival on target. Meanwhile the guards to the south would be alerted to their presence and rush north, intercepting the Bulgarians before they could complete their mission.

If that was me, Hawkins thought, *I'd want to neutralise the defenders first.* Storm the main gate to the south, clear the place of guards and marines. Seize an engineer. Someone to open the blastproof doors. Jump into a couple of vehicles and tool north to the bunkers. A journey of two or three minutes at most. Plant the explosives. Then get out again as quickly as possible.

We'll have to hedge our bets.

Form a three-sixty defensive ring around the bunkers. Eyes on all the main approaches.

They would methodically cover the ground with overlapping arcs. Sniper and spotter circling overhead, searching for targets. Anyone not in camouflage clobber or the black uniform worn by the MoD guards.

'SP Team just departed from Hereford,' Lavery said, switching back from the channel connecting him to Redpath in the Cobra room. 'One hundred minutes out.'

Hawkins noted the time on his G-Shock. 20.11. Which meant the SP Team lads wouldn't get to Coulport until around 21.50.

Almost an hour after we're due on target.

He counted down the minutes to the assault. Lavery and Bald were looking at the imagery on the tablet, identifying landing spots amid the patches of dense forest and broken ground. They decided that the roads nearest to the bunkers were their best bet. The same roads used by the forty-four-ton trucks that transported the warheads to Berkshire for routine maintenance. Therefore wide enough to accommodate a Eurocopter, with a few metres to spare between rotor blades and the surrounding foliage.

Hawkins tried to put himself in the shoes of the attackers. The Bulgarian ex-SF team. A suicide mission in all but name. Twelve-man force at the minimum. Maybe more. Armed, he guessed, with assault rifles and secondary pistols supplied from the Albanian smuggling gang. AK-47s, probably. Something widely manufactured and relatively easy to get hold of at short notice. With GSh-18 semi-automatics or similar as their secondary weapons. Plus hand grenades, maybe an RPG or two to take out the vehicles. Explosive charges in their rucksacks.

They would have collected the weapons on their way north. The Albanians would have provided them with vehicles, too. Nothing fancy. A couple of windowless vans or similar. Burner phones pre-installed with Telegram for communicating with their handlers. Plus the signal-scrambling drone, two pairs of heavy-duty bolt cutters in case they needed to breach the exterior fence. They would have spent two or three days on the ground near Coulport. Probably a rental cottage somewhere close by, Helensburgh, or Greenock. Passing themselves off as tourists. But they wouldn't be doing any sightseeing.

A bunch of guys living on cheap takeaways, smoking cigarettes and drinking vodka. Studying the intelligence packet procured by the sleepers at Plymouth. Maps and blueprints. Up-to-date satellite photographs. Orientating themselves, looking at plans of attack, escape routes, locations of the nukes. Distances and times. Calculating how many miles they could put between themselves and the bunkers once they had rigged the timers. Unaware that they were going to be vaporised thirty seconds after planting the charges.

'Fifteen minutes to target,' the lead pilot said.

20.40.

We're going to make it, Hawkins realised.

Part of him couldn't believe what the Russians were doing. The annihilation of a country's nukes. A mad plan, on the face of it. But not so insane when you parsed the details.

In a few months the US would elect a new President. The hot favourite was opposed to NATO and the war in Ukraine. Without American backing, Kyiv would be heavily reliant on its European partners for weapons and money. But no country could shoulder the burden alone. German and French support for the war was already disintegrating. Blowing up the warheads would compel Britain to follow suit.

He wondered, too, about the Russian sleeper programme. How many assets they had in the country. If they had managed to penetrate DeepSpear, with its vetting processes and background checks, where else might they have emplaced people? They could have sleepers working at every major defence and technology company in Britain – in government departments – maybe even advising the Prime Minister.

Whatever happens tonight, thought Hawkins, *it doesn't end here. Not by a long shot.*

'Ten minutes to target,' Lavery said.

Hawkins felt a tingling of anticipation. Lavery and the rest of the lads checked equipment once more. Greyhound and Bear readied themselves for top cover duty once more. Millar checked in with Varma again, getting news from Whitehall. The Bulgarian sleepers had been taken into custody. *Santana Perez* was being towed back to port. Another armed unit had pounced on the Albanians as they unloaded the coke from the charter boat. Police had raided the car wash.

'Five minutes out,' Lavery said.

'Are you okay?' Hawkins asked Millar.

She gave a tight smile. 'Fine.'

'Listen to me. When we land,' Hawkins said, 'I need you to stay on the chopper with the sniper team.'

'Why?'

'Don't argue with me. Just do it.'

She gave him a curious look. For a moment Hawkins thought she might argue back, but the protest died on her lips, and she nodded, as if understanding his reasons. He wanted her to survive.

That was why he was dragging his broken body into combat. An old warrior climbing off the ropes in the twelfth round, battered and bloodied but still standing.

Hawkins didn't love his country. He couldn't give a good fuck about Britain, or Ukraine. They were just places on a map. They meant nothing to him. He was on this chopper, because of Zoe, and Millar. And Jacob.

He couldn't put right the wrongs of the past. But he could stop one more wrong from happening in the world.

Tonight, right now, he could stop the bastards from winning.

It had been several hours since Hawkins had last seen his brother's face. There had been glimpses, fleeting visions creeping in at the corners of his eyes, but nothing more. Now he saw Jacob again, in the gloom at the back of the cabin. Staring at him.

Jesus, not here. Not now.

We're about to drop into a potential firefight, surrounded by nuclear warheads, and I'm seeing my dead brother.

Hawkins closed his eyes and tried very hard to push the image away. Force it back into the shadows, the deepest recesses of his mind.

'Three minutes out,' Lavery said.

Hawkins hoped they could stop the enemy. He hoped the SP Team would reach them before it was too late. But most of all he prayed that whatever happened in the next hour, he wouldn't let his muckers down.

It's up to us now.

No one else.

'Two minutes out,' Lavery said.

They were screaming over the peninsula now. Closing in on the target.

'What the fuck is that?' Bald said.

Hawkins looked round at the Scot. He was kneeling beside Greyhound, looking outside, gesturing furiously out of the cabin side door. Hawkins edged forward, moving alongside Bear. Peered out of the open doorway, chasing Bald's pointing finger. He saw the camp at Coulport. A constellation of security lights, surrounded by the immense black mass of the peninsula. He saw the entrance road to the south of the site, the perimeter fence, the buildings clustered west of the main gate.

Then he saw the smoke.

Twenty-Eight

Hawkins looked at the scene below in mute shock and horror. A thick pall eddied into the night sky, merging with the infinite darkness. Not a small fire. But something much bigger. He couldn't pick out any details, not this far out, but the smoke seemed to be drifting up from the buildings situated behind the second gate, a hundred metres due west of the outer entrance and guardhouse.

Christ, no.
They've breached the inner defences.
We're too late.
The attack has begun.

Time became elastic in the helicopter. Seconds stretched out like minutes. Then the team snapped out of their collective stupor. Skills and drills kicking in, focusing minds. Lavery, the Birmingham native, ordered the pilot to hold off while he switched radio channels, reaching out to Redpath. Seeking clearance for an immediate action. Legal box-ticking. There needed to be a formal handover of the situation from the civil authorities to the SP Team before the assault could begin.

Bald turned away from the side door, thrust out a hand at Greyhound. The narrow-eyed sniper with the gaunt cheeks and the .50 cal rifle.

'Give us your sights,' he said.

Greyhound took one look at the mean-faced Scot, decided against arguing with Bald and handed over his weapon. A wise decision. Pissing off Bald should come with a health warning. The silver-haired Scot positioned himself in front of the open doorway, dropped flat on his front, pressed his right eye against the optics.

'What can you see, Jock?' Hawkins asked.

'Bodies,' Bald said. 'Loads of them. All over the fucking place.'

He provided a running commentary while he arced the .50 cal from left to right, zeroing in on the swirling grey plume.

'Two in black uniform outside the guardhouse. Can't be sure but they look dead. Seven in camo gear outside the barracks. Same deal. Two vehicles next to the entrance. Smoke coming out of the engines.'

Hawkins thought, *Black uniform and camo gear. Our guys. Marines and MoD guards.*

'Any X-rays among them? Any bodies in civvies?'

'Just the one.' Bald paused. 'Shit. They've lowered the stop bollards north-east of the barracks.'

'The bollards?' Millar repeated, voice cracking with anxiety. 'But that means—'

'Aye,' Hawkins said.

His heartbeat quickened. The stop bollards were the last defensive obstacle separating an attack team from the bunkers. With the concrete posts down, there was nothing to stop the Bulgarians from racing on to the bunker entrances two miles to the north.

'Where the fuck are the gunmen?' Hawkins snapped impatiently. Heart thumping madly in his chest.

Bald canted the 50. cal upwards. Still looking through the optics as he focused on the approach road leading two miles up to the underground bunkers and the explosive handling jetty.

'Vehicles heading north,' he said. 'I can see 'em now. Two Transit vans. One mile from the bunkers.'

Bald tore his gaze away from the .50 cal's sights. Looked round at Lavery. 'They're nearly on the fucking bunkers. We've got to stop them. Got to go now.'

'Can't do it, mate. Still waiting for clearance,' came the response from the Team Leader.

Bald stared daggers at him. Vein on his forehead bulging like a kinked hosepipe. Hawkins understood his mucker's rage. Brother soldiers had just been slaughtered. The bad guys were on the cusp of winning a stunning victory, and Lavery was arguing they should hang back until they had ministerial sign-off.

Bald handed the rifle back to Greyhound and said, 'No fucking time for that. It's happening now. We can't wait.'

Lavery stared at Bald. Made a split-second decision. He said to the pilots, 'Get us on to the vans, fellas. Vehicle interdiction. You know the drill.'

The chopper dipped, swooping down on the road. Rapidly gaining on the two vans making for the bunker entrances a mile to the north.

'Going dark,' Lavery ordered the rest of the team. 'No comms on the open channel from now on, lads. Chat only among ourselves.'

Everyone knew why Lavery had given the order. Conversations on the open net were recorded as a matter of routine. Anything they said on that frequency could be used against them later on. There was a world of difference between what justified violence looked like to the guy on the ground and a lawyer sitting in an air-conditioned office. Better to stick to their own channel during the fighting.

'Turn that fucking thing off!' Bald yelled at Millar. Indicating her phone. She ended the call to Varma and put her phone away. The chopper roared past the smoke-wreathed barracks block and continued north.

'One minute to target,' the lead pilot said.

Greyhound said, 'Get us in front of the bastards. We'll knock out the engines.'

He was working the .50 cal, prone-positioned, the gun secured in place with the webbing strops. Bear at his left shoulder, directing the pilot. Hawkins next to the spotter, giving him a clear view of the ground below.

Once they had pushed ahead of the vans the pilot would bring them round, putting them side-on with the enemy. Then Greyhound would stick a couple of rounds into the engine blocks. Two .50 cal bullets would have enough stopping power to knock out all the main components. Quickest way of disabling the vehicles.

As they pulled nearer to the enemy Hawkins caught a fleeting glimpse of the aftermath of their attack on the entrance. Corpses and burnt-out vehicles. The carnage told the story of the firefight. First the strike team had engaged the security guards at the front gate, dropping bodies in that area, before advancing to the area where the marines were basha'd up. Those guys would been drilled with lead the moment they had charged out of their doss-house. The attackers would have located the controls for the concrete bollards, lowering them before diving back into their vehicles and motoring on to the main target.

These guys are pros.

Ex-military, Vitanov had said. *Special Forces. Guys with criminal records.*

Veterans of the old 68th Special Forces Brigade, Hawkins figured. Or its successor, the Joint Special Operations Command. Capable soldiers. Not the worst SF unit in Europe. But not the best either. Effective in a firefight against a bunch of green army soldiers or marines. But they wouldn't stand a chance against the elite warriors of 22 SAS.

The Eurocopter had almost drawn alongside the rear Transit van, coming up on the target's left side. Hawkins felt the cabin roll slightly. Some of the other lads were steadying themselves, gripping hold of floor straps or bracing their feet against the sides of the cabin. Hawkins knelt beside the spotter, looking past his shoulder at the scene below. The two vans accelerated down the approach road towards the bunkers, moving a fast clip, chewing up the tarmac, headlights blazing in the blackness. A distance of fifty metres between chopper and vehicle now.

Bear continued relaying information over the closed channel. Greyhound stayed perfectly still, waiting for the moment to strike. The pilots were flying as low as they dared, no more than two or three metres above the thick forest either side of the road. A kilometre to the north-west, the hillside tumbled away to the oily blackness of Loch Long.

The vans came to a T-road and swung to the right. Making their final approach to the bunkers. 'Two hundred metres to the target.'

'There's no time left to get ahead,' Bald shouted. 'Take those fuckers out now. Aim for the rear tyres.'

The Blue Thunder had moved alongside the lead wagon when the vehicle's side door jerked open. Both vans instantly dropped their speed. A gunman knelt inside the van. Clutching a rifle in a two-handed grip.

There was a tongue of flame, the staccato burst of an assault rifle.

Rounds struck the fuselage, forward of the side door. Three of them.

Greyhound lined up the van, plugged it with a single .50 cal round. Spent brass chugged out of the ejector, dinked against the cabin floor. The van juddered and skidded as the driver lost control, tyres squealing before it came to a standstill. The driver in the second van had to swerve sharply to avoid rear-ending the lead Transit, veered off the road at an angle, mounted the grass verge and slammed into a concrete shed.

'X-rays debussing!' Bear exclaimed.

Hawkins saw them too. Figures in cargoes, trainers and flannel shirts poured out of both vans, regrouping on the road next to the lead Transit. All of them wielding AK-47 assault rifles.

The alarm on the second wagon wailed its distress, bleeps and squawks faintly audible above the thumping noise of the chopper.

Muzzles flashed as a trio of figures took potshots at the helicopter. Greyhound plugged one of the gunmen, the velocity of the round tearing the X-ray clean in half. Three more rounds slapped against the chopper in a furious metallic din. The cabin abruptly lurched as the pilots pulled away from the shooters, retreating to a safe distance before they levelled out again.

'Bring us closer, for fuck's sake!' Bald roared.

'Can't do it. Incoming,' the lead pilot said. 'We need to pull back before they bring us down.'

Bald couldn't argue. The pilots had lost one bird today. They weren't going to lose another. The Eurocopter rolled away from the road and made a wide clockwise loop, the pilots keeping two hundred metres from the figures on the ground.

'X-rays on the move,' Bear said. 'Heading for the nearest bunker north-east. One hundred metres.'

Out of the side door, Hawkins saw the figures jogging up the road towards the long snaking line of bunkers strung out from north to south. Access road running alongside it. Woodland to the west, bordered by a long drainage ditch. A hundred metres ahead of Hawkins a tarmacked loading bay led to the blastproof door guarding the entrance to the nearest bunker. Located at the tail end of the snake. The closest one to the Bulgarian strike team. Therefore the most likely target.

There was a six-metre-long ISO container at the side of the loading bay. Stack of wooden pallets forty metres further south. Fifteen metres north of the loading bay, a concrete ventilation shaft rose up like a periscope. A forty-four-ton army lorry, unmarked, had been parked on the roadside directly opposite the vent shaft. Shoebox lights and wall-mounted floodlights outside the bays lit up the surrounding area.

The Bulgarians are a minute away from that bunker.

'How many X-rays are we dealing with?' asked Lavery.

'Eleven,' Bear counted aloud, following them through the binos. 'Eleven X-rays. Plus one unarmed guy in civvies.'

Bald faced the cockpit, facial muscles twitching with rage. 'They've got one of the engineers. They're gonna use him to open the doors. Get us on the ground. Fucking hurry!'

The sniper picked off another X-ray as the pilots descended towards the road, five or six metres from the abandoned Transit vans. Two of the gunmen saw the guy in front of them collapse in a heap and returned fire at the approaching heli, poorly aimed bursts that missed their target. The Bulgarians turned and ran on after their mates, dashing towards the bunkers. All their energies focused on the grand prize ahead of them. With the engineer they had taken hostage, they wouldn't need to waste valuable time breaking the entry system. They would be through those doors in a matter of minutes.

They were all feeling it in the cabin. The fear. Each man dealing with it in his own private way. The magnitude of what they were about to do. The appalling risk they were taking. They were no longer going in to make a hard arrest. It was now a kill mission. If the Bulgarians succeeded in rigging up one of the nukes, that would be the end of everything. No way they could get away from the bunker in time.

We'll be incinerated.

'Stay behind me, fellas,' Lavery said to Bald and Hawkins. 'Leave the fighting to us.'

'No worries, son,' Bald said. 'We'll be right behind you.'

Giving Hawkins a look. Both thinking the same thing.

No fucking way.

We're not gonna sit out the main event.

A fate almost as bad as death, for a veteran warrior. Like staying on the substitutes' bench during the cup final.

As Hawkins looked on a pair of black-clad guards rushed out of a guard post opposite the bunkers. The last line of defence. But not an effective one. They caught sight of the approaching enemy, turned and ran for their lives. They had made it no more than two or three metres when a series of rifle cracks split the air. The guards flopped to the tarmac, like a couple of push puppets going slack.

The helicopter touched down in the middle of the road. Bald and Hawkins ripped off their wired headsets and sprinted out of the cabin, Lavery and Munro following hard on their heels, yelling at the older men to slow down. That was what Hawkins assumed they were shouting, anyway. He couldn't hear a thing over the blast of the turbine engines, the blades slicing through the air.

He seized the AK-47 from one of the dead gunmen beside the Transit van, jerked the selector lever on the right side of the receiver down to the semi-automatic setting. Going into a pissing contest with a bunch of Bulgarian ex-SF armed with only a nine-milli peashooter was asking for trouble. Ahead of him Bald must have reached the same conclusion, because he bent down to grab the AK from the other slotted Bulgarian.

The two old warriors raced on towards the nearest available cover at the stack of pallets south of the loading bay. Lungs burning, hearts pounding. They joined Lavery and Munro behind the wooden structures as the two Blades started engaging the targets fifty metres to the north, alternately firing their suppressed Colt C8s in controlled two- and three-round bursts, Bald loosing off aimed single shots with his assault rifle.

The Bulgarians dispersed, scurrying behind cover as bullets slapped into the ground behind them. The two guys at the rear of the group ducked behind the ISO container at the side of the road closest to the loading bay. Two gunmen scrambled behind the vent shaft fifteen metres further north. Three more broke left, threw themselves behind the forty-four-ton lorry. Hawkins heard Lavery uttering orders into his mic, telling the other guys on the team which targets to take.

The last three gunmen tacked right at the loading bay, going hell-for-leather towards the nearest bunker. One of them shoved the unarmed civilian ahead of him. The engineer. The guy stumbled and fell; the nearest Bulgarian yanked the man to his feet and hurried on towards the doors while the other two gunmen put suppressive fire down on the pallets, forcing Bald, Hawkins and the others to drop down behind cover.

Hawkins glanced past his shoulder. Making sure Millar had obeyed him and stayed on the helicopter. The Blue Thunder was lifting off the ground, the tips of the blades narrowly missing the tree-tops on either side. Greyhound and Bear would support the assaulters from above, taking out opportune targets among the Bulgarians. To the west, five metres away from Hawkins, the other four men on the assault team had dived behind the treeline bordering the road. They were already engaging targets, the dull thump of their suppressed rounds interrupted by the crackle of the AK-47s coming from the Bulgarians.

The throated bark of an assault rifle echoed across the road. Four rounds thwacked into the pallets an inch or two above Hawkins, throwing up a shower of splinters. There was a momentary lull in the suppressive fire, no more than a second or two. But it told Hawkins they were up against inferior opposition. A good SF team would coordinate their attack, one guy firing while the other watched his colleague. As soon as the first man had stopped firing, or reached the end of his clip, the second guy would take his place, firing at targets. A seamless transition.

Hawkins sprang up, screaming at Bald, the pair of them working in tandem. Pepper-potting forward. Bald putting down controlled rounds while Hawkins rushed three metres forwards, dropping to a prone position in a slight hollow in the ground. In the same movement he pointed the AK-47 at the two X-rays behind the ISO container and pulled the trigger, putting down four rounds of suppressive fire while Bald rushed forward and dropped down beside him in the scrape. Every Regiment operator was schooled in the importance of maintaining forward momentum in a firefight. The golden rule of any contact with the enemy. Don't stop for anything. Keep the momentum going at all costs.

Keep advancing.

Hawkins and Bald pepper-potted forward again. Making for a transformer box the size of a Mini Cooper, ten metres ahead of the pallet stack. Thirty metres from the ISO container. Hawkins fired another round, sprang to his feet and dived behind the transformer, catching up with Bald. Lavery and Munro were a couple of paces further behind, moving in a well-drilled formation as they darted forwards.

Nine rounds expended.

Which left him with eleven rounds in the mag. Theoretically. But he had no idea how many bullets the previous owner had fired. So a maximum of eleven and a minimum of none. Plus whatever else he could forage from the corpses of the other Bulgarians, once they had been taken out of the fight.

He scanned the ground while Lavery and Munro caught up with him. Making a nanosecond assessment of the battlefield. Part of what separated Blades from the average soldier. The ability to process and make sense of the chaos going on around them. Above Hawkins, sparks were zinging off the Eurocopter's cockpit as it took a sustained burst of gunfire from the three Bulgarians crouching behind the lorry. The chopper pulled back, spinning out of control, flipped onto its side and crash-landed four hundred metres away. There was a deafening tumult as the blades shattered on impact with the ground, throwing up clods of earth, rotor fragments and debris.

No time to worry about them, the voice told him.

The mission.

That's all that matters now.

Lavery shouted over the net. Hawkins couldn't hear him – he had been forced to leave his wired headset on the heli – but he must have been issuing more instructions to his mates, because Hawkins saw the four SP Team assaulters along the treeline splitting into two groups. Two of the soldiers broke left, pushing towards the drainage ditch thirty metres away. From there they could creep forward unseen on a parallel route to the road, outflanking the two X-rays safely tucked up behind the lorry, and the two other Bulgarians in cover at the ventilator shaft.

The second pair of Blades advanced towards a slight deviation in the terrain several paces ahead. They were making good ground, surging ahead of the other soldiers with impressive speed.

Hawkins was still watching them when a grenade exploded. He felt the ground tremble beneath him. Saw the hot cloud of shrapnel and dirt ripping holes in one of the soldiers, engulfing the poor bastard. The other guy hurried on, running for all he was worth before he was clipped by a couple of three-round bursts from the two Bulgarians at the vent shaft.

Lavery and Munro rushed out from behind cover, alternating between advancing and dropping flat on the ground, putting down suppressive fire on the X-rays at the shipping container. Bald and Hawkins moved simultaneously forward from the other side of the transporter box.

Lavery nailed one of the Bulgarians as he popped out from the side of the ISO container, drilling him through the head with two rounds of 5.56. Frontal lobotomy, Regiment-style. The second gunman turned and ran towards the vent shaft. Hawkins fired twice at his central mass, stitching him in the lower back. The fucker dropped hard, belly-slapping the tarmac.

Two X-rays down.

Eight to go.

Lavery and Munro pushed forward once more, the ground erupting around them as the X-rays behind the vent shaft and the lorry opened fire. They weren't bothering to aim properly, just pissing bullets in the general direction of the assaulters. Hoping to put the brakes on their advance. Hawkins broke forward, covered by Bald, and in four more strides they had reached the safety of the shipping container, shrinking behind the corrugated steel panels.

He stole another glance over his shoulder. Looked downwind at the crashed Eurocopter, four hundred metres to the south. To his relief, Millar was staggering out of the crumpled fuselage. Bear and Greyhound were kneeling beside the bullet-riddled cockpit, dragging out the two pilots. One of them was bleeding heavily from the leg. The other looked dazed. No fatalities.

But we've lost our top cover.

In the four-dimensional chess game Hawkins was playing in his head, the chances of a Bulgarian victory increased slightly.

Lavery emptied his clip, released the mag and inserted a fresh one. He was shouting into his mic, ordering the pilots and the sniper team to hang back and take care of their casualties, pending the arrival of the SP Team from Hereford. He stopped firing again while Munro unleashed a short burst of 5.56 brass at the targets to the north. The two X-rays at the vent tower, the three guys shielded behind the wheelbase at the rear of the army lorry.

Bald bellowed at Hawkins. Calling his attention to their two o'clock. Hawkins edged round the side of the container and looked. He saw the bunker doors thirty metres away. The engineer and the three gunmen accompanying him were grouped tightly in front of the keypad next to the blastproof door. A huge steel thing the size of an aircraft hangar. Five metres high and eight across, mounted on an automated sliding trolley.

One of the Bulgarians had his weapon pointed at the engineer's neck. A thickset bloke in bright blue puffer jacket and white sneakers. Another guy was dressed in a denim jacket and a yellow beanie. The third guy carried an olive-green rucksack on his back.

It looked bulky, Hawkins noted. Packed tightly with something. Such as an explosive charge or three.

They're almost inside.

Bald took a step to the right, moving out from behind the shipping container, brought up his AK. A distance of thirty metres. Aimed and gave the trigger a squeeze. Got the dead man's click.

Empty. Out of ammo.

He'd swiped a weapon with less than a full clip. Much less. Which left him with the Glock as his backup tool. An excellent firearm, in its own right. But it lacked the stopping power of the larger calibre assault rifle.

'I'm out,' Bald shouted. 'Shoot the engineer, Geordie.'

'Ain't doing it.'

'Take that fucker out!' Bald raged.

Which made sense, from a coldly logical point of view. The engineer was the key to the whole operation. If the Bulgarians managed to overrun their opponents, they would still be in a position to gain access to the warheads and wreak havoc. Kill the engineer, and even if the men of Hereford lost the battle, they would still have prevented the enemy from blowing up the nukes.

But Hawkins wasn't thinking practically. He looked at it from a moral perspective. The engineer was a civilian. He had done nothing wrong, except to be in a bad place at a bad fucking time. Stupid to agree to open the door for the Bulgarians. But understandable, when someone was pointing a gun at the back of your head. And not enough to warrant his murder, in Hawkins's mind. Not even close.

'No!' he snapped. 'I'm not killing him!'

Across the loading bay, the mechanised trolley whirred into action.

The steel door began sliding back on its frame.

Hawkins's heart was hammering furiously. Another inch or two and the Bulgarians would be free to slip inside the bunker. Bald senselessly loosed off a trio of nine-milli shots at the Bulgarians, more out of personal frustration than any realistic attempt to stop them. The rounds winged harmlessly over the Bulgarians and ricocheted off the steel doors. A moment later the Bulgarians had slipped through the entrance.

Bald turned away from the door and looked past Hawkins, screaming at Lavery at the top of his lungs in a desperate attempt to make himself heard above the incessant rattle of AK fire, the boom of a detonating grenade, the muffled reports of the C8s. The demented cries of wounded and dying men. *Theirs, not ours.* Hawkins hoped.

'Cover us!' Bald boomed. 'We're heading to the doors! They're inside!'

Lavery got the message. Either he'd heard Bald above the million other noises, or he'd read the look of panic stamped on his face, because he shouted hoarsely into his mic.

'Suppressive fire! Suppressive fire!'

Hawkins didn't know if the other two assaulters were still alive. The ones in the drainage ditch west of the road, manoeuvring round to the Bulgarians' right flank. He hoped to fuck they were still in the game.

Lavery and Munro edged out from behind the left side of the container, kneeling and taking aimed shots at the shaft and lorry further north on the access road.

That was the cue for Hawkins and Bald to rush forward from the other side of the structure. They charged across the loading bay, running as fast as their legs could carry them. Thirty metres from container to door, across a stretch of exposed ground. Thirty metres, but it felt more like a fucking mile. Rounds winged past them, slapped the tarmac inches from their feet as the Bulgarians poured down fire on them.

Hawkins and Bald kept running. Bullets cut through the air, no more than an inch or two above Hawkins. The Bulgarians were still taking potshots, despite the suppressive fire pouring down on their positions from Lavery and the others. Hawkins could hear the zip of the shots whizzing past him, hailstoning the tarmac. Like running through a swarm of bees.

Twenty metres to the door now.
Fifteen metres.
Ten.

Five.

Bald reached the bunker entrance first and charged through the opening. There was time for the Bulgarians to loose off another torrent of gunfire at Hawkins. Bullets skipped off the steel door-frame in a firework-display of sparks. He ran on, breathing hard, heart drumming furiously against the wall of his chest. Urging his broken body to move faster.

We're not going to lose.

Not today.

Hawkins took two more desperate strides.

Then he plunged inside.

Twenty-Nine

Hawkins swept into the mouth of the bunker four steps behind Bald. The lifeless body of the engineer lay sprawled on the floor just inside the doorway. Blood pumped steadily out of a hole in the back of the guy's head. Hawkins swerved the corpse and pushed on.

He took in the scene hyper-fast. All his synapses were firing, mind and body working in perfect harmony, adrenaline going into overdrive. Slowing down time in his head. Like watching a VAR replay. Heightened sensory perception. The bunker entrance led into a concrete-lined tunnel. Wide and tall enough to accommodate a truck. Bored into the hillside decades ago. An impressive feat of engineering.

Chain of fluorescent lamps fixed to the ceiling. Wooden crates along the left side of the tunnel, four metres ahead of Hawkins. Stack of steel pipes six metres further along. Industrial air-con generator four metres beyond that. A huge thing, about the size of a backhoe cab. Mounted on a raised concrete base, with metal pipes running vertically from the unit to the tunnel ceiling.

They were taking incoming from the Bulgarians. Yellow Beanie, Rucksack and Puffer were spewing bullets at the tunnel entrance. Two wild bursts. Hawkins ducked low and hastened on.

Up ahead, Bald had dropped to a knee beside the crates. Glock drawn. Putting rounds down on the three Bulgarians twelve metres ahead of him. Giving Hawkins time to race for cover. Bald's pistol flamed beneath the harsh glare of the tube lights. Bullets spat out of the muzzle, struck the tunnel wall. Yellow Beanie and Puffer dived behind the air-con tower. Survival mode.

Rucksack ran on down the tunnel.

Hawkins scrambled over to the crates next to Bald, reaching cover a moment before Puffer and Yellow Beanie returned fire. Four bullets bounced off the ground in quick succession. Another two rounds gouged out chunks of the wall above Hawkins and Bald, sprinkling mortar dust over them. Hawkins stayed low and tried not to think about the consequences of a stray round impacting a nuke in a confined environment.

In the distance, from outside the bunker, Hawkins heard the dull thump of suppressed rounds from the Colt C8s as Lavery and the other young thrusters gave the other Bulgarians the good news. None of the SP Team lads had made an attempt to hurry into the tunnel after Bald and Hawkins. They were fully concentrated on dealing with the remaining gunmen outside. The four Reg lads had just seen two of their mates get cut down. Lavery and his mates would be like animals with a bloodlust. Once the two operators in the drainage ditch surprised the X-rays from their flank it was going to be over very quickly.

Assuming those guys are still alive.

Hawkins put the struggle outside in a box at the back of his head. Closed the lid. Forgot about it. Nothing he or Bald could do to change the outcome of that fight.

He focused every fibre of his being on the threat ahead of him.

The attackers had been thwarted. Everything now hinged on stopping the enemies inside the bunker.

The Bulgarians wouldn't surrender, he knew. Even though the attack had gone badly wrong, they still had a chance to succeed. They weren't going to get out of this situation alive. The mission had become a suicide job. Their only hope was to trigger the bombs. Carry out the task set for them by their Russian masters. Save their families. Earn themselves everlasting glory in the motherland.

Hawkins thought back to the blueprints he'd studied in the chopper. The warheads were stored in crates a little way deeper into the tunnel, inside an inner cage. He wasn't sure of the distance. Or how easy it was to prise open the crates housing the warheads. He knew only that they couldn't lose their momentum.

Keep going.

Don't stop.

Not now.

Hawkins popped up from behind cover, lined up the assault rifle barrel with the air-con unit eight metres downwind of his position. Taking over suppressive fire duties. He depressed the trigger three times. Shouting at Bald to move forward while he took single shots at the Bulgarian firing from the right-hand corner of the floor-mounted tower. The lanky streak of piss with the yellow beanie hat.

Hawkins's aim was rusty. A long time since he'd done a good session on the ranges. One round struck the floor a few inches short of the target. The next two bullets flew wide of the target, hitting the cage enclosing the generator unit in a piercing metallic din. Missing Yellow Beanie. But also forcing him to take cover.

Hawkins went to fire again. Pulled the trigger.

Got the hollow click.

Stoppage.

Empty mag.

Bald ran on.

He was three metres ahead of Hawkins now. Three metres from the pipe stack when Yellow Beanie popped out of cover again. Ready to put the drop on Jock Bald.

Bald took evasive action. Pointed the Glock at Yellow Beanie, shaping to engage the target before the other guy could squeeze off a shot.

Hawkins became aware of a sudden movement in the corner of his eye. A metallic-blue blur four metres away. He glanced across the tunnel. Looking towards the left-hand side of the air-con unit.

Then he saw it.

Puffer had sprung out from behind the other side of the tower. Sweeping round to attack Bald from the latter's nine o'clock. A classic flanking manoeuvre. The oldest military strategy in the book. But also one of the most effective.

Time froze.

Bald hadn't yet noticed the new threat on his left flank. He was busy drilling holes in the guy in the yellow beanie. Pistol lighting up, the Bulgarian spasming as if someone had just bumped him with a cattle prod. All of which meant Puffer had the advantage of surprise. The guy held his rifle in a two-handed grip, stock flush with his right shoulder, left hand clasping the wooden handguard on the underside of the receiver. Right forefinger on the trigger.

Black eye of the barrel trained on Bald.

Hawkins had an instant to react.

There was no time to toss aside his rifle and reach for his Glock. The Bulgarian would have slotted Bald long before he could line up the target and shoot.

Only one thing to do.

Hawkins ran out from behind the crates. Threw himself at Bald a fraction of a second before Puffer tugged on the trigger, rugby-tackling Bald to the ground. A gunshot echoed through the tunnel. Hot pain exploded in Hawkins's left shoulder. As if someone had skewered him with a spear-tip. Unbearable. His legs buckled. His head hit the floor with a bone-jarring crunch.

The next thing Hawkins knew he was lying on his side. Bald had retrieved his weapon and rolled onto his front, pointing his Glock upwards at the Bulgarian. Who had arced his AK-47 towards Bald. Both weapons flamed simultaneously. Puffer staggered backwards, blood jetting out of the back of his head. He landed in a heap next to the metal cage.

With a great effort Hawkins climbed to his feet.

He realised, dimly, that he'd taken a round to the left shoulder. The wound hurt like fuck. Blood was seeping through his flannel shirt, flowing freely down his front. His left arm dangled uselessly at his side. The pain was intense. Throbbing. The slightest movement felt as if someone was twisting a bayonet in his rotator cuff, cutting up muscle and tendon.

He looked round. Puffer lay slumped on the floor. The life had gone out of his eyes. The mouth sagged open. Several paces away, Bald was flat on his back, clutching his chest.

Blood pissing out of the gaps between his fingers.

'Fuck,' Hawkins croaked. 'Jock.'

Bald coughed up a mouthful of blood. He had been shot in the chest. One look told Hawkins the wound was serious. Punctured lung, maybe. He needed urgent medical attention.

'The bomb,' Bald managed, weakly. 'The other one. He's got – the rucksack. Get him.'

Hawkins didn't argue. Knew Jock was right.

He left Bald writhing on the floor.

Struggled on down the tunnel.

Hawkins thought he might puke at any moment. His mouth was sandpaper-dry. Spots blotted his vision. Blood continued pumping out of his shoulder wound. He wasn't sure, but he thought the bullet had grazed his clavicle.

He limped on.

A strange calmness had swept over him. What he could only describe as a feeling of complete peace. He no longer cared whether he lived or died. The world would carry on regardless. All that you left behind, when you put aside your bodily vessel and the things you owned, were your actions. The decisions you had made. The things you had done with your life. The things you had not.

For reasons he couldn't understand, he found himself remembering something he'd once been told by a grizzled veteran in Hereford. A guy in his eighties who had once fought alongside Lieutenant Colonel Paddy Mayne. One of the founding fathers of the original SAS in the Second World War.

The old-timer had told Hawkins about a conversation he'd once had with Mayne in a bar in Egypt. Mayne had said something that had stuck in the old soldier's mind ever since.

'If we can accept that we're already dead, no one can kill us.'

Those words kept playing on a loop in his head as Hawkins forced himself on. One foot in front of the next.

One pace, then another.

Please, God.

Let me do this one last thing.

Twenty metres of teeth-grinding agony brought him to the steel cage. The inner line of defence. Thick steel bars, like a prison cell. Hawkins saw that the cage door had been wrenched open. Rucksack must have lifted the keys from the slotted engineer.

Hawkins swallowed the pain he was feeling and shuffled inside the cage.

Dozens of coffin-sized military crates had been stacked up on one side of the room. Some containing warheads. Others housing regular missiles or other types of bombs. The Bulgarian had smashed open the locks and removed the lid from one of the crates. Inside was a cone-shaped warhead, held securely in place by a set of steel rings.

The Bulgarian was kneeling beside it, like a sinner praying for forgiveness. His AK-47 propped against the wall. Rucksack at his feet.

Hawkins raised his gun.

'Stop.'

The Bulgarian stopped fiddling with the warhead.

'Turn around,' Hawkins said.

The Bulgarian slowly turned.

'Hands in the air.'

The Bulgarian held up his hands.

Hawkins shot him in the head.

He staggered over to the cone. There was a shaped charge emplaced on the side of the warhead. A big block of a Russianderivative of C4. Military-grade high explosive. Not powerful enough to trigger a nuclear detonation – the warheads were designed with multiple safety features to guard against such a possibility. But sufficient to destroy all the ordnance in that bunker. The resulting explosion would wipe out the vast majority of warheads stored at Coulport, leaving only the ones currently aboard whichever Vanguard-class sub was currently on patrol.

National humiliation.

The timer counted down.

00.28

The bombs are rigged.

Not twenty-eight minutes.

Twenty-eight seconds.

Hawkins stuffed his Glock down the back of his trousers, picked up the brick-sized slab of HE and the rucksack. He hurried out of the cage, pushing on through the pain in his body. Cradling the explosive and the bag under his good right arm. Moving urgently down the tunnel. Towards the entrance forty metres away.

One last effort. *One last thing to do.*

Outside the bunker the firing had ceased. There was a pause of silence. A voice screamed. Then a couple of short, sharp shots. Hawkins knew what those sounds meant. They were the sounds of victory. The Regiment lads, double-tapping wounded X-rays. They wouldn't be taking any prisoners today.

Twenty metres to go.

Fourteen seconds.

He stumbled past Bald, ignoring his cries for help.

Ten metres.

Figures were rushing over to the bunker from the direction of the loading bay. Four of them. Lavery was there, and Munro and Vale, and the fourth operator whose name Hawkins couldn't remember. Lavery was shouting at him, telling him that it was all over, that they had won, the X-rays were down. They were like four guys celebrating a dramatic winner in injury time.

'Out of my fucking way,' Hawkins snapped. 'This thing is about to go off.'

He barged past Lavery, swung south.

Seven seconds. Six . . .

Hawkins lobbed the charge over the ISO container with two seconds to spare. The slab arced through the air, landing on the far side of the steel structure, Hawkins bellowing at the guys behind him to get down. He threw himself to the deck.

The charge detonated. The ground quaked.

The blast wave swept over Hawkins. Debris, hot earth and stones rained down on him. Clattering against the tarmac. He became aware of a painful ringing in his ears, a hard thumping in his skull. The distant screech of alarms. Smoke clogged his nostrils, choked his lungs.

The air cleared. The blackness disintegrated. Hawkins tried to pick himself up. Found he was too weak to move. Exhaustion. The shock of the explosion. The loss of blood from his shoulder wound. All of the above, draining his battery. He was in the red zone.

He managed to turn his head towards the bunker. Lavery sprinted forward, calling out to him. He dropped to a knee, helped Hawkins sit upright. Fired questions at him. Hawkins didn't understand a word. Every other noise had been smothered by the piercing sound in his ears. As if he was underwater. Drowning, but dimly conscious of noises above the surface.

Here was Munro, applying a tourniquet and dressing to his shoulder to staunch the bleeding while Lavery stood close by, screaming into his mic.

The ringing faded. Hawkins could hear occasional sounds again now. Breaking the surface. Lavery was ordering someone to send over an air ambulance.

'Men down,' he said. 'Get that fucking thing here.'

Hawkins tried to tell them about Bald. The chest wound. They needed to deal with Bald first. Hawkins felt very strongly about that. But he couldn't get the words out of his parched mouth.

Water. He needed water. Had never been so thirsty in his entire life.

He looked back at the bunker entrance. Vale and the fourth operator were helping Bald outside. They had patched him up. First priority. Stem the bleeding. Get the patient medevacked. What they called the Golden Hour. A battlefield casualty's chances of survival were much better if they were treated within that window.

They set Bald down beside him.

'We've called an air ambulance,' Lavery said. 'On its way up from the base at Faslane as we speak. Ten minutes out. Hang in there, fellas.'

'What fucking choice have we got?' Bald croaked.

Hawkins chuckled. Felt like he was swallowing broken glass.

God, he would have given anything for a glass of water.

Munro stared at them, puffed his cheeks. 'Fucking hell. Not bad for a couple of old knackers.'

'I'm not that old, you cheeky bastard,' Bald said, hand resting on his chest bandage. 'But I do need a bloody drink.'

Munro threw back his head and laughed.

He walked off. Vale and the fourth SAS guy were dragging over the bodies of the dead Bulgarians. Dumping them like hunks of meat beside the loading bay. The cover-up was already beginning. Soon enough the SP Team would arrive to help secure the area. Then the clean-up could move up a gear. Enemy corpses would be dumped in the nearby loch or buried beneath the hillside. Somewhere no one would ever find them.

The families of the murdered guards and marines would be fed a bunch of lies. The protestors at the local Peace Camp would be questioned, their cameras, phones and laptops seized. Whitehall would want to bury the attack. Make sure it stayed that way. Even the rumour of an assault on Coulport could be hugely damaging.

Hawkins found himself alone with Bald.

'Jock, we need to – to tell Varma,' he said.

'There's a – a mole,' he went on. 'Someone tipped off the Bulgarians tonight. Someone at the Cobra meeting. They knew we were inbound. They knew.'

'Later. Tell him tomorrow. Fuck all we can do about it now.'

'But they've got a Russian agent in the government.'

Bald said, 'They won't want to know. Too damaging. Whoever it is, they'll fucking deny it. World's changed, Geordie. Can't you see? Them bastards in power, they get away with all kinds of shit now. Worst case, they'll get a slap on the wrist and be packed off to the House of Lords.'

Hawkins wanted to argue. But deep down, he knew Bald was right. The world *had* changed. Left men like Hawkins and Bald behind. They were still fighting the good fight, polishing their chainmail and sharpening their swords, while around them the old order turned to dust. But one day they would be gone, and Hawkins worried about what would happen then. When the sentries were no longer on watch, who would keep the enemies from the gate?

The pain returned. He closed his eyes, jaw clenched in agony. At his side, Bald was struggling. His breathing sounded shallow and erratic.

'You're not gonna die, mate,' Hawkins said.

'Fuck off. Course I'm bloody not.'

'Once this is over, we'll have a pint, eh?'

'Long as you're buying the first round.'

'Tight Jock bastard.'

Millar came running over to the bay. Behind her Greyhound and Bear were in conversation with Lavery. Post-op debrief.

'God,' Millar said, kneeling beside Hawkins. 'You're hit.'

Bald said, 'Don't worry about us, lass. Had bigger scratches on our cocks. Ain't that right, Geordie?'

He winked and nodded at Hawkins. Millar placed a hand on his good shoulder. Looked him softly in the eye. 'Ambulance is on the way. They're going to take you to Glasgow Royal. It's going to be okay. Do you hear me? It'll be okay.'

Repeating it, over and over, as if she needed to convince herself.

Hawkins said, 'Call Zoe. Tell her – tell her I love her.'

'I will.'

Millar held his hand in hers. Tears rimmed her eyes.

He found himself hoping for a better tomorrow. That was a frightening thought. Hawkins had lived for so long without hope, he was almost scared of it. It seemed so fragile, as if it might shatter into tiny fragments if he touched it. But maybe that was enough. Just to know that the possibility of hope still existed in this broken world.

He heard the chopper in the distance.

Help was coming.

Maybe Millar was right.

Maybe things would be okay.

Maybe.

If you enjoyed *Second Strike*,
why not join the
CHRIS RYAN READERS' CLUB?

When you sign up, you'll receive an exclusive Q & A with Chris Ryan, plus information about upcoming books and access to exclusive material.
To join, simply visit:
bit.ly/ChrisRyanClub

Keep reading for a letter from the author . . .

Hello!

Thank you for picking up SECOND STRIKE.

I started writing this book against the backdrop of Russia's continued attempts to sabotage the UK and Europe. Barely a week passes without news reports of another cyber-operation targeting critical infrastructure, or an attack on an exiled Kremlin dissident. From political interference and disinformation campaigns to using criminal proxies, the threat to this country has never been greater.

Our enemies smell blood – and with good reason. The sad truth is that our existing defences have been neglected for too long, and if we're going to keep our country safe, we're going to have to up our game.

In the months since I began work on SECOND STRIKE, the world has changed massively. Old certainties and alliances have been ripped up. The West has become a more fragmented – and dangerous – place. If we fail to step up, we could easily find ourselves facing an attack like the one described in SECOND STRIKE. Thankfully, our leaders appear to be waking up to this emerging threat. I can only hope, for all our sakes, that they're not too late.

If you would like to hear more about my books, you can visit **bit.ly/ChrisRyanClub** where you can become part of the Chris Ryan Readers' Club. It only takes a few moments to sign up, and there are no catches or costs.

Bonnier Books UK will keep your data private and confidential, and it will never be passed on to a third party. We won't spam you with loads of emails, just get in touch now and again with news about my books, and you can unsubscribe any time you want.

And if you would like to get involved in a wider conversation about my books, please do review SECOND STRIKE on Amazon, on GoodReads, on any other e-store, on your own blog and social media accounts, or talk about it with friends, family or reader groups! Sharing your thoughts helps other readers, and I always enjoy hearing about what people experience from my writing. You can follow me on X (Twitter) @ChrisRyanMM.

Thank you again for reading SECOND STRIKE.

All the best,

Chris Ryan